Blaedel is the number one Danish bestseller and author
e Detective Louise Rick crime series, which has been
shed to acclaim around the world. In her native
nark her books have sold over a million copies and she
en voted Denmark's most popular novelist three times
2007. Sara is also an ambassador for Save the Children
ves in Copenhagen with her family.

ıd out more visit www.sarablaedel.com or follow Sara on
ter @sarablaedel.

Also by Sara Blaedel

Blue Blood

Only One Life

SARA BLAEDEL

Translation by Erik J. Macki
and Tara F. Chace

sphere

SPHERE

First published in Denmark as *Kun ét liv* in 2007 by Lindhardt og Ringhof
First published in the United States in 2012 by Pegasus Crime
First published in Great Britain in 2013 by Sphere
This paperback edition published in 2014 by Sphere

A CIP catalogue record for this book
is available from the British Library.

ISBN 978-0-7515-5120-4

Typeset in Sabon by M Rules
Printed and bound in Great Britain by
Clays Ltd, St Ives plc

Papers used by Sphere are from well-managed forests
and other responsible sources.

For Leif and Annegrethe

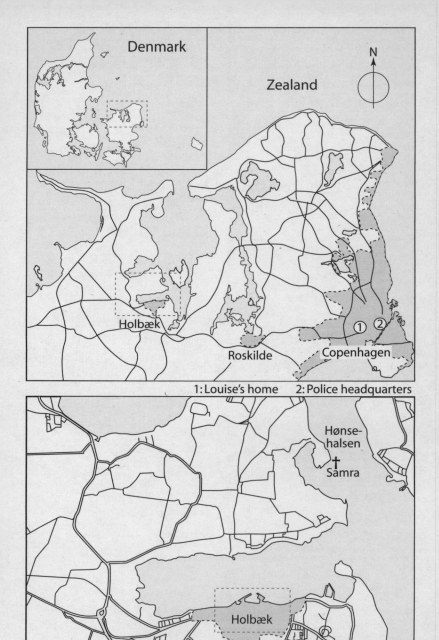

Denmark

Zealand

N

Holbæk

Roskilde

Copenhagen

1: Louise's home   2: Police headquarters

Hønse-
halsen
✝
Samra

Holbæk

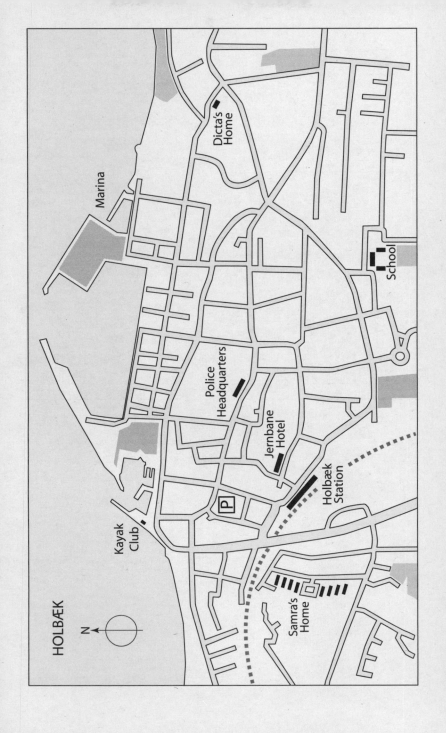

HOLBÆK

N

Marina

Dicta's
Home

School

Police
Headquarters

Jernbane
Hotel

Holbæk
Station

Kayak
Club

P

Samra's
Home

AUTHOR NOTE

When women are seen as the carriers of a family's honour they become vulnerable to attacks involving physical violence, mutilation and even murder, usually at the hand of an 'offended' male kin and often with the tacit or explicit assent of female relatives.

Navi Pillay, United Nations High Commissioner for Human Rights, 'Opinion Piece for International Women's Day: Honour Killing and Domestic Violence', March 2010

An honour killing is the murder of a family member due to the belief that the victim has brought dishonour upon the family or community.

The United Nations Population Fund estimates that perhaps as many as five thousand women and girls a year are killed by members of their own families. Many women's groups in the Middle East and South West Asia suspect the number of victims is about four times greater.

The perceived dishonour can be the result of dressing in a

manner unacceptable to the family or community, wanting to terminate or prevent an arranged marriage, engaging in heterosexual acts outside marriage or engaging in homosexual acts, amongst other things.

The most famous honour killing case in Denmark was that of Ghazala Khan, a nineteen-year-old woman who was shot and killed outside a train station in Slagelse, west of Copenhagen, in 2005 because her family disapproved of her choice of husband. Nine people, including her father, brother, three uncles, an aunt and two family friends, were convicted of murder or accessory to murder in this case.

1

She could just make out the blue flashes between the densely grown tree trunks, but she couldn't see how many police vehicles were at the scene. The forest road was bumpy, with enormous piles of firewood on either side, blocking out the bright morning light.

Søren Velin sped up, shooting small rocks against the undercarriage of the car, which skidded a little whenever the road turned. They waved him through the police blockade, and he parked next to one of the squad cars.

Louise Rick got out. The road ended at a bluff where a small path led down the last stretch to the water, which extended smooth and calm across the sound to the distant, tree-lined shore of Orø Island. From here Louise didn't recognise any of the men in the huddle at the top of the bluff, so she grabbed her jacket from the back seat and waited for Søren to lead the way.

'A fisherman found her,' explained the dark-haired,

powerfully built man who had come to greet them. He walked past Søren and offered his hand to Louise.

'Storm,' he said. 'I'm glad you were willing to help us out.' Louise shook his hand and smiled. Storm was the captain of the Unit One Mobile Task Force with the Danish National Police, and he knew as well as she did that willingness had nothing to do with why she was out here, on the shore of the sound just north of Holbæk an hour west of Copenhagen. Higher-ups had made the decision before she was even asked, and they had just been lucky that she was, in fact, also willing to help.

'We still don't know how long she's been in the water,' Storm continued as the three of them headed back towards the bluff. 'The fisherman notified the Holbæk Police this morning at eight thirty-five, saying he had spotted a motionless figure in the water. The girl had a slab of concrete tied to her torso, which was keeping her submerged under about four and a half feet of water where the body was stuck in some chicken wire. The fisherman couldn't get her loose with his oar so he called the police, who showed up along with an ambulance. The Falck Rescue squad has just recovered the body.'

Louise noticed the search-and-rescue van with its trailer for the rubber raft that they had used to recover the girl. One diver would have gone into the water to cut her free, then passed her to the other diver, who hoisted her up into the raft. Now they were loading the rescue raft back onto the trailer. Louise walked all the way over to the edge of the bluff and saw the white sheet covering the dead girl's body and the crime-scene technicians in their coveralls busy combing the shore for evidence.

'The local police have cordoned off the site, and as you can see the CSI techs are already at work,' Storm continued. 'But we're still waiting for a couple more cars.'

He interrupted his brief summary when they reached the others, and he introduced each of them in turn.

'That's Bengtsen; he's been with Holbæk's crime division since before anyone can remember,' he said with obvious respect. 'He knows everything worth knowing about Holbæk and the people who live here.'

Bengtsen nodded at her, but he kept his hands in the pockets of his tweed trousers.

Storm stepped over to a man with an olive complexion. 'Dean Vukić,' he said, and the man shook hands with Louise. There was something hypercorrect about his well-dressed style, the shirt and tie under his leather jacket making him look more like a banker than an assistant detective.

Another man offered his hand to Louise. 'Mik Rasmussen,' he said.

Like Vukić and Louise herself, Mik was in his mid to late thirties.

'Louise Rick,' she said. Out of habit she was about to add 'Unit A', but she caught herself. She quickly looked around at all the new faces. It was quite a small group, and she wondered briefly how she would fare at finding her place in this pack.

After that morning's briefing back at Copenhagen Police headquarters with Unit A – her homicide investigation unit – Captain Hans Suhr had opened the door to the office that Louise shared with her partner, Lars Jørgensen. Louise had just set her coffee cup on her desk and was asking her partner about his adopted twins, who were home sick with flu, when Suhr uttered in two short sentences that Louise's former partner Søren Velin was on his way to HQ to pick her up.

'Starting today you've been temporarily reassigned to the Unit One Mobile Task Force with the National Police,' he said, already on his way back through the door.

Louise jumped to her feet and stopped him in the corridor, wanting to know what was going on. Suhr's response was curt and clear: she'd been reassigned because she was deeply familiar with cases like this one. Then he hurried off.

Louise went back to her office and took a sip of her coffee, shaking her head in response to her partner's raised eyebrows, meaning that Suhr hadn't given her anything to go on.

'Rape, I'm assuming,' she said on her way through the door with her bag over her shoulder, adding that she hoped Lars' twins would feel better soon. As she went down the back stairwell to the exit onto Otto Mønsteds Gade she thought it must be a rape case of a certain calibre, since a local police force had called for assistance. It was only when she was sitting in the car next to Søren Velin heading out towards Cape Tuse – or more specifically, a nature preserve out there with the unusual name of Hønsehalsen, 'the Chicken Neck' – that she realised she had misunderstood her boss.

'I have no idea whether rape was involved,' her former partner told her as she started asking him about the case, preparing for what lay ahead. 'But it looks like the girl is from an immigrant background, and my understanding is that that's why Storm really wanted you on this case.'

Louise sighed. She had just wrapped up a case like this, and she was still having such a difficult time letting go of it that she was considering seeing one of the police psychologists at the

Counselling Services Unit to avoid any permanent trauma. As a young officer, she had always taken it hard whenever she was confronted with people's personal tragedies, and she had worked to learn how to handle this. Even so, she still sometimes found herself succumbing, and that's what had happened with her last case, an attempted 'honour' killing. The case had ended with a charge of aggravated assault, but Louise and the rest of her investigative team had absolutely no doubt that certain members of that family had actually intended to kill the sixteen-year-old girl, but they had botched the job, so now their eldest daughter was a vegetable in the neurology department at the National Hospital in Copenhagen.

'She was lying on her stomach,' Storm explained, pointing to a spot on their right not far out into the sound. 'We don't know who she is, but we think she's between fourteen and sixteen years old, give or take. She didn't have a purse or any type of ID on her.'

'The canine unit is on its way. Then we'll have to see whether they can find anything that could identify her,' Bengtsen interrupted, coming over to stand next to the Mobile Task Force captain. 'We can probably assume she was thrown into the water from a boat,' he continued, both hands still in his pockets and his eyes scanning the water. 'It's too deep here for anyone to have carried her out. A slab of concrete like that weighs quite a bit.'

Louise heard car doors slam and noticed a blue van now parked next to the other vehicles, and two men putting on their work clothes. She recognised one of them as Frandsen, head of Copenhagen's former Forensics Division, which had just been renamed the Forensics Centre. She walked over to say hi. Frandsen had recently turned sixty, and the Forensics Centre had thrown a big reception for him at their offices on Slotsherrensvej, in Copenhagen's Vanløse district. Louise had given him a little pipe holder carved out of mahogany for the pipe he always carried with him, even though she had never seen him light it in all the years she had known him. Whenever Frandsen pulled the pipe out of his pocket and stuck it in his mouth, she knew it meant he was concentrating.

'I guess we're back in business,' Frandsen said, pulling a large wooden box out of the back of the van. 'And here I was just getting a taste for the golden years.'

Instead of throwing a big birthday party for the family, Frandsen and his wife had chosen to spend two weeks in Thailand on holiday. They must have just got back, Louise thought. She smiled because he hadn't spent even a second wondering what she was doing at a crime scene so far from Copenhagen, a sure sign that he was wholly focused on the task ahead.

After he got all of his equipment together, he followed his team out to the bluff, and Louise walked over to the people standing with Dean and Mik, who had just come back from talking to a woman who had been out walking her dog.

'Nothing,' Dean said. 'That woman lives on a farm right around here and walks her dog through these woods twice a day.'

A big black Citroën rolled up.

'It's Skipper,' Søren said, waving at the car.

Louise had heard of him over the years. He was a fixture at the Mobile Task Force and National Police, and he had a reputation for unparalleled skill with crime-scene investigation and details. Another rumour she had heard about Skipper was confirmed by the muffled sound of music booming behind the closed windows of his car. On their way out here, Søren had told her about Skipper's enormous passion for jazz fusion, which was a complete mismatch with his understated sweater, proper Windsor knot, and otherwise distinguished and reserved appearance – including his neatly groomed grey hair combed back in a soft wave.

Louise introduced herself to Skipper, then Søren added that she had been his partner before he joined the Mobile Task Force.

'Well, then I'm sure we can't get anyone better,' Skipper said with a warm smile. 'Glad to have you with us.'

'Thank you,' she said, wondering what else Søren had told him. She watched Søren as he spoke to two of the local uniforms. He had already been with Unit A homicide at the Copenhagen PD for a while when Louise was offered her job there, and they had enjoyed a really good working relationship for a couple of years until he shifted to a new job.

The CSI techs were working on the bluff and at the edge of the water. There would be hardly any traces of DNA left on the girl because she had been in the water, but they were taking photographs of the body and the scene, bagging items from along the shore, and two men were focusing exclusively on finding footprints and tyre prints. The coroner from Copenhagen had also shown up, Louise discovered. Flemming Larsen's six-foot-six frame was impossible to miss, even though he was standing with his back to her as he balanced his bag on his knee to fish something out of it. When he turned around and caught sight of Louise, he set the bag down and walked towards her with a big smile on his face.

'Does your being here mean this girl's from Copenhagen?'

he asked, surprised, giving her a hug that lasted a bit longer than Louise would have preferred. She had worked with Flemming on many of her cases, and lately they had also been seeing each other a little outside of working hours, but no one else needed to know that.

'They sent me out here to assist the Mobile Task Force,' she replied, thinking it sounded a bit strange.

'Well, I'll be damned,' he said, smiling. 'I didn't think Suhr and the rest of Unit A could spare you. Is it permanent?'

'It's just for this case – and I guess they'll manage,' she answered, thinking that the only person at Copenhagen PD who seemed to have a problem with her working with the Mobile Task Force was Michael Stig. But that was probably just because he thought they should have picked him.

'Good luck, and give me a call some night when you've got time to go out and have a glass of wine.' He walked over to pick up his bag as Frandsen returned from the shore, announcing that the coroner could proceed with his in-situ examination of the body.

Louise followed him to the bluff and looked down as Flemming removed the sheet and squatted next to the girl. She was lying on her back on the black, wet shore of the sound, her eyes closed and the slab of concrete still tied to her stomach.

Her long-sleeved T-shirt and lightweight beige jacket had slipped off a little, revealing how the rope had dug into her skin. The coroner carefully pushed her long, dark hair to the side so it wasn't plastered to her face like yarn any more. Then he started his examination of the body.

Louise listened in as he leaned over and reported to Skipper, who had appeared with a notebook to record keywords.

'Unidentified woman found a short time ago,' Flemming began, focusing initially on the face. 'No petechiae in the conjunctiva or surrounding the eyes. Around the abdominal region a –' he studied the rope for a moment before continuing '– blue nylon rope is visible, approximately three to four yards in length, tied with a square knot, with one end wrapped around the subject's waist and the other around a concrete stepping stone measuring twenty by twenty inches. Livor mortis visible on the abdomen, which does not disappear when pressure is applied. This suggests the victim has been dead for at least four to five hours. Rectal body temperature is eighty-one degrees, and the water temperature is sixty-two.' He looked up at Skipper.

'What do you think about the cause of death – did she drown? And how long has she been here?' Skipper asked, taking a step closer.

Flemming stood up and crossed his arms as he contemplated the girl on the ground. Then he shook his head.

'I can't tell what she died from. There are no signs of force, but I don't think she tried to inhale underwater. Otherwise she'd have foam both in her mouth and around it. But obviously that may have washed off. The petechiae are sparse and reddish; she has goose bumps over her entire body, which we often see in individuals who have been in water. And there is pronounced wrinkling on the fingers, palms, toes and soles – but that shows up only after a few hours.'

He concluded by saying that, judging from the rigor mortis, petechiae and the body temperature, he would tentatively estimate that the girl had been dead somewhere between nine and fifteen hours.

'When can we get her autopsied?' Skipper asked, waving

Storm over so he could give his approval for the autopsy and lean on the coroner if he said all the autopsy rooms were in use.

Flemming looked at his watch and then at the two men.

'We can get started at one o'clock, provided you can get Falck Rescue to dispatch their bone bus out here that fast,' he said darkly.

The bone bus. Louise shook her head. The nickname had become common parlance whenever people talked about transporting a body. In some cases it was highly appropriate, but in others it seemed more jarring. Such as now. They put the girl into a white-plastic body bag, and she was ready for transport to the forensics lab in an ambulance with covered windows. Impersonal and cold for a young girl, whose identity they didn't even know.

For a moment Louise had an urge to ride along with the girl so she wouldn't have to make the trip alone, but the vehicle wasn't like an ordinary ambulance with a seat for a family member. This ambulance was stripped bare so there was room only for two stretchers, and there was a large exhaust fan in the ceiling. She pushed the idea from her mind.

After the coroner left, Storm started heading for the cars to drive back to Holbæk PD headquarters.

'That means she might have been in the water since midnight,' Storm said as he opened the door of his car. 'Let's get going.'

Louise took one last look at the scene before climbing in next to Søren, and they drove back along the forest road.

2

_____

Holbæk police department headquarters was in an elegant, old-fashioned building of red brick with white window trim, making it look both impressive and well maintained. Storm led the way, and Louise followed him up one hallway and down another before they reached the Criminal Investigation Division. The offices were arranged in a row – some detectives shared, others had their own. The latter was the case with Bengtsen: he had a corner office with windows facing both the front of the police station and the large green lawn and pond at the end of the building. By contrast, Mik Rasmussen and Dean Vukić shared a smaller, darker office where there wasn't room for much, other than desks and bookshelves.

Louise had a hard time imagining how they were going to find any room for the extra help they had called in. Earlier, Søren had told her about a case in which they had squeezed an extra detective in at a little schoolhouse-style desk out in the hallway, and another case in which they kept moving a detective around, but this time it wasn't going to be that bad because right then her old partner emerged from an empty office. He ran his hand through his longish blond hair as he looked at the weekend bag and two computer bags he had set down on the floor in front of him.

'Are you moving in?' she asked, walking over to him.

'It'd probably be smarter to wait until we know who we'll be working with, but it'd be nice to have a proper place to sit,' he said. At that moment Storm stuck his head out of a doorway at the end of the corridor.

'Everybody's meeting in here,' he shouted, waving for them to join him.

They entered what must have been the division's conference room, and Louise guessed this was probably where the Criminal Investigation Division normally held their morning briefings. The walls were painted a warm yellow reminiscent of a child's drawing, with the sun a little too heavy and saturated with colour – over the top for a small room, but the light from the tall windows here compensated for the compact feel. In front of one window they had a large whiteboard set up similar to the one they had in the briefing room at the Copenhagen PD, with bits of blue and green lines that the eraser had missed. On another wall there was a large dry-erase calendar next to an enlarged map of the area around Holbæk. Someone had decorated the opposite wall by tacking up a Matisse print, and an overhead projector was tucked away in the corner behind the door. Louise sat next to Søren, grabbing one of the lined legal pads stacked on the table with a few pens, which must have been left over from a previous meeting.

'I think he's going to split Mik and Dean up, and you'll get partnered with one of them,' Søren whispered to her.

Louise looked at the two detectives. One would be just as good as the other. It was standard procedure to form teams by mixing local and backup officers, so she wasn't even going to start hoping for any particular outcome. She had also quickly determined that she was the only woman in the group, so it might well be that the local boys were sitting here wondering about their prospects of being partnered with her. She had heard stories about local police officers calling in sick because they felt invaded when backup suddenly showed up from the Mobile Task Force and started screwing with their routines. Her thoughts were interrupted when Storm started speaking.

'Nobody has reported the girl missing, so we've put out notices to all police districts about the discovery, and we'll be going to the press with a missing-persons report,' he said, opening the meeting. 'Without a photo, initially,' he added. 'We'll stick to describing the clothes she was wearing when she was found. If that doesn't turn anything up, we'll have to release one of the forensic pictures. We just don't want to risk her parents' finding out that way,' he said, and several heads in the room shook. 'We'll set up three teams—'

At that moment the door opened, and a woman with elegant russet hair and red lips came in carrying a bag over her shoulder and a laptop under her arm.

'Hi,' she said, smiling.

'Ruth Lange,' said Storm, gesturing towards her. 'Ruth is our administrative assistant.'

Warm hellos filled the room.

'Ruth and I will hold down the command centre, which will

be here in this conference room,' Storm said, pointing at the yellow walls.

'The teams are as follows,' he continued, once Ruth had set her things on the table and taken a seat. He looked around the room. The local officers were sitting next to each other. Louise was sitting next to Søren Velin, who stood out in his cargo pants and black turtleneck jumper. Skipper was to her left.

'Skipper and Dean,' said Storm, 'you two are responsible for the site where the body was found. In other words, all of the technical evidence.'

The two men smiled and nodded to each other.

'Louise Rick and' – he looked down at his papers – 'Mik Rasmussen. We're putting you two together to identify the girl's family and social circle. We've got to find out what the motive might be. Rick has some experience working with ethnic minorities,' he continued. Louise furrowed her brow. She wouldn't have gone that far, but she wasn't going to correct Storm right now.

'Bengtsen, you and Søren Velin will handle telecommunications and question potential witnesses in the area.'

Bengtsen set his pad on the table and nodded in satisfaction. Louise guessed it was probably more the telecommunications and any subsequent wiretapping that he was happy about, and not working with Søren, because she had noticed Bengtsen sizing up her former partner. They would make an odd couple, Bengtsen with his tweed and corduroy and Søren with his very casual style.

People started talking a little across the table, especially Skipper and Dean, who seemed quite happy with each other. Louise smiled at her newly assigned partner, who gave her a quick nod then quickly looked down.

Storm told everyone to quieten down and took control of the meeting again.

'We don't know anything about the victim. Flemming thinks she was dead before she was placed in the water, but he can't say with any certainty, so we'll need to wait for the autopsy.'

Storm got up and pointed at Louise and Mik.

'And you two will attend the autopsy. I just got off the phone with Frandsen – he's the head of the Forensics Centre in Copenhagen,' he added, in case anyone in the room didn't know who he was. 'He'll make sure one of his people is ready around one o'clock so the autopsy can get started on time.'

Bengtsen grunted to show that he was quite familiar with the head of the Forensics Centre and that he also knew a CSI tech would be present at the autopsy.

Louise stood up as Storm gestured at the door.

'I've put in a request for an official car for you,' he told her. 'You can pick it up when you're finished at the autopsy. And Ruth will set you up with your own laptops.'

She gave him a questioning look at his use of the plural.

'One laptop for our internal networks and intranet, and one for the general internet,' he explained.

Of course they work on two computers, she thought immediately. The Mobile Task Force operated on a heavily firewalled secure police network, but they naturally also had access to the internet and an open email system. The laptops would be some of the new gear suddenly available to her.

'You'll also get one of our mobile phones, but keep your own with you so ours isn't busy when we need to reach you.'

As if that's going to be a problem, she thought, but she just nodded.

'We'll be staying at the Station Hotel, which is just a little way up the street across from the train station,' he said, pointing out of the window. 'I hope you'll be able to make it back from Copenhagen by dinnertime. Afterwards we'll touch base here again and keep working.'

'Sounds good,' Louise said, following him as he explained that they had cleared out an office for Mik and her to share. They stopped outside the empty office where Søren was standing with his things. He had been given a spot in Bengtsen's corner office, and as he walked past her in the corridor she could tell from the look in his eyes he was quite satisfied with this outcome.

The room she was going to be working in was small and spartan. The walls were a dull eggshell colour. The desks and two office chairs reminded her of old school furniture, with names and swastikas scratched into the desktops. Mik Rasmussen had already begun to move his things in, but Louise's area was completely empty. She went in and settled into her chair, watching Mik as he stocked his desk with paper and set out his pencils in a handleless mug from a local football club.

'Do you play?' she asked.

He looked over at her with a confused expression and then followed her eyes to the mug.

'I used to play,' he replied curtly. When she kept looking at him, he explained that he'd played football for several years with the Holbæk Ball & Sports Association.

'But we never got further than the Sjælland play-offs.'

'But you don't play any more?' she prodded, keeping the grilling going.

He shook his head.

'Now I paddle sea kayaks and teach kayaking down at the Rowing Club.'

Louise smiled. At no time during their brief acquaintance had she suspected him of being particularly athletic. He was just too lanky and reserved for her to connect him with any form of outdoor recreation.

'Do you know when they're going to notify the media?' she asked. Bengtsen was taking care of that.

'I doubt it'll go out right away, but once it does I'm sure it will get a lot of airtime,' he replied, pulling on his windbreaker.

His accent had a distinctly Sjælland ring to it, which she recognised in her own speech since she'd grown up in Central Sjælland herself. She had worked hard to rid herself of the accent, but sometimes it reared its head.

She looked at the clock and, discovering that it was nearly noon, she stood and pulled her bag up over her shoulder. They had to get moving.

'Time to go?' he asked, and she let him lead the way, through the back entrance to the car park where the squad cars were parked.

They drove in silence, and it suited her just fine that neither of them felt the need to entertain the other. Gradually, though, the silence got to be too much for her, so she broke it as they drove through Roskilde.

'Have you worked with the MTF before?' The Mobile Task Force was an elite National Police unit dispatched throughout Denmark to assist local police departments investigating serious crimes.

He nodded, and Louise explained that she wasn't permanently assigned and that this was her first case with them.

The September sun was blinding them, so he pulled the visor down and positioned it carefully before he finally started talking.

'We had a murder up here a few years ago when they called in the MTF after a couple of weeks. That was under our old boss, and for that case in particular it probably would have been smart to have called for assistance earlier, because the perp was never found. But that's not how things run any more. Now they call in assistance the moment a body is discovered.'

There wasn't a trace of sarcasm in his voice.

'How long have you been a detective?' she asked with interest. He did the tally in his head before answering.

'Eight years, but I've been here eleven. I became a uniform right out of the police academy.'

That confirmed for Louise that he was in his mid-thirties. Actually, thirty-six, a year younger than she was.

'I assume you live in Holbæk?' she said, thinking she sounded like a reporter doing a lengthy interview, although it didn't seem like it was bothering him.

'On a farm just outside town. Do you know Holbæk?'

She nodded and told him that her parents lived not far away and that when she was a teenager she used to spend all her free time at the Alley, one of Holbæk's nightclubs.

He turned his head and studied her, and she knew he was wondering whether he had seen her before.

'Maybe we've danced together,' she joked, glad that the conversation was starting to loosen up.

His eyes were already back on the road, concentrating on a couple of cyclists. He politely mumbled that if that were the case, he probably would have remembered it.

She was about to try again, but just then he turned off onto

Frederick V Avenue and parked up alongside Fælled Park across from the Pathology Lab. Flemming Larsen was waiting for them when they entered.

'Åse is already here, so let's just head up and join her,' he said, setting off towards the lift.

Louise smiled. Åse was one of her favourites among the forensic pathology staff. Not that Louise was a feminist, but the tiny woman whom Louise initially had taken as fresh out of college and green was, in fact, extraordinarily competent and thorough.

Åse had her very own quiet style whenever she set to work photographing a corpse, moving on to the lesions on the body and internal organs, and it was clear that she considered every detail important. Now she was ready to go, waiting for them in the little corridor into the autopsy section in her scrubs with blue medical booties carefully secured over her shoes.

'So, we meet again,' Louise said.

Mik went straight into the rear autopsy room, which was commonly called the murder room. It was twice as large as the other rooms where autopsies were performed so there was room for any law enforcement officials who were supposed to observe. Louise and Åse stayed outside talking while they waited for the fingerprint expert to finish taking the body's prints – he would run a comparison on the girl, in the faint hope of identifying her that way. When Flemming asked them to come in, they walked past the line of smaller autopsy stalls where other forensic pathologists were working. They continued to the autopsy room, joining the forensics team in charge of preparing the body. Mik Rasmussen was sitting on a stool in one corner with a pad of paper on his knee, ready to take notes when the actual examination got going.

Louise grabbed another stool and sat next to him. They kept back while Åse pulled her camera out of her camera bag and started taking pictures of the fully clothed corpse from various angles while speaking quietly to Flemming. When she had finished the examination, the other forensic techs stepped forward and removed the girl's clothes. Åse took pictures of each garment separately, and then at last they were ready to start on the external examination.

During a brief break, Louise stood up and stepped forward to take a close look at the naked girl. She looked so very young. Her long dark hair lay out over the table; around her neck she was wearing a thin gold chain with a tiny heart. She had no make-up on. Obviously it could have been washed off by the water, Louise thought, but there was no dark residue around her eyes.

She stepped back again when Flemming and Åse were ready to continue. The coroner reiterated his comments from the examination at the crime scene: 'No clear signs of violence, no signs of pathology or specific identifying marks.'

Mik scooted his stool over to the windowsill on the back wall so he could use it to hold up his notepad, and he wrote extensively as everyone continued speaking behind him. Flemming Larsen also repeated that there were petechiae in and around the victim's eyes, and then the forensic techs went over every inch of the girl's body, using an arsenal of cotton swabs to dab for evidence before turning the body over.

Åse was taking pictures of every detail the whole time. When Flemming finished examining the back of the body, he straightened up.

'The top left side of the neck shows two yellow, slightly

rounded abrasions,' he announced. Åse stepped closer, and together they bent down.

'These are quite unusual and were sustained after death. I can't exclude the possibility that they occurred during transportation here,' he said, asking the men standing in the corner by the door to open the girl up.

Louise stepped out with the others while the forensic techs did their work, finishing half a cup of coffee in Flemming's office before being called back into the autopsy room.

The body had been opened with a long, straight cut, and the internal organs had been lifted out in one block and rinsed. Now the last stage of the autopsy could get under way. The light from Flemming's work lamp that hung from the ceiling by its long arm was intense, reflecting a glare out into the room wherever it struck the white tiles of the end wall and the shiny surfaces of the stainless-steel tables. A long hose hung over the deep sink where the block of organs lay, with the shrill sound of regularly spaced drips whenever a drop of water hit the basin.

'She is a healthy young woman,' said Flemming, mostly directing his comments at Mik and his notes. 'Her last meal was rice and beans.'

He worked a little more in silence until he continued: 'There is no water in the lungs or sphenoidal sinus, so there is no indication that she drowned, but she was underwater for a few hours. She has acute hyperinflation, the lungs are large and pale, which may be because she had difficulty breathing, but I can't give you a cause of death,' he said, completing the autopsy.

Everyone said thank you, stepped out, and pulled off their masks and white coveralls. Louise hung back a moment to talk with Flemming before following Mik over to the lifts to head down to the car. They had agreed that he would drop her off at the Polititorvet, the large, red-brick neoclassical building that housed the Danish National Police headquarters, where she could pick up the car she had been assigned. Then she would stop off at her apartment in Copenhagen's Frederiksberg neighbourhood to pack a bag.

3

Louise did a quick walk-through of her apartment, her weekend bag in her hand. She packed both warm- and cold-weather clothes. Even though they were halfway through September, they were still having days so hot that shorts and T-shirts seemed like overkill.

Her answering machine was blinking. She pressed play and walked over to the windowsill to grab the vase of flowers she had bought the day before. It would be easy enough to take the flowers wrapped in a bit of newspaper to her room at the Station Hotel in Holbæk.

'... *you can call any time today. It would be nice to know if we're all set to get together tomorrow or if I should just wait on standby until it suits you to call me back—*'

Camilla Lind's voice was cut off by the answering machine's shrill beeping sound.

'Yeah, yeah, yeah,' Louise said to the machine, reaching for the phone.

'Hi – and I'm sorry . . .' she began, heading off Camilla's initial reproach for her laxness in returning calls. 'I've got to cancel for tomorrow.'

'Well, then let's set up a different time to meet up,' Camilla said.

Louise's best friend worked on the crime desk at *Morgenavisen*, and she was used to Louise's cancelling when she was working on a case. In turn, that usually also meant that Camilla could expect to get some kind of story lead out of her. Their jobs were connected in a way, even though they approached homicide cases from different angles.

Even so, Louise was a little surprised that Camilla didn't protest more vigorously, which left her feeling guilty. She knew that her friend could really use her support, and she wanted to be there for her too. It just couldn't be right now.

'I'll give you a call in a couple of days,' she promised, explaining that she was on her way out the door.

Then she hung up and changed her voicemail greeting: 'This is Louise. I'm not checking my messages, so call me on my mobile. Bye.'

Camilla Lind stepped up her pace. She needed to make it to Markus's school on time and then take the metro with him all the way back to the Frederiksberg Community Centre so he wouldn't be late to his break-dancing rehearsal at Hot Stepper again. She had planned to buy a bottle of water and some fruit for him on the way, but she dropped the idea when she looked at her watch at Nørreport Station, bounding down the stairs instead and darting onto the train in a quick leap.

She was disappointed that her date with Louise had fallen through. Camilla had been looking forward to slumping down onto Louise's couch and venting all the thoughts and feelings that were filling her. But after talking with Louise, Camilla had called the Copenhagen PD to find out what was up, since Unit A was apparently involved. Camilla sensed that they were giving her the runaround when the duty officer insisted he was unaware of any new case. Annoyed, she quickly packed up her things, shut down her computer and headed out the door. On the way, she ran into her editor, Terkel Høyer, who was coming to see her with a missing-person report from the Holbæk PD involving the body of a teenage immigrant girl.

Camilla quickly realised that her working day wasn't over yet after all. Both of her colleagues were out: Kvist was using up some extra holiday days he had earned, and their intern, Jacob, was in Australia with his girlfriend for the entire month of September, so everything was riding on Camilla. Her editor just nodded when she announced on her way out that she would be back as soon as she'd dropped her son off at home. Her mobile phone was already in her hand so she could get hold of her irreplaceable babysitter, Christina, and have her watch Markus after his rehearsal.

'Be back as fast as you can,' Terkel called after her.

With her back to him, she raised one arm in the air in acknowledgement. She knew where he stood: the paper should be in on the story from the get-go. She agreed. The stories of eighteen-year-old Ghazala Khan, who had been shot by his brother on the square in front of Slagelse Station in September last year, and the even younger Sonay Mohammad, who was slain by his father in February 2002 and thrown into Præstø harbour, had filled many front pages and garnered a great deal of media attention during their investigations and subsequent trials. So obviously they should run with this story too.

Markus was waiting for her on the pavement in front of his school, wearing his backpack, and she could tell that he was looking for her. She started running towards him, waving as soon as he spotted her. Hurrying hand in hand, they raced off and made it just before the rehearsal began. Markus quickly changed his shoes and put on his hoodie and baseball cap while Camilla went to the food court to buy a bottle of water and a banana for him. Then the door closed, separating her from the loud pounding music and the fifteen tough eight-year-old kids – fourteen boys and one girl – who would spend the next hour practising the Baby Freeze and various other moves. She sat down on a bench in the lobby for a moment.

Christina had promised to be at the community centre in forty-five minutes so she could take over when the rehearsal finished. Then she and Markus would go home and have some dinner together. Camilla was already braced for a fairly late night before she could make it back home herself.

She had just stood up when she saw him – and sat back down again, heavily, as though two powerful hands had given her a rough shove to the chest. She knew instantly that he had been watching her, and her stomach turned as he approached. She couldn't stand up, and instead sat and looked up at him as he spoke.

'For the love of God, you've got to stop calling me and sending me emails,' he said. 'You have got to respect my boundaries and stop contacting me.'

Then he was gone. Out the door and down the street. Camilla felt as though the whole interaction had played out in slow motion, and yet she had not had time to react or say anything.

She sat there, frozen. Anger and pain filled her, both fighting to take over. She wanted to run after him and make him understand. Tell him that she needed to stay in touch. That she needed him, and that they had been good together. But she couldn't stand up; her muscles felt weak and useless. He ignored her phone calls and didn't respond to her email. He didn't want her. It was over, and that was unbearable.

She just sat there and collected herself, deep stomach pains converging at her diaphragm. Finally, she got to her feet and started walking back to the metro.

4

'The body of an unidentified teenage girl was found this morning in Udby Cove on Cape Tuse north of Holbæk. The girl is approximately fourteen to sixteen years old and appears to be of Arab origin. She has long, black hair and was wearing a beige summer jacket over a dark blue, long-sleeved T-shirt, faded Miss Sixty jeans and white Kawasaki shoes. If you have any information about this girl, please contact Holbæk Police.'

Louise heard the missing-person report break on the news on the local P3 radio station as she drove back to Holbæk. It was almost five o'clock when she parked behind the police station. Upstairs in the corridor she nodded at Mik Rasmussen, who was talking with a colleague.

Inside the sun-yellow command centre, someone had set up a small fourteen-inch TV that was playing in the background at low volume, and there was coffee in the pot. Ruth, the administrative assistant, and Storm were talking to Bengtsen about coordinating the first interviews with witnesses who might have known the girl. A communications guy was walking around, running a few extra outside phone lines, and Ruth was just getting a large database system up and running.

'Have you taken a look around the Station Hotel?' Ruth asked. Louise shook her head and said she would drop her things off when they headed back there for a bite to eat.

'Have we got any leads from the missing-person report?' she asked with interest.

'A few tips have come in, but not really anything we can use,' Ruth replied.

'But we have ten men circulating a description of the girl in town, so I don't think it'll take long for something to turn up,' Storm added as he stood up. 'Let's head over to the hotel and grab something to eat.'

Ruth flipped the lid of her laptop shut and pushed aside the stacks of binders, pens and pads that she had been quick to requisition before the investigation got going. No one was going to have time to keep filing requisitions for everything they would need once the case was really under way. The mobile command centre was almost ready.

At that moment one of the four telephones in the office started ringing.

'DNP Unit One Mobile Task Force, Ruth Lange speaking,' she said, pulling back her voluminous hair.

'Okay, send her in. We'll come and get her.' She hung up and looked at Louise.

'There's a young woman in reception who thinks the victim we found may be a friend of hers. Can you go and talk to her? I just told your partner he could go home for a few minutes before dinner.'

Louise nodded and poured a cup of coffee from the thermal jug in the middle of the table before she grabbed a pad of paper and a ballpoint pen in case her computer hadn't been set up yet. The coffee sloshed over the rim and down the side of the cup, burning her fingers as she walked down the corridor. Swearing, she set the plastic cup down on the desk a little too hard, causing it to slosh more. She quickly wiped her hand on her trousers and went out to meet the witness.

A tall, very pretty, very young, blonde teenager was walking in slowly, uncertainty in her eyes.

Louise approached her with an outstretched hand and a welcoming smile.

'Hi, I'm Louise. Let's go in here.' She pointed towards her office, which still seemed unoccupied and cluttered although her partner had already put his things away.

'Would you like a glass of water?' she asked as they stepped in. The girl shook her head and sat down on the edge of the hard wooden chair that Louise had pushed towards the end of her desk.

The bags containing her laptops were still the way she had left them, but she left the pad of paper where it was, hoping that a little informal chat would get the girl to relax.

'What's your name?' Louise began, leaning back slightly in the office chair.

'Benedicta, Dicta for short ... ' The girl cleared her throat and repeated her name a little louder. 'Dicta Møller. I'm in ninth grade at Højmark School,' she continued.

'And you're worried that the girl we found out at Hønsehalsen may be someone you know?'

It wasn't uncommon for girls to worry about their friends and contact the police if a girl was reported missing in the media.

'There's a girl who's in ninth grade with me; she wasn't in school today,' Dicta began.

Louise didn't rush her.

'She and I were going to get together this afternoon, and I haven't been able to get hold of her. She's not answering her mobile, and no one answers when I call her at home.' Louise nodded and waited again without saying anything. 'I've been calling all afternoon.'

'Do you think she might have taken off somewhere with her parents and forgotten about your plans this afternoon? Something unexpected may have come up.'

Dicta thought for a moment as though the possibility hadn't occurred to her, but then she shook her head.

'She wouldn't have forgotten this. We were going to go through the photos,' she said, now with more strength in her voice. 'She was over at my house yesterday after school, and we talked about it then. One of the photos is going to be published this weekend in the paper.'

Louise asked her to explain what kind of photos she was talking about and what paper she was referring to.

'I'm a model,' the girl explained. 'I model for a few stores, including Boutique Aube, and the paper is supposed to run their big ad on Saturday. The photos were ready, and Samra was supposed to come to the photographer's to take a look at them. So she wouldn't have just taken off.'

Tears started streaming down Dicta's cheeks, but she continued: 'She would never do that. She keeps . . . '

Dicta's emotions overwhelmed her, sounds pouring out in a completely incomprehensible mess. Louise held out her hand to stop the flood of words.

'What does your friend look like?' she asked when the girl had calmed down a little.

Dicta straightened up and carefully dabbed the tears so they wouldn't ruin her make-up, as though she had only now discovered that she was crying.

'She has long, dark hair.'

Louise sat up and grabbed her notepad.

'And is your friend ethnically Danish?' she asked, waiting for the next crucial answer.

'No,' the girl replied hesitantly, as though she were afraid that was the wrong answer. 'She's from Jordan.'

'Does she have any distinguishing marks that you can think of? Or things she usually wears?'

Dicta fell silent, picturing her friend in front of her.

'She usually wears a watch. It's a Dolce and Gabbana knock-off. I bought it for her in Thailand – and she's also got a ton of bracelets. You know, bangles, where each individual one is thin, but you can wear a lot of them at the same time.'

She used her index finger and thumb to indicate a width that Louise estimated at about four inches. 'Anything else?'

'Nothing that she wears regularly, but she does have jewellery.'

'What about her clothes?' Louise asked instead.

'Just the usual. Jeans and T-shirts . . . She often wears a top with a little blouse over it, and she has a beige jacket like they mentioned on the news on the radio.'

Louise glanced down at the girl's feet and saw a pair of black Kawasakis. She pointed at them.

'Does she have a pair like those, too?' she asked, knowing that most of the girl's friends probably had them. She couldn't understand how the floppy little trainers managed to stay in style. They'd been popular when she was the girl's age, as well.

Dicta nodded.

'We bought them together; hers are white.'

The girl stopped, unable to think of anything else. Louise didn't pressure her, instead saying, 'Okay, I've got all this information written down. The last thing I'll need is just your friend's full name and address, and also how to get hold of you in case we want to talk to you again.'

'She always replies to text messages. I've tried texting her, but she doesn't reply,' Dicta said, instead of giving Louise what she had asked for.

'What's her name again?' Louise asked before Dicta started talking.

'Samra al-Abd. She lives on Dysseparken, apartment 16B,' the girl said. She seemed to consider her words before continuing. 'She comes over to my house a lot when her parents let her, but her father can be pretty strict; sometimes she's afraid of him. And now she's suddenly missing . . . '

Louise tried to reassure her by repeating that there could be any number of good reasons why her friend had missed school or blown out their plans to get together.

'There's no need to assume the worst,' she said. Louise knew that lots of people saw ghosts in broad daylight when it came to persecuted immigrant girls and their fathers. Still, she had to admit that many of the things Dicta had told her might well indicate this was the right girl.

'Could you give me your friend's phone number?' Louise asked, watching Dicta take her mobile phone back out and browse through her contacts. Louise took down the number and also asked for her friend's home number on Dysseparken.

The girl pressed the button a few more times and gave Louise the parents' phone number.

Once she had written down both numbers as well as Dicta's, Louise nodded towards the mobile phone and asked if Dicta happened to have a picture of her friend on it.

A moment later Dicta passed her phone across the table and told Louise she'd taken the picture outside school the week before.

Louise quickly leaned forward and took the phone, but the picture was taken from so far away you could see only the long, black hair and a blurry face. There was a certain similarity between Dicta's friend and the dead girl, but it was impossible to tell for sure if it was her.

'I can't really make her out properly in this one,' Louise said, handing back the phone. 'Do you think you have a better photo?'

The girl shook her head: she had had more pictures on her old phone, but she had lost it, she explained.

'I might be able to find one at home,' she offered. 'I'd be happy to bring one in tomorrow.'

'It's a deal. Then hopefully we can rule out your friend from our inquiries,' Louise told Dicta. She thanked the girl for coming and walked her back out to the reception area. Then she quickly went back to the command centre, but it was empty and the lights were off. She surveyed the offices, but Bengtsen was the only person still at his desk.

'Did everyone else go over to the hotel?' she asked. Bengtsen nodded without looking up from his copy of *Venstrebladet*, Holbæk's left-leaning daily newspaper.

Louise went back to her office and found Storm's mobile phone number so she could call and update him on her conversation with the girl. 'Hurry over here and get some food,' he said curtly. 'Then we'll go over it after we've eaten.'

'If it really is the friend, shouldn't we get in touch with the parents right away?' Louise objected.

'Of course, but we also need to eat; it's going to be a long night,' he said. 'Afterwards we'll check out what other leads have come in on the missing-person report, and then we'll know where we stand before we start talking to people.'

Louise would have continued protesting, but then she remembered that Storm called the shots. Instead, she went back in to see if Bengtsen wanted to join her.

He shook his head, but this time his eyes left the paper, and he looked at her.

'Aren't you going to eat?' she asked.

'Yes, but I prefer to eat at home,' he said, briefly explaining that she needed to head left when she left the police station, and then take a right. Then she'd come to the Central Station Square where the train station and the Station Hotel were located.

'See you later,' Louise said, heading back to retrieve her bags from the car before she set out on foot towards the hotel.

5

Last night he cut deep gashes into his own face. He can't take it any more; I have to keep an eye on him.

Camilla's eyes filled with tears as she read the old email. She was still deeply upset that Henning had turned up at the community centre to tell her to her face that she should stay away from him. When she got back to her office at *Morgenavisen*, she immediately checked her email to see if he had sent an explanation, but there was no word from him. So she sat there, depressed, skimming through his old emails instead.

They used to talk to each other, she and Henning. They both thought their relationship was strong enough to handle what had happened in Roskilde. Camilla couldn't recall ever being so determined to fight for a relationship. Not even when she and Tobias had started drifting apart when Markus was about a year old.

A few weeks after Henning's brother was arrested, they had lunch at one of the colourful eighteenth-century restaurants on Franciscan Square, right off the pedestrian shopping district. After coffee, they sat holding hands across the table, promising each other that their relationship would survive, despite the trauma they had shared as a result of the headline-grabbing online-dating case involving several brutal rapes.

'It's settled. It will always be the two of us,' he said, and at the time his words had filled her with relief. But then every-thing suddenly went to hell – culminating in that email he'd sent saying he had to focus on taking care of his brother.

Now, as she sat staring at her screen, she would have given anything in the world to just let go of him and move on, but she couldn't. He filled her thoughts, and she was close to exploding from the pain of longing to have him back in her life. He was the man who had finally shown her what it felt like to come home. He was the one: she had known it after their first week together.

Her hands were still trembling a bit as she opened the door to her editor's office to announce that she was back.

Terkel Høyer was sitting behind his desk and didn't look like he was going to be heading home anytime soon either.

'No word from Holbæk since they issued the missing-person report,' he said.

Camilla had been on the crime beat at *Morgenavisen* for several years and had got pretty good at reading her boss. She could sense that he was all fired up about running something in the paper the next day.

'We've got to include every angle on the story. You're going to have to get someone local to talk, otherwise we'll just be rehashing what we did out in Slagelse in the first few days after Ghazala Khan was killed. There wasn't any depth to our coverage, and people lost interest.'

Camilla watched him for a moment. She didn't actually think there was anything strange about readers' avoiding the tragedy of an entire family joining forces to beat their daughter to death because she'd sullied their familial honour by marrying someone they didn't want her to. Camilla really couldn't blame readers for turning their backs on that one in disgust. At the same time, she understood what Terkel was saying. Over time, all the reporting on cases like these started to sound the same, so their coverage of this case would pack more of a punch if she could land an interview with a member of the family. That probably wouldn't be so easy to accomplish, but she could certainly take it on as a challenge.

'And then of course you'll byline a report from Holbæk with local reactions and whatever else you can dig up.'

'But we still don't know if the girl is actually from there,' she pointed out.

He conceded her point but thought it wouldn't hurt to stick to the plan all the same.

'I talked to Storm,' he explained. 'The MTF already has a team in town. It's probably not a bad idea to stick close to them. He agreed to give us an update on the case by phone later tonight, once they've got a little more information to put out. You stay here and write that tonight so we can run it in the next edition, and then drive out there tomorrow morning.'

Camilla nodded and thought about Storm, whom she had a great working relationship with. He didn't have the same aloofness from the press that several of the other lead detectives had, which undeniably made it a little easier to enjoy friendly rather than irritable interactions with the police.

She went back to her office to pull out her calendar. Sometimes she was organised enough to jot down her family's and friends' plans. This was usually limited to her mother in Skanderborg, Markus's dad and Louise. She started by calling Tobias to find out if he could take their son a day earlier than planned. This week he was supposed to pick Markus up from school on Friday and keep him until Monday morning, but if he didn't have other plans he was usually more than happy to take Markus for an extra day.

She sent a text message and quickly got a reply that that plan was okay: Tobias would pick Markus up on Thursday afternoon. So that was covered. Camilla briefly pondered calling Storm and asking if he had any more information, but she decided to give him a couple more hours. She still had plenty of time until her deadline. Instead, she printed out the missing-person report to have it ready, and then she went down to grab a bite to eat.

Louise carried her weekend bag into reception, and the woman at the counter handed her the room key along with a message that the others were already at the restaurant. She hurried up to her room with her bag, quickly scanning the large, airy room – yellow walls, gaudy curtains around the large windows. The décor included light-coloured birch furniture, a large framed America's Cup poster from 1987 and a painting of the crowns of some trees densely packed together under a blue sky. Next to the bathroom there was a small dressing table.

She went into the bathroom and washed her hands,

splashing a little cold water onto her face. Then she removed her hair band and shook out her long, dark curls before gathering them back into a ponytail. That would have to suffice. Before heading to the restaurant, she sat down on the bed and dialled the two numbers that Dicta Møller had given her, but no one answered either call. Dicta's friend's mobile phone went to voicemail, and her parents' landline rang and rang until Louise hung up.

'I ordered something for you,' Søren said, as she walked into the restaurant, 'but you should tell them what you want to drink.'

They were the only diners, and the waiter was busy talking through the swinging door that led off to the bar. She walked over to him and ordered a Coke before taking the empty seat her former partner had saved for her at their table.

'So you think it may be this girl's friend?' Storm asked as she sat down.

'Can't rule it out. There are several similarities,' Louise replied, looking at him.

He was speaking from across the table four seats away from her, so she had to raise her voice.

'She said her friend is from Jordan, she has a beige jacket, and she wears white Kawasaki shoes. I think we have to take her information seriously and follow up on it.'

Storm nodded.

'How long has it been since she was heard from?' he asked.

'She wasn't at school, and she missed a date with her friend this afternoon, so it's only really been today,' Louise replied.

'None of those things are uncommon,' said Mik, who was sitting across from Storm. 'What was her name – the girl you talked to?'

Louise hesitated until she realised he was asking because he thought he might know her. That's how it was with small-town life, she reminded herself. People knew each other.

'Dicta Møller,' she answered, adding that the girl and her missing friend were in ninth grade at Højmark School.

Mik shook his head; apparently the name didn't ring a bell. Holbæk wasn't quite that small.

'Shouldn't we focus on our food now? That way, we can throw ourselves back into our work afterward,' Storm suggested, apparently forgetting entirely that he had started the whole conversation.

The waiters started bringing in huge plates of Wiener schnitzel, with slices of veal as thick as phone books. The meat was served with pan-fried potatoes, peas, anchovies with lemon, and horseradish on the side. Gravy was set out in a little boat next to each place setting. Normally Louise would have lost all appetite when confronted with an enormous portion like this, but the last thing she had eaten was some porridge she'd dished up at seven that morning. So she tried to ignore the oversized portion, reminding herself that there was no shame in not cleaning her plate ... She could just hear her grandmother: *No shame in not cleaning your plate* ... Nowadays, if anything, there was more shame associated with overeating. After dinner, several of the others ordered apple cake with whipped cream, while she made do with coffee.

She could already tell what direction things would go if she was to be living and eating with a pack of hungry men like this for any period of time. Not that she was some kind of delicate lettuce eater, but she was going to have to keep an eye out. Otherwise she'd just end up having to run off the weight during her morning jogs.

'Let's regroup in the command centre for our briefing,' Storm said when everyone was finishing off their coffee. They split up and left the restaurant in small groups, chatting away.

Bengtsen was waiting for them by the time they got back. He had made a fresh pot of coffee, and had a baking sheet of chocolate cake on the table in front of him.

'It's from Else,' he said, passing it around.

Louise tried to call the two numbers for the girl and her parents again, but since there was still no answer, she sat next to Bengtsen and was happy to take a piece of cake. She had regretted not ordering the apple cake almost immediately, even though she felt as if she were bursting at the seams.

'Is Else your wife?' she asked, slicing a corner off the cake and tipping it onto a piece of paper towel. She had decided to ignore the somewhat rigidly square grid Bengtsen had begun when he took the first piece.

He nodded, drawing the ends of his narrow lips up only just enough that Louise dared interpret it as a smile. But whether the smile was an expression of a lifelong devotion to his wife or whether it was because he was a little shy about having food made for him, she couldn't say. She was quick to praise the cake as soon as she had got a bite into her mouth.

'How did it go out at the crime scene today?' she asked Dean, who was sitting on her other side and who had loosened his tie a bit. 'Did anything turn up?'

'The Frogman Corps has been doing dives up and down the cove, but they haven't found anything,' he replied, referring to the elite special forces unit of the Royal Danish Navy. He poured her a cup of coffee before saying that forensics had kept the girl's beige jacket out at the scene so the dogs would have something to go by.

'Various things have been collected from the scene,' he continued, but he was interrupted by Storm, who asked him to speak up so everyone could hear.

Dean Vukić looked around and reiterated that the divers hadn't found anything they could link to the girl or her murder and that the canine units weren't finished yet.

'There are some tyre prints we'll research. And we have several footprints that we need to take casts of. And the CSI team has secured some evidence from the soil in the form of cigarette butts, chewing gum, mucus from globs of saliva that will be checked for DNA, and then we'll see what we have,' he said.

Yes, we'll see, Louise thought. But first they had to find out who the girl was.

'We haven't found a purse, bag or mobile phone,' Dean finished after a pause.

Now it was Mik's and her turn, and Mik updated everyone on the autopsy.

'We're obviously ruling out an accident, given the concrete slab she had tied to her waist,' Storm stated when he'd finished.

'What about suicide?' Søren asked.

'In that case she would have had to jump into the water from a boat,' Skipper said, but he added that they had not come across any unmoored boats in their survey of the area.

'If she had been attacked at that location, there would have been prints in the dirt or on the bluffs near the water,' said Dean, who had spent the whole day working with the CSI team. 'There were no signs of any struggle. And, again, some kind of boat would have been needed to get her so far out into the water.'

'There are some boats moored out at Hønsehalsen that the fishermen use,' Bengtsen interjected, who evidently had in-depth knowledge of the area.

'All those boats are accounted for,' Skipper said. 'They're all moored, so she couldn't have used them herself, in any case. But we should take a closer look at them.'

'Most likely she was killed somewhere else and taken out to Hønsehalsen,' Dean added. 'Otherwise, the dogs would have responded at the scene. We ran the dogs through the little marina with all the dinghies too, and they didn't find any-thing.'

Everyone nodded and seemed to agree.

Storm was sorting through some scraps of paper as though they were playing cards.

'These are the tips that have come in response to the missing-person report so far,' he said, dropping them non-chalantly on the table. 'Probably nothing of much interest. All of the girls are native Danes, but let me flip through them quickly,' he said, fishing out his glasses. 'There's a Lisette Andersen, age seventeen, from Kalundborg. Her mother called in. Her daughter has short blonde hair.'

'Didn't it say that our girl has long dark hair and might be Arab?' Søren asked pessimistically, disqualifying Kalundborg. 'A Tove Mikkelsen called in about her daughter, age twenty, from Roskilde, but she pointed out that her daughter looks very young and could well pass for sixteen.'

'We get a couple of hundred missing-person reports about teenage girls every year,' Ruth interrupted, looking at the men around the table. 'Some of them make their way to Christiania,' she went on, reminding them of the appeal of Copenhagen's downtown hippie commune, 'or they get settled into a co-op building or communal house somewhere and come home again once the exoticism of their adventure has faded and they miss hot baths and decent food. But there isn't anything you can say when a mother is worried that something has happened to her daughter.'

'True enough, but there's no reason to spend more time on that now,' Storm replied, instead asking Louise to tell Bengtsen about her conversation with the teenage girl. Bengtsen had not been at the dinner at the hotel restaurant, so he didn't yet know anything about Dicta Møller's visit.

She quickly updated him on the conversation and on the similarities that were of interest.

Bengtsen nodded several times as Louise spoke.

'Given so many things that match, we definitely need to get hold of Ms Møller's friend or her parents so we can figure out what's going on,' he said. 'We can't proceed with the investigation until the body has been identified.'

'I've called her and her parents' numbers a few times, but there isn't any answer at either number,' said Louise.

Storm looked from Louise to Mik Rasmussen.

'You two drive out there right away. We've got to determine whether we've found the right girl. And then we'll go from there.'

6

'There's a lot of ethnic diversity in this neighbourhood,' Mik Rasmussen explained as they parked next to some townhouses at the end of a large block of flats. The townhouses were made of yellow stone, and there were two apartments in each.

Samra al-Abd and her family lived in one of the upstairs units. From down in the car park, Louise could make out a faint light in the one room at the front of the building. Not much light, probably from a single lamp, she guessed, walking closer. The downstairs neighbours were clearly at home. That unit had lights on everywhere, and she could see someone through the window.

They walked up the stairs together and rang the bell. As they waited, Louise jotted down the name on the door: Ibrahim al-Abd. There was no woman's name. After a few minutes and several rings they gave up and went down again.

'Let's just go and talk to the neighbour,' Louise suggested, walking over and ringing the bell on the ground-floor apartment before her partner could object.

The door was opened, almost before her finger had released the button, by a woman with a crutch under one arm. Louise introduced herself and asked if the woman knew if her upstairs neighbours had been at home over the course of the evening.

The woman at the door took a small step back when she learned they were with the police, but at the same time a spark of curiosity gleamed in her eyes.

'Is anything wrong?' she asked.

Louise shook her head and said that she assumed not, but they had a question for the family upstairs.

'Have you seen their daughter at all today?' Mik asked over Louise's shoulder.

The neighbour seemed to think about it and then shook her head.

'I don't think I've seen any of them today at all. But you could check if their car is in the car park. Maybe they all went out in the car together.'

Louise stepped aside so Mik could move in closer. 'What kind of car is it?' he asked.

'It's a run-down thing, red.'

'What make?'

Louise was already sure this woman was clueless about makes and models, so they would have to take whatever she said with a pinch of salt.

'A Honda,' the neighbour said, after a long pause.

Louise took a notepad from her pocket and wrote, *Red car, older-model Japanese. Check vehicle registration.*

'How many kids do they have upstairs?' she asked before they left.

'Four. Two older ones, and two little ones,' the woman said, explaining that the younger children were Aida, a girl who was four, and Jamal, a boy of about two.

Louise and Mik said thank you and apologised for disturbing her. The neighbour stayed in the doorway watching them until they got back to their car.

Just as they were driving out of the car park, Louise yelled, 'Stop!' There was a red car parked there matching the description. She jumped out and went over to an older-model red Peugeot 306. She wrote down the vehicle registration number and walked back over to her partner.

'Should we just try to go upstairs again and see if they'll open the door?' she suggested, but she could tell that he really wanted to get going and thought they had already done enough.

'You can wait,' she said. 'But it does look like their car is here.'

Mik stayed in the car with the engine running while Louise ran back upstairs and pressed the bell. She stepped away and looked in through the window next to the front door. She could see the kitchen, and it was completely dark. There was a bedroom on the other side. Louise leaned over the railing and peered in. That was the window with the light on, but the room was empty and the door to the hallway closed. It was a girl's room, she thought.

After pressing the doorbell a second time, she went back down and walked over to the other side of the building, but everything upstairs was off and dark, Louise noted. So she returned to the car.

The drive back to the police station took ten minutes, and they agreed that Mik would check the car's registration in the motor-vehicle registry when they arrived to find out whether the Peugeot was registered at that address. Again Louise had a feeling he was eager to get the job done so he could go home.

'Not much new information. No one was home,' she reported to the others sitting in the command centre. 'But what we do know about this girl fits the description we have. Samra al-Abd is from Jordan. She has long hair, and her clothes also match the description pretty well.'

'We need to find someone who can come to the Pathology Lab and identify her,' Skipper said, filling his mug with coffee.

'With her parents' permission we could take Dicta in to do that,' Søren suggested. 'We have to be sure it's someone who knows the deceased well.'

'She's too young,' Bengtsen interrupted. 'We should only use Dicta as our very last option. It's too much for a girl that age to be confronted with a corpse, even if it turns out not to be her friend.'

It surprised Louise to hear him make that objection.

'What about her class teacher from school?' she suggested. 'She would know her student well enough that we can trust what she says.'

Storm nodded and asked her to get in touch with the teacher so they could get the identification done that night.

'The press has started pushing for more details. But I'll take care of them,' he continued.

That sounded sensible: it wouldn't be much help if everyone was taking calls and they didn't have a chance to coordinate the information before it leaked out.

Louise got up and left the meeting to call Dicta and get the name and number for their ninth-grade teacher. Mik had stayed in the office to check the red car in the motor-vehicle registry. He had an answer ready when Louise came back.

'It's good enough: it belongs to Ibrahim al-Abd,' he said, pronouncing the name slowly and trying to put the stress on the right syllables. 'The address also matches,' he added. 'And there was a mobile phone number registered for the same name, but the phone seems to be switched off.'

'We should be prepared for things to go late tonight,' Louise said. She told him about the impending identification before dialling Dicta's number and waiting for the girl to answer. Mik and Louise had family living in the area around Holbæk, so the task had fallen to them. To her surprise he nodded absent-mindedly and stood up, pulling on his jacket.

'Well, I've got to run a quick errand.' Then he left the office without another word.

'Jette Petersen,' Dicta said when Louise got her on the line and asked for her teacher's name. In the same breath Dicta asked if it was Samra who had been killed.

The anxiety in this question was palpable to Louise even over the phone.

'We don't know yet. But we are certainly taking your concern seriously,' she said to dampen the girl's fears. Then she asked if there were any friends Samra might be staying with. 'Does she have a boyfriend?' she asked more specifically.

'No,' Dicta said quickly. 'She's not allowed to have a boyfriend or anything like that, and she doesn't usually get permission to go out that much. Sometimes she bends the rules, but that's mostly when she's supposed to be coming over to my house and her father won't let her.'

Louise wrote this down. If it proved relevant, Louise wanted to hear more about how Samra managed to sneak out and be with her friends, but she would not probe into that right now. As they were talking, Dicta found their class teacher's phone number, and she gave Louise both her home number and her mobile.

'Thank you so much, and I apologise again for bothering you,' Louise said before hanging up. Louise could hear Dicta's voice choking up as they said goodbye and knew perfectly well that calling her had only added to the girl's worry.

Louise glanced at her watch as she dialled Jette Petersen's home number. It was nearly half past nine, a bit late to be calling people; but the way things were, they couldn't wait until the next day.

'This is Helge,' a man's voice said.

Louise introduced herself and asked to speak to his wife. She didn't think it was necessary to fill him in on the reason for her call.

There was a moment's silence, then the teacher got on the line. 'Yes?' she said, a little coldly.

Louise introduced herself again and apologised for the late call.

'I'm calling because I'd like to talk to you about one of your students.'

'Has something happened?' Jette asked anxiously.

Louise heard a chair being dragged over the floor. Based on her voice, Louise guessed the woman was middle-aged, but it was hard to say – she could also be younger and just a little tired.

'That's what we're trying to find out,' Louise answered. 'And I need your help.'

'Who are you talking about?' the teacher asked quickly, and

Louise could tell she was holding her breath, waiting for the answer. Probably not because hearing one name would be any less bad than hearing another, but because the teacher was nervous about what was coming.

'This is about Samra al-Abd,' Louise said.

'What's happened?' Anxiety seized the teacher's voice, making it shriller.

Louise explained that the police had received a visit from Dicta Møller, who linked Samra with the girl who had been found dead early that morning.

'Oh, I heard about that. But it didn't occur to me it might be one of my kids!'

'It's certainly far from sure,' Louise hastened to say. 'But there are some similarities, which means we have to look into whether it could be Samra or not. How long has Samra been in your class?'

'Ever since she moved to Denmark four years ago. She started fifth grade just after the summer break.'

'We haven't been able to get hold of Samra or her family, and despite the late hour I'm afraid I need to ask if there's any way you could accompany me to the Pathology Lab in Copenhagen tonight and tell us if the deceased girl is your student.'

'Of course.' Her voice grew slightly hoarse, and she was breathing deeply. 'I can be ready in ten minutes.'

'That's very good news. We'll pick you up,' Louise said, silently cursing the fact that her partner had just taken off. They could have the girl identified before midnight if they got going now.

She went out and found Storm, telling him she was ready to drive to Copenhagen with Samra's teacher.

'If you leave now, I'll get Bengtsen and Velin to see if they can track down any family members who might know where the parents are.'

Skipper and Dean were sitting with Ruth, reviewing the technical evidence that had come in during the day so it could be entered into the database. They had turned up some tyre tracks, which might be of interest, and the technical investigation would continue the next day.

'Well, I'll be on my way,' Louise said, but at that moment she saw her partner walking towards her, ready to go. She couldn't help thinking it was some kind of retribution that he'd ended up having to make this late trip into Copenhagen even though he was obviously itching to get home.

7

Samra's teacher lived in a yellow house on the outskirts of Holbæk. Forty-five years old, Louise guessed, plus or minus. She was an attractive woman with her short, dark hair tucked behind her ears, her glasses pushed up on top of her head, and her lipstick a subdued hue. Her voice made it clear that she was not quite as composed as she seemed, and she was clenching her hands tightly together in her lap.

They didn't talk much in the car. Mik assumed the role of chauffeur– he hadn't uttered a word since they left the police station. He drove with a local's familiarity through the residential neighbourhoods named after various flowers, and he nodded subtly when Louise volunteered to walk up to the teacher's door by herself.

Now Louise sat leaning her head against the window on their way to Copenhagen for the second time that day. Jette Petersen obviously had her mind on her student, who might be the victim in this case.

Before they left Holbæk police headquarters, Louise had phoned the on-call Pathology Lab technician in Copenhagen, asking to have the body brought out: it would be ready for viewing when they arrived.

'Is it normal for Samra to miss a day of school?' Louise asked, breaking the silence and turning around in her seat to look at Jette.

She quickly repeated that they still weren't at all sure that the victim was Samra al-Abd, but this was the only relevant tip they had received on the missing-person report. And obviously the fact that they weren't able to get in touch with either the girl or her family was a contributing factor in their suspicion.

'Well, she misses a day every now and then. Most of the students in this class do. But she hasn't had any major absences. In fact, it's fairly uncommon for her not to show up,' the teacher said after thinking a bit.

'What's her family like?'

'I don't know much about them,' Jette replied. 'Samra has a brother, Hamid, but I only know him by sight. He's a few years older than she is, I think. He only attended our school for a year before moving on to the business school.' Jette paused, then went on, 'She's a very pretty girl, and I got the impression several times that the parents had the son keep an eye on her. He was often standing around waiting for her at the end of school, and then he'd accompany her home. Occasionally she would run into trouble if she stayed late after school or if we had a special-topic week and were working on class projects into the early evening. The last time we did that, Samra asked me to call her parents at home to confirm that she would be staying at school that late. So I guess you could say they keep a pretty close eye on her, but she never complains about it. I probably couldn't put up with it myself, though.'

'What's your impression of her parents?'

'I've met them only a few times. Her father showed up just once for a parent-teacher consultation; apart from that I haven't seen him. But last winter we did "Food Week". We have several immigrant kids in class, so we spent a week focusing on different food cultures, and we invited all the students' parents for an evening in the home-ec classroom and asked them to prepare a special dish together with their children. It was really great – homey and pleasant and fun – and we ended up with a huge buffet of Danish and international dishes. Samra's mother, Sada, is a lovely, sweet woman. That night we laughed a lot and ate a lot, and I don't think I might otherwise have had the opportunity to talk as freely with the mothers had it not been in a format where they were serving their food to us. Everyone's dishes came with lots of funny stories. Sada had her two littlest ones with her as well, Aida and Jamal, and Samra's sister was a big hit strolling around the room in her little white apron, holding her mother's fancy serving dish in those dainty hands of hers and asking, "Would you like any more, ma'am? Sir?"' Jette smiled at the memory.

'Does Samra have relatives in the area?' Louise asked. 'Or further away, for that matter, that her family might be visiting?'

'They do have some family here in town. I'm not sure whether they're on her mother's or her father's side, but Samra definitely has a cousin. She's in the other ninth-grade class, but I have her for maths,' Jette said. 'Also, I think there's an uncle who lives somewhere around Ringsted, or somewhere between Holbæk and Copenhagen, I'm not exactly sure. But during the holidays last summer I ran into Samra at a flea market in Ringsted, and I think she said she was visiting family. My sister lives just outside Ringsted,' Jette said by way of explanation.

'Do you know what her uncle's name is?' The teacher shook her head.

Louise knew that Bengtsen and Søren were already trying to locate members of Samra's extended family; with a bit of luck the families shared the same last name. She wondered if she should ask any more about the girl but decided to wait until she knew whether it was actually Samra al-Abd whose body was lying out, ready to be ID'd.

A man was waiting to let them into the Teilum Building, which was otherwise dark at this late hour, and he led them through the waiting room to the left of the main entrance, around a corner and then through the door into a smaller waiting room. He asked them to take a seat on the blue sofas and wait for a moment. There was a box of tissues on the table, and the blinds were rolled down over the window into the viewing room, where Louise knew that the girl was already lying.

The technician opened the door to the room, and he asked Jette to come in. Louise stood up and walked over to the door. He had pulled the white cloth down to reveal the girl's face, and her hair was neatly arranged over her narrow shoulders. She had no wounds or bruises. She looked the way you often hear: like she was asleep.

It was over after the first glance. Jette nodded and confirmed that the dead girl was fifteen-year-old Samra al-Abd, who was a student in her ninth-grade class. Louise nodded at

Mik, who stepped out to make the phone call so they could start focusing the investigation.

The teacher placed her hand on her student's cheek and let it rest there for a moment as she looked at Samra's face with her eyes shut. Jette's eyes were filling up as she turned, and Louise left her in peace as the tears started flowing freely.

When Mik came back in, to Louise's great surprise, he stepped over to put his arm around Jette's shoulders and stood there for a moment comforting her. Louise couldn't hear what he said, but she noted that the teacher stopped crying, and shortly after she heard him ask if Jette was ready to go back to Holbæk. She saw the small nod, and they slowly began to walk towards the exit. Louise stayed back a bit as Mik helped the teacher into the car.

They drove back in silence. There were suddenly a number of important questions to ask, but Louise didn't feel it was the right time to ask them. It was late, and Jette was sitting with her eyes closed, taking deep breaths as though she were struggling to regain control over the emotions that had suddenly sprung a leak within her. Her willingness to come had been an enormous help to them.

Louise received a text message from Søren, who wrote that the family in Ringsted had been located, but they were going to postpone getting in touch with them until morning, hoping that would allow them to inform the parents first.

Before dropping Jette off, Louise asked her not to mention anything at school. They wanted to make sure that the family had been told before they heard the rumours in town. They agreed to meet the next morning when the teacher had a free period in her timetable so they could talk about Samra.

'Goodnight, and thank you so much for agreeing to do this so late in the evening and at such short notice,' Louise said.

Mik got out of the car and shook the teacher's hand goodbye.

'Do you know her?' Louise asked as he pulled away from the kerb.

'I know who she is, and she knows who I am, that's about it. But it's never nice to take a blow like that while other people are looking on, let alone people who know you.'

Louise just sat and watched him, surprised by the thoughtfulness that had shone through Mik's reserve and awkwardness.

'I'm heading home, if that's okay with you,' he said when they arrived back at the police station. After they dropped Jette off, they had stopped at Dysseparken 16B to inform the girl's parents, but there was still no answer at their door.

Louise nodded at her new partner and said goodnight before heading up to see whether the others were still at their desks. The lights were off in most of the offices, but Ruth Lange was sitting at her desk working. Ruth told her that everyone had just taken off and they would regroup again at eight.

Louise sat down in her office and found to her satisfaction that the IT guy had managed to set up her two laptops, so she would be ready for the next morning. She took out her personal mobile phone and saw the long list of messages from Camilla, all asking her to call. But now it was too late.

She turned it off and flipped it shut, and then started walking over to the hotel with an extra key that had been dropped off for her that opened the main door to the hotel when the front desk was closed. She suspected there wouldn't be anyone at the front desk this late, but she still went over to see if she could get anything to drink and take up to her room.

Søren Velin was sitting in one of the roomy armchairs in the lobby waiting for her. With two beers.

'Hey,' he said.

She smiled and sat down. There was a pack of cigarettes on the table, but she quickly looked away. She had relapsed and started smoking again over the summer but had decided to quit again.

'How's it going?' he asked, holding out a beer to her.

'All right,' she replied. 'We got the girl ID'd.'

He nodded, then said, 'Actually, I meant how are you doing?'

'I'm all right, too.' Louise said.

'What about your partner? Is he okay?' he asked, and Louise took care not to say too much because she knew she couldn't afford to complain.

'I haven't really figured him out yet,' she said. 'It's like we're not communicating on the same frequency.'

'Well, everything is pretty new. Are you still happy about being in Unit A back in Copenhagen?' he asked, shifting the subject away from the local situation.

She nodded and asked if he had plans to come back.

'Yes, but I don't know when,' he replied. 'Right now things are going well here.'

'What about at home? Are you guys able to stay connected with you gone so much?'

'Actually, it's working pretty well,' he said. 'As long as Lisbeth is enjoying working from home, I think we can make it work.'

Søren and Louise had been partners back when Søren's wife was deciding to leave her job and start up her own web-design business, so Louise had been privy to all the considerations that had entailed.

'With her working from home, it's possible for her to take care of Sofie alone, and things have been working really well for them when I'm away.'

Louise estimated that his daughter must be about two and a half now. She still thought that the girl's name was a little pretentious, and she knew Søren had preferred the spelling 'Sophie', but he hadn't won that battle.

'Are things going well with her job?'

Although Louise knew that his wife designed websites, she had no idea whether it was a proper business or more like a hobby.

He nodded. 'For the time being, at least, and if things change we'll obviously have to sell Strand Boulevard,' he said, referring to their place in an affluent neighbourhood to the north of Copenhagen.

Yes, and buy somewhere out in Hvidovre or smack-dab on City Hall Square, depending on which direction things go, Louise thought, picturing one of the beautiful old brick buildings with ornate, wrought-iron balconies near the fancy hotels across from City Hall. But Søren was right. You had to adapt.

'How about you?' he asked, lighting a cigarette. 'Did you keep the apartment after Peter moved out?'

She nodded. 'That was my place when I was single too, before he moved in,' she reminded him.

He smiled. 'Ah, right. And do you think there will be two names on the door again at some point?'

She shook her head and loosened up a bit. There weren't many colleagues she felt like inviting into her private life, but back when Louise and Søren used to be partners, he had managed to break down her barriers, and she felt a little of their old familiarity starting to rekindle.

'At first Peter wanted to move back in. Or, I don't fucking know exactly what he wanted, but in any case he had second thoughts about the break-up at one point.'

When Peter had dumped her for someone else after eight years together, Louise had told Søren everything. It was some other girl Peter worked with. Then shortly after he had moved in with that girl, Louise found him standing in the stairwell outside her place, asking if they couldn't work things out after all.

'I just couldn't,' Louise said. 'And when I thought the whole thing through carefully, I came to see that the right thing had happened – it probably should've even happened a little sooner!'

Søren nodded, but at the same time asked if she wasn't saying that with the benefit of hindsight.

She shrugged.

'I spent a whole month with Camilla and her son in the South of France. We rented a little house and sat gazing out over the water drinking Kir and talking through everything that had happened to us at the start of that summer. I don't think I'm seeing it this way just because he's gone. We were too different and we wanted different things from our lives.'

She got lost in her thoughts for a bit while he nodded.

'Yes, but it can be hard to get perspective on stuff like this while you're in the middle of it, especially if two people's everyday routines seem to work without major conflicts.'

She conceded his point, but reminded him that there had been a few clear signs along the way.

'For example, I never thought about joining him when he would fly to Aberdeen for work.'

'Well, you're not exactly the archetype of the follow-him-loyally-at-his-heels housewife,' Søren replied drily.

'No, but I probably would have gone with him if he'd been the most important thing in my world,' she said, taking a sip of her beer.

'Do you miss him?'

She nodded. 'I miss him as a person, but I don't miss our life together.'

'Incidentally, what happened with Camilla after that arrest down in Roskilde? Is she still together with that guy's brother?' Louise shook her head and suddenly felt overwhelmed with fatigue.

'No, they broke up before we took that trip to France. The whole thing knocked all the wind out of her, and I don't really know what I should do to help her. The only sensible thing for her to do is forget him and move on.'

Søren stood up and grabbed another beer, and she nodded when he asked if she wanted to share it.

'I feel like giving her a firm shaking. The relationship between those two was completely lopsided, but instead of getting angry and flicking him off, which is much more her style, she's doing just the opposite.'

'That doesn't sound like the Camilla Lind I know,' Søren conceded, lighting another cigarette.

'Uh-uh, not the one I know either.'

'The best thing would be if she met someone else who completely swept her off her feet,' he said after a moment's thought.

'You're right. But that kind of thing just doesn't happen that often, and certainly not when you need it to.'

Louise glanced at her watch and downed the rest of her beer. 'I think I'm going to call it a night,' she said, standing. 'It's been great seeing you again – thanks for the beer. Next time they're on me.'

'Same here,' Søren said. 'I'm looking forward to working with you again.'

They went up together and parted ways at the top of the stairwell.

It was nearly half past nine the next morning when Ibrahim al-Abd arrived at Holbæk police headquarters. Louise had just returned to the office and grabbed a cup of coffee, and her hand was on her phone. Earlier that morning, Mik Rasmussen and she had visited the family's flat again. Since there was still no answer, Ruth Lange helped them look up where the father worked, which was a lumberyard by the harbour. When they arrived there, the manager said Ibrahim had just left.

He was a small man with thick, black hair and a solid, well-groomed moustache. Louise had been about to leave for Højmark School and her appointment with Jette Petersen, but she cancelled when Storm asked her to come with him to notify Samra's father.

'Let's go in here,' Louise said, leading Ibrahim into the office. She asked him to take a seat on the chair next to her desk and nodded at Mik, who had already grabbed an MP3 recorder that he was setting up from where he was sitting. She offered the father coffee and water while she prepared for the conversation. She was just about to shut the door, when Storm waved her out into the corridor.

'Try to get him to tell you a little bit about his daughter before you tell him that she's the person we ID'd.'

Louise raised an eyebrow and stood there for a moment but then nodded and turned to walk back into her office.

'You wanted to talk to us about your daughter?' she began. He nodded and said he had left work when he heard the news at nine that morning, which had included a report about the dead girl the police had found.

'What is your daughter's name?' Louise asked.

'Samra al-Abd,' the girl's father said, pronouncing her name clearly. He added that his daughter was fifteen years old and was in the ninth grade.

'How long has she been missing?'

He shrugged his shoulders all the way up to his ears and, holding out his palms in despair, said it was hard to know. 'We haven't seen her since she said goodnight and went to bed on Tuesday night.'

The night before she was found out by Hønsehalsen, Louise thought, feeling sorry for the man – in a moment he was going to find out his daughter was dead. Still, she wanted to try to get as many facts as possible about Samra al-Abd as long as the father was talking.

'What about the next morning when she was supposed to go to school?' Mik asked. 'Didn't you notice if she left for school?'

He was obviously also determined to get the father to explain himself, and he watched the man intently as he answered.

'No, my wife doesn't get up when our older kids leave for school.'

He went on to explain that he had to be at the lumberyard at six thirty himself, and three mornings a week his eldest son had a job there too, before his business-school classes started.

'He and I are already gone when Samra gets up.'

'Has your daughter disappeared from home and stayed away for a whole night before?' Mik asked.

At first Ibrahim shook his head, but after thinking for a

while he said, 'Sometimes the other young people she hangs out with infect her, like a rotten apple in a basket.' He looked accusingly at Louise for a moment, as if she bore part of the blame. 'So it can be hard to work out exactly what she's up to.'

'What other kinds of things does your daughter do?' Louise asked, seizing the opening.

She could see how torn he felt as he contemplated what to say.

'She doesn't always listen to what we tell her,' he said finally. 'Then she comes home when it suits her.'

'Does she often come home late?' Mik wanted to know.

'A few times it's been several hours past what we agreed on,' said Ibrahim.

'But right now we're talking about almost thirty-six hours – has she ever been gone so long before?' Louise asked.

'No, which is why I think something must have happened. She wouldn't dare,' the girl's father replied, and Louise noted that Samra apparently had reason to fear her father's reaction.

'Does your daughter have a boyfriend she might be staying with?' Louise asked, following every movement in his face.

His expression suddenly seemed less open and he shook his head.

'She's too young for that sort of thing. She's fifteen,' he said, looking Louise straight in the eye when he replied. Louise felt as though she were gazing directly into the abyss of a father's deep worry.

If he considered a fifteen-year-old girl too young to have a boyfriend, then he also probably believed the girl was too young to marry off, thought Louise, making it fairly unlikely that it was an 'honour' killing triggered by a conflict in that area.

Louise excused herself for a moment and went to ask one of her colleagues to check on whether there were any past reports of violence in the family. But when she entered the command centre, Ruth Lange had already foreseen Louise's request and had a printout of the information ready for her.

'We've got one report against the father for domestic violence. His wife filed it a year and a half ago. Apparently he beat both her and her daughter, and subsequently the wife stayed at a women's shelter in Nykøbing Sjælland. Other than that, we don't have anything on him or the elder brother. The father came to Denmark in 1998, while the rest of the family did not arrive until 2002. At that point, the youngest hadn't been born yet, and the little sister was still an infant. They come from a town fifty miles south of Amman, Jordan, called Rabba. Since early 2001 he has been working at Stark, a lumberyard down by the harbour,' said Ruth.

Louise hurried back to her office and sat down quietly so she wouldn't interrupt the interview.

'Do you have a picture of her?' Mik asked.

Samra's father gently pulled out a photo from his jacket pocket. He set it on the table. It must have been taken on Midsummer's Eve: Samra was wearing a light-coloured summer dress and you could see the bonfire in the background. Her long, dark hair fell onto her shoulders, and she was holding her little sister's hand. Both of them were smiling widely for the photographer. It struck Louise that she actually hadn't known whether Samra wore a headscarf, but apparently she hadn't.

'Is she the girl you found?'

Louise glanced at Mik, who nodded to her, then she turned to Ibrahim. 'I'm deeply sorry to have to tell you that your daughter's body was found in the water out by Hønsehalsen in Udby Cove.'

All the colour drained out of his face. His shoulders slumped, and a moment later tears burst from his eyes, and a long screeching sound was pulled up and out of him from somewhere deep within. As the sound made its way out into the room, the girl's father rose with a jerk and started to pace back and forth, crying out that it couldn't be true. The words were ripped into pieces by a stream of Arabic they didn't understand, but there was no mistaking the despair in them.

Louise approached cautiously, pulled the man back towards the chair, and tried to get him to calm down.

'My little girl,' he repeated between deep sobs, sitting with his face hidden in his hands.

The air in the office was heavy with misery and grief. Finally Ibrahim calmed down a little.

Mik turned the MP3 recorder back on and made an attempt to restart the interview.

'We need to ask you some more questions about your daughter's disappearance.'

The father looked at them with a distant gaze and tear-laden eyes.

'How did it happen?' he asked, his thoughts still preoccupied.

'We don't know quite yet,' Mik said, making no mention of the rope and concrete.

'Could you please repeat for us when you and your wife last saw Samra?' Louise asked, turning the conversation in another direction.

'Tuesday night, when my wife said goodnight to her at eight thirty.'

'Yesterday one of your daughter's school friends came forward when she heard we had found a dead teenage girl. Didn't you see or hear the news yesterday?'

Ibrahim al-Abd was frozen, sitting as if encased in ice for a moment before he shook his head and his face cracked.

'Was it on TV? So then everyone knows what happened—'

'We put out a description,' Mik interrupted him. 'No picture was shown.'

Louise couldn't tell from Ibrahim's face whether he thought it was good or bad that the missing-person report had gone out.

'Last night we visited your flat to try to talk with you and your wife, but no one answered. Where were you?' she asked.

It took a moment before Samra's father replied.

'At my brother's house in Benløse, outside of Ringsted,' he explained, and Louise just nodded.

'How did you travel down there?' she asked. 'By car?'

Tears were making his eyes shiny again.

'We drove,' he continued, diverting attention from his fresh bout of weeping.

'When did you come home?'

'Midnight; maybe one o'clock, I think.'

'But you didn't answer this morning either, when we called by again,' Mik interjected.

The man looked over at him and explained that he and his son had gone to work.

'My wife is very worried – she didn't sleep at all. After my son and I left for work, she took the little ones to her sister's house.'

'When we went to your flat last night, your car was parked

in the car park, and it was at just past ten. Does your wife have a car?' Louise asked.

He shook his head, but she had known the answer already. No other cars were registered to their address.

'If you didn't drive your car, then which car did you drive?' He didn't seem to understand what she meant.

'You drove down to your brother's house, you say. But your car was parked in the car park last night,' Mik clarified.

'No, no,' he said, jumping up from his chair and pacing back and forth again. 'We didn't drive. My son drove.'

'There is no vehicle registered in his name,' Louise interrupted.

'He's buying one. It's not all worked out yet, but he'll get it settled,' the father assured them.

Louise asked for the car's make and registration number, but Ibrahim could only say it was an older-model BMW.

'Could I just get your brother's name and phone number?' Louise asked, to be on the safe side, so they could compare that with the information Søren had dug up.

Ibrahim sat back down and gave her both.

'What happened. . . ? What happened to her?' he mumbled again, rubbing his forehead hard with his thumb and forefinger as his face once more took on an absent look.

Mik took over and pointedly asked Samra's father to describe in detail the period of time when he was last with his daughter.

Ibrahim calmed down a little, and Louise could see him pulling himself together and preparing to go through the last time he had been with his daughter. They waited as his breathing became regular again.

'Tuesday,' he said, savouring the memory of the weekday.

'I was down at the boat,' he continued; 'I have a small sailing boat moored in Holbæk's marina.'

Louise asked him to clarify where it was and wrote a note that she should have someone look into how long it took to sail from Holbæk over to Udby Cove, where the Hønsehalsen peninsula jutted out.

'When did you get home?' Mik asked after they had noted all the details about the boat so they could find it later.

'Around seven o'clock.'

'Was Samra at home when you came back?'

He thought carefully before nodding.

'Did anything particular happen that night?' Louise asked.

He shrugged slightly and said they had had a visit from family.

'Who from?'

Louise was starting to get annoyed at the way they were having to drag everything out of him. She had hoped that they would be able to get him talking without having to squeeze each word out so they would have his own description and sequence of events to go by.

'My brother,' he replied.

'From Benløse?' He nodded.

'You see a lot of each other,' she noted.

'That's normal in my family.'

'Was Samra with you?' Mik asked.

Ibrahim shook his head and said that she had spent the whole evening in her room. 'She was doing her homework,' he added.

'But you said goodnight to her?'

Again there was a pause before he explained that his wife usually took care of that sort of thing.

'I was in the living room.'

'We know that you were reported for domestic violence previously against your wife and daughter. Will you tell us what happened?' Louise asked.

Ibrahim winced and looked down at the table.

'Have there been problems between you and your daughter since then?' Louise continued.

He still didn't respond and they let him sit in silence. 'It was a misunderstanding,' he finally said. 'Nothing bad. I lost my temper.'

'What set off your anger?' Louise asked quietly.

'It was my son, and Samra stuck her nose into it.'

'How?'

'It's not her place to make a fuss about the way I raise my son,' he said simply.

'What did your son do?' Mik wanted to know.

'He lied to me. But I had misunderstood and made a mistake. I apologised, and my wife came home. You can see that everything got sorted out.'

Mik coughed briefly before meeting the father's eyes and asking: 'Did you kill your daughter?'

Ibrahim al-Abd's face shut down completely and he started crying and shaking his head vigorously. He looked back into Mik's eyes without shame.

Louise and Mik looked at each other and agreed that that would have to be enough for now. They asked him to give them his son's mobile phone number so they could get in touch with him.

On his way out, Ibrahim turned in the doorway, tears still running down his cheeks, and asked, 'Can we see her?'

They both nodded and said they would call him about a

time when he and his wife could drive over to the Pathology Lab in Copenhagen and see their daughter one last time.

He nodded his thanks and zipped his jacket all the way up to his throat before turning around and heading down the corridor past the offices where everyone was hard at work on the investigation into his daughter's murder.

Louise stood watching him leave until he disappeared out the door.

8

Louise and Mik sat in their office with Storm and told him how it had gone, and Louise called Samra's teacher and principal and asked them to notify the students before the news got out.

'We need to find out how that family works,' the lead investigator said. 'If her father or another member of the family did this, we need to close in on them before they start covering their tracks with uncles and alibis.' Then he stood up and strolled down the corridor, summoning everyone to the command centre

Louise felt strangely relieved that Storm had just said straight out what everyone undoubtedly suspected. Yet another 'honour' killing, or liquidation of women, as some had begun calling it, because they could not accept that there was anything 'honourable' about such an act.

Louise had brought the picture of Samra with her. She tossed it out onto the conference table so it could make the rounds.

'This is how she looked in June, so about three months ago.'

At that moment, the door opened and a young man came in balancing two white boxes in one hand. Storm had ordered fancy open-topped sandwiches from the local bakery.

'Here are your sandwiches,' the man said. Following him was a girl with plates, silverware and napkins.

Bengtsen got up and returned a moment later with a blue lunchbox that he set in front of himself.

'Aren't you having any?' Skipper asked, nodding at Bengtsen.

'No, I prefer to eat what I bring from home.'

'We're definitely going to have to meet this Else soon,' Skipper said.

Bengtsen ignored him and started opening his lunchbox, and Louise hurried to reach for a Veterinarian's Midnight Snack – an open-topped sandwich of buttered rye bread topped with liverwurst, corned beef, aspic and red onion – before anyone had a chance to call dibs.

'Did the father say anything?' Søren asked, getting everyone's attention again now that they had food on their plates.

'He said he got home at around seven on Tuesday night,' Mik said, wiping his mouth, 'and his daughter was home then. They had a visit from the uncle from Benløse, but Samra was in her room, and he has not seen her since.'

'Ibrahim al-Abd also has a sailing boat moored down at the marina,' Louise added, looking at Storm.

He set his knife and fork down, and a deep wrinkle appeared over his brow as he let that information seep in.

'So far we've got only the one crime scene. We need to get the girl's room and the rest of the apartment searched in a hurry – we can do it under the pretext that there may be important information about her disappearance. Then we should bring the mother and brother in immediately, and of course we've also got to get the sailing boat searched, as well as the dinghies anchored out in the cove.' He paused briefly. 'In addition, we need to ID her closest friends, so we'll be able to get their take on the relationships within the family.'

The boss looked around and asked who else they should get hold of.

'The father's brother in Benløse,' Mik said quickly.

Storm nodded and repeated that everyone related to the al-Abd family needed to be brought in as soon as possible.

'And you two need to help with all the interviews,' he told Bengtsen and Velin, adding that they were also responsible for obtaining a printout of the girl's mobile phone records.

Søren said that Samra's phone had not yet been found, but he had already requested a court order for the phone company to turn over all of the information pertaining to her phone number so they could get a list of all calls, times and cell towers.

Storm nodded in satisfaction.

'Shouldn't we call in an interpreter?' Louise asked. 'Based on Mr al-Abd's statement, his family speaks and understands Danish, but aren't we obliged to make sure that everything is being understood correctly?'

'We'd better,' Storm conceded and then looked at Bengtsen. 'Who do you usually use for cases like this?'

Bengtsen said that there was a woman they had been extremely satisfied with in the past who worked as an interpreter at Holbæk Hospital.

'Couldn't it present a problem if we use someone local?'

Louise interjected. 'Interpreters can be more loyal to the interrogatee than to the police. If we want to be sure that the interpreting is correct, we should use double interpretation and bring in one of the department's own interpreters.'

She spoke from experience. The first crucial interrogations in the Nørrebro case had gone horribly wrong because the interpreter turned out to be from the same area in Pakistan as the suspect. That meant he did not dare convey the uncomfortable questions the police were actually asking, and instead he made things up.

'Rick is right,' Søren said. 'We don't have any way to control for that, and Holbæk is a small town.'

'We've got a good guy, Fahid, so let's see if he's free so he can assist her,' Storm said and asked Søren to get hold of him. Then he turned to Skipper and Dean, who were following up on the technical investigation. 'We've been looking into the family's cars.'

Louise briefly updated the others on the old BMW that Samra's brother was apparently in the process of buying, and on the father's red Peugeot.

'I understand you've already got something around the crime scene that might be of interest?' Storm continued, asking them to report.

Dean explained that they had secured several tyre prints, but one in particular was interesting. Close to the bluff, the forensic techs had found a print of a tyre manufactured by Bridgestone with the brand name Europa II 195/50 R15 82V.

'So it's a fifteen-inch tyre, and that's a little unusual,' Skipper added. 'Most of us drive on sixteen-inch tyres. Bridgestone explained to us that this tyre is unique in its design and size, and it was for sale in Denmark for only a short period of time. A car dealer here in Holbæk, Hans Just, sells Bridgestones, and he said that on 10 March 2006, he sold a red Peugeot 306 to an Ibrahim al-Abd who lives on Dysse-parken and that vehicle had just had four completely new tyres put on, brand Europa II 195/50 R15 82V.'

'That car needs to go into forensics,' Storm said. 'They'll secure the tyres and put on some equivalent ones before he gets the car back, and then of course we can go over the interior in detail. We also want them to investigate the BMW, and I want that to happen today.'

Dean and Skipper seemed happy with that and got ready to return to work.

Louise got up as well, and on her way out of the command centre she tossed her paper plate and plastic cutlery into the bin. She liked this phase of an investigation, when the tasks were assigned and everyone was scrambling to get going on them.

9

When Louise got back to the office, she first called Samra's teacher to get the names of the school friends Samra had been closest to. She also called Dicta Møller and left a message on the girl's mobile phone.

It only took a minute before Dicta called back. Louise could hardly hear what she was saying and asked her to speak louder.

'Are you in the middle of class?' she asked.

Dicta explained that she had stayed home from school. She was sick.

'I'd like to talk to you, if you think you are ready for that,' Louise said, sensing that the girl was about to cry.

'Hmm,' Dicta said. Then came a sniffle and the girl inhaled deeply.

'I just heard,' Dicta cried, releasing the emotions she had been trying to hold back. 'The school called, but of course I knew immediately.'

Louise offered to drive to Dicta's house so she wouldn't have to come down to the police station. It would be helpful to get Dicta's views as quickly as possible on how Samra's family worked.

She told Mik across the desk that she wanted to drive out and have a quick talk with Samra's friend, and they agreed that Mik would continue questioning the family members. Then Louise could join back in once she returned.

She hurried down to the car park, tucking the slip of paper with Dicta's address in her mouth as she pulled on her jacket and opened the car door. She felt privileged to have been assigned her own vehicle. Back at the Copenhagen PD, a number of cars were allocated to each investigative team, but that didn't mean there was always one free when she needed one.

She had no idea where Holbæk's Østby neighbourhood was in relation to the police station, but she keyed the address into the car's GPS and praised the technology and the satellite that were both now set to guide her to the Møller family home. Normally she considered it a point of honour to have some feel for a place, but the only thing she knew in Holbæk was the town centre. She didn't have a very good handle on anything outside that. But when she saw the route, it dawned on her that instead of a car she should have asked them to issue her a bike. Even though the address was on the edge of town, it wasn't very far, and it would have done her good to cycle out there.

She soon found herself in a showy neighbourhood of newly constructed family homes not far from Beach Mill Meadow Park and the sound. The houses were close together, and Louise drove down the streets slowly, curiously checking out the homes on either side. All were built in individual styles with impressive driveways, and several houses had sunporches facing the street or were in a functionalist style with sleek surfaces and lines, while others were done in an older style with arches and balconies. Although the residents had clearly gone to some trouble to turn their houses into something unique and special, there were three things they pretty much all had: Poul Henningsen designer lighting, either outdoor sconces on exterior walls or conspicuous table lamps in windows facing the street; Swedish-style white wooden benches, and large lion statues carved from white stone gracing the driveways.

Louise inhaled all of the details. There were kids' bikes in most of the driveways, and she didn't doubt that this was a neighbourhood for privileged children. Yet you couldn't feel much life on a Thursday morning like this, probably reflecting the fact that both parents had to work to afford to live here.

If she hadn't already known that Dicta attended one of the city's normal state schools, she would have guessed that parents living here would sooner send their children to the hundred-year-old Stenhus School in Holbæk, one of Denmark's largest university preps, or to any of the city's other private schools. But apparently the Møller family had not chosen to make that sort of thing a priority.

The Møllers' house had a white plaster exterior with a large balcony that went all the way around the top floor. Louise guessed that the view was impressive: the sound, the marina, open fields, forest and the city. Parked in the driveway was a large new SUV. Louise was a little puzzled. As far as she had managed to find out, both parents worked in Holbæk; the father had a chiropractic clinic on the main street, and the mother worked part-time as a medical secretary. Yet they had opted to equip themselves with a Jeep Grand Cherokee with yellow licence plates, normally reserved for business cars that were eligible for lower fees. It irked Louise when people who didn't have a really good reason chose to drive big, heavy cars like that.

As she approached the front door, she heard fierce barking. There was a wall to the right of the house with a white gate in the middle. She had the feeling there might be a nice pack of medium-size dogs just on the other side, and she got a glimpse of the shadow of a German shepherd and an Old English sheepdog before she quickly took the three steps up to front door and rang the bell. *Ding-dong*. The sound echoed and only agitated the dogs more. Now there was barking from inside the house too. Louise wondered if she should have asked Dicta to come down to the police station after all. Not that Louise had anything against dogs, but all the noise and frenzy was annoying as she tried to gather her thoughts and prepare her questions.

Dicta was wearing a grey tracksuit, she had no make-up on, and her long blonde hair was gathered into a loose ponytail. Her panic of the other day were now entirely gone. Louise was standing opposite a young girl who was either trying to be a grown-up or striving to give an impression of maturity. Pale and deeply upset, Dicta invited Louise inside, into something Louise would have described as a laundry room – or scullery, as people still called them where she was from. A woman was busy grooming a large black poodle there.

The woman wiped the dog hair on her hands onto an apron that was mostly covered by a picture of a dog jumping through a car tyre. Underneath was written: *Stockholm 2006.*

'Hi, I'm Anne Møller,' she said, offering her hand to Louise. 'Dicta's mother.'

The latter comment was superfluous. Not only did the two of them resemble each other uncannily, but the woman also looked at Dicta with the concern on her face that only a mother could have for her child. 'I came home as soon as Dicta got the call from school,' she went on. 'She called me at the medical practice where I work.' She let the dog go and pulled her shoulder-length blonde hair behind her ears as she explained that she did competition-level agility trial training and trained other people's dogs for them. Those were the dogs running around out in the garden right now.

That explained all the barking, and probably the SUV, Louise thought.

The poodle was interested in her and began to sniff.

'Charlie, down,' Dicta's mother commanded. The dog hesitated only for a moment before going under the dining table and lying down.

Anne Møller asked Louise to follow her into the kitchen, where she pointed at the large oval Piet Hein table that filled the room.

'Do you drink coffee? I just put a pot on. My husband is on his way home. He just has to pass off his patients to the two chiropractors who work for him at the clinic.'

Anne's speech seemed a bit frantic and her cheeks were flushed. During pauses, her eyes would dart over to see how her daughter was doing.

Louise had taken a seat opposite Dicta and had the sense that the girl was tuning out her mother's stream of words. Dicta sat with her eyes trained on the table, her mind clearly somewhere else entirely.

'Do you take milk? I'll just warm some up!'

Louise looked up at Anne and said cold milk was fine, but Dicta's mother ignored her and placed a jug of milk in the microwave.

After clicking the door shut and punching in the heating time, she appeared to calm down. She came over and stood behind Dicta, laying her hands on her shoulders. She had taken off her apron and was dressed classically in a light-weight cardigan over a white blouse and beige linen trousers. Her face looked fresh and youthful with nice, smooth skin.

'It doesn't make any sense at all. Samra was just here a couple of days ago,' Anne said.

She started stroking her daughter's arms and then walked over and took out a plate and filled it with chocolate biscuits. She did the whole thing reflexively, because there was something safe and reassuring about setting out cups and biscuits on the table.

Louise looked intently at Dicta, saying she wanted to chat with her a little about Samra's friends and her relationship with her family.

Dicta slowly raised her eyes towards Louise, as though it were a long trip back to reality, and Louise gave her plenty of time once she finally began to speak. Mechanically, the girl took a biscuit from the plate and broke it into small pieces so the crumbs fell on the table as she rattled off the names of three other girls from school she knew Samra spent a fair amount of time with.

'I only know one of them really well,' Dicta said. 'She's my friend too; the other two I don't know that well.'

Louise wrote down the names and signalled that the mother was welcome to come over and sit with them. She'd been hovering in the background since they started talking. Now she brought her cup over and sat down.

'I think they mostly hung out together at school,' Dicta continued, regaining her composure a little. 'Samra hardly ever got permission to take part in anything that happened after school hours.

'Her parents were really strict,' she went on. 'She was supposed to go straight home and do her homework,' Dicta said. 'And she often had to help look after her little sister and brother, too.'

Louise detected a sweet sort of pride when Dicta explained that her friend Samra had been one of the smartest students in their class – but then you'd darn well expect that, Louise thought, if you were forced to pore over your schoolbooks for so many hours every day.

'You're good kids,' her mother interjected, stroking her daughter's cheek.

Dicta looked at her as though she didn't understand where that comment had come from, finding it out of place.

'She was a good kid,' Dicta stressed, turning her eyes back to Louise.

'You work hard too,' the mother insisted.

Dicta ignored her, and Louise hurriedly stepped in.

'But her parents did give her permission to come over here?' Louise asked.

'Yes, but definitely not quite as often as Samra would have liked, as far as I understood.'

Anne was the one who latched on to that question, and Louise listened in interest as Anne explained that she had met Samra's mother several times.

'At the medical practice where I work,' she said. 'She stops by there relatively often, either by herself or with the two younger children, and then we always chat about the girls and their school. She knows that Dicta is a stable, sensible girl, and that probably contributes to their feeling comfortable having their daughter at our house. But I never got the impression Samra was allowed to spend much time with anyone else after school either.'

'She also got permission to sleep over here,' Dicta said, adding that she hadn't got permission to sleep over at Liv's, another of the girls in their clique.

They heard a car engine stop and a door slam shut. Anne got up to go out and prepare her husband for the fact that there was a police officer visiting, Louise guessed.

He was a tall, handsome man, blond with bright blue eyes. It wasn't hard to see where Dicta got her looks from with these parents, Louise thought, standing to shake his hand.

'I'm Henrik,' he said once Louise had introduced herself and explained why she was there.

He gave his daughter a kiss on the cheek before going to get a cup from the cabinet and joining them.

'It's so terrible, you can hardly bear to think of it,' he said.

'I can't think of anything else,' Dicta said.

He looked with worry at his daughter.

'Of course you're thinking of her,' he said, turning to look at Louise. 'It's just so incomprehensible when it's a girl you know. It's been all the talk at the clinic this morning. People are afraid this will lead to something more.'

'It might, too, if there's a killer on the loose in town,' said Anne.

Henrik looked at his wife, and Louise could tell that he was about to say something reassuring when Dicta suddenly stood up and left the kitchen.

They sat watching her go.

'The police still don't know much?' Henrik asked, looking at Louise. She shook her head.

'We've started interviewing the family and are looking for witnesses who might have seen Samra during the period of time we think she went missing. But it's a gap that extends over twelve hours, from when she said goodnight to her mother in her room at eight thirty until she was found the next morning.'

Neither of the parents asked Louise whether the police thought the family was behind it. And she was happy about that. She looked over towards Dicta's room to assess whether enough time had passed for her to go in to talk to her more.

'She was a good kid,' Dicta's father said, using the same wording that his wife had used earlier. 'Even if her family had a different set of rules for her than the ones her friends lived under, it seemed like she accepted them. There was no anger in her voice and she talked openly about the things that were off-limits to her. I actually had quite a lot of respect for that. We also hear about girls at school who are very disruptive to class unity because they let all their pent-up frustrations spill over onto their classmates.'

Charlie, the poodle, had come in and was now resting his soft, furry head in Louise's lap. She scratched behind his ear.

'Many of these young immigrants are put into an unreasonable situation – especially those who come here after spending their childhoods in another country,' Anne added, backing up her husband. 'They get pressured to step into a life they are never given full access to. That has got to be frustrating, especially for young people who aren't that aware yet about the differences between Muslim and Danish ways of life.'

Louise listened without interrupting. She liked Dicta's parents, and it wasn't hard to see why Dicta's friends liked to spend time at her house. They were very down-to-earth and forthcoming.

'Nor is it easy to come to this country,' the father continued. 'It's not like we're trying to meet them halfway. That much is clear here, even though Holbæk is a relatively small town. Lots of immigrants have moved here, and it's obvious when you visit our schools or walk around in town.'

'But he doesn't mean that just in a bad way,' Dicta's mother hastened to inject.

'No, of course not,' her husband said quickly, 'but the tension has been growing more visible in recent years.'

He stood up and walked out to find his jacket and pull a pack of cigarettes from the pocket.

'Do you mind?' he asked before he tapped one out.

Louise shook her head, hoping in a moment of weakness that he would offer her one. But he didn't, probably assuming he was the only one with a nicotine addiction.

'The children of immigrants are placed in state schools, which causes many Danish families to choose private schools for their children – which is pretty much a ridiculous system,' he said, 'particularly at the secondary level, from seventh grade up. They may be good at reading and writing, but they have no idea who the prime minister is because they never watch Danish TV or read Danish papers, and it doesn't help that there aren't any Danish students in class to pick these things up from. It leaves our state-school classrooms full of only disadvantaged students with limited resources. And that's not good for anyone.'

'I assume that's why you're sending Dicta to Højmark School, which is state, right?' Louise asked.

They both nodded.

'Some Danish kids have to stay in the state-school system if we don't want the country to crack down the middle,' Anne said, her voice sounding tired, as though she had had to explain her position one too many times.

Louise thought of Camilla, who was of the opposite opinion when it came to her son, Markus. He was attending a private school because Camilla felt he had only a limited number of years to attend school and so his experience had to be as close to perfect as possible – and she definitely didn't want him held back by students without family resources who slowed the pace down for everyone. For a moment Louise was happy she didn't have kids herself, because she found herself torn between the two points of view.

She stood up and said she just wanted to see if Dicta was ready to continue. The poodle's eyes followed her, as though he were trying to figure out whether she was going to come back or whether he might as well take a nap.

She knocked quietly on the door and waited for Dicta to say come in. The room was large and bright with its own French doors opening out onto the garden. Several posters were hanging on the walls, but, considering the girl's aspirations of becoming a model, Louise was surprised there were no pictures of herself. When Louise asked about that, Dicta pulled a photo album off a shelf and flipped through the last few pages in it. Then she went to the wardrobe and got out a box that was crammed so full, its lid would no longer stay in place without a rubber band.

'My parents don't know much about this,' she explained as she opened the box and carefully spread the pictures out on the bed.

'Surely they can't help but notice when the pictures are printed in the paper,' Louise said.

Dicta laid out the last picture. 'They do know a little bit about it. Just not that I'm working on becoming a professional model, and that we've taken so many pictures.'

Louise looked at Dicta and thought she had a curiously grown-up way of relating to this modelling career that she hadn't even really embarked on yet. They must be the photographer's words she was using.

'Who took the pictures?' Louise asked, contemplating one where Dicta was sitting on the deck of a sailing boat with her long blonde hair fluttering in the breeze and her feet hanging over the edge. She turned the photo over to see if there was a copyright notice on the back, but there was nothing.

'His name's Michael Mogensen; and he's the best in town,' Dicta said, sitting up straight. 'We've spent a lot of time taking the pictures for my portfolio. Now I'm just waiting for him to finish them. There's something about the background he needs to correct in Photoshop; but once that's all set, the portfolio will be ready to be submitted to the major modelling agencies.'

Louise smiled at her. Dicta had a youthful joy and exuberance when she talked about her dreams, and at the moment it was just sweet – but it didn't take a professional's eyes to see that there was something naïve and rigid in Dicta's poses, which a more talented photographer would probably have done something about.

'It sounds exciting,' Louise said.

She fished out a picture in which Dicta was standing between Samra and a man who was in his mid-twenties.

'That's Michael,' Dicta explained. 'He's a staff photographer at *Venstrebladet*.' She sounded a little impressed that he had taken on the responsibility for shepherding her to the top.

Louise looked at the picture for a long time. Samra had a big smile on her face and her hair hung loose. It had been taken on a summer's day down by the water. Louise recognised the bridge out to Holbæk's public beach, and she thought she could just make out the red-painted main building and little changing cabins in the background.

'He looks nice,' Louise said, examining the average-looking guy with blond hair and thick eyebrows.

'Did Samra have her photos taken too?' Louise continued, asking out of curiosity.

Dicta shook her head. 'She just came with me a couple of times. Her father would totally flip out if he knew.'

Dicta stacked up the pictures and put them back into the box before carefully hiding it away again and making sure it was hidden by other boxes and a bag in the bottom of her wardrobe.

'Was she seeing any boys?' Louise asked once Dicta emerged again.

It took a while before she answered. 'What do you mean by seeing?'

Louise was angling again to find out whether Samra had a boyfriend, or whether there was a boy she had had an especially big crush on.

'She wasn't allowed to do that stuff,' Dicta continued.

'Not being allowed to do something is not necessarily the same as not doing it,' Louise tried to say, in a way that would not force Dicta to snitch on her friend for breaking her family's rules. Dicta herself obviously felt other people didn't necessarily need to know everything about Samra's life.

Louise asked how Dicta perceived Samra's relationship with her family.

Dicta shrugged, and when no answer was forthcoming, Louise stepped over and opened the door to leave.

'Over time, she preferred spending time here more than being at home,' Dicta said finally as Louise stood in the hallway, 'but that may also have been because there was always so much noise and so many people at her place,' she continued, following Louise.

Louise went back out to the kitchen and said goodbye to Dicta's parents, who were still sitting at the table talking softly, but they got up and came outside with her.

'Did Samra mention anything about her family recently? Did she give the impression that anything wasn't as it should be?'

Louise glanced at the parents to see if they understood where she was headed with this line of thought.

Dicta's shoulders sank a little, and, without warning, all the tears she had been holding back suddenly flooded out. Her slender body began to shake as though convulsing from some intense cramp, and then the sobs emerged. Charlie got up uneasily from his place under the table and watched Dicta. The tremors increased, and Dicta's father took his daughter in his arms and rocked her gently back and forth.

'Had you noticed anything about Samra that might indicate

she was afraid of something the last few times you saw her?'
Louise repeated, persisting with her question despite the sobbing because the question might well have been what triggered
it.

Dicta didn't answer, and her father closed his arms tighter
around her. Louise nodded at him and said goodbye to
Dicta as she let the mother accompany her the rest of the way
out.

They stood on the front steps as Anne said she thought she
had noticed a change in Samra recently. She said Samra had
seemed sullen and sad.

'She used to enjoy helping me out a little with the dogs, and
when I was training them in our dog run out in the back
garden. But lately she's been staying up in the bedroom with
Dicta. Maybe they just had a lot of homework to do, or a lot
of things to talk about.'

Louise nodded. It was impossible to know, if Dicta didn't
want to say what was going on. Louise thanked Anne for the
coffee and asked her to tell her daughter that she could call or
stop by at the police station at any time if anything else came
up.

She was just stepping off the end of the driveway onto the
pavement when a blue station wagon drove up and parked at
the kerb, and she immediately recognised the photographer as
he got out of the car and started walking up towards the front
door.

'Hello,' she said, offering a hand. 'Detective Louise Rick.
I'm with the Holbæk Police Department.'

The man shook her hand and introduced himself. 'Michael
Mogensen,' he said, seeming a bit hesitant.

'I know,' Louise said, smiling. 'I was just looking at the

pictures you've been taking of Dicta. Those are some big plans the two of you have been cooking up there.'

He nodded a little self-consciously.

'I'd really like to help her. It would be fun for me as well if she got discovered and became famous.'

'I noticed that you also knew Samra.'

'Yes, a little,' he said. 'I promised Dicta I'd drive her out to Hønsehalsen cemetery so she can lay a bouquet of flowers and light a candle.'

The door behind Louise opened.

'I'm just coming,' Dicta yelled, disappearing back into the house. A moment later she returned, wearing a jacket and ready to go.

Louise went to her car and smiled at them as the photographer gallantly opened the station wagon's door for the young woman.

10

When Louise got back to the police station, she met Samra's father and a woman in the hallway. She guessed it must be the mother, Sada, because she was wearing a headscarf and keeping her eyes stiffly trained on the floor. They were following Søren Velin to the corner office where Bengtsen and both interpreters were ready for them. Louise nodded to them and hurried to her own office. Once there, she cautiously knocked before entering and found her partner in the middle of questioning Samra's older brother. Without interrupting, she took a seat and listened in.

'Where'd you get the car from?' Mik asked.

'From a friend, like I said!'

There was no trace of anger in the young man's tone, just a stubbornness that told them they shouldn't count on finding out any more than he'd already told them.

'But it isn't your car?' Mik continued. Samra's brother shook his head.

'Does that mean other people might have used it in the last week?'

There was no response.

Mik Rasmussen leaned forward and asked, 'Did you use the car on Tuesday night?'

Hamid nodded. 'I wasn't anywhere near Hønsehalsen.'

His Danish was very good considering he'd only been living in the country for four years, Louise noted, although he did have a tough time pronouncing Hønsehalsen.

'I'm not saying you were,' Mik interrupted. 'I really just want to know if anyone else might have driven that car out there.'

Samra's brother shook his head.

'Did your sister have a boyfriend?'

Mik had changed topics so quickly that it seemed as if Hamid needed a moment to reboot before he answered the new question. He shook his head.

'Who do you hang out with?'

'People from school.'

They had determined that he went to trade school, and in addition to a morning job where his father worked, he also had an after-school job at the local Kvickly supermarket. Ruth was already working on getting a list of his classmates in case they needed to talk to them.

Louise leaned back to listen in on the interview. She was surprised that her partner was being so aggressive with his questioning. Louise was more a fan of the cognitive interview method, in which you guided the subject through an explanation in his own words at his own pace. She had always found that more productive. But every now and then it just failed to get anything out of a subject, and then of course you had to be more aggressive.

'Does it bother you when girls have male friends?' Mik asked, changing topics again.

'Why the hell would I care about that? Girls can have male friends. What kind of silly preconceptions do you have?'

'So you feel that way even when your sister is involved?' The tone the question was asked in was filled with a confrontational sarcasm.

There was a bang as Hamid slapped his hand against the desk instead of responding, and in a way Louise couldn't blame him for losing his temper if the interview had been going like this from the beginning.

'Was your sister dating anyone?' Mik asked again, in a more subdued tone.

The brother shook his head and hid his face in his hands as he shrugged his shoulders.

Mik set down the pen he had been holding in his hand. 'That's enough for now,' he said and asked Hamid to wait until the interview had been typed out so he could read through it and sign it. Once that was done, Mik said, 'It may be that we need to talk to you again.' He followed Samra's brother to the hallway and held out his hand, but the young man ignored it and just scurried off.

'I guarantee you that got to him,' Louise exclaimed as Mik stepped back in and closed the door.

'He spent the first half-hour evading everything I asked about, so I did that to get a reaction,' Mik responded, and Louise got the sense that he had taken her comment as criticism. Instead of getting into it, she started focusing on her computer to avoid spoiling the mood just because they approached things differently.

'All right. I admit that he got to me, too,' Mik said after

they had each sat staring at their screens for a few minutes. 'But I'm having a hard time accepting his attitude towards immigrant girls and their male acquaintances. There must be a fundamental acceptance of what's permitted for girls. And yet here it seems like everything is divided into two categories. There's plenty of tolerance towards immigrant girls in general, but that tolerance is severely curtailed when it has to do with the female members of your own family.'

Louise thought about that for a moment and then nodded. 'She was kind of viewed as the family's property and then suddenly that turns into something else,' she said, remembering what a sociologist from the University of Southern Denmark had explained to her when she was on the Nørrebro case.

'That's really the crux of it when you're talking about honour and shame,' Louise continued after a moment. 'In families where those concepts are significant, people don't care that much about honour or shame when it doesn't have to do with their immediate family members. And in those cases when something does happen to offend the family's honour, it doesn't become dangerous until someone from the neighbourhood starts talking about it. As long as the problem is only known within the family's four walls, no one has to react to it. It's so strange that there's such a huge difference between the world in general and the inner circle.'

Mik watched her while she talked, and she could tell that he wasn't putting much stock in her explanation. But that was one of the important things she had learned during the case she had just wrapped up. It wasn't until it became publicly known that the family couldn't control their own daughter that the girl had to die. In the case in Nørrebro, the death sentence had been pronounced by an uncle and his three sons.

They wanted the girl killed before any of the other girls in the family became infected by her loose behaviour.

'The world is a strange place. I don't understand that way of thinking,' Mik admitted, shrugging his shoulders.

Louise smiled at him and said that there weren't many Danes who did.

'Jette Petersen is here,' Ruth announced from the doorway. She asked if they were ready for her and when they wanted the classmates to come in.

'Maybe we ought to see about borrowing a room at the school so we can do it while school's in session tomorrow?' Mik suggested and received a nod of confirmation from the administrative assistant.

'That'll save us a ton of coordination. Good idea,' Louise said, standing up to go to receive Samra's teacher.

'I'll write up the parents' and brother's interviews and update what we have in the case file on the family from before,' Ruth said before heading back to the command room.

Storm came in to ask them if they could also talk to the women's shelter the mother had stayed at to find out what information they had on the family. Louise took a seat on the edge of her desk as he spoke.

'We just need to find out if the parents were having problems with the girl, before we latch on to our suspicions,' Storm said.

'I'll call the shelter right away,' Mik offered, pulling out his papers and flipping through them. He left the office to find somewhere quiet to call from so Louise could start her conversation with Samra's teacher. Louise followed Mik into the hallway and asked Jette Petersen to come in.

'Would you like some coffee?' she asked.

The teacher looked tired, as if she'd been crying. Her eyes were red and there were streaks of mascara under her bottom lashes.

'We told the students right after their lunch break,' she said, 'and then we gathered Samra's classmates in the hall afterward and told them what had happened. It was the single worst experience of my twenty years of teaching.'

Louise let her sit for a moment.

'I'd actually thought the girls would take it the hardest. But several of the boys reacted quite strongly. Also in a somewhat unfortunate way.'

'In what way?' Louise asked.

'Obviously they were all really shocked, but I don't think they'd ever thought much about the fact that Samra and two of the other students in the class who aren't ethnically Danish came from different cultures. But now suddenly they're all aware of this and cursing all immigrants and wanting them to go home. Of course, they're mostly reacting to the feelings of helplessness and grief,' she said after pausing to think for a moment.

Louise nodded.

'There've already been journalists outside the school asking the students about Samra's family. About whether they'd tried to force the girl into an arranged marriage, whether maybe that was what triggered the killing. And that kind of thing is enough to stir up trouble among the kids.'

'But there wasn't anything like that, as far as we know,' Louise said.

Jette Petersen shook her head.

'Now we just need to help them stick together and talk about what happened so we don't end up with a worse schism in the class – or the school, for that matter. No one has been sentenced yet and we don't know what happened, but they've already made up their minds,' Jette said and then in the same breath added that it was both good and bad that the newspapers had been featuring stories about honour killings so prominently because of course that affected the kids' opinions about what must have happened when a girl like Samra was suddenly murdered.

Louise agreed with her, but had a hard time seeing how it could be any other way. At the moment, she couldn't think of a single murder case where a young immigrant girl had been killed and it wasn't the family that was behind it. But of course you had to be careful about leaping to conclusions, even though that was also where the police had been focusing their investigative resources.

Both women sat for a moment, lost in their own thoughts, then Louise asked Jette to describe Samra, both how she fitted into the class socially and as a student, anything that might help the police put together a more nuanced picture of the girl that could lead them to a motive.

_____

11

'It's clear she was very well liked and got along fine in class,'
Louise said, addressing the others in the command room later.
'Her parents didn't forbid her from attending class events and
other activities at school, but even so, there were problems at
times. Sometimes her father wanted proof that she was really
at school if there were late classes or something.'

'And Jette Petersen didn't have the impression that Samra
had much to do with her classmates outside of school hours,'
added Mik, who had been present during the last part of the
conversation.

'As we already know, Samra occasionally saw a couple of
the girls,' Louise continued. 'For the first few years after she
started school here in fifth grade, she played handball with a
bunch of kids from school, but that only lasted a couple of
years. Then she quit.'

'Something happens around the time girls start puberty,'
Dean explained. 'When they transition from childhood into

puberty, they no longer have the same freedom. Up until that point their fathers are in charge of their upbringing and they are welcome to play and spend time with other kids their age. But once the girls menstruate for the first time, all that's over. Then the upbringing becomes the mother's responsibility and their freedom is noticeably curtailed. And if things go wrong for a girl, it's the mother's fault. So they're kept at home and not allowed to hang out with boys the way they could before.'

'Are you Muslim?' Louise blurted out. She knew he was from the former Yugoslavia and was now married to a Dane, but she wasn't sure it was polite to ask.

He shook his head. 'Catholic,' he replied. 'But where I come from, there were a lot of Muslims.'

'Well, then your familiarity with the cultural concepts will give us a head start,' Skipper said.

Louise noted that, when viewed from the outside, their little group was quite diverse: a woman, a couple of older men with years of experience and strange habits, and a couple of young bucks who really wanted to make their mark. She smiled at Dean when he responded, 'Now I'm afraid of disappointing you.'

For a second he looked self-conscious.

'So we'll assume that Samra al-Abd didn't have that big a circle of friends. She occasionally spent time with some of her girlfriends after school and at the weekend, but she was kept on a relatively tight rein at home,' Storm concluded, looking at Louise and the others to see if there were any objections.

'I agree that she was under very tight control from her parents,' Søren Velin said, and gave a recap of his and Bengtsen's interview with the parents. They had both denied knowing anything about their daughter's disappearance.

'They say that their daughter didn't have many friends and preferred to spend time with her family,' Bengtsen began before pouring some coffee into a plastic mug. 'Yet her father maintains that he didn't really get worried about her being gone until she still wasn't home when they got back from visiting his brother in Benløse. And that sense of worry was only reinforced when he heard the news on the radio the next morning at nine.'

Now it was Mik's turn to report. 'I spoke to the women's shelter,' he began. 'She was there six months ago, and the woman I talked to remembered the family quite well. She said that Samra was rather beaten up when they arrived. It appeared she'd been hit, but she wouldn't talk about what had happened. So they got the story from her mother. The family voluntarily returned home after about five days, and there haven't been any more reports of violence since then.'

Everyone in the room sat digesting that for a moment before Storm spoke again.

'The preliminary results are back from the technical inspection of the father's boat,' he said. 'They didn't find any traces to suggest that he'd been carrying a concrete slab in the boat. There's no doubt it would have left scratch marks. There was also nothing to suggest that the boat was the scene of the crime. They're still studying the pictures.'

Storm looked over at Skipper. 'You head out to the house and examine her bedroom.'

Skipper nodded and his hair billowed gently.

'How's it going with the mobile phone printout?' Storm asked. This was aimed at Bengtsen and Velin.

Bengtsen pointed to the table in front of him where there were two sheets of paper.

'It's here,' he replied. 'She mostly sent text messages and we've located the numbers. Her family and some of the girls from school. No unknown numbers, no surprises,' he said, sounding disappointed that he didn't have anything more helpful to report.

Skipper and Dean stood up to go and help the crime-scene technicians examine the girl's room.

'Remember to check if she had access to a computer,' Storm called after them, and Dean turned in the doorway. 'And if she did, obviously bring it back,' he continued, and then directed his attention to Bengtsen and Velin.

'We need to set up audio surveillance in the home,' he said and suggested that that be done the next time the family came in for questioning.

That was Søren Velin's specialty and he nodded right away, so Louise guessed that he'd already done the prep work for that. 'Maybe you should head out there while the others are working on the bedroom just so you can get an overview of the apartment. We have a warrant, so there's no problem with your having permission to be there,' Storm said.

Velin nodded again and Louise could tell that he must have already been by the place and presumably had a very good idea of what he would need to be able to set up the audio surveillance there.

'The phone is easy, and you'll know best how to capture the conversations that take place in the various rooms.' Storm avoided going into detail. The custom was that only the officers who set up the equipment would know where the devices were located. 'Check the place out and get everything ready so we can start the surveillance tomorrow.'

'We should have it up and running today,' Bengtsen cut in. 'It would be crazy to wait until tomorrow.'

There was a second of silence. He was right.

'Well, then we need to get the family out of the house again,' Storm said, without showing any sign of irritation at having been rebuked by the local officer.

'We're not ready for our next questioning session yet. We need a little more time to prepare,' said Ruth, who was responsible for gathering all the details about the family's background and past.

'Then we'll do something else,' Bengtsen suggested. 'We'll invite them to come in for an update on where things stand in the case. Then we can also set up a time for them to go to see the girl's body. It'll be totally informational, no questioning, just an update of what our plans are, what the school has told the other students, and the fact that they're having a moment of silence for Samra tomorrow at noon. We also owe it to them to prepare them a little for what's going to come now that the press is starting to get interested in the case and in them in particular.'

The others nodded. They hadn't had a chance to discuss that yet. Of course the family should be provided the same courtesies others would be in that situation, even if suspicions were starting to point in their direction.

'We mustn't treat them as if they've been charged,' Mik Rasmussen added. 'They're just suspects.'

Louise could tell by looking at Søren that he was starting to get irritated. No one had been treating Samra's family as if they'd been charged; but even though he and Bengtsen were looking as hard as they could for witnesses who might have seen Samra and they were receiving assistance in those endless interview sessions from local officers from the Holbæk Police, it hadn't led to anything, and that meant that for the time being the suspicion was still focused on the family. So he seemed to think treating them with kid gloves was a little bit of overkill.

Louise looked out the window as she listened. Suddenly she remembered how it had occasionally driven her crazy that Søren's patience was as fragile as crystal. He wanted action and progress the whole time. It would do him good to get out and mess around with his eavesdropping equipment, she thought.

'Right. We'll just invite them in for some coffee and pastries and I'll have a chat with them,' Storm said as he sent everyone out the door.

It was after five and there was no guarantee the family would even be home, but everyone agreed that this was the right approach.

Storm waved for Mik and Louise to remain behind as they were starting to follow Søren down the hall.

'We need to pay the uncle a visit and find out what happened when he visited the family on Tuesday night,' he said. 'And at the same time, find out why Samra's parents visited him in Benløse the following day, when they'd just seen him.'

'I'll get hold of him, then Louise and I can drive down there this evening,' Mik said, pulling his car keys out of his jacket pocket. 'The uncle has a shop, so he won't be home until after he closes at seven.'

They took the back stairs down to Mik's car to drive out and invite the al-Abd family in for a chat. In the yard, Bengtsen and Velin were checking to see if they had all the necessary equipment for the audio surveillance and they agreed that Louise would send them a text message once they knew the family was safely lured out of the house.

Half an hour later, Louise and Mik came back with Samra's parents, and Storm ushered them into a meeting room next to the police chief's office. Back in their own office, Mik familiarised himself with what Ruth had printed out about the uncle and his family. There wasn't much, just a little about the business he owned, his wife and kid's social security numbers, information about their immigration and residency permits. Louise offered to bring her partner a can of coke if he needed a pick-me-up.

'Good thinking,' he said, tearing himself away from the papers for a second while he explained that she would find whatever she needed in the cafeteria.

Her tour of Holbæk police station had not included the cafeteria, so she stood in the doorway, a little lost.

'Fourth floor,' Mik said.

She walked out to the secretary's office and took the stairs up. The passport and DMV offices were on the first floor, and administration, the police's legal department and the cafeteria were on the fourth.

There was a small group of officers around one of the tables when she walked in. She said hello and felt their eyes following her as she walked over to the vending machine. Something told her it wasn't because she was a woman but because she was an outsider. Even from a distance she could tell there was only Pepsi and Faxe Kondi. Irritated, she wondered why she couldn't just get a Coca-Cola, but with the men's eyes on her back she couldn't bring herself to spin around in disgust and walk back out empty-handed. She decided to just get something for Mik and give up on anything for herself.

On the way back, she met Ruth, who was headed for the hotel with her bag over her shoulder to take a nap before dinner. She smiled at the Pepsi in Louise's hand and said there was a bunch of cans and bottled water down in the command room.

'The investigation would grind to a halt if the boys were forced to drink that stuff,' she said, and apologised for not having mentioned this to Louise sooner. 'There's also a cupboard full of crackers and things for the days when we're forced to skip breakfast or work drags out late into the evening.'

Louise thanked her for the information and returned to the office to give her partner the Pepsi. They decided that they wouldn't let the uncle know they were planning to visit him that evening. He shouldn't have any time to prepare.

When Mik stood up and said that he had to go home before they set out again, Louise decided to follow Ruth's example so that she would be fresh for their visit to Benløse. She grabbed her bag and headed for the hotel, speculating with a little annoyance as to whether her partner had some kind of busybody wife since he was always having to check in at home and then come back.

12

Louise glanced at her watch as she entered the hotel and confirmed that she could just squeeze in half an hour of relaxation before they were supposed to meet for dinner. On her way to her room, she stopped by the restaurant to pick up a cup of tea. She had her back to the tables, waiting for the waiter to return from the kitchen, when she heard a familiar voice say, 'There's tea in the pot over here ... and warm milk, if that's any enticement.' She spun around in astonishment.

Camilla was sitting at a table way over in the corner. Louise had walked right past her without noticing her.

'What the hell!' Louise exclaimed. 'When did you arrive?' She stepped over and gave her good friend a hug.

'I got here this morning, and I'm only staying until tomorrow for now.'

'You're writing about the case?' I don't even know why I'm bothering to ask, Louise thought, as soon as the question was out of her mouth. Of course word had already got out. Obviously *Morgenavisen* was going to run the story.

Camilla poured tea into a second cup and set it on the table. Then she proceeded to scold Louise.

'Now, obviously it's not like I'm entitled to know everything, but you darn well could have told me that you'd been assigned to the Mobile Task Force. That's exciting news!'

Louise took a seat and filled the rest of her cup with warm milk. 'It's going to be a challenge,' Louise admitted, instead of starting in on the excuses. 'Do you know Storm?'

Camilla nodded and said they'd known each other since he'd been put in charge when the Mobile Task Force was resurrected in 2002, after having been dismantled a couple years earlier and merged with the Forensics Department.

'Storm's a great guy,' Camilla said. 'And, after all, Holbæk is practically like coming home again.'

'Well, it's a way from Roskilde to Holbæk,' Louise pointed out. She and Camilla had known each other ever since they went to Roskilde High School together.

'We used to get drunk and make out with boys here in town,' Camilla pointed out to Louise, but then she apparently forgot all about reminiscing and instead drew Louise's attention to the notepad lying on the table in front of her. 'I have to get to work now,' she said, explaining that she had a meeting with Storm later that evening, and that until then she was planning to poke around a little.

Louise realised right away what that meant. Camilla was going to do her best to find someone who had known Samra.

'The girl's mother ran off to a women's shelter several times. A woman doesn't just do something like that unless she has a real reason,' Camilla said, obviously sure that part of her story lay there.

'She went to the shelter once,' Louise corrected, realising too late that in doing so she had just confirmed what Camilla was probably only guessing at.

'Was Samra rebellious?' Camilla asked.

Louise shook her head to indicate that Camilla wasn't going to get anything else out of her.

'Either she didn't want to get married or she had a Danish boyfriend . . . ' Camilla ploughed on, undaunted.

Louise shook her head slightly at Camilla and got up to leave. 'The others will be down here in a bit. We're meeting for dinner in fifteen minutes. I'm just going to pop up to my room beforehand,' she said, excusing herself and thanking Camilla for the tea.

Camilla walked Louise out to the lobby, where she wrapped a crocheted shawl around her shoulders and pulled her shoulder strap over her head so her bag rested securely on her back.

Louise gave her a hug as they parted and hurried up to her room to wash her hands and splash a little water on her face before joining the others for dinner. Running into Camilla had reinvigorated her, and she didn't feel the least bit tired any more.

Louise regretted not having passed on the dessert as soon as she stood up from the table after dinner. Strolling back to the police station, she spotted Mik, who had pulled over to the kerb, waiting for her. She turned to head towards him, but at the same time noticed a figure leaning against a streetlight a little way behind the car. When she got closer, she recognised

Dicta Møller, even though the girl was wrapped in a large scarf that covered the lower part of her face and wore a cap pulled down to her eyes. Louise motioned to Mik that she was just going to run over and talk to the girl.

'Hi,' she called out before she got too close so as not to frighten Dicta. 'Are you feeling better?'

The young girl shook her head and asked Louise if she had time to talk. She had been to the station to ask for Louise and had been told she would be back around seven.

Louise thought it over quickly. Then she strode over to the car and explained that Dicta was there to talk to her.

'I'll just head down there alone,' Mik said without hesitation and agreed that it was important they find out what the girl had to say.

'Do you want to come inside, or would you rather go to a café?' Louise asked, realising Dicta might tell her more now than she had with her parents present.

The young girl thought about it for a moment, as if she were contemplating where it would be least embarrassing to be seen – at the police station or at a café, where people could see that she was talking to a police officer. Finally she chose a café that was located at the end of Ahlgade. Once they got there, Louise realised there wasn't much risk of running into anyone else Dicta's age. Yellowed lace curtains were drawn over the large windows, so the late-evening sun had no effect on the dark atmosphere in the café, and the wall sconces cast a greenish sheen over the room, leaving the customers in a shadowy darkness. They ordered soft drinks and chose a table in the back.

'How did your trip out to Hønsehalsen go?' Louise asked. 'I assume they didn't let you go all the way out.'

Dicta shook her head and said that Michael had got one of the policemen out there to lay her bouquet down by the cliff. 'When you're a photographer, you know most of the people in town,' Dicta said and smiled a little.

'How did it go with the pictures? Did they turn out well?' Louise asked, pouring coke into her glass even though she wasn't sure it was entirely clean.

Dicta shrugged.

'I haven't seen them. I didn't want to. He just drove me home again afterward.'

The answer fell short, not leaving Louise with any easy way to keep the conversation going, so she waited for the girl to start telling her why she had been waiting for her outside the police station.

'I came to tell you that I'm not sure something I said was true,' Dicta finally began. 'I don't know if it's true that Samra was afraid of her father, and I'm afraid I might have told you something incorrect.'

Dicta said this very tersely, and it was as if the self-confident air she had had during her visit to the police station had disappeared. Louise found herself sitting across from a hesitant little girl, who had been scrutinising every single word she'd said and had immediately developed a tummy ache.

'She liked her parents,' Dicta continued. 'But she just wasn't ever allowed to do anything and it's been like that since her mother found a picture of one of the boys from our class. It was in Samra's purse, hidden in a bunch of other stuff.'

After a long pause, during which they sat there facing each other in silence, Dicta started to explain how Samra had falsified her school timetable after the summer holidays when they started ninth grade.

'She always had to be home right after her last class. But on Monday and Tuesday, when we got out earlier, she wrote extra classes on her timetable to give herself some time to hang out with the rest of us. We promised not to say anything because she said something terrible would happen if her father found out about it.'

'So what did you guys usually do?' Louise asked.

'We either hung out at school or went to my place. Every once in a while she'd come down to Michael's studio or to a café where she knew she wouldn't run into anyone. There was this one time when we bumped into her dad down on Ahlgade at a time when he thought she was still in school. He was furious even though she told him one of the teachers had been sick and we'd had a free period. He wouldn't even listen to her and he ordered her to go straight home.'

Louise listened without interrupting.

'Her brother's allowed to hang out with his friends in town. I didn't get why her parents treated the two of them so differently,' Dicta said, sounding offended on her friend's behalf.

'He's older, and he's a boy,' Louise said, knowing that a Danish teenage girl was not going to find that answer sufficient.

'Yeah, but he got into fights and all that kind of stuff,' Dicta replied indignantly. 'I just didn't think it was fair.' She took off her scarf and hat and her blonde hair hung down almost to the edge of the table.

Louise just nodded.

'Samra didn't think so either,' Dicta continued. 'That's why every once in a while she would run away.'

Louise couldn't blame her. But she did think there was

something wrong with parents moving an eleven-year-old to a country with such a dramatically different culture and putting her in school there without making it possible for her to fit in and be like the other kids. It was only natural for a girl like that to try to fit into her new life. Danish kids who moved from one part of the country to another would try to do exactly the same, but they would have a much easier time adjusting. In this case, there was this ominous demand that girls had to adapt, but only to a certain extent, otherwise all hell would break loose.

'Did it seem like her parents were pressuring her to maintain their traditional culture?' Louise asked, interested.

It took a little while before Dicta responded, but eventually she shook her head. 'Not pressuring, no. She felt like her parents' attitude towards tradition was normal, you know? But sometimes it irritated her.'

'Had you noticed anything about Samra? Had anything happened lately that had affected her?' Louise asked.

'Just that she had been a little quiet lately, but she didn't say anything, so I don't know if there was anything wrong.'

'Which boy from class did she have a picture of?' Louise wanted to know, flagging down the waitress at the same time so she could pay.

Dicta hesitated a little, as if she had revealed something that was going to make her tummy hurt later.

'His name is Mads, but that's over. He's dating Emilie now.'

'Has she dated anyone else?' Louise asked as they were on their way out.

An older man with a pint of porter and an aquavit in front of him watched their movements with interest.

'No, they weren't dating,' Dicta interrupted loudly to

emphasise that Louise had misunderstood. 'She just liked him. I don't even think he knew about it.'

'Okay,' Louise said, holding the door. 'Was there anyone else she had a crush on or was maybe interested in? I mean, I suppose it's practically unavoidable at your age.'

When that went unanswered, Louise asked instead if Dicta had a boyfriend.

The girl quickly shook her head. 'I'm making my modelling work a priority,' she said, explaining that she and Michael Mogensen had devoted a lot of time to taking those pictures, and that they were going to help her reach the next level in her career.

Louise was taken once again by the way the girl expressed herself and her very grown-up attitude towards her modelling. Not that it surprised Louise to see a girl that age going after her dreams in such a purposeful way, and after all, Dicta was a pretty girl.

It was almost nine o'clock when Louise returned to the police station. Mik wasn't back yet. She considered waiting for him, but she was tired; and since his mobile went straight to voice-mail she figured he'd turned it off, either because he was still with Samra's uncle or because he was already back at his own home. She powered down her computer and started walking back to the hotel.

13

When Camilla stepped across the threshold of the al-Abd family's apartment in the yellow-brick townhouse a little after eight thirty, she noticed how densely packed the place was with furniture. Dressers, shoe racks, a display case, a row of hooks above so that a thick blanket-like layer of clothes hung over the rest. She smiled and introduced herself to a short, thin woman who only came up to Camilla's shoulders and wore an attractive black scarf over her head.

'I'm Camilla Lind. I'm with *Morgenavisen*,' she said, and then hurriedly continued, 'I'm so sorry about what happened to your daughter.'

Even though it was the most glaring cliché to fire off at the woman, Camilla meant it. After she had arrived in town the day before, she had taken a spin through Holbæk town centre to track down some teenagers who had known Samra and were willing to talk about her. The picture of the young immigrant girl that had emerged was basically no more heart-rending than if it had been any other young girl who'd been killed in the same way, but it also didn't help make the situation any more comprehensible.

Extremely sweet, helpful, fun, smart ... it had been a long list of superlatives. But what had struck Camilla most was how raw the teenagers' grief was. They had been genuinely floored by a level of pain and turmoil that they didn't comprehend. They understood that the worst had happened and they were responding to it, but they had in no way been prepared to have the foundations of their lives yanked out from underneath them that way. The safe and innocent world they'd known had disappeared all of a sudden, pushing them several steps closer to the seriousness and sorrows of life.

'I'd really like to talk to you a little,' Camilla continued.

Sada al-Abd started retreating back into the apartment, eyes cast down to the floor. Camilla knew she was thirty-seven years old and that she understood and spoke some Danish. She heard a young child's voice from inside the living room, and a second later a cute little girl with dark curls dancing around her head came to the doorway, casting a slightly shy glance at the female stranger. In the background Camilla spotted a little boy, who was sitting on the floor playing with some blocks.

The mother said something to her daughter in a language Camilla didn't understand, and the girl smiled, her mouth full of chalk-white teeth that would have made a great ad for Arla, the dairy company, and disappeared back into the living room to join her little brother.

'I didn't want to bother you,' Camilla quickly told the mother. 'But I was talking to some of Samra's friends in town yesterday and they told me such nice things about your daughter. I thought you might like to hear what they said.'

She waited to see how much of her Danish the mother seemed to understand. The woman's eyes were still trained on the floor, but she nodded weakly at Camilla's words. However, as soon as Camilla finished talking, the woman shook her head and softly said, 'You have to go.'

Camilla stood there for a moment, looking at the Jordanian woman. She couldn't tell if there was fear mixed with the profound grief emanating from her.

'We could always meet somewhere else to talk?' Camilla suggested, making another attempt. 'I'm going to have to write about this story, with or without your cooperation. But it would be better if you would talk to me.'

Again the woman shook her head.

'I can't talk to you.' She spoke in thickly accented Danish, but she was very understandable.

Camilla sensed movement behind her before she heard a voice say, 'What are you doing here? Leave us alone.'

A man had entered without her having heard him, and when she turned around he was standing right behind her.

'You must not come here and bother us ... '

The man's voice grew louder and Camilla tried to explain that she was not trying to bother anyone, that she just wanted to talk to them about what had happened. But everything she said was drowned out by his yelling.

Then he turned his rage on Sada. 'What did you tell her?' he yelled.

She shook her head. 'Nothing.'

'I'm calling the police,' he screamed at Camilla. 'You need to get out of here NOW!'

She watched how he punched the buttons on his phone, shifting angrily from one foot to the other in his eagerness to get through. Sada stood still, as if nailed to the spot, her eyes on her own feet, as Ibrahim moved to the living room to talk.

Camilla moved a step closer to her and said, 'I know you reported him for abuse and spent some time at a shelter, but then you came back to him. How could you do that to your daughter?'

The mother jumped as the import of the words hit her. She looked up and stared Camilla right in the eyes but didn't say anything.

The man's infuriated voice was echoing in the background. He had finally got through to a human.

'I'm staying at the Station Hotel and I hope you'll decide to talk to me. But I'm going to be writing my articles whether you do or not.' Camilla nodded a quick farewell before the husband returned.

As she walked down the stairs, she briefly contemplated whether she ought to call the Holbæk Police herself and let them know she was the one who had stopped by to see the family and triggered this enormous outburst of anger. But that might be blowing things out of proportion, she thought.

The sun was shining, enveloping the car park between the buildings in a soft, golden sheen, and there was some warmth in its rays despite the season. Camilla buttoned her cardigan and climbed into the driver's seat of her car. Well, that didn't go well, she thought. It would be hard to recover from that beginning. She supposed the ball was in Samra's mother's court now, since Camilla hadn't had a chance to say she would come back. The father would skin his wife alive if he found Camilla interviewing her in the apartment. Plus there were the two little kids. It would end in chaos.

*

'I'm going to kill that whore.'

'You mustn't say kill. Or die. What are you doing to us? Can't you understand that they're going to come and take my children away from me if you say things like that? Stop it!'

The heated voices could be heard in the background, but the interpreter's monotone translation remained calm and unaffected by the things that were being said.

'You're ruining it for us, and we'll all end up in there . . .'

'In jail,' the interpreter explained, glancing up at Louise, who was standing with the rest of the team, listening in on the audio surveillance feed.

'For God's sake, don't ruin anything else,' the interpreter continued, concentrating again on the unintelligible words whirling around the Danish police officers' heads.

Again a man's voice on the tape: 'I didn't say kill. I said I'll hit you!'

'Why are you saying these things?'

'I'm going crazy. I'm going to kill myself too.'

'You mustn't say that word at all. They're going to take my babies away from me.'

The woman started crying loudly.

'Get out, get out! I don't want to hear any more . . .'

A door slammed and Storm impatiently asked for the tape to be stopped so they could discuss what they'd just heard.

During the morning briefing, Storm had informed them that they were going to have to do without him for the rest of the day. With a little embarrassment he had explained that he certainly knew it was impractical and that it was coming at an unfortunate time, but the appointment had been made a long time ago. He was going to teach a continuing education course at the Police Academy Centre in Avnø and he had to be there until ten o'clock that night because they were having a big farewell dinner.

Louise got the sense that he was anxious to get out of there, but he obviously also felt like he had to be present while they prepared, before bringing Samra's family back in for another round of questioning an hour later.

They were brought into the interrogation room at ten o'clock. The National Police's staff interpreter, Fahid, had arrived early that morning so he could listen in as the family woke up. Normally they would have had the audio material transcribed and would have waited until they had the translated transcript in their hands, but Storm had decided that there was enough time pressure in this case that they had to skip that step. So instead they had the interpreter doing a simultaneous interpretation directly from the tape, which would allow them to pick up the last few important details before the couple arrived.

'He calls his daughter a whore,' Søren Velin said, offended. Fahid shook his head and explained that it wasn't Samra but the female interpreter who was being called a whore.

'He's accusing her of stabbing him in the back during the questioning. He's very upset during this conversation,' Fahid said. 'They were apparently just visited by a journalist, who was standing in the doorway talking to his wife when he came home, and he feels like everyone is against him.'

'What was that stuff about the kids?' Louise asked.

'That has to do with the problems stemming from Sada's stay in the shelter. A note was placed in the file that the state was considering removing the two youngest children from the home if the internal family problems continued.'

'She's accusing him indirectly of having killed their daughter,'

Skipper concluded, referring to the statement that the father mustn't ruin anything else.

'I don't get it,' Louise said heatedly. 'He was completely crushed when he found out the murder victim was his daughter. What the hell kind of charade is this?'

Mik nodded in agreement. He was apparently also having trouble reconciling how this could be the same man who'd been so upset to learn of his daughter's death.

They stood around quietly, digesting what they'd heard, before moving into the command room and taking their seats around the table. Storm pulled on his jacket, grabbed his computer bag and the large, square black briefcase containing all his teaching materials, and then he was out through the door with a brief nod.

Ruth had a stack of plastic folders ready, which she handed out. 'Here are all the facts on the al-Abd family,' she said. 'About their stay at the shelter, too.'

'The father can be a real prick,' Bengtsen began, explaining that he had some peripheral awareness of Ibrahim al-Abd, both from the local street scene and from Stark, the company where Bengtsen's brother-in-law was in charge of the department where Samra's father and brother worked. 'But he's also very well liked by his co-workers. As long as things run smoothly, he's cheerful and amenable, but he's got a short fuse.'

'I can believe that,' Mik said, rubbing his nose and seeming lost in thought for a moment.

'Well, in spite of everything, Samra's mother must have some backbone,' Louise said, thinking it would take guts to report your husband for domestic abuse and then end up going back home again. 'She's not a coward.'

Skipper got up and took a handful of cans and bottles out of the fridge and put them on the table, sending the bottle opener around.

'Nah, but if the father was responsible for Samra's murder, then it didn't really pay off for the mother to have reported him for his violence, did it?' Velin contributed.

'The father's brother in Benløse says that he visits Ibrahim and the family every Tuesday evening,' Mik said, glancing down at his notepad. 'He describes Samra as a sweet girl, but at the same time said that there had been a few problems lately, trouble getting her to stay away from the boys. The Danish boys.'

'That sounds a little exaggerated,' Louise exclaimed in surprise.

'Did he want to go into any more detail on that?' Dean asked.

Before Mik had a chance to respond, Louise interrupted, telling everyone about the picture Samra's mother had found in her daughter's purse.

When Louise finished, Mik shook his head and said the father's brother wouldn't say anything concrete. 'He doesn't generally consider Ibrahim to be particularly violent, but he did say that if that kind of thing happens, of course you have to take action and get the girl in line before things get totally out of hand.'

'But we're not talking about a dog that needs a little behavioural correction,' Skipper commented.

'It doesn't make any sense that a fifteen-year-old girl would do anything that went so much against her parents' wishes that they'd rather kill her,' Ruth Lange said, plopping down onto the edge of the table.

'This kind of thing isn't logical,' Skipper countered. 'We'll never accept that things like this happen. And I don't give a damn if this is part of their religion,' he continued.

'Cultural tradition,' Louise interjected, but she really didn't want to get into that with a group of co-workers she'd just met. It was easier to have this conversation with people who knew each other, because every time someone made it clear where they stood on this issue, you found yourself in deep water.

'It doesn't have anything to do with religion or Islam. Honour and shame are part of their cultural heritage. Men fight for their honour and fear that women are bringing shame to them. Therefore all women must be controlled so they don't mess things up for everyone,' Dean explained.

'There's also that thing about some families regarding women as property, thus making it totally okay to beat them and treat them as chattels,' Velin said, both indignant and baffled that people could think like that.

Dean nodded at him, agreeing that unfortunately that was not uncommon.

'Did the father's brother say anything else?' Bengtsen asked, putting an end to their contemplations of global cultural differences. 'Did he say why Samra's parents went out to see him in Benløse again so soon, when they'd just seen each other?'

Mik sat there studying the folder Ruth had given him, and then shook his head. 'Just that it was because they were worried about Samra.'

Before they wrapped up the meeting, to get ready for the next round of questioning with Samra's parents and her older brother, Louise reported on her conversation with Dicta Møller the previous evening.

'It turns out that Samra tinkered with her school timetable to give herself a couple of free periods each week when she could escape her parents' control for a little while, so she did occasionally do something they didn't know about,' Louise concluded just as the phone rang to let them know the al-Abd family had arrived.

Louise and Mik walked to their office together.

'I'll be back from the school as soon as I've spoken to Samra's friends,' Louise said. 'And we'll see if I can twist anything out of them.'

They had agreed to split up – Mik would interview Samra's family while Louise went to talk to her school friends – and they had both turned down the offer of help from a couple of local assistant detectives. Louise realised she had misjudged her new partner when she had assumed he was lazy. He actually took more work on himself than he assigned her.

'Good luck,' he called after her as she walked away.

'Same to you. You'll need it more.'

Mik smiled at her and tipped his chair back a little, running his hand through his hair and making a face. 'I suppose I'll have to try to go a little easier on Hamid if I want to keep him from shutting down right away,' Mik said, and for the first time Louise got the sense that her new partner didn't feel so uptight with her any more.

'I'll see you,' she said, stuffing her car keys into her pocket on her way out.

14

Louise looked around the empty staffroom. There was a long table and several small clusters of sofas, stacks of books and newspapers, and a few empty coffee cups that had been left behind. It was bright and airy with a couple of coloured reproductions hanging on the walls, and though it was an old school, it had obviously been renovated within the last few years. She had an appointment with the four girls who'd been closest to Samra. The school had been closed for the rest of the day, but Jette Petersen had asked permission for her class to meet for a memorial service in the hall before Louise took over.

'I'll just get them all out the door,' Jette had said when they had spoken that morning.

Maybe she should have waited until Monday, Louise thought, walking over to the window, but then the whole weekend would have passed before she got a sense of the girl's circle of friends. She saw a minibus parking along the pavement, emptying its load of small children with wet hair and swimming gear in their hands. She followed them with her eyes as the herd disappeared across the playground.

The door opened and Louise turned around and said hello to a man, who gave her a funny look, obviously wondering who she was.

She introduced herself and explained that she was waiting for Samra's teacher. Jette Petersen's co-worker just nodded at her and walked over to the table that served as a kitchenette and poured water into the coffee maker.

'It's a sad story,' he grunted when he had finished. The machine started gurgling a second later.

Louise quietly agreed with him.

'But who says the family's behind it?' he asked, nodding at the morning papers that were sitting on the long table. Both front pages prominently featured the words 'honour killing'. 'She may just as easily have been the victim of a crime the family wasn't behind. Isn't that kind of jumping to conclusions?' he asked in a tone that made Louise feel as if he was holding her accountable for the coverage.

She hurried to say that of course someone else could easily have been behind it. 'But there's not really any motive to suggest that,' Louise continued, trying not to sound defensive.

Silence hung in the air between them and she took a seat. The coffee maker finished gurgling and the man pulled a couple of clean mugs out of the dishwasher. He asked her if she wanted milk or sugar. She said 'Milk, please' and asked if he might know anything the police hadn't heard yet, since he had brought all this up.

He shook his head and said that it just seemed to him as if they were taking the path of least resistance. 'You're going after the easiest target,' he said, taking a seat. 'If it had been a Danish family, you'd be searching for the perpetrator every-where but inside the family.'

Really? You think so? Louise thought. 'The second we have any other leads to follow, I promise you we will.'

'Even though Holbæk isn't that big, there are crazy people here too. We've had a number of rapes—' the man began.

'Well, Samra wasn't raped,' Louise interrupted sharply. 'She was murdered, callously and cold-heartedly. She was asphyx-iated and had a concrete slab tied to her waist.'

'Yeah, well, you don't know it was the family,' he said once more.

Louise sighed and conceded that he was right. No, they didn't know. 'But I can tell you that two of my colleagues have been looking for witnesses since she was found and no one saw her leave her parents' home,' she said, thinking about all the interviews Bengtsen and Velin had done in Dysseparken and the neighbourhood around the large residential area where the family's apartment was located.

'But that also means no one saw her father drive off with her,' he pointed out, and again Louise had to concede. Samra could easily have left home without having been noticed.

'You're just starting out with the assumption that the family is guilty—'

The door opened and he stopped talking.

Louise got up and walked over to put her mug in the sink. 'We're not assuming anyone is guilty,' she said, standing right across from him. 'We're following the leads we have as we continue to investigate the case.'

She was starting to get irritated and turned around to greet the girls – Dicta Møller and three others – Jette Petersen was ushering into the staffroom.

'We can go down to the classroom, which is at the end of the hall,' Jette said after they'd greeted each other.

'Great,' Louise said, leading the way without saying good-bye to Jette's colleague.

Two of the girls, Fatima and Asma, were from immigrant backgrounds. Liv was Danish. Louise pulled a couple of tables together so they could sit across from each other. Jette Petersen sat down a little way in the background as an observer.

'I'd really like to get a better sense of who Samra was,' Louise began, looking at the girls. 'As far as I've understood, you four were closest to her.'

She was prepared for the crying and gave them plenty of time as it rapidly set in. The memorial service in the hall must have been tough on them.

'She's my cousin,' said Asma, the thinnest of the girls, whose pretty, slender face was framed by a headscarf that was so tight-fitting that Louise couldn't see a single strand of hair.

Louise sat for a moment, watching her, because it would have been hard to find someone sending more mixed signals than this girl. Of the four, Asma was the most provocatively dressed, so the demure head covering seemed completely at odds with her plunging neckline and tight skirt. Louise's eyes moved on to Fatima, who was a little stockier and seemed more relaxed about her appearance. She was wearing a pair of baggy trousers and a stylish pink T-shirt and had a lot of unruly black curls framing her face.

Louise got back down to business and explained that she had already spoken with Dicta and that what she hoped to get out of today's conversation was an impression of who Samra had hung out with. Who had known her? What kind of person had she been?

She looked first at Fatima. 'Our families know each other. We moved to Holbæk because my father grew up with Samra's father back home in Rabba. So I played with her a lot during the years we've lived here.'

Louise was particularly struck by the girl's use of the word 'played'. That wasn't a word Dicta would have used about the time she spent with Samra.

'When did you see her last?' Louise asked. She had thought about whether or not she ought to meet with the girls individually, but had decided that having them all here together might help them loosen up.

'We saw each other last weekend,' Fatima said and nodded at Asma, adding that Asma had been there with her family too.

Asma explained that her mother was Sada's sister. Asma was in the same grade, but in a different class.

'How do you guys think Samra was doing?'

'She was doing well,' Fatima answered without hesitation, but then she gave Asma a questioning look. Asma, however, was lost in her own thoughts and didn't reply.

'Do you also think she seemed to be doing well when you were together last weekend?' Louise asked the girl's cousin, when she didn't respond.

Asma hurriedly nodded, and Louise felt herself starting to get a little exasperated. 'You know, I'd heard that she seemed like she was under a little pressure lately, but you guys hadn't noticed that?' Louise prompted.

Fatima shook her head, but Asma looked Louise in the eye and said that there were times when Samra wasn't that happy.

'Had she been like that lately?' Louise asked.

Asma shrugged. There was something vulnerable about her, evoked by her provocative sense of style and her covered hair. She didn't look at all cheap in her tight-fitting clothes, it was more like she radiated a strong sense of feminine elegance, one that she was just too young to carry off and that wasn't fully realised because she was hiding one of the most feminine of bodily adornments: her hair.

'Did Samra say anything to you? She must have needed someone to talk to?' Instead of waiting for an answer, Louise asked the girls who they talked to when they were sad.

'Each other,' all four of them replied.

Dicta added that she also talked to her parents, and there was nodding all around the table. The others obviously did too, when all was said and done.

The silence in the classroom was oppressive until Louise asked if anyone thought the family might have been planning a wedding for Samra and that maybe that was what had been making her feel pressured.

Suddenly everyone was talking over each other.

'They wouldn't do that,' Fatima exclaimed loudly and was interrupted by Liv, who exclaimed, 'Well, they could just forget about that!'

'My aunt and uncle aren't like that,' Asma said, once everyone had calmed down. 'They're not into that kind of thing.'

'But that's what you Danes always think about us, isn't it?' Fatima mumbled angrily.

'Samra would never have put up with that. She was way too independent to accept a decision like that,' Liv interjected, and the other girls agreed.

Louise studied Liv for a moment. She was hardly the first

person Louise would have picked as one of Samra's closest friends. Her leather jacket was worn, and the red T-shirt with the black dots she wore underneath it was faded. Louise couldn't figure out whether the girl's hair was standing up in stiff tufts because it was beyond greasy or if she'd painstakingly achieved this look with multiple hair products, and it was hard to tell what colour her eyes were behind all that thick black eyeliner.

'Well, good, we'll forget about that then,' Louise said. 'Do you think Samra would have sneaked out of the house at night without telling her parents?' she asked instead.

Both Dicta and Liv nodded, while Asma and Fatima took a little longer to contemplate the idea before they also acknowledged that she might well have done that.

'Samra's parents usually went to bed around ten, because her father had to get up early,' one of the girls added.

'Who would she have gone to visit if it wasn't one of you guys?' This time there was no rapid outburst of answers.

'She was very cautious,' Liv said, pulling her leather jacket tighter around her, as if she were a little uncomfortable talking and having the others' full attention. 'If they found out, her father would have been furious and then she would have been grounded for months.'

Dicta agreed with Liv and said that Samra had been grounded a few times in the past.

'You can't just fucking do that! I dare my parents to even try such a thing,' Liv said, her tone indignant. And Louise could imagine that they wouldn't easily get away with that.

'Her parents hadn't seen her since her mother said goodnight to her on Tuesday evening. They thought she'd gone to school the next morning. But by the time the alarm clock rang at eight Wednesday morning, Samra was already lying out in Udby Bay.'

Louise knew it would be hard on them to hear her say it so matter-of-factly, but she felt she needed to shake them up a little. They weren't giving her anything, and she had to get them talking if she was going to make any headway.

'Did she show up at any of your homes on Tuesday night?' Louise asked, and she was prepared when all four of them shook their heads. 'Did any of you go out gallivanting with her and you're not mentioning it now because you don't want your parents to find out?'

Her voice had become sharp, and she noted the look the teacher shot at her, but she didn't stop. She studied the young girls to determine what was going on behind their expressionless faces, but none of them seemed to be trying to cover up a lie.

'She must have disappeared in the evening or at night,' Dicta said softly, when the silence became unbearable.

Louise had the sense that a wall was being erected between the group of girlfriends, and it wasn't hard for her to work out what they were divided over. Accusers on one side and defenders on the other. Against the family and for the family. She was also afraid to put any words into their mouths, but they were dealing with facts here and she had to confront them with those. If anyone could come up with an alternative chain of events, they were more than welcome to do so.

'I've already asked Dicta, but now I'm asking the rest of you: do you know if Samra had a boyfriend or a friend whom she saw in secret.'

Louise was ready for loud protests from Fatima and Asma and looked at them in surprise when they just shrugged and said there wasn't anyone they were aware of. Dicta repeated that there hadn't been anyone.

'You wouldn't know shit about it,' Liv remarked caustically to Dicta. 'The only thing anyone can talk to you about is your hair and your advertising jobs.'

'Modelling jobs,' Dicta corrected her.

'I just mean it's not like Samra would have wanted to tell you anything – if there was anything to tell – since you're always off in your own egocentric universe.'

Louise considered interrupting, but before she had a chance, Dicta managed to do so herself.

'Give me a fucking break, will you?' Dicta swore. 'I don't think I spend any more time on my hair than you do, so just drop it.'

Louise's eyebrows were halfway up her forehead. There was something out of place about a rant like that spewing out of Dicta's pretty young mouth, but it was effective. Louise had obviously misjudged her. And it surprised her just as much that Liv took it without any kind of comeback.

'Do you know something?' Louise asked, directing her question directly at Liv. She had made it sound like she did.

'I don't know what it was, but I think there was something,' Liv replied cryptically.

'Well, how about a few more details, please!' Louise's tone was a little harsh, harsher than she'd intended, and again she noticed a look from the girls' teacher, who obviously wanted to protect her students.

Liv shook herself, as if she had promised more than she could deliver. The young black-haired rebel oscillated between feigned bluntness and paralysing insecurity, which once again caused her to pull her leather jacket tighter around herself. But actually there was nothing flippant about her charm, Louise noted, studying Liv with interest as she began her response.

'I don't know anything about any boyfriend,' Liv explained, 'but it's very clear that there was something. Something had hurt her, she had been upset, something had been painful.'

Dicta looked sceptical.

'Well, I certainly didn't notice that,' Dicta said, looking over at Fatima and Asma. 'Did you guys?'

'Maybe, but not the way you mean,' Fatima told Liv. 'I think she seemed happy, as if she had butterflies in her stomach.'

Louise looked at each of the girls in turn. This was almost worse than no information at all, she thought. Everyone was going off in a separate direction.

'At some point did she maybe confide something in one of you?' Louise asked, hoping that her last question was down-to-earth enough and suitably open and naïve that it would appeal to something in their teenage compulsion to confide in someone. But all four of them shook their heads.

Louise thanked them for their time and for the information they'd given her. She said goodbye to Jette Petersen and thanked her for her help as well. Then she left Højmark School and drove back to the police station with the sense that she hadn't got very far.

15

'We know you used to call the school office and ask about your sister if she was even ten minutes late coming home from school. And now you're claiming you don't know shit about what she liked to do?'

Louise heard the voice through the door, just as she was about to enter her office. She stopped, quickly realising that her partner's plan of maintaining a more convivial tone hadn't gone so well. Louise considered going to the command room to wait until Mik had finished questioning Samra's brother, but ended up standing there in the hallway for a bit while Hamid heatedly defended himself and claimed it was all a bunch of lies.

'You used to follow her on your moped when she walked home after visiting her friends. Am I making that up too, or shall we accept that as credible since Dicta Møller's parents say they saw you several times?'

Louise ducked out again before Hamid had a chance to

answer. She knew Mik had the upper hand. Samra's class-mates had already described several incidents to Louise confirming that Hamid had indeed followed his sister.

Louise went in to see Ruth and sat down with a cola in her hand. 'How did Mik's interview with the parents go?' she asked, hoping that he'd got a little more out of them than she had from her visit to the school.

Ruth leaned back in her chair and pressed her cherry-red lips together, placing her hands behind her head and pushing her ample orange mop of hair upward to form a crown over her head. A look of annoyance slid over her face.

'To put it mildly,' Ruth said, 'this has not been a good day. Storm decided to leave us.' Then she explained that the mood had been rather tense after the day's questioning sessions. The administrative assistant leaned forward slightly, letting her hair fall back into place.

'Ibrahim al-Abd started waffling about what time he came back from the marina on Tuesday night and when his brother went home. If Storm had had time to attend to his responsi-bilities here, maybe he could have forced through a detention order for the father, but the deputy police commissioner didn't think we had enough to hold him.'

'Couldn't you just call Storm on his mobile?' Louise asked.

Ruth irritably shook her head. 'He's not picking up and hasn't responded to the messages I've left. Maybe giving his PowerPoint presentation down there will eventually earn him another star on his lapel further up the ladder somewhere, but he'd be doing a hell of a lot more good right now if he were here.'

Louise pictured the look on Samra's father's face when they'd told him about his daughter. 'If we forget about statistical probabilities and everything we have to go by so far, I'd say I'm reasonably sure the father didn't know it was his daughter's body that had been found,' Louise said. 'It would be almost impossible to fake the kind of despair and impotence he gave off.'

The administrative assistant shrugged.

'They haven't given us a thing – either the mother or the father – that would give us the slightest reason to cross them off the list of suspects. One minute the father is yelling and screaming and making a big scene because the police suspect him of having something to do with his daughter's death, and the next he's refusing to say anything about the family's acquaintances and what Samra had been up to in recent weeks. He's completely shut down. The mother cried most of the time and didn't say anything that could lead us further. We let them go, and we'll have to see what Storm says whenever he finally gets back,' Ruth said.

'Are you going to be in town this weekend?' Mik Rasmussen asked after he'd said goodbye to Hamid, who had given the policeman a very obstinate look and a barely perceptible nod before quickly scurrying away.

Louise nodded. Before Storm left, he had made it clear that everyone was going to be staying in town over the weekend. Not that he was expecting all that much to happen, but he wanted to be able to call in his troops if there was a sudden breakthrough. It didn't bother Louise. She was in no hurry to go home to her empty apartment.

'I'm teaching a sea kayaking class for beginners tomorrow,' Mik said. 'If you want to give it a try, stop by.'

Louise stared at him blankly. 'Sea kayaking?' she repeated.

Mik nodded and smiled at the look on her face. 'We go out on the sound,' he explained. 'It's amazing. I think you'd actually really like it.'

Louise started laughing. 'And just what makes you think that? It sounds strenuous, cold and wet. Definitely not something for me.'

'You wear a wetsuit, so you won't get cold when you're in the water,' he countered. 'Besides, you don't need to paddle all the way out to the Sjællands Odde peninsula on your first trip.'

'Isn't this a little late in the year to start kayaking?' she asked, trying to shoot down the idea, but her partner brushed that aside, explaining that as long as they were wearing wetsuits, they could keep going until well into October.

She stood there for a moment, watching him as he gathered his papers into a neat pile. Then he shut down his computer and said he was heading home to do the next feeding.

'Feeding?' she asked. Now she was totally in the dark.

He explained that one of his hunting dogs, a black Lab, had had puppies who were three weeks old now and that the mother needed all the food she could eat so she could produce enough milk for them, which is why he had to go home several times a day.

Suddenly things made sense, and she had to smile.

'The Rowing Club is behind Hotel Strandparken,' Mik said on his way out.

She waved after him, but her mobile phone rang just then; and when she saw that it was Camilla, she pushed the office door shut with her foot before answering.

'I don't think we'll be working that late tonight,' Louise answered when her friend asked what time she'd be finished.

'There's a restaurant down by the harbour that looks promising. Let's meet there at eight. I'll have my articles turned in by then,' Camilla said. 'Maybe some of the others would like to join us. You guys can't keep hanging out at the Station Hotel, and it's usually pretty easy to tempt Søren Velin into tagging along.'

Louise had no doubt he could be tempted. When they'd worked together in Unit A, Søren had been known as a joiner. She headed down the hall to find him and hadn't even finished talking before he'd suggested they start with a beer at the pub before heading to dinner. Skipper stopped as he walked by and asked what time they were meeting.

'Who's going to convince Bengtsen?' Louise asked, heading down the hall to see if Dean had left yet.

'I will,' said Ruth, who had appeared in the hallway without Louise's noticing her.

Suddenly Louise had the impression that the prospect of a little socialising had improved everyone's mood. They'd all been buried in work since the group had been formed. Now people's voices sounded more upbeat.

They all had more than one beer at the little microbrewery, which was in walking distance from the hotel, and when they made it down to the restaurant by the harbour they agreed it probably wasn't the best fit for them. They were well past the point where appetisers and quiet conversation were what they wanted. So they decided on a nearby Indian restaurant instead. The group was a little too big for the one table that was available, so they all had to squeeze to fit, but that didn't seem to bother anyone. Not even Bengtsen, who had ordered an orange juice at the pub to begin with, although that had only lasted until Camilla stuck a foamy draft beer into his hand.

Louise sat crushed between Skipper and Søren, and she was well entertained because Skipper pulled his iPod out of his pocket and started showing off his knowledge of fusion jazz. She listened intently, trying to hear the tranquillity in the notes, but kept getting thrown off because the music constantly switched tempo and style. She noticed that he smiled whenever she grimaced.

'Do you like it?' he asked.

She felt like she'd been caught and shrugged her shoulders a little.

He said a lot of people felt that way about this kind of music; they either loved it or hated it. The people who loved it took pleasure in the unpredictable notes, and the ones who weren't captivated described it as irritating noise. He explained that he'd been in a band when he was younger.

'Now we just mess around for fun, whenever I get together with a couple of the other old guys back home in Svendborg.'

Louise turned to look straight at him and really had a hard time picturing him with a saxophone in his mouth. Skipper was in his mid-thirties and in great shape, muscular in an outdoorsy way. It was much easier to picture him with a golf club or a fishing rod, now that she thought about it.

Søren ordered another bottle of red wine while Ruth and Camilla made Dean retell a story that had made them erupt in raucous laughter, so that everyone else could hear it too.

'Shortly after I arrived in Denmark, I was living in a refugee centre in Lyngby,' Dean began, getting everyone's attention. 'And the only funny thing I have to say about that period is that we discovered that on the door to the boss's office it said

"Peder Pedersen". And where I come from, Peder means gay. So you can appreciate why all the kids laughed every time they saw him and the rest of us had a little trouble taking the head of the refugee centre seriously. The guy resigned after just two weeks.'

The laughter spread around the table and Søren generously refilled people's wineglasses.

When they were having coffee after dinner, Ruth got a call from Storm, who had just returned to the Station Hotel. For a second it sounded like he was considering joining the party, but that was only until Ruth made it clear to him in succinct, unambiguous terms how irritated she was that he hadn't been there doing his job when they'd needed him.

Louise followed the conversation from the other side of the table and smiled, thinking that it must have taken years of working together closely for Ruth to achieve such a sharp tone without his taking it the wrong way. Louise was yanked out of her musings when Skipper spoke to her.

'So, are you happy with Unit A and Suhr?'

She nodded, and reminded him that he too had worked in Unit A once upon a time.

'But that was many years ago,' he said. 'A long time before Hans Suhr became chief of the homicide division. He and I worked together back near the dawn of time at Station 3, or Bellahøj, as they call it now.'

Well, she supposed it shouldn't surprise her that Skipper and Captain Suhr knew each other. They were sort of the same calibre of men, even though it was hard to spot a gruff side to Skipper. But maybe that was because she didn't really know him yet.

'I've been there three and a half years and so far, so good,' she replied, explaining that she was in Henny Heilmann's group.

Skipper knew Henny too, of course, and told Louise a couple of anecdotes, ending with a story about Thomas Toft, who had seniority on the investigation team Louise was currently part of. She laughed out loud when Skipper called him a stubborn terrier who wouldn't let go once he'd bitten into something, because that was the perfect image.

After coffee, they split the bill and set off to go check out Holbæk's night life. Dean and Søren led the way, heading back to the pub, where they had live music, and Louise gladly accepted the pints Skipper passed across the table to her each time he returned from a trip to the bar. As she let herself into her hotel room a couple of hours later, she noticed she was a bit tipsier than she had realised, and it didn't take many minutes from the time she lay down in bed until sleep overcame her.

16

Camilla was lying in her hotel room reading through her own article in *Morgenavisen*. They'd been out late the night before, and they had had plenty of beer and wine with their food. That had been nice. Bengtsen had stubbornly denied that he'd let Else down on a Friday night because of Ruth's special persuasive abilities. He had insisted to Camilla that he was very social as long as the company was right, so she'd taken it as a compliment that he'd chosen her as a tablemate, and she made sure he was aware that in the future she would include him on her list of police sources.

The paper was featuring her story prominently, with a set of statistics on recent honour killings. She'd hoped all the way up until her deadline that Samra's mother would show up so she could interview her, but as much as she had hoped for that, she was also very sure that it wouldn't happen. And it certainly wouldn't happen now that her boss had thoughtlessly rewritten the headline for the article Camilla had written about the mother's visit to the women's shelter. *Samra's mother failed her*, it now said, and with those words her last chance of an interview disintegrated, Camilla thought angrily.

Camilla felt rotten about the headline. Something in the pit of her stomach contracted when the words jumped out at her. Plus there was no way she could retract it, since the title promised quite a bit more than the article actually contained. She had carefully described the police report about the father and how Sada had sought help. That was all information she'd got from the police. It wasn't like she'd been poking around to find that out on her own; and nowhere in the article did she suggest that the mother had failed her daughter and that this had cost the girl her life.

Camilla had spent most of her Friday afternoon trying to find someone who would talk to her about their impressions of Sada al-Abd, both as a mother and as a wife. It was hard to get anyone to talk, but she had finally managed to find two other immigrant women who dared to speak to her, and they had been very positive and had told her in their limited Danish how Sada devoted all her time to her children, especially the two little ones. On the other hand, when Camilla brought up the spousal abuse Samra's mother had been subjected to, the two women shut down. Either they didn't know anything about it or, more likely, they dared not get involved in that kind of thing. That was something you kept in the family.

Camilla quickly skimmed through the rest of the paper, and was lazily lounging around in her hotel bed when the phone in the room rang. She tripped over her suitcase as she darted to answer it. She had packed her things before breakfast and was planning to head back into Copenhagen later that morning.

'There's a guest in the lobby who'd really like to speak with you,' the person at the front desk said.

'Is it Louise Rick?' Camilla asked.

'It's a foreign lady who says she needs to speak to you.' Camilla felt herself trembling and sensed instinctively that something unpleasant was coming.

'I'll be right down,' she said and put on her shoes.

The woman was sitting in the large dark-brown armchair to the left of the front desk. Her face was hidden behind the same veil Camilla recognised from the day before. Camilla took a deep breath and straightened herself up before walking over and saying hello.

There was a girl manning the front desk, one she hadn't seen before, and Camilla noticed that she was watching them with curiosity.

'Come,' Camilla told Samra's mother, nodding towards the restaurant. 'Let's find somewhere where we can talk in peace.'

She said it so loudly that the girl behind the desk quickly looked away.

Sada al-Abd still hadn't said a word, but she rose and followed Louise. The restaurant was empty. All the same, Camilla asked the waiter cleaning up after breakfast if there was a place where she and Sada could speak undisturbed. He showed them into something that might have been the hotel's conference room, although it did not look as if it was used very often. There was a heavy, stuffy odour in the room and a layer of dust over the rectangular rosewood table that filled the room lengthwise.

When the waiter left, shutting the door behind him, Camilla turned to Sada, ready to take whatever the woman was going to dish out.

'You mustn't write things like that,' Sada exclaimed in despair.

Camilla was completely unprepared for how loud Sada was and pulled back reflexively.

'How could you do that?' Sada stepped towards her and started crying loudly and shrilly, as if she were pushing out the pain from all the way down in her diaphragm.

Camilla stepped further back, now standing silently and watching Sada, until she sensed that the rebukes were over. When she saw Sada collapse into quiet, miserable sobs, Camilla put her arm around her shoulders and led her over to a seating area by the far wall.

Once Sada was sitting down, Camilla stepped out into the restaurant and asked the waiter to bring them some tea. Then she sat down across from Samra's mother and let her cry. When the tea finally arrived after a long wait, the woman was still crying.

Camilla felt the knot in her stomach again, but didn't want to admit it was there. Her article had been restrained, but she felt a fierce rage at her boss and the sloppy way he came up with headlines. Besides, it never cost him anything, but that damn well wasn't the case for her. Here she was, sitting across from the woman they'd maligned who very obviously couldn't take any more pain.

Camilla poured tea into two large floral teacups copied from the best of traditional English style and passed one to Sada in the hope that it would distract her from her crying.

Sada reluctantly accepted it, avoiding eye contact with Camilla as if she was ashamed of her angry outburst. After she took her first sip, she finally said something: 'I have always taken good care of my children.'

Camilla was about to speak when, after a long pause, Sada continued.

'Now they're going to take my children away. But what do you care? You don't understand,' she said, wringing her hands together.

Not caring was not Camilla's problem at the moment. Her boss had sold her out, and it was going to cost him. But she actually did care about Sada too, although she was irritated that the woman hadn't come to see her until now that the article was already written and printed instead of the day before so they could have talked to each other beforehand. At any rate, Camilla began by defending herself in a way that could easily be interpreted as an attack.

'No one needs to understand or accept anyone being abused to the point that they have to go to a women's shelter,' Camilla said. She knew this might put an end to the woman's willingness to talk, but on the other hand she felt it was necessary to indicate where she stood.

But her statement didn't seem to bother Sada al-Abd. The woman just shook her head. There was obviously something else Camilla didn't understand.

'Try to explain to me what led up to your going to the shelter. What I especially want you to explain to me is why you went back to him,' Camilla said.

'Why should I?' Sada asked. 'You're just going to write whatever you want anyway.'

Camilla had certainly heard that one many times before. 'You wrote that I killed my own daughter.' Sada spoke quietly with a determination in her voice. The tears were gone and she seemed almost fearsome.

'I didn't write that you killed her,' Camilla exclaimed

indignantly, wishing that instead of accusing her, the mother would start talking. 'I wrote that you went to a shelter for help and that shortly after that, you went back to your abuser.'

Camilla took a sip of tea and again asked Samra's mother to talk about what had happened when she went into hiding with her children.

Sada drank a little more of her tea and it looked as if she were fighting some kind of battle within herself. Camilla had the sense that the woman across from her really wanted to tell her story, but that she was afraid it might have consequences if she did so.

'I won't write anything until you've given me permission,' Camilla said. 'And I'll let you read through it before it goes to print.'

That was really all she could offer Sada, but it seemed to have an effect.

'My husband got mad at Hamid, our older son,' Sada began. 'Hamid didn't want to hand over some money he'd earned, and that made Ibrahim so mad, he started hitting him.'

Camilla sat on the edge of the sofa, listening. She had brought her bag down with her, and she pulled out a notepad and started taking notes. Sada didn't seem to notice and kept talking.

'He was hitting Hamid hard, and I tried to stop him.'

'You fled with your children because you tried to come between your husband and your son?' Camilla stated in surprise, a little shaken. She knew that Hamid had not gone to the shelter with the other children.

The woman nodded.

'If it was your son Ibrahim was mad at, why were you the one who had to flee?'

'Samra was also yelling at her father and defending her brother. My husband can get very angry. He lashed out with his hands many times and said he would kill the little ones if I got involved again.'

'And did you?'

'No, but he hit Samra to show that he meant it.'

'Didn't he threaten to kill Hamid?'

Sada looked directly at Camilla and maintained the eye contact for a long time.

'He would never kill his eldest son,' she finally said.

Camilla had her notepad in her lap and sat for a bit, gathering her thoughts. She bent her head back to stop the shivers that were running up and down her spine.

'So you reported him to the police and you all got out of there?' Sada nodded.

'How could you go back to a man who had threatened to kill your children?' Now she set down the pad, sensing how the room seemed to close in as she asked her question. 'Why?'

Tears began to flow down Sada's cheeks once more. She cried a little without a sound. 'Loneliness,' she finally whispered so softly that Camilla had to lean forward to hear her. 'If I had left him, we would have had no one. I might have been okay, but it wouldn't have worked for the children. Our lives would have been shut out.'

'What do you mean?' Camilla asked. 'You would have been free.'

The thin woman shook her head. 'Freedom is not the same for me as for you.'

Camilla sat motionless.

'I would rather be home with my husband than be free and lonely.'

Camilla didn't understand what she meant.

'Why would you be more lonely when you weren't with a man who would hit you?' Camilla asked.

'If you don't belong anywhere any more, then you have no one. Then no one will talk to you. You don't get invited anywhere. The children are not allowed to play with other children, and there's not even any guarantee you will get to keep your last name. You will be totally alone, an outcast.'

Camilla was speechless at the way Sada rattled this all off, as if it had come straight from some kind of list of rules.

'Who says all that?' Camilla asked.

For the first time a glint came into Sada's eye that could have been mistaken for a small smile.

'It's not something anyone says. That's just how it is, and how it has always been for those who bring shame to their families.'

'Yeah, but you damn well can't avoid things happening in a family that will make waves, and you don't necessarily have to become an outcast because of it,' Camilla said heatedly. It wasn't that she hadn't heard of honour and shame before, but this all sounded completely crazy to her ears.

Sada sat for a moment before responding, as if she were searching for the right words.

'It's only in the closest family that honour and shame really mean something. If it's someone you don't know, who cares? Then it doesn't mean anything.'

Camilla had no idea what Sada was talking about.

'There can be conflict within a family without it necessarily resulting in any consequences. It's only once the extended family hears about it that things can get tricky.'

'You mean if other people start talking about it?'

Sada nodded. 'You don't want that,' she said. 'You don't want anyone speaking ill of your family.'

Camilla was with her so far. She urged Sada to explain what kinds of issues could be so important that they would result in abuse or expulsion. Because she did not understand.

'I can certainly appreciate that some people might feel it was impinging on the family's honour if one family member did something wrong, but I can't understand how this would result in such a physically violent outcome,' Camilla said.

'Danish families also expel people,' Sada said, after pausing a moment to think.

Camilla was about to protest.

'Paedophiles, for example,' Sada continued.

Words failed her, but Camilla understood what Sada was saying and her eyebrows shot up. 'That's not a fair comparison,' Camilla exclaimed in her shock.

Sada nodded and said that that was precisely the same way one might be excluded from a family unit in her culture. 'People who do that are the worst kind of scum. No one wants to be with them and people won't protect them either,' the slender immigrant woman said.

Silence prevailed between them, as the thoughts slowly settled into place in Camilla's head. She regretted promising she wouldn't write anything without obtaining permission first, because it was pretty easy to see that she wasn't going to get it in this case. She sensed a peace between them, as if all the air had gone out of a balloon. But she also sensed that a new intimacy was burgeoning between them, which was what made her decide not even to try to pressure the woman for permission to use anything from their conversation.

'Would your husband have been able to kill your daughter

if she had violated the family's honour?' Camilla took a deep breath once that question was out there. It had been burning away at her since they'd sat down, but she hadn't even contemplated whether she dared ask it. Now it was done.

She noted that Sada's shoulders rose a smidge when she understood what she was being asked, but then slowly fell back into place again as she answered.

'He might. But our daughter didn't do anything to violate our family. On the contrary. She was our pride. He took care of her,' she said, taking great pains to emphasise the words, making them unwavering.

'Are you afraid of him?' Camilla asked.

Sada looked at Camilla in surprise and then responded with a convincing 'No'. Then she continued, 'On those occasions when something happened, he had a reason to react. He didn't have one in this case.'

This statement made Camilla suspect that Ibrahim had hit Sada more than once. It had happened before, but just hadn't been reported to the police.

'I'm not afraid of my husband,' Sada went on, 'even though he can lose his temper and do stupid things. But I am afraid that they will come and take the little ones away.'

'Who will?' Camilla asked, her thoughts still on the rest of Sada's family.

'The government. I won't be allowed to keep my children after what you wrote.'

And with that, they were back where they'd started, but the feeling in Camilla's stomach was totally different now than the one she'd had when Sada had started scolding her.

'They're not going to take your children away. You're a good mother. They have no reason to.'

'They don't know how it is. They only see what's in the paper.'

'Well, I don't believe that,' Camilla said, but she knew that the other woman wasn't entirely wrong. Camilla had stoked the fire and possibly set something in motion that she had not understood the repercussions of, but she hadn't been thinking about her article as something that could have this type of direct consequence. Now she regretted that she hadn't just written a sentimental piece about a town where some teenagers were grieving the loss of a good classmate.

Repercussions, Camilla thought, afraid it was a word that was going to follow her for the entire case.

'I'd really like to write about what you told me today. It might help your case.'

'No, no.' Sada vigorously shook her little head. 'You mustn't.'

'I don't need to say the two of us talked. I can write something about honour and shame, about the loneliness and fear of becoming an outcast, and why it might be necessary to act as you did.'

'No one will bother reading that to try to understand,' Samra's mother said, suddenly sounding tired.

Camilla smiled at her.

'You leave that to me. I'll just throw something together.'

Before they stood up, Camilla pulled out her card with the paper's number and her own mobile phone number on it. 'Call me. Also if you just want to talk,' Camilla said. 'I'll be back in Holbæk again next week.'

Sada nodded and took the card.

'Take care of yourself,' Camilla said as they parted. 'And thank you for coming.'

She stood there outside the hotel watching Sada walk across Banegård Square to catch a bus she could take home.

17

Louise quietly coasted down the street and parked next to a red wooden building with a big sign that said HAMAM. She sat looking at it for a bit, wondering, until it suddenly dawned on her that she had once read an article about a Turkish bath opening in Holbæk. She and Camilla had even toyed with trying it out. So this is where it is, she thought, getting out of the car.

The Rowing Club was on her right, and a little way out in the water, along a pier, were the Oceanside Baths – a redwood building with a number of small, attractive cabins all painted white. She wondered for a second if she shouldn't head back up the road and try to go in through the clubhouse to find Mik, or if she should go down to the water and see if she could get through that way.

'Hi!'

He had spotted her before she saw him. He was standing along the shore in a wetsuit and a life jacket, which wasn't buckled shut yet, but what she noticed first were his bright-yellow plastic clogs. Attractive they were not and yet they were all the rage, but they were one of the last things she would have expected to see her not-all-that-hip partner wearing. He was standing with a bunch of men and women in wetsuits and fluorescent yellow-and-orange life jackets. There was a line of sea kayaks, ready to put into the water, and she realised she had interrupted the class, which was already under way. A little embarrassed, she walked over and greeted the others.

'I got one out for you,' Mik said, pointing to the red Dagger-brand kayak, which was the one furthest away.

She walked over and stood next to it and listened along as he explained that the sea kayak had two sealed compartments, which meant it couldn't sink, and they also served as storage space if you were going on a trip.

He held something up that looked pretty much like a skirt and explained that it was a spray skirt, which you attached around your waist before you climbed into the kayak and then pulled taut and secured over the opening.

'Start from the back,' he said, demonstrating how to secure it. 'That way you won't get water in your kayak. It will come off easily if you capsize in the water, so don't be afraid of getting stuck if that happens.'

Louise looked around at the other students, listening attentively to his explanation. Personally, she didn't have the slightest desire to capsize, whether she had one of these skirts on or not. She was having a hard time paying attention. It was totally discombobulating to see Mik Rasmussen in the role of kayaking instructor.

He showed them how far to pull their kayaks out into the

water before climbing into them, and then he came over to Louise and said that he'd laid out all her equipment for her up in the changing room.

'But you didn't even know I was going to come,' she protested, as they walked back up to the clubhouse.

'Of course you were going to come. No one ever turns down a free kayaking lesson,' he said, holding the door open for her.

She refrained from commenting that that had more to do with the fact that she didn't have anything else to do today and that kayaking had just been an alternative to an afternoon at the movies.

'Did you bring your swimsuit?' he asked. She shook her head.

'Then you'll have to make do with underwear under your wetsuit, but I hope you brought an extra set, otherwise you'll be uncomfortable once you've been in the water.'

'Yeah, but I'm not going in the water,' she protested.

'Well, we'll see.' He found her a life jacket and asked if she wanted to wear a parka underneath. 'I don't think it's cold enough for you to need that,' he added helpfully.

Louise just nodded, hoping he wasn't expecting her to start pulling on the wetsuit while he stood there watching.

'Come down when you're ready,' he said, turning his back to her. The suit was still a little wet, and she was already having regrets as she felt the clammy neoprene against her skin. She kept her trainers on, feeling annoyed that she hadn't given any thought to what she ought to bring, but she hadn't really been planning on coming. She didn't even have a towel, which was really dumb, she realised.

The others were already sitting out on the water when

Louise reached the shore. Mik was standing there waiting for her as he yelled his instructions to the class. He helped her with the kayak and held it while she climbed in. He carefully pushed her the last little bit out into the water.

'Find the balance point,' he said and she took the paddle he passed her.

'The curved side should go down next to the water,' he reminded her.

She turned to give him an irritated look, but noticed how the kayak started tipping when she turned around. She quickly straightened back up and took a first cautious stroke in the water. She let the paddle rotate in the palm of her hand and switched to the other side. Then she started moving forward, stroke by stroke. It surprised her that she didn't feel more unsure of herself, so close to the surface of the water, but it felt good. Gradually, she reached the other students, who seemed to have enough control over their paddles and kayaks that they could manoeuvre around without bumping into each other.

Mik had hopped into his own kayak and was already on his way out. 'We're going to paddle down to the other side of Strandparken,' he yelled. 'And when we return, I'll show you how to get back up again if you land in the water.'

In the beginning her arms hurt, especially the left, but then she straightened her back and stretched it out at a right angle and could feel that things were going better. Once they'd rounded the hotel and were on their way back, she realised she was actually enjoying this. She had never pegged herself as a water-sports enthusiast, but this was great. The autumn sun was shining low in the sky, and she was gliding through the water very peacefully. She'd quickly worked out how to control the way you turned by back-paddling so the motion of the water acted as a brake, and the boat would slow down and start to change directions.

'If you fall in the water, you'll need to do an assisted recovery,' Mik explained as the kayaks bobbed in a group in the water in front of the Rowing Club. He had everyone's attention.

'First you empty the water out of the kayak. Let's just try. Hop in,' he said, and for a second Louise thought he was talking to her. She held her breath until she realised he was talking to a guy with long hair behind her. The man was down in the water quickly and Mik paddled over to him and positioned himself alongside.

'Start by flipping the kayak over and emptying out the water,' he instructed, and, along with the long-haired man, he pulled the kayak up over his own so the front part was resting on his.

'The water empties out like this,' he explained as he demonstrated. 'Then you have to get back in.' He turned the kayak over again and pushed it into the water so it was parallel to his. 'You support it while your buddy climbs in.'

Louise was glad it wasn't her. It didn't look easy. Although on the other hand, I probably ought to learn what to do in this situation, she thought. Just then, she felt a sharp jerk on her own kayak and before she had a chance to react, she was halfway over and just barely had time to wonder if her spray skirt would come loose so she wouldn't be trapped under the water. But it had already come free and she was out by the time her kayak was floating bottom up beside her.

'Sorry!' exclaimed one of the older men, who had accidentally bumped into her.

'Well, I suppose you two might as well do the next assisted recovery,' Mik said.

Louise got the kayak flipped over and drained the water out of it. She quite easily crawled up so she was lying on her stomach with her legs half down into the hole. With her kayak being held good and steady, she slowly turned around so she was lying with her head over the back end, and cautiously slid down into the kayak. She felt victorious having succeeded on her first try.

'Bravo!' Mik yelled, paddling over and giving her a high-five.

There was a good feeling in her body when the class ended shortly after that and they helped carry the kayaks back to where they were stored. Mik offered her one of his extra towels and she headed in to the changing room to get dressed. She wrung out her underwear and although she wasn't crazy about wearing her jeans and T-shirt with nothing underneath, she decided there was really no way around it.

'That went extremely well,' her partner complimented her as they walked out of the clubhouse together.

She smiled and thanked him for having enticed her to try it. 'It was a lot more fun than I thought it would be,' she admitted.

Just after she'd arrived in Holbæk, her mother had invited her to come over for dinner since she was so close, and tonight was the night. Her brother, Mike, and his wife, Stine, would be there too, along with their two little terrorists, and as she drove back to the hotel to get some dry underwear she realised she was actually looking forward to spending a nice evening with her family.

18

It was almost eleven when Louise, full and in a good mood, pulled into the car park by the hotel. In the car on the way home from her parents' house, she had decided she would go for a run the next morning before work. She walked over to the train station on the other side of the street to look at the big map of Holbæk and the surrounding area that was posted by the entrance. She was trying to decide whether to drive out and go for a run in the woods or make do with a run along the shore, following the sound out of town.

She was preoccupied with planning her route when, with disgust, she registered the sound of someone throwing up behind her and turned around. At first she didn't recognise the person, doubled over with one arm on the railing around the train station's bike racks, supporting herself as the vomit poured out of her in waves. Then she realised who it was.

'Dicta! What's going on?'

It took a moment before the girl shakily stood up. Louise

hurried over and put her arm around Dicta. She found a pack of tissues in her pocket and took one out, using it to dab the remaining vomit away from the girl's mouth and chin.

Even from a distance, she'd sensed that Dicta was pretty drunk, and they wobbled as Louise started walking towards the hotel with her. She got her seated in the restaurant, which had been empty of guests for a while. Then Louise went into the kitchen for a glass of water and found a bag the girl could throw up into if necessary. She set the glass down in front of Dicta and took a seat next to her.

'What did you do?' Louise asked.

Dicta didn't respond, didn't even look at Louise. She seemed to be falling asleep. Louise took a firm hold of her shoulder and shook her. 'Where have you been? Hello!'

The girl shook her head a little and tried to focus her swimming eyes on Louise's face. A spasm overtook her and Louise only just managed to get the bag in place before a new wave of vomit erupted from her mouth.

Goddamn it, she thought, as some of it hit her hand. She went back to the kitchen and washed her hands, found a new bag, and went back in to ask the question again.

'In Copenhagen,' Dicta finally answered. 'All day,' she said, looking up at Louise.

'And what were you doing in Copenhagen besides drinking yourself into a stupor?' Louise asked, trying not to sound like a mother.

For a second it looked like Dicta was going to throw up again, but it was just a tremor that ran through her body. She rubbed her face and looked at her hands in astonishment at the colours from her make-up that had rubbed off.

'I was working,' she said in a weak voice. She looked wretched, and Louise felt bad for her. She guessed it was the first time Dicta had got really drunk.

'A modelling job?' she asked.

Dicta nodded, and now such obvious tremors ran through her body that Louise was beginning to fear that it wasn't just alcohol she'd consumed.

'Did you take drugs? Pills? Or smoke something?' Dicta vehemently shook her head.

'I just drank champagne.'

Louise forced her to drink some more water and relaxed a little to hear it had just been champagne. Although that could be bad enough when you were fifteen and almost certainly hadn't had it before. It struck Louise that she probably ought to call the girl's parents instead of sitting here herself with the sad dregs of their daughter.

'What about your parents?' she asked. 'I have to call them.' Dicta shook her head again.

'Were you with your photographer?' Louise asked, already prepared for the scolding the *Venstrebladet* photographer could look forward to after dropping off his young model outside the train station in this condition.

Dicta suddenly looked childishly proud in the midst of all her misery as she told Louise that she'd been photographed by one of the big-name photographers.

'He photographed Lykke May too,' she said, clearly assuming that Louise would be familiar with the name of one of Denmark's most successful models.

'Can you give me a few more details? I'm not quite following. How did you end up with him?'

Dicta had perked up a bit.

'I'd seen his name in a few magazines, and then yesterday I called him and he invited me in for a photo session.'

There were a few too many Ss in 'session', and she struggled to get control of her pronunciation as she continued.

'I took the train in this morning and we met at Café Ketchup and had brunch. His studio is right next door.'

Louise was a little surprised at how uncomplicated and familiar she made it all sound.

'Do you usually go to Copenhagen like that?' she asked. 'It sounds like you're familiar with the cafés.'

Dicta shook her head and said that she'd never been there before – she'd just read about it. She and Liv had been to Copenhagen over the summer holidays, but otherwise she usually went there with her parents.

That reminded Louise that she had to contact them. 'Do your parents know that you're back?'

'They think I'm at Liv's house,' Dicta said, brushing aside Louise's objections.

'But they know you went to Copenhagen?'

This was starting to sound like an interrogation and Louise noticed Dicta receding into her own world again, so Louise restrained herself and let the girl go on with her story.

'His studio was really impressive compared to the one Michael has here at home,' Dicta said, describing the walls with the different photographic backdrops and a bunch of lights and filters to tone down the light.

'What does Michael Mogensen have to say about your finding yourself another photographer?'

'He doesn't know I went there. Michael's totally not in the same league. Tue says that too,' she said, explaining that the Copenhagen photographer's name was Tue Sunds and that he had already explained to her over the phone that if she was really dreaming about making it big on an international level, she was going to have to stop wasting her time in a tiny town like Holbæk.

'Michael is really just small potatoes, a provincial photographer,' Dicta said with a level of disdain that was the result of her visit to the big city.

'Why did Tue Sunds want to meet you on a Saturday?' Louise interrupted when the question occurred to her. 'I hope you didn't take your clothes off for him.'

Dicta turned to face her angrily, and there was something comical about the gesture because she still hadn't regained full control over her speech or coordination. She flung out her hands, whacking the back of one of them against the edge of the table.

'Are you crazy? I wouldn't do that!'

'Did you two go anywhere else?' Louise asked.

The girl sat for a bit before responding that they'd only been to the café and then he took a couple of pictures of her.

'Just a couple?'

That didn't seem like very many considering the man had spent his Saturday on this. In that case, it was probably a desire to maximise his income, Louise supposed.

'I mean, he is a professional,' Dicta retorted quickly. 'He's totally not like Michael, who spends several hours on a single pose. Tue works for the big magazines.'

'But you didn't get home until now? Or had you already been back in Holbæk for a while when I met you?'

Dicta obviously had to think about that one for a minute. Maybe she just couldn't remember how or when she'd come back.

'I took the train home and had just got back. And then standing there outside the station I suddenly had to throw up.'

Louise shook her head at the girl.

'What did you guys do for the rest of the day?'

'We went out and drank champagne to celebrate our new collaboration.' Dicta sounded proud. 'He said one of the heads of the big modelling agencies often came to the same place and that he would introduce us.'

Louise sat there with her arms crossed.

'Did you go back to his place after that?' she asked, and Dicta nodded so that her long, blonde hair fell down over her face in wisps.

'We drank more wine and ate the sushi and caviar he ordered and then I had to go home.'

'Did you sleep with him?'

Dicta melodramatically widened her eyes and gave Louise a shocked, offended look with her groggy eyes.

'You have no right to ask me that. He thinks I have a lot of potential.' Again Dicta had trouble speaking clearly. 'He says I could make it as far as Lykke May or Louise P.'

'Did he do anything to you against your will?' Louise asked when Dicta didn't respond to her question.

'What do you mean?' Dicta seemed genuinely not to understand.

'Did he force you to do anything you didn't feel comfortable with?' Louise really couldn't put it any more clearly than that.

Dicta closed her eyes and hid her face in her hands as she shook her head. After a while, she moved her hands again and gave Louise a dark look. 'You're like my mother. Why don't you believe that amazing things can really happen?'

Louise was about to defend herself, but saw how tired and wretched Dicta looked. 'Of course they can really happen. I just want to make sure that he didn't take advantage of you. You're a little off balance these days after what happened to your friend. That can make it harder to make good decisions.'

'He didn't. He just thought I was pretty, and he really wanted to help me. We kissed a little. Okay?'

She added the last part out of spite and Louise couldn't tell if that covered everything that had happened. But she wasn't actually all that concerned as long as the girl hadn't been molested on top of being marinated in a large portion of champagne.

Louise stood up and helped Dicta to her feet.

'I'll drive you home.'

Dicta stood there unstably on her feet and looked as if she wanted to protest, but Louise started pulling her along right away.

It was dark in the big house when Louise parked outside, but by the time she reached the front door Charlie had already started barking loudly and several lights along the driveway switched on. She rang the bell and supported Dicta while they waited for the door to open.

'No one's home,' Dicta said after they'd waited a while. Louise looked at her in surprise.

'Then why are we standing here waiting for someone to open the door?' Louise asked, helping Dicta as the girl tried to extract her keys from the little chest pocket of her jeans jacket.

At first the girl didn't answer, then she shrugged and laughed a little foolishly. 'I forgot it was the weekend,' she said, getting the door open without letting the dog out. 'My mum spends most of her weekends at dog shows or agility courses, and my dad goes along. Otherwise they'd never see each other.'

She spat that last sentence out and had obviously heard the explanation repeated so many times that it had become a kind of mantra. Louise had the sense that it was more that Dicta didn't care about her parents' priorities, not that they upset her. Louise stood just inside the front door watching the girl slip off her jacket and toss it on the floor. Once she had ascertained that Dicta was heading for her bedroom she yelled goodnight and shut the door to drive back to the hotel.

19

'What are we doing about those tyres?' Storm asked, irritated, looking at Skipper and Dean.

It had been more than two weeks since Samra had been found, and the whole group was sitting around the table in the command room. So far they hadn't got anything out of the crime-scene investigations or the dinghies that were out there, the search of the al-Abds' home, or the string of witness statements that Louise and Mik had spent the intervening weeks on along with Bengtsen and Velin. They'd trawled through everything – acquaintances, work relationships, family, neighbours. Storm had even considered whether he ought to have Interpol send one of them to Jordan to speak to family members there, but it would have a big impact on the investigation if that kind of questioning was to be permitted and he still hadn't found a way to justify it.

Skipper reached for a little stack of papers he had on the table in front of him.

'Well, there is a report here from the crime-scene investigators that we've been working with for the last few days. They compared the tyre tracks secured out at Hønsehalsen with the tyres of Ibrahim's red Peugeot. In one of the treads in the crime scene track they found a milled groove, which was measured at 1.3 millimetres deep. In comparing that to the corresponding tread on the Peugeot's four tyres the corresponding depths were measured at 1.4 on the left front tyre, 1.7 on the left rear tyre, 1.6 on the right front tyre, and 1.8 on the right rear tyre,' he read from the pages and then set them down again. 'Therefore, there are no specific parameters that can serve as a basis for identification between the plaster of Paris cast from the scene and Ibrahim's car,' Skipper concluded. 'But we also can't rule out that the impressions at the site were made by his car. The tyre impressions are of the same dimension with an equivalent pattern and wear. We'll just never be able to prove it.'

'All right, then let's drop that,' Storm said gruffly. 'There's no reason to throw more resources in that direction.'

He went on to explain that there hadn't been anything in the dinghies that were close to where the body was found, nothing besides remnants of fish blood, which had aroused interest at first until Dean reminded everyone that Samra hadn't bled.

Louise sighed and looked around at the rest of the team. She sensed that they had all been banking on the tyre tracks being unique and matching the car Samra's father usually drove. There was no doubt that Samra's body had been dumped into the water from a boat, but the family could easily have driven her out to the site and then just rowed her out from there instead of crossing the entire sound with her in the boat.

Since they couldn't rule out the possibility that the tyre track had been made by any random driver, Skipper and Dean had issued a press release asking people who owned cars with the same type of tyres to contact them if they'd been out at Hønsehalsen in the days before the killing. There had also been a great deal of talk about tyres and tyre tracks in the media and on the police's home page. But no one had come forward.

'We have to keep looking,' Storm said, nodding at Bengtsen. 'Should we expand our search for witnesses?'

Bengtsen stopped him by thrusting a hand up in the air. 'We've talked to a lot of people over the last couple weeks. It would be a total coincidence if we suddenly found someone who'd seen the girl. It isn't likely.'

'Well, then we'll focus on the audio surveillance of the family, and we may have to consider putting some pressure on them to see if there's any reaction.'

Søren seemed to support that decision. 'We'll keep going with the digital room bug, and there's a wiretap on their landline too,' he said.

Storm nodded and appeared satisfied. Louise was hardly as satisfied. They'd been working hard the last two weeks, mostly routine work, in the hopes that they'd overlooked something, but nothing new had turned up. She thought about Dicta. Louise hadn't talked to her since that night at the hotel, but maybe it was most considerate to let that episode be, she thought, getting up as the meeting ended.

'There are women strong enough to fight their way out of the iron grip their damned families keep them locked in. They break free to escape forced marriages and violence and mentally ill husbands who feel so overly confident that they own these women that they rape them around the clock and dominate them and damn well believe that they have the absolute right to use them any way they will.' Camilla was working herself up to maximum volume. She took a deep breath and lowered her voice. 'But that's a tiny fraction compared to all the women who stick around and put up with the whole thing because they don't have the same strength.'

She was sitting across from Terkel Høyer in his office and had just turned in two articles for the next day's paper, but when she saw the look on his face, she realised that she couldn't even count on a mention on the front page.

'It's been over two weeks since the girl's body was discovered, but instead of going to the police and pressuring them to reveal whatever the hell they're doing, you turn in two articles about honour and shame and about women who never get a real chance to integrate into Danish society, because, according to you, they're bound by cultural traditions.'

Camilla kept a straight face.

'What the hell are you thinking?' thundered her editor. 'Our readers couldn't care less about cultural traditions if they cause a couple of parents to kill their daughter. No one is ever going to accept that kind of thing in Denmark, no matter what the girl did to get on her family's bad side. If they choose to live in Denmark, then it's up to them to fucking follow our cultural norms! You're not going to get anywhere with that angle, and you can't cram crap like that down my readers' throats. This paper does not condone that kind of thing in any way.'

Ah, so now they were his readers, Camilla thought. Her voice was icy as she got up to stand in front of his desk. 'I don't agree with you,' she said simply. 'What I wrote has nothing to do with getting Danes to accept this. But it can't hurt to try to understand where it's coming from, to get to the bottom of why people are doing these things, which we very obviously don't understand and which of course we will not tolerate. Your readers may well be stupid, but I don't fucking think they're that stupid.'

She spun around and a couple of steps later, once she was out of the office, she slammed the door shut behind her so the wall shook. She did it again when she got to her own office just to get some of the rage out of her system in an efficient way.

Camilla sat down at her desk and looked at her screen: loneliness was worse than fear. She had promised Sada some sort of redress in the paper and she was ready to go to some lengths to make good on her promise. But right now that felt rather impossible. Terkel was going to have to back down a little first, or she was going to have to come up with some news from Holbæk. There just wasn't any news, though. Obviously she'd been keeping tabs on developments the whole time. What was he thinking?

The whole time since Sada had come to see her at the hotel, Camilla had been working on those two articles on the side, along with everything else she'd written. She had spent a lot of time getting all her research in place, talked to women who had managed to break free, and even with a Pakistani woman whose husband had kept her locked in their small apartment and brutally raped her whenever he wanted to have sex, which was at least once a day. If she begged him to leave her alone, he beat her.

Camilla had striven to distinguish between religion and

culture in the articles, to explain that the two things didn't have anything to do with each other when it came to concepts like honour and shame.

When you lose your honour, you lose your worth as a person and a social being, Camilla had written, linking that to the Arabic saying: *Honour is what distinguishes people from animals.*

It had shaken her that honour killings in the Middle East were increasing instead of decreasing. And there was obviously a big difference between the shamefulness of an act and the consequences of it. Women's sexuality was worst of all, for example, being unfaithful and having sex outside marriage. Only after that came hardened criminality. She shook her head and felt deeply indignant on behalf of her sex.

Camilla had determined that the consequences of such an act depended a lot on where you lived. In traditional families in rural areas, honour and shame meant much more than in modern families in urban environments, so obviously it was impossible to generalise. She had also made a big deal of elaborating on that.

When she was nearly finished, she had stumbled across something that had made her consider whether she ought to write the story at all, because there was something about it that she had obviously misunderstood and she wondered if she would ever truly comprehend the whole thing.

In the Koran it said that you mustn't force someone to marry against their will. So how the fuck could parents still be forcing their wishes on their children? But there was obviously also something cultural going on, Camilla realised. She just didn't see how people could so blatantly go against the Koran, since it made it so clear. She had decided not to include that in the article, but the book was sitting there as a reminder on her desk and she had to admit that it all was quite complicated. So she had gone to see Terkel with her two articles, which she considered important to the debate that had been raging in the press since Samra's murder.

Now in a fit she had crumpled them both up and tossed them into the corner of her office. She swung her legs onto her desk and sat there, lost in thought, her eyes focused on the many drawings Markus had made for her, which she had dutifully hung up on the wall as a border all the way around her desk.

She had actually been planning to drive to Holbæk that evening to find out if there'd been any progress that hadn't percolated out of the police command room yet. Markus was with his dad, so that would have worked great. But after her run-in with Terkel she suddenly didn't care. It was one thing for him to have his opinions, but it surprised her that he had voiced them aloud. It was inappropriate for an editor to so openly take sides.

It made her jump when he flung open the door without knocking and fired off his torrent of words in one breath: 'If you can find some kind of Danish angle in your articles, we'll run them. Otherwise, forget it. We're not publishing a manifesto here.'

He was gone before she'd processed what he'd said, and the door had already clicked shut by the time she yelled that it was too a manifesto if he was going to be so freaking one-sided that he wouldn't even listen to the other point of view.

20

'We're going to release the body,' Storm said from their office doorway, and then asked if Louise didn't need to take a spin back to Copenhagen to water her plants. If so, could she swing by the Pathology Lab and bring back the certificate? The family had requested permission to fly Samra back to Jordan so she could be buried in Rabba, where she'd grown up and where her grandparents still lived.

'I'm sure my plants would love that. I suppose I might as well do it now?' she said, looking from Storm to Mik, who both nodded.

'Of course, you could also stay for a cup of coffee before you go,' her partner coaxed once Storm had left. 'Bengtsen brought in some of Else's macaroons.'

Louise smiled and held up both hands to fend off the offer.

In the car she called Flemming Larsen's direct number and said she was on her way in to the Pathology Lab to pick up

Samra's death certificate. Did he have time to go for breakfast or a cup of coffee?

'I'm going to have trouble getting out of here,' he said and explained that he was about to start an autopsy. 'But if you want, we could have a cup of coffee here when you arrive. I'd really like to see you before you leave town.'

Louise laughed into her headset. The tall pathologist was a master at making her feel like she was special, which made her cherish their friendship.

'I'm in the basement,' Flemming said. 'Just come on down and we'll get the death certificate all sorted out too.'

When she arrived at the Teilum Building, she said hello to one of the pathology techs whose name she couldn't remember and found out that Flemming was in the first room on the right at the bottom of the stairs.

Her heels echoed. She'd been down to the cold-storage rooms several times, but had never attended a post-mortem there. She wasn't usually there until they did the formal autopsy. She knocked and waited a bit before pushing the door open.

'Hi,' Flemming said, walking over to her in his white lab coat. Louise stayed out in the hallway, but saw that the deceased on the table was an older man. She received a quick peck on the cheek from Flemming.

'Give me ten minutes and I'll be ready. I picked up some pastries across the street from the cafeteria at the National Hospital,' he said, indicating a chair a little further down the hallway.

'I'll wait,' she said, smiling at the fact that he'd gone out of his way to pick up pastries for her.

Down the hallway a heavy steel door opened and a man in

a gas mask came out. She raised her eyebrows at Flemming, wondering what that was about.

'They've just started embalming your Jordanian girl,' he said. 'That has to be done before she can be sent abroad. Have you ever seen how they do that?'

Louise shook her head and followed him as he started walking towards a glass window in the wall. Through the window she could see a small room dominated by a steel table, which was screened by a thick plastic curtain on all four sides. Above that, there was an enormous exhaust fan, and Samra's naked body lay on the table.

'They slowly fill her up with formalin,' Flemming explained, pointing to a pump next to the body. Several tubes were attached with needles to the girl. 'About four or five litres will be pumped in via the major arteries, also filling the lungs and the chest cavity. The formalin will cause her organs to shrink a little, and then they'll keep for quite a long time after that.'

The pathology tech in the gas mask came back, rolling a zinc coffin in front of him.

Louise stood there for a bit, looking at the girl. You couldn't tell that her earthly remains were being preserved. She still looked like she had when her teacher identified her in the presentation room.

'Once she's been through a few Muslim burial rituals, the coffin will be sealed, and then she'll be sent home to Jordan, where the actual burial will take place,' Flemming said.

He went back to finish his post-mortem exam, and Louise took a seat to wait for him. The sentimental side of her, which she still struggled with from time to time, really wanted to see them apprehend the culprit before Samra left Denmark. Not because her departure brought up any technical problems; all the evidence had been secured. Louise knew she would just feel more confident that justice had been done if she could say goodbye to the girl secure in the knowledge that someone was going to be punished for having robbed her of her young life. Instead, Samra was being sent away without their knowing anything at all.

'There. Time for a coffee,' she heard Flemming say, pulling her out of her reverie.

His office wasn't particularly big, and there were stacks of papers and folders everywhere. He cleared off a chair for her and stepped out for a moment, returning with two cups and plates bearing a chocolate croissant and a Danish pastry with rum frosting, which he squeezed onto the last available spot on the desk.

'How's it going in Holbæk?' he asked as he poured the coffee.

She shrugged, not up to explaining that they really hadn't got anywhere. Instead she told him that she'd tried sea kayaking.

'Sea kayaking!' His outburst was just as surprised as her own had been when Mik invited her to try it.

She smiled and nodded, breaking off a piece of pastry. 'It's amazingly fun,' she admitted, one eyebrow shooting up when Flemming set down his cup of coffee and said it was something he'd been wanting to try for ages.

'I've just never got around to it, but now I have a good excuse. It would be fun if we went kayaking together next spring.'

Louise brushed some crumbs off her blouse.

'Well, I can't promise that I'll be so hooked that I'm still doing it then, but if I am, that sounds nice,' she laughed.

When they finished the coffee, she stuck the death certificate into her bag and said goodbye with the agreement that they'd go out for a couple of beers once she was back in town.

'I can't understand how this happened. How could this happen?'

Ibrahim's voice was husky and unclear, but the interpreter translated without adding any emotion to the words.

'You stopped taking care of her.'

'Sada is accusing him,' the interpreter explained.

Louise had let her bag and jacket drop to the floor as she joined the others back at the police station.

'Of the murder?' Storm asked, interested, leaning over the oval table, where they were all sitting tensely, listening to the previous day's recordings. They hadn't got much out of the tapes over the last couple of weeks, but now that the girl's body had just been released, her parents were suddenly discussing something that might be related to what had happened.

'I never stopped.'

The Mobile Task Force's own interpreter sat listening with concentration before he repeated the words in Danish.

'Why do you even talk to him? Why don't you shut the door on him?'

'He humiliates me. I won't find any peace until he's dead. He's ruined us.'

'Who is Ibrahim talking about?' Louise asked.

The interpreter stopped the recording and thought for a moment before shaking his head and saying, 'It could be a friend, an acquaintance, someone from the family. I don't know. But it could also be himself. If he killed his daughter and is convicted, I would interpret that as self-reproach.'

When he turned the playback on again, they heard deep sobbing and a sentence so drowned out by the sobs they had to play it several times before Fahid was able to tell them what had been said.

'It would have been better if she weren't dead, but alive.' Again Fahid turned it off and looked at them.

'That is a very strong expression he used there,' he explained. 'He means they might have been able to find a different solution than taking her life.'

'Well, then, he's admitting it, isn't he?' Skipper exclaimed.

'No, I wouldn't interpret it that way. I would sooner say he's acknowledging that someone is responsible for her death and that he might know who it is. I don't consider it a direct admission.'

'You still don't think they should be questioned about what they're saying here?' Mik asked, looking at Storm, who shook his head.

'They shouldn't find out we've been listening in on them until we arrest him, if we're going to. We can use this in court to get the court order extended if that's necessary. If we need to, we can confront them with the most important sections of the recordings and ask them to explain themselves. We can also easily compare things they haven't disclosed and false statements up until that point if they don't know we're listening.'

It was obvious that Louise's partner did not agree with that plan, but he gave in and continued paying attention as Storm signalled to the interpreter to continue.

Sada's clear voice filled the room.

'I told you you shouldn't kill her. She could have got married.'

Ibrahim was still crying when he again said something. 'I didn't do it. She was my daughter.'

'Who did it, then? It was your fault.'

'There's a very unpleasant atmosphere between the two of them. It is completely obvious that his wife is accusing him, but he is denying it. I think he sounds extremely unhappy,' Fahid said once the sequence had finished playing.

'Does he say anything we could charge him with?' Storm asked, not allowing himself to be moved by the sympathy the interpreter seemed to be feeling for Ibrahim.

'No, quite the contrary. He seems agitated and unhappy.'

'He's alluding to a third person, isn't he?' Louise asked, her eyes on the interpreter.

She couldn't tell if Fahid was feeling trapped, as if his loyalties were divided, or if he had really changed his opinion on the father partway through this session. At first he had seemed like he believed Ibrahim was incriminating himself, but now he was leaning towards believing Ibrahim was profoundly unhappy.

'Something about this family isn't right,' Skipper said in his calm, deliberate manner. 'That story Camilla Lind wrote about the rabbit made that quite obvious.'

Louise had been disgusted when her friend had called her one evening after talking to Samra's friend Fatima, who had related an episode that had taken place a month before Samra was killed. One night Samra's parents served their daughter's pet rabbit for dinner, but told her it was chicken. It was only after she'd eaten it that her father asked her to go out to the garden and look in the empty rabbit hutch. Camilla's story had taken up the whole front page that time.

'Yeah, but that doesn't mean they killed her,' Fahid

objected, eyeing them steadily. 'Ibrahim explained that he'd done that to punish Samra, because she'd come home so late one night after visiting her aunt and uncle in Benløse. They had had a clear agreement that she would be back at a specific time. And yet she didn't get home until several hours after that.'

'That's quite a severe punishment for a young girl,' Mik said, staring at the wall.

According to Fatima, Samra had run straight into the bathroom and thrown up until there wasn't anything left in her stomach, and after that she refused to eat, no matter what her mother served her.

'Why don't we just charge the family?' Velin asked, looking at Storm in irritation, as if he was losing faith in his boss's ability to make decisions.

'Because we'll get more out of waiting until we're sure that we have enough to hold them on,' Storm replied sharply.

The interpreter finished his work, and Louise walked back to her office with Mik with an uncomfortable sense that the atmosphere at work was becoming rather tense. Good thing the weekend was almost here, so they wouldn't all have to spend every minute in such close quarters for a couple of days.

21

On Saturday morning, Louise was on Ahlgade trying to pick out a face cream when someone grabbed her arm and spun her around. Anne Møller said hello with a big smile, and Louise immediately got the distinct sense that Dicta's mother had not heard about her daughter's overindulgences. She also decided that the mother didn't need to hear about it from her.

'Hi,' Louise said, smiling back.

'You've practically moved out here to the boondocks for good,' Anne joked. Then she asked Louise if she wasn't getting tired of eating at the Station Hotel every night.

'It is starting to get a little old,' Louise admitted.

'If you want, you're very welcome to come over and eat with us. Dicta comes home for dinner, even if she usually goes back over to Liv's afterwards. She's starting to do a little better, but of course the whole thing is still a terrible shock to her. As it was to all of us, of course,' she hurried to add. She went on to say that she'd seen Storm on TV the evening before and understood that some family matter was behind the killing, not that that made the crime any more understandable, but at least there was no reason to walk around feeling afraid there was some maniac on the loose.

Louise hadn't seen the report, but thought maybe her boss ought to have kept his statement to himself, since he didn't want to detain the suspects yet. She politely declined the dinner invitation with an off-the-cuff excuse.

'I'm afraid I'm getting together with one of my colleagues tonight,' she said. 'Perhaps we could do it another time?'

'Of course.'

'I'm glad to hear that,' Louise said, seizing the opportunity to break the conversation as an employee walked over to them. She quickly said goodbye to Dicta's mother.

An Indian summer. Wish I knew how long this weather was going to hold out, Louise thought that afternoon as she cycled out to the Rowing Club. It was a week into October and the sun still felt warm. She'd borrowed an old men's bike from Mik and was pedalling hard, so her pulse was up and her body covered in sweat. She was slightly out of breath as she rode down the gravel path to the Rowing Club and the Turkish baths.

After the class the previous weekend, Mik had persuaded her to keep going with Beginners' level 1 and 2, which were each four hours long. At the same time he had emphasised that she didn't need to try to be the best. She should just be satisfied to learn enough techniques so she felt safe going out paddling on her own.

But it just wasn't that easy. From the very beginning, all some of the men could talk about was when they would finally learn to do an Eskimo roll. When the first beginners' course ended, they'd practised turning around and doing a half roll, and Mik had got them all worked up by promising that in the next class he would teach them how to go all the way around. Louise had felt sort of left out, but she had still said 'Of course' when he'd asked her earlier in the week if she was ready for Beginners 2. No matter what, it was better than sitting around looking at the inside of her hotel room.

She zipped up her life jacket, tossed her bag containing a change of clothes next to the shed, put on a hat with a visor so the sun wouldn't blind her, and she was ready. There were six of them, two women and four men, and she was intent on ignoring their boyish outbursts and putting the daunting task of learning to roll the kayak all the way around out of her mind.

'I'd rather get soused than learn how to roll a kayak,' she'd said when Mik leaned in over her desk the day before and asked if she was going to give it a try too, when all the men rolled their boats.

Now she took a couple of deep strokes with the paddle and moved quickly away from the landing platform. The sun glimmered on the water, shrouding Cape Tuse on the other side of the sound in a lovely golden mist, and it filled her with calm as her kayak shot out and her mind lost all sense of time. By the time Mik got his kayak into the water a couple of minutes later and the lesson was under way, she had put all thoughts of work and murderers behind her and just wanted to follow the others further out.

She left her bike there afterward, climbing into the passenger seat of Mik's car and driving out to the farm with him. She was still laughing and he was still complimenting her.

Before the lesson was over – and while the four lumbering men in the class had fooled around with their paddles sticking up in the air and the water sloshing around them because they couldn't succeed in finding the right angle that would get their kayaks to flip all the way around, without having to bail out partway – Louise slid up alongside Mik. She had spent the day's training session learning to fall into the water and then right the kayak again on her own using her paddle and a bilge pump to empty the water out. She had tipped her kayak many times before she started feeling secure that she would be able to do it some day when she was out on her own. Now, without making a face, she tapped him on the shoulder with her paddle. Then she put her weight out to the side and put her paddle into the water and, with all her might and the technique he'd just shown the guys, she disappeared underwater and came up again, becoming the first of the students to successfully complete the eagerly discussed full roll.

At first Mik didn't realise what she'd done, even though she was sitting there in front of him, soaking wet, with a huge grin on her face. It wasn't until the men in the group started catcalling that he exclaimed, 'What the hell are you doing? You can't just do a roll like that!' But then he started clapping too and smiling at her, impressed, while tactfully not mentioning the fact that this was probably due more to astoundingly good luck than to her technique.

Louise's heart was still pounding and she was a tad shaken that it had even occurred to her to do that. She couldn't comprehend how humiliating it would have been if she hadn't made it all the way around. At any rate, she couldn't help but be glad that she could still get it into her head to do things without overthinking them to death.

'So, I guess that means you picked the Eskimo roll instead of getting drunk?' Mik said when they were standing around the clubhouse afterward having a drink.

Louise nodded, but still agreed when he suggested they celebrate her Eskimo roll with a beer back at his farm.

They drove out past Strandmølleengen and Holbæk Marina, which was full of pleasure boats. The road narrowed as they continued out towards the golf course and Dragerup, where Mik's red U-shaped farmhouse stood. The roof was thatched, the house freshly whitewashed, and the timber framing had been tarred over that summer. Everything looked like you would expect for a Copenhagen dweller who moves to the countryside and puts his all into realising the dream of a pastoral idyll. But Mik wasn't from the city; he'd taken over the farm from his parents and fixed it up himself with the help of a couple of friends and the local roof thatcher.

'Do you want to see the puppies?' he asked once they'd got out of the car.

Louise followed him to the house, but then quickly took a step back when an exuberant wirehaired pointer came running out and started dancing around them until it lost interest and continued around behind the house into the garden. Mik waved for her to follow and then went into the kitchen, where the puppies were sleeping in a big basket.

'They're not always this calm,' he said, leaning down and petting the mother, a black Lab, who stood up when they came in.

Louise kneeled next to the basket and stuck her hand down to touch the soft puppies, who were beginning to move. A second later they were wriggling. They came tumbling over to curiously sniff her hand and then started nudging it. Mik picked up a puppy for her. She put her cheek down next to it and felt its muzzle against her skin. When it started getting fidgety, she carefully put it back in with the others and stood up.

'Every time I get close to a puppy, I forget I don't want a dog,' she said, shaking her head and smiling. Then Mik said that one of the puppies was still for sale.

She followed him as he grabbed two beers from the fridge and they strolled back out into the garden.

'Shall we sit here?' He gestured to a wooden bench bearing the inscription DAD'S BEER-DRINKING BENCH.

Louise winced to think Mik didn't have enough taste to acquire a nicer bench, but at the same time had to concede that at least the view couldn't be better. She stood for a second, enjoying the sight of the fields and woods on the other side of the road.

'Don't you ever miss the countryside?' he asked once she'd sat down.

She shook her head and said she would probably never miss it enough to move back.

'But every now and then I do need to get out of the city,' she admitted, looking at the horses in the corral in the field opposite them.

'Do your folks still live out here?' he asked, watching her as she took a swig of beer.

She nodded and smiled at him. Not because he was asking about her, but because she'd misjudged him. She didn't have to pull every word out of him. He was the one who was grilling her, which surprised her a little.

She told him about her parents' place, which was between Roskilde and Holbæk, and said that her brother still lived out there, not in an old farmhouse, but in a house in a new development that didn't have even a smidge of the charm her folks' country home or his farm had.

'Actually, what is the difference between a country home and a farm?' she asked, then volunteered an answer to her own question: 'Isn't it mostly that you tend a farm, while a country home is just for fun?'

Mik nodded. That pretty much summed up the definition. 'How much land do you have here?' she asked him. 'Are you growing anything?'

'Almost seventy acres, but I lease it to the farm over there.' He nodded towards the large farm on the other side of the narrow road, the one with the horse corral. 'They have the machinery and a barn.'

Mik brought them another two beers and a blanket Louise could wrap around herself.

'My parents are dead, but I'm sure I told you that,' he said after he sat down again.

Louise nodded.

'My mum died this spring, but it's been almost six years since my father died. His heart just stopped one morning while he was out checking on the cows. But if he had to go, I couldn't imagine a more fitting way for him to do it.'

Louise watched him as he spoke. He sagged a little and was picking at the label on his beer bottle, but he didn't seem as if he felt any pressure to tell her about himself.

'It didn't take more than a few months after my father died for my mum and I to move. She couldn't manage this whole place on her own and I had a small house on Fasanvej in town.' He nodded in the direction of Holbæk. 'And then I have a sister in Dubai. She moved there with her husband almost ten years ago and I really doubt they're coming back. The kids go to a European school and she stays at home and does her thing, so she wasn't interested in taking over this place.'

Louise explained that her parents hadn't bought their country place until she was old enough to start school. Before that, they'd lived in a big apartment in Østerbro. 'My mum's a ceramics artist,' Louise explained. 'She needed more room, a bigger kiln, and space for her potting wheel.' She spoke the words slowly with enough of a pregnant pause in between them to make it clear that she had not inherited her mother's creative abilities.

'What does your dad do?' Mik asked out of curiosity.

'He's an ornithologist,' she replied, and then quickly elaborated. 'He works for the Danish Ornithological Society a couple of days a week doing conservation and preservation work, and he edits their journal. He's one of those guys who lives his whole life with a spotting scope around his neck.'

Suddenly Mik laughed out loud, and something boyish came over his face that Louise hadn't seen before. She smiled and waited for him to explain what was so funny.

He shook his head a little before saying that that was the last thing he would have imagined.

'I pictured him as maybe a detective or a lawyer. How the heck did you end up in the police?' he asked, looking at her with interest.

She gave him a look of mock affront. 'Why? Is that so odd?'

'I don't know. With parents with skills and abilities like that, I would have thought some of it would have rubbed off on you.' He said it as if she'd been cheated out of something marvellous. The same way you might if a couple of very attractive parents had produced a really ugly baby.

An awkward silence settled between them as she contemplated this. Why had she chosen to join the police?

He interrupted her thoughts.

'Would you like an Irish coffee?' he asked so quietly that she had the sense he didn't want to bother her if she was actually trying to explain how she ended up in her job.

She nodded absent-mindedly, her thoughts locked on both her parents. It had never occurred to her that she could have followed in her mother's footsteps. She didn't think she had even a hint of creativity in her, but she had never really put herself to the test to see if that was true.

Mik came back with a tray of mugs, coffee, whipped cream, brown sugar, a bottle of Tullamore, and three large, square candles that were stacked up on the tray, threatening to tip over onto the coffee things.

'I grew up with birds,' Louise said as he put brown sugar and whiskey into her cup, mixed them together, poured coffee over them, and topped it off with freshly whipped cream. 'I got bird posters, bird books and stuffed birds, while all my friends were getting Barbies and pop-music posters. And my mother walked around in her work clothes all the time covered in splotches of clay with a towel around her hair. I didn't want to look like that when I grew up.'

'Did you rebel?' he asked, handing her the cup.

'Maybe, but that's not how I saw it. I didn't go in a different direction to defy my parents. I just did it because what they did didn't interest me. I went to one of those forest kindergartens in Langelinie as a kid, one of those places where school is held outdoors all day regardless of the weather. I know they chose that because they wanted what was best for me. But I really would have rather gone to a kindergarten where you sat on little chairs and drew or played with puzzles and cleaned up nicely after yourself after each meal, instead of relying on the public toilets out by the Little Mermaid statue and never eating a hot lunch, just sandwiches from our lunch-boxes, even in the rain.'

Mik listened without interrupting.

'I like there to be some kind of structure, so you have some-thing to adhere to.'

They'd finished their drinks and when he offered her another, she was well aware it was time to say no, thanks and force herself to be on her way. He'd said she could borrow his bike, since they hadn't brought along the bike she had on loan from the Rowing Club.

Instead, she nodded and held out her cup. She thought about the next morning. How smart was it to show up to work with a hangover? Sure, tomorrow was Sunday, but they were going to meet anyway. On the other hand, hadn't they pretty much been working around the clock for the weeks the case had been open? They needed to unwind a little.

He stood concentrating, letting the whipped cream slide down onto the warm coffee so carefully that it spread out like a white comforter over the blackness.

She didn't have a chance to stop herself. Before she knew it, she was on her feet, still wrapped in the blanket, starting to kiss him. Somewhere in the very back of her mind she heard stern warnings that what she was doing was extremely unwise, but she ignored them, letting the blanket fall as he reached around her shoulders and pulled her towards him. She stretched, standing on her toes, to press her cheek against his and noticed the short stubble against her skin in the few pauses between the volleys of kisses that ran back and forth between them. Nibbling, yearning, hungry and indulgent.

Where did that come from? she wondered when her brain started sending signals again that had to do with things besides him and his mouth. They still hadn't made eye contact, she didn't dare, couldn't deal with what she'd set in motion, but also didn't want to run away from it.

'Do you think this is wise?' he asked, his mouth against her throat, as both of his hands slid up over the skin on her back.

She sought out his mouth again even as she shook her head. It wasn't wise at all, and wasn't she supposed to be the one saying that? Truly, it was anything but wise. They shared an office, and they were still going to be sharing it the next day and the day after that. No one knew how long she was going to be in Holbæk. But they had already crossed this line, so no matter what they did it was going to be awkward and totally wrong to see each other at work after this, she thought. And besides, he wasn't her type at all. Not the way he looked, not his interests, or his Dad's Beer-Drinking Bench. All he had going for him was that he hadn't turned his head away when she kissed him.

She released his lips and inhaled in short bursts to calm her breathing.

'Let's stop here,' she said, releasing her firm hold on him, but nonetheless willingly allowing herself to be pushed along as he guided her backward, both hands on her hips, away from the Irish coffee towards the house. As they walked slowly so she wouldn't stumble, her eyes bore into his to determine how big a catastrophe this was. What did he think of her? Had she pressured him into this? Did he feel like he couldn't turn her down? How crushing a failure would it be when he said this was all a mistake? That they should have stopped before they even started. He didn't seem the type to turn down a colleague, so maybe she'd already really overstepped his boundaries. And he had already suggested that this wasn't particularly wise. The thoughts were whipping around in her head, but she couldn't read anything from his eyes. They were just blue eyes smiling at her and they didn't seem to be suffering from any kind of crisis of conscience or harassment.

After he settled her onto the sofa and brushed her dark curls away from her face, he carefully pulled her sweater up over her head. After that her blouse, and finally he unbuttoned her jeans. He sat there caressing her stomach, letting his fingers glide gently over her body, until his hand settled softly around the back of her head and he leaned over and kissed her. Kissed her tenderly and intensely, slowly, the whole way down her body.

'Now we kind of have to keep going, don't we?' he asked, once he'd pulled his own shirt over his head and loosened his belt.

Louise nodded in silence without opening her eyes. They kind of did have to keep going now.

22

The melody was so insistent and the volume rising such that it couldn't be ignored. Louise did a rapid damage check inside her head before opening her eyes to be confronted with the mess she'd got herself into the night before. They had ended up in his bed after first making love on the sofa, then on the living-room floor. She had no sense of when they had collapsed from exhaustion. Actually, that's not so bad, she thought.

Mik's mobile phone was ringing, and she shook him. The worst thing was that at one point he had whispered to her that this seemed like something she had really needed and she had hungrily agreed with him. After which she had really let go and abandoned herself to a level of enjoyment she could scarcely control.

To hell with the fact that she'd whispered a bunch of words she couldn't really recollect now, she thought. What did it matter that she had let him see her like that? Well, maybe that wasn't totally inconsequential. And she wasn't proud of it either. She couldn't believe she'd sold herself out by admitting that she had needed a man. That she was under-stimulated, and that she possessed a level of desire she herself couldn't control once it had been let loose. She had a hard time excusing herself for that.

Mik had the phone to his ear and was talking quietly, intensely. He was already out of bed and standing by the dresser, pulling out clothes. Louise could feel him looking at her, but she kept her eyes closed so there was no contact.

'You're going to have to wake up,' he whispered, stroking her cheek.

'What time is it?' she mumbled, not wanting to face reality.

'Almost six.'

He leaned over and kissed her until she opened her eyes and their eyes met. It wasn't as bad as she had feared. He smiled at her and she focused on his left front tooth, which was missing one small corner. Then he straightened back up and explained that that had been the duty officer down at the station on the phone.

'They just got a 911 call from a woman who found a dead teenage girl in the car park behind Nygade,' he told her. 'That's the street that goes up to your hotel.'

Louise was out of bed and on her way to the living room, where her clothes lay in a heap on the floor. He followed her and kept talking as she got dressed.

'They've already started cordoning off the area.'

He gave her a serious look as she pulled on her socks, and then he went out to tend to his dogs before they left the house.

'It looks like one side of the girl's head was crushed and she was very badly beaten,' he said, walking back into the living room with his car keys in his hand.

Louise cast a quick glance around the living room to see if she'd forgotten anything.

'I'll catch a ride over there and—' she started, but was interrupted when he reminded her that that would make it very obvious to everyone else that the two of them had spent the night together.

That hadn't even occurred to her, but she quickly agreed that he was right.

The October morning was still dark, and while he drove around the small turn and back in past Holbæk Marina at a pace that made it clear he'd driven that route countless times, she sat next to him speculating.

'How am I going to slip into the hotel if they're cordoning off the area?' she finally asked, suddenly unable to assess the situation.

'I can drop you off a little way away, if you'd like. But I don't mind in the least if the others see us together. I mean, it's not like we did anything illegal.'

'We shouldn't arrive together,' she said, a tad harshly. 'I'll wait over at the station for half an hour before I head over.'

He didn't remark on her stern pronouncement, but pulled over to the kerb so she could grab her bag from the back seat.

Louise was standing there with her bag and the car door open when she realised this was all too ridiculous.

'I'll just walk in there,' she said, blowing him a kiss.

He shook his head. Then he got out, walked around the car, and kissed her goodbye – not a long kiss, but with an intensity that gently settled reassuringly around her.

'Talk to you soon,' she said, once their lips had parted. 'Definitely soon.'

He got back in and drove the last four hundred metres past the police station over to Nygade.

23

Louise walked along Jernbanegade in the early morning with her kayaking bag over her shoulder and the feeling that she'd been in a dream for the last eight hours, a dream in which she couldn't completely take responsibility for her actions or vouch for her own conduct. She had pushed the thought of yet another body to the back of her mind and was too tired to think about it until she reached the hotel and the local police and the red-and-white-striped tape with the word 'Police' printed on it at regular intervals, with which they were just cordoning off the area. Then she spotted Storm and Skipper, who were standing under a large streetlight outside the hotel's small outdoor seating area, well dressed, their hair nicely done, with their hands in their pockets, looking out over the empty early-morning pedestrian shopping street.

She looked down at herself. She was wearing the same clothes as she had the day before, her hair was more tousled than curly, and she had forgotten to bring a hair band that could hold back her dark mane. She quickly ran a hand through it and as she walked the last few metres tried to make herself a smidge presentable. She had one foot on the steps leading up to the hotel's front entrance when Skipper spotted her.

'Good morning, Rick.'

She stopped mid-motion, turned, and started walking over towards them.

'Good morning,' she said, dropping her bag with a thump. Neither her temporary boss nor Skipper looked at it, nor did they comment on her arriving from outside the hotel.

They nodded over towards the police cars, most of them with their lights on, and asked if she'd heard all the commotion.

She shook her head, watching Mik's outline disappear into an alleyway next to Gyro Hut.

'There's a teenage girl with a crushed skull back there,' Skipper said, pointing in the direction in which Mik had disappeared.

'Do we know which teenage girl?' she asked, to get them talking and make it seem like she was on the ball. But she was completely unprepared when Storm turned to her and nodded.

'It's Dicta Møller.'

Suddenly the beer and Irish coffee were churning around in her like a centrifuge. She tasted bitterness as the bile from her stomach shot up into her mouth. But she held it back. She had vomited once before in front of a male colleague, and that was something she was only going to do once in her career. She sank, supporting herself against a lamp post.

The fatigue was suddenly so overwhelming that it made a very real situation seem unreal. While Louise had been revelling in her own pleasure, Dicta's skull was being smashed in. Not that she would have been able to prevent it if she'd been asleep in the hotel, but somehow it still seemed unseemly.

'I'm going to run upstairs and take a quick shower,' she said. 'I'll be down in ten minutes.'

She didn't wait for a response, already on her way up to her room.

What the hell was going on here? she thought, feeling for the first time in a long time like she didn't have a handle on things.

Pretty, sweet, young Dicta, who should have been a star, was now a victim. And the thought that this was how she was finally going to get her picture in the paper was unbearable, Louise thought sadly as she wrapped up her shower with an ice-cold rinse and hurriedly threw on some clothes.

The ambulance was still there. Storm and Skipper had moved over to the car park, where they were now standing with Søren Velin and the ambulance paramedic, who had established that Dicta was dead. Her old partner nodded at her sombrely as she reached them.

'This is nasty,' Velin said. He pulled her a little way away from where the body was located, as he explained that a woman had found it when she was bringing some clothes over to the Salvation Army donation bin after finishing her night shift at the hospital. The area was still illuminated by a couple of big portable spotlights.

Louise could just make out Dicta, lying at the edge of the car park. Quickly surveying the area, Louise counted eleven cars. At the far side, out by the ring road at the end of the car park where Dicta was lying was a large building that housed Nordtank. And Lindevej ran between the ring road and the car park, but that was quite a small street. At the perimeter of the car park down by the main street was a small service station. And out by Nygade was the back of the Gyro Hut. Louise spotted Dean, who was helping cordon off the area, and noted that the only person she hadn't seen yet out here was Bengtsen.

Søren Velin said that one side of Dicta's cranium had been crushed. He spoke so softly that Louise had to strain to hear the words. Maybe he was trying to spare her or himself a little of the gruesomeness of what had happened.

'She obviously took a lot of blows to the face and definitely also to the body,' he said. 'Her clothes are covered in blood.' He explained that the local police had locked down the scene when they arrived and now everyone was just waiting for the crime-scene technicians and the coroner, who were on their way.

'But it looks ghastly.'

She stared at him, astonished. He didn't usually react like that, and if he was putting it that way, she had no doubt he meant it.

'What did you do with Bengtsen?' she asked after a brief pause.

'He went to the hospital with the woman who found the body. He was the first one here and since she didn't have anyone who could go and stay with her, he did it. He'll stay with her until she calms down.'

Louise stood there for a bit before she started walking over to the body of the girl whose secrets she had been in on. She sank down into a squat when she reached her and sat there for a bit, looking at the dead figure. Just as Søren Velin had said, the side of her face was crushed, and her long blonde hair was stuck in the thick bloodstain that radiated from her head like a dark shadow. A little further away on the asphalt lay a yellow hair band tinged red with blood. Louise rested her elbows on her knees and supported her face in her hands. Under her jacket Dicta was wearing a small yellow top. She had got dressed up and had been looking good before she left her house to visit Liv. Louise felt a jab of pain in her chest as she stood back up to return to the others.

Camilla had arrived in Holbæk late on Saturday night. She had decided to drop the whole thing after her run-in with Terkel, but in the end her stubbornness compelled her to head back out there anyway and see if she could get any further on the story. Even if it robbed her of her Sunday, it would be a victory after their spat if she came home with something none of the other journalists had. She had called Louise from the road. Even before Camilla left Copenhagen, she was looking forward to meeting Louise at Bryghuset and chatting for a while over a beer, but Louise's mobile phone just kept going to voicemail. Camilla gave up around midnight.

Then early that morning, the sirens from the first responders' vehicles sliced through the walls of her room at the Station Hotel with their high-pitched howl. She had strolled out to the car park to check, but they'd cordoned off the area around the body, and with all the police tape she couldn't get close enough to see anything, so she called the desk officer at the station to find out what had happened. And when he wouldn't tell her anything, she called Storm directly.

She hadn't got any more than the name out of him, but that had been enough to start with, and she had promised to keep it to herself until the girls' parents had been informed. Camilla had known whom he was talking about right away. In the days following Samra's death, she had interviewed Dicta along with a couple of other girls from Samra's class. When she finished talking to Storm, she went back to the hotel to dig out her notes from her conversation with the girl, and after that she went down to the restaurant and got the chef to make her a little breakfast. She picked up a copy of *Ekstra Bladet* that the chef had sitting next to the stove along with a pot of coffee. She tried to get hold of Louise again, but her mobile was still going straight to voicemail, so Camilla went back out to the restaurant with her breakfast to wait until there was some news from the police.

She saw the picture in the paper, read the brief text, and then jumped up, dropping everything. It all happened so quickly, her coffee sloshed onto the tablecloth and the bread basket tumbled to the floor.

With the paper tucked under her arm, she ran out onto the street and over to the car park. Storm and Skipper were standing there talking, but she ran right past them and continued to where Velin stood to ask him about Louise. Just then she spotted her friend coming over from the other end of the car park, where the body was. Her face was blank and her eyes trained on the ground. Camilla ran over to her, holding out the paper.

'You have to see this,' she called from a distance.

Louise looked up and was about to protest, but Camilla ignored her friend's rebuff and pulled her over to a walkway between the walls of two buildings, so they were away from the others. Camilla unfolded *Ekstra Bladet*, turned to page nine, and pointed to a large colour photo of an almost-naked Dicta Møller.

'This is today's paper,' Camilla said, waiting for a reaction. Dicta's long blonde hair was falling down over her breasts.

Her body was turned slightly with her head tilted a tad, and one hip pushed forward in a diminutive white crocheted bikini, which was tied together by a thin string, leaving little to the imagination if you were the kind of person who was attracted to young girls.

Louise slowly reached for the newspaper and studied the picture. 'Well, she doesn't look like that any more,' she said.

'How does she look?' Camilla quickly seized the opening her friend had given her.

Louise stood there for a moment, appearing to consider whether she could tell Camilla anything.

'One whole side of her head is caved in after multiple powerful blows,' Louise finally said. 'I would imagine that most of her cranium is crushed, and her face is one big bloody pulp.'

Camilla put her arm around Louise and they stood like that for a bit. She knew Louise had had a fair amount of contact with the girl and that she must be working hard now to contain her emotions so they didn't overwhelm her. Camilla gave her shoulder a squeeze, and Louise folded up the paper and gave her a little smile.

'Thanks for showing me that,' she said, preparing to join Storm and Skipper.

'I know the photographer who took this picture,' Camilla called after Louise. 'He's a disagreeable chap. Sad that she fell into his clutches.'

Louise stopped and walked back over. 'Disagreeable in what way?' she asked.

'Not in a way that I think would lead him to crush a girl's skull, but certainly a girl's heart. I always sort of got the sense he was ambitious, and there've been a few stories going around about him that haven't cast him in a good light.' Camilla explained that there had been rumours of violence. 'Although not against the girls, as far as I know,' she hurried to add, before saying that, on the other hand, there had been rumblings about how he couldn't keep his hands off the young girls who came to his studio. 'But that's not to say – well, I don't know how much is gossip and how much is the truth. He's never been convicted of anything as far as I know, and of course he's quite active professionally. So it could well be that he just has a bad reputation,' Camilla added, so she couldn't be accused of having contributed to spreading the rumours.

'Interesting,' Louise said. Then she said that she had just been asked to drive out and inform Dicta's parents.

Camilla stood and watched her as she walked away with the newspaper under her arm.

24

Louise stopped twenty metres from the Møller family's drive-way. She had driven two wheels up onto the pavement and was sitting in the cruiser with her phone pressed to her ear. Before she'd left, she had told Storm about *Ekstra Bladet* and shown him the picture. Now he was calling her on her mobile, instructing her to tell Dicta's parents about it.

'Oh, no,' she exclaimed. 'I don't know if I can make myself do that.'

'It's going to be hard to keep it hidden,' Storm quickly retorted. She conceded that he was right. Obviously they would end up seeing it.

'Maybe you can ask them a little about how much they knew about her free time, while you're discussing it with them,' he suggested.

'We'll see,' Louise replied curtly, still not having the faintest desire to bring it up.

She shut off her phone and drove the last little bit to the

driveway. It was only a few minutes before eight in the morning, but there were no cars in the garage and the house looked empty.

Louise was suddenly afraid that they could have left early to go to a dog show, because it might be hard to find them then.

The police usually sent two people to inform a family so that one officer wasn't alone if the parents had a violent response to the shock, but in this case Louise had opted to talk to them by herself because they already knew her. However, she had arranged with Storm that he would keep one officer ready to assist her should that be necessary.

The dogs out back started howling as Louise walked up to the front door and held her finger on the bell for a long, sustained ring. The dog inside came galloping and acting very fearsome. She pushed the button again and heard the chime of the bell spreading through the house. She did not hear the gate in the wall to the garden opening, so she jumped when Dicta's mother was suddenly standing in front of her with a cheerful morning greeting and a large bowl in her hand.

'I was just out with the dogs. I usually run them early in the morning, and then we do our training later,' she said, holding out the bowl as if that explained why she had it.

Louise nodded and said that she'd come to speak to the woman and her husband.

Anne Møller gave her a questioning look, but there was no trace of worry to be seen in her apparently candid face.

'There's coffee made. Henrik just popped out to the bakery.' She opened the door and held the dog. 'But Dicta isn't here,' she added, still leaning over Charlie with a grip on his collar. 'She's spending the night at Liv's.'

Anne set coffee cups out on the table and it wasn't until they were sitting across from each other that a shadow came over her face.

'You didn't come over to talk about Dicta, did you?' she asked, to encourage Louise to begin.

The coffee in the cup was steaming and the milk had turned it a creamy, golden colour.

'I would really like to speak to both you and your husband. How about if we just wait for him?'

Now that that was said, the worry was more palpable. Louise sat up when she heard the car door shut. A second later, Henrik Møller was standing in the doorway, looking at her in astonishment.

'You're here so early,' he said, walking over to shake her hand. Dicta's mother stayed seated in her chair, following her husband with her eyes, but clearly hadn't yet had the thought that something awful had happened. That wasn't the source of the worry that was evident in her eyes. Just apprehension.

Henrik Møller had tossed a bag of breakfast rolls and the newspaper onto the kitchen table and walked over and took a seat next to his wife, as if he were expecting that this would all be wrapped up quickly so they could return to their quiet Sunday-morning routine.

Louise took a deep breath and jumped in.

'Early this morning, Dicta was found in a car park behind Nygade,' she said slowly. 'I am very sorry to be the bearer of such terrible news. Your daughter is dead, and there is no doubt that she was murdered.'

Both parents were still looking at her with expectant expressions, as if any signals to or from their brains had ceased the second Louise spoke those words. It took a few more seconds before the expressions on their faces changed.

'Dead? Murdered?' Anne Møller stammered, not seeming to understand how this had anything to do with her.

'How can she be dead?' Henrik Møller asked, his voice extremely calm. 'What happened?'

Louise started to explain. 'She sustained a number of powerful blows to the head.' Louise paused to allow the parents a chance to respond further.

Dicta's mother was sitting completely still, nodding automatically. Louise doubted she could even hear what was being said, so she turned to look at the father.

'Extremely powerful blows,' Louise emphasised, hoping he wouldn't ask her to go into more detail.

'My darling little Dicta,' Anne Møller croaked hoarsely. Then came the reaction as she collapsed into tears.

'Did she die quickly?' Henrik Møller asked, reaching out to hold his wife's hand.

They always wanted to know the same thing. All parents wanted to be reassured that their children had died without pain and without fear.

'Is that what the big emergency response in town was for this morning?' he continued. His voice was no longer as controlled and his eyes were shiny. 'They were talking about it at the bakery.'

Louise nodded and told them about the woman who had gone down early that morning to drop off some clothes in the Salvation Army bin.

'We don't know exactly what time the attack happened,' Louise acknowledged, explaining that it could have been any time between midnight and when she was found a little before six. 'We have one witness who works at the Gyro Hut, who says that Dicta definitely wasn't there when he got into his car last night. We got hold of him early this morning and he's the only one we've talked to so far who was at the location so late. The owner of the gyro place lives upstairs from his business and contacted his employees when my colleagues were looking for witnesses.'

'What was she doing out so late? She was supposed to be staying at Liv's,' her mother said disconsolately to no one in particular.

Her husband lit a cigarette and inhaled deeply.

'So, Dicta was planning to spend the night at Liv's last night,' Louise repeated. 'What else did she do yesterday?'

'She was out most of the afternoon,' Anne replied mechanically. 'She left as soon as we'd finished lunch. I went out to look at a new dog, and after that I took my car over to the shop. They're going to service it on Monday morning. When Dicta came home, we ate dinner and then she went over to Liv's.'

Anne's voice was monotone, like a report being read, and there was no way to tell from her intonation that she was actually talking about her daughter.

'I drove out to the golf course after lunch, along with Anne. Dicta walked,' Henrik Møller explained, 'and I didn't get home until evening.'

With a heart-rending scream, Anne leapt up from her chair so fiercely that it tipped over backward.

'No, no, no,' she shrieked with so much passion that it seared its way into Louise's skin.

Henrik was at his wife's side in an instant, pulling her to him. He started rocking her soothingly back and forth, like a child he wanted to comfort. He seemed composed and all his attention was directed at her. He tenderly stroked her hair, and Louise left them alone until Dicta's mother had calmed down a bit.

Henrik moved his chair right over next to his wife's so he could sit and hold her while they kept talking.

Quiet settled over the room and Anne looked at Louise, her face streaked with tears, her head resting limply against her husband's shoulder, as if every last bit of muscular control had left her. Only small, almost imperceptible tremors ran through her.

Louise felt the knot in her stomach and turned her attention to Henrik.

'Did you talk about anything before she went over to Liv's?' Louise continued, aware of how awkward it was to ignore the mother's agonising pain.

'I think she was talking about the two of them going to the movies,' Anne whispered with her eyes closed.

There were good reasons for and against telling them about the *Ekstra Bladet* photo, Louise thought. She almost couldn't bear to do it because she was pretty sure they weren't aware of their daughter's Copenhagen adventure. On the other hand, it would almost be worse if they didn't know about it and happened to hear from somewhere else that a photo of their daughter posing practically naked had appeared in the paper the same day she was found murdered.

Maybe they already know, Louise thought, permitting a third option.

Without allowing herself any more time for reflection or to come up with any other excuses, she just asked flat out if they knew that Dicta was that day's page-nine girl, and if they knew anything about the Copenhagen photographer who had taken the picture of her.

The silence in the kitchen was deafening. Finally Henrik spoke.

'Let's see it,' he said and didn't sound as if it surprised him.

'You knew pictures had been taken?' Louise asked, surprised at having misjudged him.

'Well, there's knowing and then there's knowing ... She didn't tell me, but I definitely knew she was up to something we weren't involved in,' he said.

'What sort of nonsense is this?' Dicta's mother exclaimed, suddenly back with them again. 'She wasn't involved in anything we didn't know about. She wasn't like that.'

Her voice began to choke up, but Henrik's vehement response stopped her crying. 'If you didn't know anything about this photo in *Ekstra Bladet*, then she must have been keeping something hidden from us.'

Louise cringed. Suddenly she found herself in the middle of a much-too-private conversation.

Henrik's wife didn't react, didn't even look at him, but sank deep into her own thoughts until she quietly spoke again, asking, 'Why that newspaper? Why that kind of picture?'

'You knew that she wanted to be a model, right?' Louise asked.

'Don't all young girls?' Henrik responded. 'I don't think she dreamed about it more than many other girls her age.'

'But unlike many others, she managed to get in touch with a photographer here in town,' Louise continued. 'And she had been used as a model for a couple of local stores.'

The girl's mother nodded and said that she was well aware of her daughter's dream, and that they had also talked about how that was all right as long as they were proper pictures and it didn't get in the way of her schoolwork.

'I met Michael Mogensen and saw the pictures he's taken of her. She's a beautiful girl,' Dicta's father said, sounding somewhat proud.

'Do you think this was the same person who killed Samra?' he continued, staring through the kitchen window and scratching Charlie behind the ear.

Louise shrugged and responded that she could easily understand where he was coming from, but the way things looked currently, that didn't seem to make sense.

'There's nothing similar about the two deaths, so it's hard to directly compare them. Samra's death seemed carefully planned, while your daughter's murder looks like an impulsive act. In terms of profiling the culprit, each of those things pulls the investigation in a different direction,' she explained. 'But of course that's something we'll look into.'

'Can I see her?' Anne suddenly asked. 'I would like to see my daughter as soon as possible.'

'I'm not sure that's a good idea,' Louise said softly. 'It might be better for you to remember Dicta the way she looked the last time you were with her.'

'Will there be an autopsy?' Henrik interjected, and Anne squeezed her eyes shut tight.

Louise nodded.

'I'm assuming that it will take place as soon as later today,' she said.

It was as if picturing Dicta's autopsy happening triggered something in Henrik. He bent his head, supporting his forehead in one hand, and visibly crumpled over the table.

25

Louise had just returned from Dicta's parents' house and was sitting in her office with a cup of coffee when Mik came in and shut the door behind him. On his way over to his desk, he leaned over and kissed her on the forehead.

'What a morning,' he said, sitting down behind his computer. Louise didn't know what to think about the intimacy that suddenly existed between them. It was unavoidable, but she didn't like it and it could easily get ugly, she thought. All the same, she smiled at him.

'We have to talk about what happened last night,' she said after looking at him for a minute. Normally she did not do things that were rash and poorly thought out. The last twelve hours, she'd done nothing but.

He looked at her and smiled. 'Didn't you think it was nice?' he asked in a teasing tone, which immediately made her pinch her eyes shut a little. 'We don't need to make a major deal out of it,' he said, beating her to the punch. 'Obviously it wasn't particularly smart. But now it's happened, and I had a lovely night.'

'We share an office!' Louise exclaimed, irritated at his relaxed attitude.

He nodded. 'I still think it was lovely, and I promise I can control myself.'

Louise couldn't help but smile. He had just kissed her, but apparently that didn't count, she thought, shaking her head. 'Of course we can control ourselves, but it never should have happened, and I know it's my fault,' she said emphatically. 'But promise me anyway that we'll keep this just between the two of us.'

He grinned and Louise put her head in her hands, suddenly overwhelmed by the wave of fatigue that she had suppressed while she was with Dicta's parents. Now it came back full force. The few hours of sleep had made her sensitive to the cold, and her body was weak and tender from the unfamiliar amount of lovemaking it had all of a sudden been subjected to.

She glanced over at him, not feeling very proud of the situation. And now of all times that she had finally gained her freedom, she thought. Which she had actually been longing for for many years, but just hadn't got around to doing anything about. She sat for a bit, lost in her thoughts, until she suddenly heard Camilla's voice in the back of her mind: 'Now is the time to hook up with a few lovers. Lovers are so liberating; there's no pressure of having them around permanently.'

Louise smiled down at her clasped hands and thought that actually that was what Mik was, a lover. She just wasn't used to that. What were you supposed to do with them after you made love and you got back to everyday life? Where did you stash them when you were finished with them, and how did you get them back out again? Or did you just scrap them all from time to time?

She pushed her hair back and looked over at him. 'I'm tired, but it was nice,' she said, meaning that sincerely. 'Still, I wish we'd managed to sleep a little more. Oh, and now to face a day like today.'

Louise thought about Dicta and pictured the girl. 'How did it go at her parents' place?' Mik asked.

She told him how Anne and Henrik Møller had reacted and that they really wanted to see their daughter if possible.

'The message from Pathology was that they were going to do the autopsy this afternoon, and we're supposed to be there.'

Louise couldn't bear to think about the autopsy or the new investigation that was just starting up. Instead, she stood up to get more coffee. She asked if he wanted any.

'I'll come with you and find out if there's anything new. We've got in touch with a bunch of people who work close to the car park, but I think we'd better take a drive out and see that friend Dicta was supposed to spend the night with,' Mik said.

Storm and Bengtsen were sitting with Ruth in the command room with steaming coffees in front of them when Louise and Mik walked in with their empty mugs.

'We just got her mobile phone back from the tech guys,' Storm said, once they'd sat down. He pushed the phone across the table and asked Louise and Mik to read the last set of text messages in Dicta's inbox.

Louise pulled her chair close to Mik's and they both leaned over to read.

'They must have been sent while she was with Liv,' Louise commented when she saw the time.

'We'll drive over there and talk to the friend before we head into Copenhagen,' Mik added, and received a nod before Storm continued.

'Velin is working on printing out all the phone info so we can see which antennae it was routed through for the last few days,' he said.

'This number doesn't have a name entered, but it belongs to Tue Sunds, the girl's photographer,' Bengtsen said, but Louise had already figured that out after having read the first of the messages, which said, Unfortunately, I have to cancel for this evening.

Louise reached over and took the phone out of Mik's hand and scrolled down to the next message, the second that had come from Tue Sunds within a short time window.

Yes, of course you mean something, but not in that way. Please stay away from me.

She moved to the next one.

No, we can't meet tomorrow either. I never promised anything. You're done, history. Stop bugging me.

As if she were a child he had brought to a sweet shop and not a young woman who didn't understand the harsh rules of reality.

Don't threaten me and stop coming here, otherwise things might get uncomfortable for you.

That was the last one, and it had been received a little after ten thirty.

Louise didn't even want to look when Mik switched over to the sent messages. She couldn't bear to see how Dicta had begged to try to avoid Tue's rejection.

What a pig, Louise thought, as she drained her coffee cup and got up to accompany Mik on a visit to Liv, the last person Dicta was known to have seen.

Louise hardly recognised Liv without the thick black eye make-up and the black clothes. Her hair was still black, but she was wearing totally normal clothes, and there was nothing provocative or rebellious about her as she stood there at the front door and let them in. She'd heard what had happened and had been crying, and she certainly hadn't finished crying yet. They promised her parents they would make it quick and followed the girl into the dining room, which was dominated by a large window with a panoramic view of the garden. They were looking for simple, straightforward answers. What time had Dicta left Liv's place on Saturday night, and what was she planning on doing?

Liv didn't even need to think about it when she reported that Dicta hadn't left until a little after eleven, although she'd said earlier that she would be leaving around eight thirty because she was supposed to meet up with her photographer. Liv had assumed she meant Michael Mogensen, but she hadn't asked about it because she was mad that Dicta had used her as an excuse to go out without her parents' permission.

Liv said they'd watched a little TV, but that Dicta had seemed distracted and kept looking at her mobile phone and sending text messages; and when she finally left, she seemed more depressed than when she'd arrived.

They thanked Liv, and Louise said that they might need to come back and talk to her again.

Liv nodded and stood there watching them go as Mik pulled away from the kerb and turned the car onto the suburban street.

'It's hardly even worth discussing it with you,' Camilla snapped into her phone so gruffly that people at the other tables in the café looked at her. 'You're so goddam judgemental, you've got me wondering if I can even keep working for your newspaper.'

She would never have dared talk to her boss this way if he hadn't stepped on her toes by trashing her articles on Sada. And because he was quite aware that he had exposed a very unseemly side of himself, and she knew he would go to great lengths to cover that up.

'I completely agree that it's the same as admitting we were wrong,' she continued. Her voice was back down in its normal range, so the other café guests had returned to their conversations. 'But we were wrong, and right now there is no indication that the al-Abd family killed their own daughter in some kind of honour killing. Quite the contrary, it would appear that there's a murderer on the loose in town.'

She listened and patiently took deep breaths while Terkel Høyer spoke.

'I can't keep smearing the family in the absence of any new information to point in their direction,' she repeated into her phone. 'There must be a reason the police haven't arrested the Jordanian girl's father yet.'

Her editor kept insisting that they had to keep going with the approach they had picked – their angle – so they didn't suddenly start working against their own stories.

'Well, now. You were actually the one who skewed the story so hard from the beginning,' Camilla said again when he started blaming her for having stuck to such a hard line in the articles she'd written from Holbæk. She listened for a bit and then sighed tiredly. 'If you print the two articles in the paper tomorrow and refrain from linking them to the killing of Dicta, then you will already have changed the tone, so the paper's stance isn't so severe.'

Camilla could picture Terkel. It wouldn't be that easy for him to do, but he wasn't so stupid that he couldn't see she was right. 'I'm planning to stay in Holbæk for the rest of the day,' she said, 'but it might be a good idea to get someone to look into that photographer who took the pictures of Dicta for *Ekstra Bladet*. I know the police are interested in him,' Camilla said, wrapping up the conversation.

She didn't have to pick her son up from football until six, so she had plenty of time before she had to drive back to Copenhagen. Markus was playing in a tournament, so he wouldn't be finished until five thirty. Camilla had tried only once to be there, ready at the school gates when the team returned home, sweaty and in high spirits in their oversized football shirts with the team logo on the front and their own last names on the back, and her effort had not been well received. First they had to eat a few pieces of crispbread slathered in Nutella and hold their post-game strategy meeting so they were ready for the next match. She either had to wait while they did that or come back half an hour later.

She called Louise in the hopes of luring her out for a cup of coffee, although she guessed Louise wouldn't take her up on it now that there had been another murder.

'A quick one,' Louise said. 'I have to go in and observe the autopsy in two hours, and I could definitely use a pick-me-up before that.'

Surprised that her friend hadn't taken more convincing, Camilla switched off her phone and hurried to the café further down the main street.

'Look at the state of you,' she exclaimed when she spotted Louise.

Louise yawned loudly and nodded as Camilla suggested a latte and some water.

'Didn't you get any sleep last night?' Camilla asked, concerned. 'What time was Dicta found?'

Before the coffee had even arrived at the table, Louise was filling Camilla in on her evening and night, the words pouring out of her mouth in one long stream. When the coffee was consumed and Louise was still only in the middle of her story about her visit to her colleague's farm, Camilla got up to order more coffee.

'With him, really?' Camilla asked, incredulous. 'He's pretty much as close to the opposite of Peter as you can get, if that's what you were going for. The man wears Wranglers, for Pete's sake!'

'How do you know that?' Louise asked right away.

'I notice that kind of thing,' Camilla said with a grin. 'He also wears police-issue Ecco shoes.'

'Henning wore sandals,' Louise reminded her.

Camilla's eyes sank down to the marble top of the café table, feeling a momentary stab of pain. Yes, he'd been wearing sandals and, worse still, socks the first time she met him, but she'd fallen for him anyway.

She looked up and smiled at Louise.

'Well, are you going to see him again?' Camilla asked.

'I don't see any way around it. I see him all the time. There's actually no way I could avoid seeing him,' Louise said.

'If it didn't mean anything other than a bit of fun, well, then it's already over,' Camilla said, trying to smooth things over. 'Was he good to you?'

Louise smiled and nodded. 'He was very good, really sweet, and I can't remember it ever being like that before. But it felt so strange. That's the part I'm not crazy about.'

'Then I suppose you'll just have to do it again, so it starts to feel more familiar,' Camilla said, trying to sound suggestive enough that her friend would get over her shyness at having flung herself into something she had no control over.

'No thanks. I think that was enough,' Louise said. 'I'm not sure he thought it was a particularly good idea either, although he may be handling it a bit better.'

'You mean that maybe you seduced him against his wishes?' Camilla was not opposed to getting a few more details out of her friend.

'You certainly might say that.' Louise grinned sheepishly, and Camilla smiled at her. In Camilla's mind it didn't really matter what Louise needed to do to shake off Peter's shadow. Which made her think of Henning, which made her stomach hurt. If anyone was stuck on a relationship that was over, it was clearly she, and she just couldn't see any light at the end of that tunnel.

They paid and Camilla grew serious again. 'What do you have on the new case?' she asked before they parted ways.

Louise seemed to be considering whether she would answer, but eventually said that they would be bringing the Copenhagen photographer in for questioning.

'We don't have anything, but we'll have to see what the autopsy shows,' Louise said, looking at her watch, as if the time were getting away from her. 'It appears that there may be something to the rumours you told me about this morning,' she said before stepping out onto the pavement and setting her course towards the police station.

Camilla watched her go, then she pulled out her mobile and called Terkel Høyer again.

'You should work the Tue angle, hard. He had something going with the girl,' Camilla said succinctly and then stood there for a second before heading back into the café and ordering a glass of organic Søbogaard fruit juice, while she tried to get her thoughts in order. She wanted to write a story for the next day's paper with quotes from several of Dicta's classmates and a summary of the mood in the town. Then, once her censored articles came out, she would contact Sada again and ask for her reaction to the murder of her daughter's friend.

26

To Louise, as she and Mik arrived at the Pathology Lab late that afternoon, it felt like the day would never end. She'd had her eyes closed most of the way there in the car, thinking that it was just typical that on the one day she didn't show up to work perky and well-rested, of course that would be the day all hell broke loose. But her father had once told her something that now rang profoundly true: if you're up to partying all night, then you darn well ought to be up to doing your job the next day!

Åse was already there, and Flemming Larsen was getting prepared as they walked into the autopsy room. It was the same set-up as before, aside from the fact that it was now Dicta's beaten, ill-treated body that was lying on the table waiting to be examined in minute detail by professional eyes and hands. Louise took a couple of deep breaths, and her hand brushed against Mik's as she walked past him to lean up against the wall. A strip of images from the CT scan of Dicta's skull was hanging in front of a large light box to the left of the door.

'Can you tell what happened?' Louise asked, looking at Flemming.

He walked over and stood next to the light box and pointed up at the first picture.

'It is evident that she sustained several severe blows to the left side of the head and there are many bone fragments. The advantage to a CT scan, in a case where the injuries are as severe as these, is that we can see the lesions inside the skull. When I open it up a little later, most of her cranium will just fall apart, which can make it hard to tell how the blows impacted,' Flemming explained, turning to start securing Dicta's bloody clothes. After that, every centimetre of her naked body was meticulously examined for particles. Åse leaned over several times and dabbed a piece of tape against her bare skin in the hope of removing some evidence, and Flemming used cotton buds to search for anything that could be used for a DNA analysis. Meanwhile, Louise leaned against the wall, following along, prepared to work all night if that would bring them a step closer to whoever was responsible for this crime.

'There are fresh abrasions and subdermal hematomas on the chest.' Flemming pointed to the large, dark splotches scattered above and below the girl's breasts. Then he leaned over and drew the big round operating lamp further down over Dicta's body.

'That looks like maybe a footprint,' he said, making room for Åse, who moved in with her camera. 'I think she was kicked after she fell down.'

Rage, Louise thought, everything she saw in front of her

radiated so much rage. It had been unleashed and transformed into raw violence.

Flemming cautiously allowed his hands to feel all the way around the head injuries before he walked over to the cabinet at the end of the room to retrieve a set of electric hair clippers, which he plugged in and used to start shaving the long blonde hair off the left side of the girl's head.

Louise closed her eyes for a second. It was almost unbearable to see Dicta's pride and vanity being peeled away from her, leaving her bald and naked.

'Let's see how the skin looks,' Flemming said as he switched off the clippers, long tufts of light-blonde hair strewn in heaps on the floor. 'She was severely beaten,' he said, confirming that the whole left side of her cranium was caved in.

Åse took her pictures and said it looked like there were more contusions.

She made room for Flemming, who leaned over Dicta's head and studied it in detail. Then he straightened up his six-and-a-half-foot-tall body and stood there for a moment before he said, 'I'd say we're dealing with a pattern injury here.'

'What do you mean?' Louise asked from over by the wall. Flemming pulled the lamp closer and asked Louise to come closer.

'Can you see those marks there? They appear to be identical. She was struck multiple times with a blunt object, which seems to have a distinctive appearance. It has two rounded protrusions spaced three centimetres apart.'

'Do you have any guess what it might be?' Louise asked, cursing her own tiredness as Flemming shook his head.

'Nothing other than the fact that it's heavy and if you found the object of interest, I could easily tell you if it was the one.'

'Well, then, that's what I'll try to do,' she said, smiling at him. 'What about the cause of death?'

He stood there looking at her for a moment before he answered.

'Dicta Møller asphyxiated on the blood from the severe cranial lesions. It ran down into her throat as she lay unconscious in the car park.'

Images from the crime scene pushed their way in front of Louise's retinas, but she forced herself not to react, not to think about how long Dicta had lain dying in the car park, alone and without anyone coming to her aid. Louise took a seat on a stool by the wall while Flemming completed the examination. She didn't get up until Mik put away his notes. Then she followed him down to the car in silence.

Louise didn't get back to the hotel until around 8 p.m. Before she went up to her room, she stopped in the restaurant to order a little food she could take upstairs with her. When she and Mik had returned from Copenhagen an hour earlier, the others were already eating, but she had declined the invitation to join them. The image of Dicta was still too clear in her mind.

Ultimately, however, hunger had won out and now she made her way up the stairs, balancing a brown wooden tray with a hamburger, boiled potatoes, and all the trimmings.

It was ten past three when she woke up with the tray on her stomach and the TV on. It was a miracle that the potatoes hadn't tumbled onto the bed while she slept. She got up and brushed her teeth before climbing into bed again to sleep for the last few hours before the alarm clock went off at six thirty.

27

The next morning was set aside to question the photographer Tue Sunds. The interview was going to take place at the Holbæk Police Station, so the plan was for Louise and Mik Rasmussen to pick him up in Copenhagen at eight and bring him out to the provinces. When she opened her eyes a couple of minutes after six thirty, she fantasised for a minute about calling first just to make sure he'd be home, but she knew that idea was out of the question. Their arrival should catch him unawares. So she swung her legs out of bed and set her feet on the rough hotel carpet.

She quickly made herself a cup of Nescafé with the electric kettle with which she'd equipped the room; then she was ready to meet her partner. They had agreed that he would pick her up in front of the hotel at seven.

As Louise stood outside in the cold October morning air, she realised she had a couple of butterflies fluttering in her stomach. The drive to Copenhagen was going to be long, since she and Mik would be alone together in the car. The day before, Louise had dozed on and off, but today the silence in the car would be so oppressive there would be no way to keep it from feeling a little awkward, she thought, pacing up and down to stay warm. The train station across the street was already in full swing. The waiting taxis had nothing to do, but the town's commuters were busy trying to make their morning trains into the city.

She waved at him when he pulled over into the loading zone in front of the hotel, coming to a stop right next to the kerb in front of her.

He had brought freshly buttered morning rolls with a thermos of coffee. The milk was in a little Tupperware jug, and she smiled at him when he told her to help herself. She hoped that he had inherited the jug from his mother. There was just no way she was going to have a thing with a man who bought himself Tupperware products, she thought, ruefully acknowledging that she might already have done precisely that.

'How thoughtful. Did you get up early?' Louise asked, and by the time she had poured coffee for both of them, Mik was already heading down Roskildevej towards the highway at a decent pace.

'Yeah, you could say that,' he said with fatigue and explained that one of the puppies had been having stomach trouble all night and had had diarrhoea all over the hallway and kitchen.

'It's unbelievable what can fit into such a small tummy,' he said. 'But the little guy was whimpering so much that in the end I had to call the vet.'

Louise looked at him with concern and offered to drive, because now that made it two nights in a row he hadn't got more than a couple of hours sleep, but he shook his head and said that he still had a little bit of charge left in his batteries.

'How's the puppy now? Is he doing any better?' It was hard not to be concerned about the little furball.

'He was sleeping when I left,' Mik said and added that he'd enlisted his neighbour, who would look after things until he got home.

Louise smiled at him. After all that, he'd still managed to bring coffee and rolls for them. She gradually started to relax.

It was five minutes to eight when they rang the doorbell of Tue Sunds's large penthouse apartment, which was unsurprisingly located in the heart of an exclusive part of the inner city, right up under the roof of an old red building on Grønnegade. It was a combination apartment and photo studio, as far as Louise had understood from Dicta the night she picked her up in front of Holbæk Station.

They had to ring the buzzer several times before the photographer came and opened the door, barefoot and dressed in a bathrobe. They'd obviously caught him in bed, and Louise had the fleeting thought that now she would be confronted with whatever new young model had taken Dicta's place. But her thought was interrupted when Mik spoke.

'Tue Sunds?' he asked.

The photographer nodded.

'We're from the Unit One Mobile Task Force,' Louise continued, really pulling herself together to be polite. 'We're working on a serious murder case. Do you have anything against coming back to the station with us for questioning?'

Sunds took a step back and ran his fingers through his hair. 'Yes, I do. Now just isn't a good time,' he responded, shaking his head a little. 'Can't do it. I've got appointments all day.'

'Would it be possible to move the appointments to another day?' Louise continued, in the same polite tone, avoiding looking at Mik.

'No, it's not something you can just rebook,' he said with a touch of condescension and amazement that she could even imagine his being a man with appointments that could just be changed at a moment's notice.

Now Mik took over. 'Yes, well, let me phrase it this way. If you don't accompany us of your own free will, we will be forced to place you under arrest.'

Louise looked at her partner. There was quite a contrast between the cheerful, considerate side of him that she had begun to get to know – the way he treated the high-school teacher, herself and, for that matter, his dogs – and the way he dealt with people professionally when it came to situations like this.

'Then you'll have to arrest me,' the long-haired photographer responded provocatively, his unwillingness radiating from him.

'This pertains to Dicta Møller, who was found murdered in a car park in Holbæk yesterday morning,' Louise said. She hoped that opening the bag all the way would make him see that now was not the right time to be flexing his muscles. 'We know you knew her, and that you were supposed to get together on Saturday night, but that you cancelled your get-together.'

He seemed puzzled about how she knew all this, but didn't ask. Seething, he pulled his bathrobe tighter, like a coat.

'Dicta?' he said, making them repeat that she was the one they were referring to.

'You know the person we're talking about?' Mik asked.

The photographer responded with a nod and confirmed that he knew the girl, but said he did not know she'd been murdered. He also confirmed that he had cancelled a get-together with her, but did not provide any more details.

'It can hardly have escaped your notice that she died,' Louise interjected. 'She is one of your models, and her face was in all the news broadcasts last night, and she's front-page news today.'

'I haven't seen them,' he responded stand-offishly, casting a glance down at the newspapers lying on his doorstep. One of his own photographs showed her young face. He walked over, picked up the papers, and started reading one.

Mik took the newspaper out of his hand and said that he would accompany Tue inside his apartment while he put some clothes on.

Louise was following Tue Sunds's facial expressions with interest, but there was very little going on in that taut, polished, sunburned face. He's older than you'd think, it occurred to her, guessing that the photographer wanted to appear younger than he really was. That being the case, the Bordeaux-and-black-striped terry-cloth bathrobe didn't suit him at all.

He was more respectably attired when Mik came back down with him five minutes later. Once on the street, Louise climbed into the back seat with him. He didn't ask what had happened to Dicta until they'd crossed Kongens Nytorv and were on their way along Kalvebod Wharf.

'We'll talk about that once we get to Holbæk,' Louise responded tersely.

At first the photographer sat with his teeth clenched,

watching the heavy morning traffic coming towards them, but once they were out on the highway, he leaned his head back and closed his eyes and sat like that, off in his own world, the rest of the way to Holbæk.

Louise grabbed a mineral water, a jug of coffee and two cups before walking in and turning on her laptop. She'd sent Mik home to check on his dogs and rest for a bit while she handled the interview with the photographer. At first her partner had been reluctant to accept the offer, but ultimately he'd conceded.

Tue Sunds was pacing around restlessly when she entered the office. She asked him to have a seat and offered him coffee. As she poured, she asked if she could get him anything to eat. They had taken him right out of bed, so he hadn't had any breakfast yet.

He sat down and accepted her offer. Out in the hallway she ran into Velin and asked if he could bring some bread from the cafeteria while she prepared to question the photographer who had taken the page-nine picture of Dicta. Five minutes later, there were two slices of French bread on a white paper plate, butter and marmalade each in small packets next to it, and they were ready to get started.

'I'm rather surprised to be here,' Sunds started as he opened the butter packet. 'I don't have a damn thing to do with this case.'

Louise could see that he was starting to build up some resentment, which she hurried to quash by saying that she didn't think he did either.

'Well, then, why am I here?' he asked.

'Because I would really like to hear you tell me about your

relationship with Dicta. You sent her some messages rejecting her quite cruelly last Saturday after you cancelled your appointment, and you weren't particularly eager to come when we asked you to.'

'Yeah, but do you suspect I killed her? Because that's totally absurd,' he continued. 'It's true that I wasn't able to see her last Saturday after all, and maybe I was a little harsh when she didn't seem to be getting the message, but I didn't see her at all that day, so there's no way I could have murdered her.'

Louise let him talk on for a bit and then she asked him to tell her why she should believe that he hadn't committed the murder.

He seemed puzzled for a moment, but then started speaking again. 'First and foremost, I wasn't in Holbæk. Aside from that, I actually liked her.'

Now this was starting to get interesting, Louise thought.

'It would also be totally foolhardy to take the life of a model I actually thought I could make some money from,' he continued.

Louise smiled at that last comment, which was stated in a slightly milder tone, with a hint of irony.

'Obviously,' she said. 'And that's exactly the type of thing that would help convince us that you're not our murderer. So if you don't have any objections, I'd like to ask you a few questions that might help me shed a little light on Dicta's life and your relationship with her.'

He nodded that that was fine. It would have been pointless for him to respond any other way, Louise thought.

'How did you come to be in touch with Dicta Møller?' Louise asked after Tue Sunds had eaten both slices of bread. And when he didn't respond, she continued, 'How does a

SARA BLAEDEL

young girl with no contacts in Copenhagen find her way to you specifically? You're not that famous, are you?' she asked, leaning back a little to take the sting out of her words.

He cleared his throat before answering. 'No, of course she didn't know me.' He smiled with exaggerated modesty. 'But I understood from her that she subscribes to *Sirene* and *Bazaar* magazines, and I've had big fashion spreads in both magazines in the last few months. That's where she came across my name, and it wasn't hard for her to find me online.'

Louise was familiar with the two fashion magazines targeted at teenage girls.

'So she called you?' she asked, looking him in the eye as he slowly nodded.

'Yes, she called my studio.'

'Is that normal, for young girls to contact you that way? If that were the case, I'd imagine you'd probably spend all your time doing nothing other than taking calls from starry-eyed teenage girls.'

He smiled a bit and shook his head. 'It's not normal at all. I thought it was quite impressive that she had the guts. They usually send their pictures to the modelling agencies. But Dicta wanted to hire me to shoot a few portfolio shots of her that she could use for submissions. She was very ambitious, and I could tell that she was really willing to fight to make her dream into a reality.'

'What was she supposed to pay for them?' Louise wanted to know.

'Normally six thousand Danish crowns. That's the price for the shoot. But I said I'd do them for her for three thousand crowns. She paid for them with her confirmation money.'

'And did she then owe you the other half?'

Sunds fidgeted imperceptibly in the chair and let his hands rest on the desk. Then he shook his head. 'No,' he replied. 'There was nothing about how I'd bill her for the rest if she made it big. Three thousand crowns was the agreed price.'

Louise sat for a little while, watching him, but couldn't interpret his composed face as he sat there looking at her with his bright blue eyes. Then he leaned back and wove his fingers together behind his head.

'What you're really asking me is if I was expecting anything else from her because I offered to do her pictures for half price,' he said, and now he was the one whose eyes pierced Louise.

She nodded and waited.

He sat and thought for a moment before he began to speak. 'I have an eighteen-year-old daughter. I got divorced from her mother four years ago, and one of her friends was spending a lot of time at our house around that time. My own daughter never harboured any dreams of becoming a model. She wants to be a vet and just started veterinary school, but her friend was very taken with the modelling world and used to tag along in the studio when I was working with professional models. I actually thought she was thinking about becoming a photographer, that's why I let her watch. But she wanted to be a model and kept pressuring me to give her a break, like under the table, even though I explained that I couldn't just start using a completely unknown girl when magazines booked me for an assignment. Besides, they choose their own models.'

He paused for a moment before completing his story: one day his daughter's friend had gone to the police and reported him for rape, and at the same time she let the story leak out.

She couldn't be charged with making a false statement because of her age, but she was examined by a gynaecologist and the exam showed that she wasn't telling the truth. Although it happens that the hymen can remain intact after a rape, it is rare, and after the events she'd described it certainly wouldn't have been possible.

'I didn't do anything more about it, apart from talking to her parents, because the most important thing for me was that they understood that the story was a lie. I've always gone out of my way to treat young models considerately.'

Louise had a copy of the police report in front of her. Ruth had had it waiting when they got back from Copenhagen, and Louise could see that a caseworker had been there during the questioning, which was standard procedure whenever someone underage was involved. Something had obviously gone wrong in terms of updating the case, because it didn't say anywhere in the paperwork that the preliminary charge had been found to be baseless.

'There's also a report of assault?' Louise said, pulling out another piece of paper.

'The same day the girl went to the police, she sent an email out to several of the magazines and papers I work for and to the biggest modelling agencies in the city, telling her story.'

There was something generous about the way he talked about the girl, as if he didn't really want to accuse her of such poor behaviour.

'She was a little girl, my daughter's friend. At that point, my daughter didn't have any room for more upheaval in her life.'

Louise was starting to get irritated, but reined herself in. He was almost being too selfless about what he'd been subjected to for Louise to take him seriously.

'You beat a man up so severely that he was in the hospital for a long time with facial injuries,' she fished, to put an end to what she interpreted as a self-aggrandising defence soliloquy.

He nodded.

'The story about the girl was making its way around the city. A few people knew how it all fit together. I got the girl's parents to write a letter to the people the girl had contacted, in which they explained that the report was made up. But not everyone who had heard the story received such a letter and the incident you mention happened one night after I'd had a little too much to drink and was maybe a little touchier than usual, so it all got out of hand when another photographer started egging me on.'

Louise nodded and asked him to explain in more detail.

'There's nothing more to say. I just couldn't stand to listen to any more whispering behind my back and didn't feel like I should have to keep defending myself for something I didn't do. So I lost my temper.'

Louise nodded. 'Did Dicta have what it takes to make it as a model?' she asked, picturing the tall girl with the prominent cheekbones. Louise had no doubt that the girl had radiated charisma and the boys certainly turned to look at her in the street, but forging a career was a totally different matter.

He contemplated that for a bit before he started nodding.

'I think she had a reasonable shot. She was just too impatient. She expected the agencies to line up the instant they heard about her, and it just isn't that easy,' he said. 'She apparently posed a little for a photographer up here and he succeeded in building up her image of herself into something really amazing in her own mind, but reality isn't like that.'

'She was actually used as a model here in town,' Louise said to vindicate Dicta a little.

'It's a hell of a long way from a picture in a free small-town newspaper to the big magazines,' he said, and in an instant arrogance swept the relaxed look off his face.

'Well, actually, it was *Venstrebladet*,' Louise pointed out, grabbing the chance for a new angle. 'Give me an idea how many visits it takes to a celebrity photographer to get three thousand crowns' worth of portfolio pictures.'

That shook him a little, but he didn't respond.

'And does it often happen that you drag it out all day and invite the model out for sushi and other goodies after the pictures are taken?'

He didn't say anything, so she kept going.

'Last Saturday around eleven p.m., I ran into Dicta in front of the train station here in Holbæk. She was so drunk, she was hunched over in the middle of the bike racks throwing up.'

He was about to say something but she interrupted him and kept going, her voice still calm and steady.

'A visit to a café and sushi up in your penthouse apartment. Why did you want to impress her when she was already in high spirits from the adventure she had set out on?'

He sat there with a wrinkle in his brow, which showed that his rage was building; she discreetly followed his attempts to control it.

'I think you misunderstood that,' he said finally. 'Did she tell you that story? It's true that we ate brunch and that I invited her out for a glass of champagne after the pictures were taken. I usually do that when I wrap up a job.'

'But she made up the part about your opening multiple bottles that night?' Louise asked, watching him.

He nodded.

'Did she also make up your eating sushi together?'

He said that Dicta had been hungry before she went home.

'She had the money to pay you three thousand crowns, but not to buy herself a hot dog at Nørreport Station?' Louise let the question hang in the air, and then continued: 'How many times did you see her after that day?'

She could see that he was going to deny that he had seen her at all since then, so she reformulated the question. 'How many times did you have contact with her?'

He remained silent.

'She came by a couple of times,' he finally said, 'so we could pick which pictures would go in her portfolio. But otherwise I didn't see her.'

'Did you agree to her sending that picture to *Ekstra Bladet*?' Finally some response was visible in his eyes. They squinted, nearly closed, and darkened. 'What fucking picture?'

Louise explained about his picture of Dicta appearing in *Ekstra Bladet*.

'I didn't fucking send in any picture. How do you think it makes me look if people see my name next to a page-nine girl?' he asked, outraged and angry.

Louise couldn't restrain herself. 'I don't give a rat's ass how you look. How do you think Dicta looks? Now, you tell me what the fuck went on between the two of you. I don't want to hear any more bullshit about you and your actual intentions.'

He pulled back slightly in his chair and seemed more surprised than threatened.

'There's nothing else to tell.'

Louise took a deep breath before she spoke again.

'I'm sorry I got all worked up. But I actually knew Dicta Møller in connection with another case we're working on, and it was terrible to see her lying down there in the car park with her skull crushed.'

He had once more pulled his compassionate look down over his face when he said that that was perfectly all right, but his eyes were hard again when Louise repeated the question about how his photo of an undressed Dicta had ended up in *Ekstra Bladet*.

'She must have sent it in herself,' he said, almost snorting the words.

Louise stood up and went to check with Storm if it might not be a good idea to hold off on pressing Tue Sunds any harder until they'd ransacked Dicta's room and had maybe found more that would help them get a picture of the relationship the two of them had had.

'Agreed,' Storm said and then told her that Dean had been in touch with *Ekstra Bladet*'s photo editor, who had just got back to him with the information that the picture had been sent in by the girl herself with a return envelope that was addressed to her own address. Dean had also checked that the account the money was supposed to be deposited into was Dicta's.

Louise leaned against the wall and stood there for a moment, feeling how the energy that had been coursing through her during Tue Sunds's questioning had now suddenly left her body.

Storm left her in the hallway. He was going to see Søren Velin, who was studying Dicta's laptop with a technician.

Louise returned to her office and told Tue Sunds that an officer would be ready to take him back to the city within ten minutes. She held out her hand politely and thanked him for coming in.

'Did I really have any choice?' he asked, as he gathered his white sweater up off the floor, where it had slid, and tied it around his waist.

'Yes, you could have refused. Then we would have been forced to arrest you, and then I wouldn't have thanked you so nicely afterward,' she replied, following him out.

28

Louise was scurrying to the command room for a meeting with the others and hadn't noticed their presence until she heard a hoarse male voice behind her.

'Did that man have something to do with the murders?' Ibrahim al-Abd asked from the row of chairs along the wall. Sada was sitting next to him, well hidden behind her veil, which was wrapped tightly over her face.

Something had happened to his face since she'd seen him last. Something dry and stiff had come over it, like bread that had been left out too long. He had expressed intense grief when they had last been together; now he expressed nothing, and his eyes watched her with a lacklustre gleam. She walked over and sat down next to them.

'We came because we're afraid the new murder will make you forget about our daughter,' Ibrahim began. 'I presume now you're probably only interested in the Danish girl, whom Samra knew?'

Louise mollified them by explaining that murder investigations didn't work that way. You didn't just drop one case because a new one came along.

'Obviously, at the moment, we're trying to identify who murdered Dicta Møller. But you can rest assured, we're still doing everything we can to find out what happened to your daughter.'

Sada gazed at her with a dark, unhappy look, which made Louise want to put her arm around the woman and comfort her. Instead, she said that the police would really like to speak to them at some point in the near future, to find out what they knew about Dicta and the two girls' friendship.

'Please don't let our daughter end up on the back burner,' Ibrahim pleaded. His voice cracked, and his wife looked down at the grey-laminate floor.

Louise knew what he meant. So she tried to calm them by explaining that a team of eight people was still working on their daughter's murder, working what must be described as expanded hours.

'We promise to let you know as soon as there's anything new,' she said, holding out her hand as she stood up to join everyone else in the command room.

'Was it the same killer?' Storm asked as she opened the door.

The others were sitting around the table and the meeting was under way.

Bengtsen shook his head and was backed up by Skipper, who had extensive training in criminal profiling.

'The two girls' murders can't be compared.' Skipper stood up and walked over to the whiteboard, where he drew the two girls as stick figures and wrote 'organised' and 'disorganised' over their heads.

Louise pulled out a chair and accepted the cup of coffee Søren handed her.

'One murder was committed by someone organised, one by someone disorganised,' Skipper continued. 'The organised one was thinking about his or her own safety and planned how to dispose of the body in advance, and we can certainly assume that the culprit doesn't live in the proximity of Hønsehalsen. The act suggests that there was a relationship between the killer and the victim.'

Everyone seemed to agree.

'The murder of Dicta Møller, on the other hand, appears to have been committed by someone disorganised, and in terms of motives I think it's obvious that it was an emotional act stemming from a feeling like revenge or jealousy, for example. It was a spontaneous killing, and the murderer could easily have been seen from one of the surrounding apartments. Everything suggests that the location where the body was found was also the scene of the crime.'

Louise had noticed that there were first- and second-floor apartments with windows looking out over the car park and had thought that the murderer was lucky no one had seen anything.

Storm stood up and moved to stand next to Skipper, from where he addressed the room.

'At present there are no commonalities between the murders of these two friends. Thus we will continue to investigate the two cases individually,' he said, adding that of course they should remain more attentive than usual to the coincidence that both girls were in the same class at school.

'A number of the ninth-grade parents have already called,

expressing serious concern,' Ruth interrupted. 'They're afraid more students in the class may be in danger.'

'I have a hard time believing that we're dealing with a murderer who has set out to systematically wipe out a whole school class,' Storm said, running his hand through his hair, 'but of course it's impossible to rule that out at this point.'

He turned to Bengtsen and said, 'Maybe you should drop in on the ninth-grade class and fill them in on our work. A little information often goes a long way in calming people's fears.'

Bengtsen nodded and said he'd do that right away.

'We should talk to the local photographer who worked with Dicta,' Storm said and looked at Louise.

She sat there for a moment as Bengtsen left and the others stood to go. She was thinking about Dicta Møller and all her dreams. Yes, when Mik came back, they'd have to get hold of Michael Mogensen, but first they had to go out and take a look at Dicta's room. There must be something there that could advance the case.

29

The Pastor was sitting in the kitchen with Dicta's parents when Mik and Louise came to the front door. Both Anne and Henrik Møller came to greet them when they rang the bell. Sitting on the counter were bouquets of flowers, still wrapped in cellophane, along with small white cards that hadn't been opened or read yet. The pastor stood up and shook hands with Mik and Louise.

'It appears that sorrow has settled over our town for the time being,' he said.

There was something very forthright and confidence-inspiring about him, and there was a peace in the kitchen even though the grief was also palpable and visible in both parents. The mother's eyes were red and puffy, her nose bright and shiny and rubbed almost raw from wiping and countless handkerchief dabs. The father's face was ashen and withdrawn, his eyes glassy, but there was no sign of tears.

So he hasn't got that far yet, Louise thought, but it will come. In some people, the crying and flood of tears happened right away, while in others the grief had to take root in all of their cells before the reaction came.

'We would really like permission to look around Dicta's room. Do you have anything against that?' Louise asked, after they'd both said no-thank-you to coffee or joining the parents at the table.

'Of course we don't have anything against that,' Henrik said immediately. He stood up and led the way and opened the door, but remained frozen in the hallway as if he didn't have the strength to go into the bedroom that still contained so much of his daughter's spirit in all the things that were in there.

They could hear that Anne had started crying again and the pastor was comforting her. Louise turned her attention to the girl's room. She'd been there before, but with Dicta, and hadn't been so interested in the things in the room but instead had been focusing more on what the girl had told her.

There was a big round disco ball hanging in one corner of the room above a small circular table that was so covered in thick, pink pillar candles that there was only space for an old-fashioned alarm clock with a bell on top. The bed was a futon, which was currently made up as a sofa adorned with two cream-coloured pillows.

At the end of the bed, hidden behind the open door, hung a large mirror with bare bulbs screwed into a wood frame all the way around it, like you might see in a theatre dressing room or like a professional make-up artist might have. Under the mirror hung an open shelf with more hair and beauty products, make-up and perfumes – along with curling tongs and hair straighteners – than Louise had seen gathered anywhere else, even at Camilla's place. Overwhelming and completely unnecessary for a young woman with the appearance nature had imbued Dicta with, Louise thought. Along the opposite wall there was a narrow desk and a tall bookshelf. To the left of the desk a little stereo system was mounted on the wall and in the corner there was a tall, narrow CD holder.

A Fatboy beanbag chair filled up the space just to the left of the door. The trendy, oversized version of the classic 1970s beanbag chair was pink and matched the candles on the table. On the floor next to that, there was a big pile of fashion magazines. A quick glance showed that they were *Costume*, *Eurowoman*, *Sirene* and *Bazaar*. There was also a TV and a small black iPod on the table under the disco ball. The only thing missing was the computer Bengtsen and Velin had already picked up. On the wall over the desk, there was a photo collage that Dicta had made herself with pictures of several of the biggest international models on catwalks from around the world.

'She was a beautiful girl,' Mik said, as Dicta's father stood in the doorway.

Henrik nodded and asked if they needed him to stay while they looked through her things.

'No, we can manage on our own,' Louise hurried to say. It would be better if she and Mik could talk undisturbed without worrying about offending the girl's parents.

'We'll see if she wrote anything about her meetings with Tue Sunds,' Louise said once she'd taken a seat on the sofa to get an overview. Mik had gently put his arms around her waist as he slipped around her to enter the room and she could still feel his hands on her body. It irritated her that she was receptive and, besides, it wasn't okay that he touched her that way. He would never have done that before their night together.

She followed him with her eyes as he opened Dicta's wardrobe and started slowly flipping through her hangers. Not surprisingly, the wardrobe was crammed full. The floor of it was littered with shoes and boots. The room overall was neat and tidy on the surface, but as soon as you opened something, an awful mess was revealed. This young woman obviously had not yet developed any sense of order, or she just hadn't been interested in that.

Louise got up and started with the bottom shelf in the bookcase. It was mostly textbooks and three-ring binders; the two shelves above that were books, children's and young adult; and then there were computer games, The Sims and The Sims 2. Louise was guessing they hadn't been used in a while, because there weren't many kidlike things left in the room any more.

Then there was the shelf with the photo album and a thin scrapbook. Louise took both of them over to the sofa to look through.

A lot of pictures had been taken of Dicta. Louise could see that this must have been done over a long period of time, possibly over a year, because she had changed over time. Louise left the album sitting on her lap and flipped open the scrapbook. Several stores in town had used Dicta in their ads, and Michael Mogensen had also used her often as a model in the photos accompanying stories in the local paper. There were also clippings showing her as a movie extra. He had apparently done what he could to make her dream of a modelling career come true, Louise ascertained, lingering for a bit over the clippings Dicta had pasted on the front page of the scrapbook and drawn a thick border around with a felt-tip marker. They were quotes from a couple of the biggest names in Danish modelling.

Remember your goals. A single picture can ruin your career.

That was surely true, Louise thought, letting her eyes move down to the next frame.

The first time you see your picture on the cover of *Vogue*, the sky falls and the world opens up. That's the best.

Dicta had double-underlined 'the best'. Louise read the first quote to Mik.

'Then why the hell did she send a picture to *Ekstra Bladet*?' he asked.

Louise shrugged. She started looking through the rest of the shelf to see if maybe there was a calendar or day planner that Dicta might have written something in. Something like that might also reveal how many times she'd been to Copenhagen, and Louise would take great satisfaction in slapping it down on the table in front of Tue Sunds and asking him to provide some more details on his first statement.

'It was probably, like Sunds said, because she was impatient to be discovered,' Louise said after a long pause.

Mik had picked up a little sports bag from the bottom of the wardrobe. He started spreading out the contents on the floor. Skimpy tops, short skirts of both denim and softer material. He picked up a narrow yellow belt and a small white bikini the size of the one Dicta had been photographed in.

'Could this be the one she took to Copenhagen?' he asked, checking the bag's exterior pockets. A small picture of a young, very blond-haired boy fell onto the floor as he pulled out a flowered, worn, standard-size notebook with the word 'private' written neatly in a white field on the front.

Mik sat down with his back against the open wardrobe door and opened the book. Louise watched him, curious.

'Read it out loud,' she urged, annoyed at his silence.

He skimmed a few more pages then looked up at her. 'It isn't Dicta's.'

Louise gave him a quizzical look.

'"My big brother got a job at Kvickly today",' Mik read. 'Dicta was an only child.'

Louise nodded, and he turned the page in the book.

'"Saving up for a bigger cage for Snubby". This was written last summer,' Mik said, after glancing at the date in the top corner, but Louise was already up off the sofa. She snatched the flowered notebook out of his hands before he had a chance to react.

'It's Samra's,' she said, sitting down with the book in her hands. Flipping through it, she could see that the young girl had started the diary in May of the previous year.

'There are big jumps in the dates every once in a while, and somewhere near the end, several pages are missing,' Louise said after having quickly skimmed it.

Mik had got up from the floor and had come over to sit

next to her. They sat in silence and read until they came across a poem Samra had written about her white rabbit.

> You and me. Me and you.
> We'll never get out.
> You in a cage. Me behind a wall.
> We are the same. We'll never be free.
> But happiness can touch us now.
> Your soft fur and tiny nose
> undo the big knot within me and make me
>   happy inside.
> Thank you. I love you, my little furry
>   animal.

'That's the one they killed and served to her to punish her for coming home late,' Louise said drily.

After some searching through the pages, she found the episode in which her parents had made their daughter believe that they were eating chicken and only after the fact did they tell her it had actually been Snubby.

'"I will never, never speak to Father again, and I will not eat Mother's food. I told them I was going to live with Dicta. Father went ballistic and started hitting me."'

'How can parents treat their children like that?' Mik asked, and Louise shrugged. Even though neither she nor Mik had children, it seemed totally incomprehensible.

Louise flipped through to the last entries in the diary. Something in her resisted poking her nose in somewhere that had been another person's most confidential and private space, but, given the situation, the diary could obviously be an important key to the investigation.

'"I got permission to go home to Grandma and Grandpa's for Christmas. I'm flying to Amman on my own and then they'll pick me up there. Maybe everything will work out. Father is sweet."'

The short sentences in the naïve handwriting had been written the day before Samra died. She must have hidden the diary in the bag when she was at Dicta's place that Thursday, Louise thought.

'That doesn't make sense,' Mik said, looking blankly at Louise, who left the book sitting in her lap while she tried to think it through. They started reading their way backward through the diary and sat there in silence after reading each page.

There was a soft knock on the door and Henrik Møller stuck his head in to ask how it was going and if they'd like a cup of coffee.

They declined, and Louise showed him the book and pointed to the bag.

'Did you know that Samra had a few things hidden in your daughter's wardrobe?' she asked.

He stared at her with a puzzled face and then looked down at the contents of the bag, which were spread out on the floor in front of the wardrobe.

Then he shook his head and said that it was possible his wife knew something about it. He stepped out, and a moment later Anne appeared at the door.

She nodded when she saw it and said that she actually had known that but hadn't given it a thought. She apologised, saying she was sorry many times.

'It was some of the clothes her parents wouldn't allow her to wear. Maybe I shouldn't have turned a blind eye to it.'

Louise showed her the diary and asked if she was aware of

that as well. But Anne shook her head. She had never pried into the bag's contents.

'Did Dicta keep a diary as well?' Mik wanted to know before Anne left.

The mother shook her head again. Not as far as she knew.

'Did she have a calendar or day planner?' Louise asked.

'Yes, she had a nice one from Louis Vuitton that she got as a Christmas present. Maybe it's in the living room. I can look for it,' she offered and walked out.

A moment later, she was standing in the doorway with the large brown monogrammed planner, holding it out to them.

Mik took it and said they would really like permission to take Samra's bag and its contents and Dicta's planner back to the station so they could go through them there instead of taking up the Møllers' time, but Louise wasn't paying attention. She felt the blood surging through her body. Her intuition told her that the diary was important and at the moment she couldn't think of anything other than getting back to the station and being able to study it in peace and quiet.

'Dicta went to Copenhagen four times after she had those first pictures taken,' Mik said once they were back at the police station. 'He obviously photographed her several times, or at least the planner has them listed as "photo sessions", but she went into the city twice in the evening, and for those it says "Restaurant".'

Louise was absorbed in a drawing that covered two pages of the flowered diary. At the top right-hand corner of one page, someone had drawn a picture of a girl's face, a girl with long, smooth hair like Samra's own. Tears were flowing from her eyes and the tears filled both pages. The ruled pages were filled with itty-bitty, round tears densely packed in next to each other.

She flipped to the next page, where she read: *He did the worst to me and says it's my own fault.*

There were very short, incoherent sentences filling the pages around the crying girl's face.

> *If I say anything, he'll give away my secret.*

Mik was still talking on the other side of the desk, but Louise had blocked out his words and felt something contracting inside herself.

She flipped further ahead in the book.

> *They were laughing together as we ate. The whole family was there, and my mother was in the kitchen.*

Louise interpreted the small scenes as a form of short prose, taken out of context, but the fragments of a teenage girl's pain were far more alarming and powerful the way they appeared here in short excerpts.

> *I will never, never trust anyone again. How could he do that to me when he says he loves me?*

Louise stood up and walked out the door with the diary in her hand. She didn't notice Mik's questioning look and didn't hear him get up and follow her.

Storm was sitting in the command room talking on the phone when she walked in. Louise stood in front of him and waited impatiently for him to finish.

'We need to bring Samra's parents in now,' she said as soon as he hung up.

She showed Storm the section where the pain was depicted graphically in dense teardrops and explained where they'd found the diary.

'A few pages were ripped out, but what's here says plenty,' she said, summarising briefly the gist of what she'd managed to read.

He read a little himself before standing up and handing back the diary. Then he went to find Skipper and Dean and ask them to drive out and bring in Samra's parents.

'They should bring the brother,' Louise called after him. She was starting to see the outlines of what Samra might have been subjected to.

Then she returned to her office and her close reading of Samra's tormented pages.

30

By the time Louise had read most of Samra's diary, she had a knot in her gut.

The pages drew a picture of a young girl who was torn. On the one hand, she was trying to meet her parents' expectations and demands, while at the same time she tried to adapt to her new country and new friends. It was clear that she was having a hard time finding the balance between these two in her own identity. Was she Danish or was she still a Muslim girl from Jordan? Louise read between the lines that what Samra was really trying to achieve, with so much effort, was to be a Muslim Danish girl, which on the surface sounded easy enough; but when you read the diary, you realised it was obviously far from it.

Louise had been taking notes on the things that would be of particular interest when they started questioning Samra's family again. It was clear in a couple of places that Samra had started having thoughts of love – at least, emotions had begun to occupy a more visible significance in the words she wrote. Louise guessed that she might have fallen in love, but it was not clear that she had begun a relationship. She had written short poems about what she thought it would be like for two people to share a life. *The person I love and me*, she wrote in her script. She also wrote a story about what it would be like when they went up to the old Crusaders' castle in Jordan together and sat looking out over the valley and then after that walked home to her grandmother's house and drank tea and ate sweet cakes.

Louise was a little surprised that Samra dreamed of walking home with her boyfriend in Rabba instead of along the sound in Holbæk.

'Did you know that your daughter kept a diary?' Louise asked, once she'd brought Ibrahim in.

He did not appear to understand what she meant.

Louise held up the diary so he could see it. 'Do you recognise this?' she asked instead.

He hesitated and shrugged. 'Maybe.'

'It's your daughter's diary. Where she wrote down her secrets.' His face remained expressionless, so she continued.

'This book gives me reason to believe there's something you're not telling us. Something that made Samra very afraid. In several places she expressed outright fear that she might have to die.'

Ibrahim looked away, but didn't say anything.

'Did you kill your daughter?' Louise asked bluntly after several minutes of silence.

He shook his head.

'I could never hurt my little girl,' he finally said just as Louise was giving up on hearing him say anything.

'I know that you hurt her. It says that clearly here in the book, but that happened long before she died. Something occurred during the last few months of her life. What was it that made her so unhappy and afraid?'

He thought about it for a long time before he said anything. 'Maybe something at school?' he suggested.

Louise shook her head. 'I think your daughter had a secret she was trying to keep hidden from her family. But she didn't succeed and then she became really, really scared.'

Ibrahim went pale, but remained silent.

'Did she have a boyfriend?' Louise asked, even though Dicta had already told her that Samra had never said anything that would suggest that.

Ibrahim didn't make eye contact, but he shook his head.

'It's strange,' Louise said, 'that I thought it was you she was afraid of, but this here confuses me.'

She read the last page of the diary out loud and stared intensely at him to take in his reaction.

She read, 'I got permission to go home to Grandma and Grandpa's for Christmas. I'm flying to Amman on my own and then they'll pick me up there. Maybe everything will work out. Father is sweet.'

Now Ibrahim hid his face in his hands and sat silently rocking back and forth.

Louise cleared her throat.

'I think you should tell me about this. The fact is, we know that something happened. And it won't just go away because you sit there hiding,' she said, trying to sound kind.

While she waited patiently, she wrote on a piece of paper

that she didn't think he knew about the diary. She got up and walked into the office next door, where Mik was questioning Hamid. Without saying anything, she set the piece of paper on the desk and waited while he wrote back to her: 'Hamid does. And the bag.'

She returned to Ibrahim, who lifted his head as she entered. 'I didn't hurt my daughter,' he repeated after Louise was seated.

'You mean other than killing her pet rabbit and forcing her to eat it.' It slipped out before she could stop herself. She instantly regretted it, because now she was going to have to do some coaxing if she was to have any hope of getting him to talk. Idiot, she thought to herself, rubbing her face with both hands. She watched him as he sat there like a statue, then she sighed and said: 'Maybe it wasn't you who physically killed her. But I think you know what happened to her and what she was afraid of. She writes that she had lost her faith in the people who loved her. And the people she was referring to were her family. In other words, you. My colleague is sitting next door talking to your son. He's not as reluctant to tell us what he knows. For example, he was well aware that his sister hid a bag of clothes at her friend's house. Clothes she didn't dare keep at home because you wouldn't allow her to wear the same things her classmates wore. Hamid also knew about the diary, and I think he was aware that his sister confided in Dicta Møller.'

At that moment, something struck her, and she got up and left the office with a quick apology. Storm and Ruth were sitting in the command room, studying the big whiteboard where details about Samra's life and actions during the period leading to her death were written in blue ink. Next to that was a similar summary of Dicta's final days. Bengtsen and Velin had reconstructed the days up to the time when Dicta had been found in the car park.

Louise stood there in the doorway and talked a little too fast. 'Could Samra's family be behind both killings?'

She explained that Hamid had just admitted that he knew about the bag and the hidden clothes and the diary at Dicta's house.

'If Samra was really hiding a secret that would be so damaging to the family's honour that they felt they had to kill her, wouldn't it be possible that they went one step further if they realised that she had confided in her friend from school?'

A thoughtful silence settled over the room as they each tried to picture that scenario.

Ruth got up and walked over to the window, where she gazed out over the square in front of the old police station. Grass and big trees filled the space between the building and the pavement on Jernbanegade.

A couple of uniforms were called in to keep an eye on Samra's family members and make sure none of them left the police station while the team was quickly gathered.

'You're on to something,' Storm said, nodding at Louise. 'That would also explain why the one murder was so carefully thought out and the other seemed very impulsive. If they felt threatened by what Dicta knew, they would have acted fast.'

'Let's arrest the father and son for killing Samra,' Velin said. 'Then we can add charges later to cover Dicta's murder.'

'Yeah, or we could charge them with both killings from the get-go,' Skipper suggested.

Louise was sitting on the edge of the table.

'We don't know what secret she was hiding,' Mik reminded them. 'Let's be cautious now not to read too much into this.'

'No, but we know there was one and we know she feared for her life. That's enough for me right now,' Skipper interjected. 'What we don't know is which of them killed her. That's why we charge them both.'

'Often the person chosen to do the killing is the person the family can most easily do without,' Dean explained. 'That can either be someone who doesn't have anyone else to look after or someone who isn't able to contribute by sending money back to the remaining family members in the old country. Of course it also happens that that person is sometimes a minor,' he concluded.

'You're saying you think it was Hamid who killed his sister?' Bengtsen said.

'I don't know what I think. I'd really like a little more to go on before I sign up to anything. I'm just telling you what kinds of considerations I would expect people to contemplate in families living according to strict cultural traditions,' Dean hurried to add.

Storm had remained silent, but now he cleared his throat to interrupt their conversation. 'I'm not sure we have enough right now to hold them on,' he said, 'but we'll do it and then gamble on more coming out during questioning. We may also get lucky and have something turn up if we do a new search, and then we have to hope it'll be enough.'

'What about Sada?' Louise asked.

'She can go home to the two little ones, and then we'll follow the audio surveillance closely and have it interpreted as we go. We can easily guess that there will be increased activity if we're holding her husband and oldest son,' Storm replied. He asked Ruth to get hold of the interpreter they'd had listening to, transcribing and translating the tapes from the last several weeks in instalments of several days' worth at a time.

'It's Monday, October ninth. The time is four fifty-five p.m. You are under arrest for the murders of your daughter Samra al-Abd and her friend Dicta Møller,' Louise said when she returned to the office.

Ibrahim jumped as if he'd received an electrical shock. He stared at her with his eyes wide, after which he collapsed in his chair with his head bowed and his chin resting on his chest.

Louise thought for a minute that he'd fainted and moved over to him. For a brief instant she saw Mik standing out in the hallway with Hamid, ready to walk him down to the uniforms downstairs so the arrest could be processed.

'I have to ask you to follow me,' she said quietly, watching him as he slowly collected himself and stood up.

Neither the father nor the son said anything as their names were entered in the arrest log and they were searched, their possessions placed in clear plastic bags.

'We'll walk you over to the cells,' Louise said, holding the door for them. Ibrahim had kept his eyes on the ground, but now he raised his head and gazed right into Louise's eyes with a profoundly unhappy, silent look, as he almost imperceptibly shook his head.

Two officers were waiting in the cell block to accept the men. They said hello to Mik and nodded at Louise. Before they took Ibrahim and Hamid away, Louise stopped them and walked over to the two arrestees.

'If there's anything you want to say, just ask to talk to Mik

Rasmussen or me,' she said and then watched them as they started walking down the hallway towards the cells.

Louise and Mik returned to their office and started reading through all the previous transcripts of questioning sessions with the family members before they started with the father and son again.

It was only just seven when the deputy chief of police walked into the office and said he wanted to order a preliminary examination that same day so they could get it over with.

Louise was up out of her desk chair so fast that it shot backward and slammed into the wall.

'Out of the question,' she said, giving him a stern look. 'We need the full time, and we have twenty-four hours for the questioning we need to get through.'

Mik was also standing, but he said nothing.

The deputy chief paced back and forth a little bit before he leaned against the wall and looked from Mik to Louise.

'I read the whole thing and I'm not sure I have enough to keep them in custody,' he finally said.

Louise pulled her chair back to her desk and sat down.

'But this isn't a presentation of the evidence. You just need to convince the judge that there is reason to suspect that if we let them out, they could sync up their explanations and sway other people,' Louise said and referenced section 762 (1), paragraph 3. 'Now just give us a little peace to do our work.'

The deputy chief hesitated. 'Fine. We'll hold off on the preliminary examination until tomorrow afternoon,' he said. 'But by then, I will expect you to have something more for me.'

31

At ten past eight the following morning, the group was once again gathered in the command room. There was a pot of coffee, and Velin had stopped off at the bakery on his morning jog to make sure there were some Danish pastries too.

'We're going to search the family's home again,' Storm began, once they had all helped themselves. It was obvious that there'd been a break in the case, but at the same time the mood was tense and focused. The deputy chief of police had dropped in again to make it clear that he would appreciate it if they had a little more for him before he had to appear for the preliminary examination, but Storm had calmly said that if the man just had faith that the case would hold, then he already had enough.

Now Storm looked at Skipper and Dean. 'Go through everything, you two,' he said. 'And you should tear things apart. We need something more to connect the family to Dicta Møller's murder and we have to find the murder weapon.'

They received a brief description of the presumed weapon with the two distinctive rounded protrusions that Dicta had been hit with. According to Flemming Larsen, it had to have a certain heft.

'The crime-scene technicians finished at the site yesterday, and two of them will join you out at Dysseparken,' Storm continued.

'Do we know that the murder location is the same as where the body was found?' Mik asked, looking at Skipper and Dean, who had helped process the car park.

'Yes, there's no doubt about that. She was bleeding so much, we would have found traces of blood elsewhere in the car park if she'd been transported there,' Skipper said.

'It's sheer coincidence that no one saw the attack,' Dean said, shaking his head. 'It was so violent.'

'It may also be a coincidence that it happened right there,' Storm said, repeating that it was still his guess that there had been strong emotions associated with it.

'Rage,' Louise suggested. Storm nodded.

Bengtsen briefly cleared his throat and then said, 'Could that young girl have tried to use what she knew to pressure Samra's family? Just a thought. But maybe that could have been the provocation?'

Everyone around the table went silent, trying to picture that. 'What the fuck did she want to get out of it?' Skipper asked.

'I couldn't say. But if Dicta felt sure that Samra's family had murdered her friend, we certainly can't rule out that she confronted them with her suspicion. Maybe the brother, whom she knew better than the parents.'

Storm shrugged.

Louise's first impulse was that the theory was way out there, but on second thought she decided not to say anything because ultimately she just couldn't figure out what had been going on in Dicta's head. If she had sent her own pictures in to *Ekstra Bladet*, she had already stepped well beyond what Louise would have imagined she would do; and she had also sneaked off to Copenhagen and gone traipsing around with a much older man without filling anyone in on her adventures.

Seen in that light, it was hard to dismiss the idea that it might have occurred to her to use what she knew against the family. If she had done that, it surely wouldn't have been to pressure them, Louise thought, but to let them know that she knew something and it wouldn't have been very well thought out. It just made the picture of an immature, naïve young girl all the more clear. All in all, that fit quite well with the Dicta who'd shown new sides of herself during the time Louise had known her.

'We can't rule out that she was seeking justice for her friend's death, if Samra had confided something to her, and she may well have confronted Hamid with it,' Louise said, reminding them that even the first time she'd appeared at the police station, Dicta had expressed her concern about the family's role in connection with Samra's disappearance. 'Maybe she hoped she could get them to turn themselves in.'

'That's not a bad theory. Let's bring them in from the cells so we can proceed again,' Storm said, wrapping up the meeting.

'What the hell are you doing?' Camilla shouted when she burst into Louise and Mik's office five minutes later. With no make-up on and her bed-head hair gathered into a loose ponytail, she stood flinging her arms around, wearing grey sweatpants and a sweater, which was enough to show that she'd come darting out of her hotel room the second she got off the phone. No doubt that was also the reason Mik didn't recognise her right away, even though he'd met her before. The last time he'd seen her, she'd been dressed the way her vanity required her to be: in a skirt, shoes with impressive heels, a little form-fitting jacket, and perfect make-up. Louise had never understood how Camilla could stand to put all that on just to go to work, but that was one of the discussions they had that never got anywhere, in the same way Louise could never make her friend understand how she could leave her apartment without make-up.

'Are you people stupid, or what?' Camilla railed on, now that she had decided Mik wasn't going to throw her out. 'What are you trying to achieve?'

Her loud yells had brought Storm to the doorway, where he stood listening, without Camilla having noticed.

'Good morning, Ms Lind,' he said with a smile when Camilla finally spun around and stared at him crossly.

She stepped towards him. 'Are you getting desperate? Or are some guys higher up starting to breathe down your necks?' she asked, glaring at him.

The lead investigator seemed to be enjoying this, and on some level Louise was impressed at her friend's courage, because crime-beat reporters depended on being on good terms with guys like Storm. At the same time, Louise was also embarrassed for her. Camilla could act as if she owned the Danish media, and on many occasions that was far from flattering. But she did have a point.

'You must see how you'll look if you end up having to release them,' Camilla told Storm.

Storm was looking serious again and asked if it might not be a good idea for Camilla to join him for a quick cup of coffee. Louise didn't have trouble figuring out that it didn't particularly serve Storm's interests that news of the arrests had leaked out, since he wasn't sure yet that the judge would allow the two men to be kept in custody.

Louise looked over at Mik.

'What just happened?' he asked.

If he had been a comic-book character, his jaw would have been hanging down to the floor, Louise thought and smiled at him.

'Camilla's right,' she finally said after a moment's thought. 'If the judge lets them go, we're in for a trip through the wringer because it'll look like the arrests were based solely on racial profiling.'

Mik sat up straighter.

'But we actually did arrest them based on something,' he reminded her. 'And we can't go overboard on the political correctness just to protect our reputations,' he continued, irritated.

Louise sat for a moment before saying she didn't agree. She was just trying to provide her best guesstimate about how things would look if the judge let Ibrahim and Hamid go.

'We have enough to keep them in custody,' Mik said tersely and asked if they should get started on the questioning so the deputy chief would feel prepared when he presented the arrestees to the judge.

Louise nodded and got up. She glanced at him over her

desk as she gathered up her papers and acknowledged that now was not the time for them to lose their nerve.

Camilla was still worked up when she left the police station. She went back to the hotel and had breakfast in the restaurant. She was sitting at a table by the window, looking over at the train station, when she spotted Sada, who was trudging towards the hotel with her eyes down, holding hands with Aida and Jamal. Camilla got up and went out to greet her, and with her arm around the slender woman's shoulder and Aida's little hand in hers, she brought them into the restaurant.

'Have you had anything to eat?' Camilla asked, pointing into the next room where the continental breakfast buffet was still set up. Camilla had ordered à la carte because she hadn't felt up to sitting with all the other hotel guests, mostly consisting of German and Danish tradesmen, who populated the hotel on weeknights. Camilla had only seen Samra's little sister once before. That had been the time she had almost been thrown out of the family's apartment by an enraged Ibrahim, but apparently that hadn't had any negative impact, because now the little girl smiled and handed Camilla her doll.

'Oh, for me?' Camilla said, smiling back.

Aida nodded and followed Camilla's suggestion to go in to the buffet, even though her mother and little brother were seated at the window table and appeared satisfied with cups of tea.

Camilla wasn't used to little girls, but she just couldn't resist this one. Her heart went all soft when Aida looked at her with those delightful, kind dark eyes.

Sada gasped when she saw two large pastries on her

daughter's plate, but she didn't say anything. Not even when Aida climbed up onto a chair next to Camilla instead of sitting by her mother and Jamal. Sada just sat there looking down and stirring her tea.

'They're going to end up in jail,' she said finally, setting down her spoon.

Camilla really wanted to comfort her and said that nothing was certain until they'd seen a judge, but at the same time she said that she'd been to the police station to find out what had made them decide to make the two arrests.

'They found your daughter's diary at Dicta Møller's house,' Camilla said.

Storm hadn't told her much beyond the fact that the diary seemed to connect the two cases.

'Haven't they told you anything?' Camilla asked when Sada didn't react to the information.

'The police say that they're not coming home right now,' Sada said, arms desperately wrapped around herself, as if she were trying to warm up her fingers. 'I don't know what's going to happen.'

Camilla wished she could reassure the woman, but that might be raising false hopes.

'Can you tell me what you think the police might have read in Samra's diary? They wouldn't arrest two men if they didn't have a reason to,' she said.

Sada didn't say anything, but Camilla had the sense that she was struggling internally and that it was a battle in which doubt and trust were playing major roles.

'I don't know anything,' she finally said and took a little sip of her tea.

Aida had finished both pastries and her mother pulled a

sketch pad and a box of puzzle pieces from her purse and spread out a small blanket on the floor and asked Aida and Jamal to sit down and play.

Without objections, the girl went over to her mother and took the things her mother handed her, and a second later the two kids were both busy down on the blanket. That would never have worked with Markus, Camilla thought.

'Do you know what this might have to do with Dicta Møller?' Camilla persisted, even though she was afraid of putting too much pressure on Sada.

'They were friends,' came the answer.

'You mean that your daughter might have confided in her friend?' Camilla fished. That was also her guess at the police's connection.

Again there was a nod.

It was hard to tell if Sada was telling the truth or if she didn't dare divulge what her daughter had been hiding. But now at least she admitted that there had been something.

'Let's try to think about it from the police's perspective. Are they assuming it was an honour killing?' Camilla started, asking Sada to think through what might have triggered Ibrahim's rage. She had a strong hunch that deep down inside, Sada was afraid her husband's temper had got away from him and that in a fit of rage he had killed their daughter, but Sada categorically rejected that.

'That kind of thing never happens as long as no one outside the family knows about what took place,' Sada slowly explained, as if she were trying to select each correct word individually. 'My daughter didn't do anything that our family is aware of.'

Camilla asked her to explain herself a bit more clearly.

'When girls are killed, it's because you can't defend the family's honour to the rest of the family – I mean, the extended family.'

Sada reached out for Camilla's white paper napkin and asked to borrow a pen.

She drew a little circle.

'This is my immediate family, at home on Dysseparken.' Then she made a larger circle around that.

'This is the rest of our extended family who live in Denmark,' she explained.

Yet another ring around those.

'This is the entire extended family back home in Rabba.'

She looked earnestly at Camilla and set the tip of the pen down on the outer circle.

'When the extended family knows there are problems with a daughter, they will want you to get her under control. If you can't do that, things can turn out badly.'

She moved the pen in to the innermost circle.

'We loved our daughter. If there are problems, then you help your child. Things don't turn out badly here.'

Camilla tried to follow. 'What you're saying is that the rumour that something is wrong has to make it further than this small nuclear family before it would result in an honour killing?'

Sada nodded.

'And the problems that involved Samra weren't something that anyone outside your immediate family knew about?'

Sada shook her head, apparently not realising that by doing so she was confirming that there had been problems. She stood up quickly and packed up her daughter's playthings as she thanked Camilla for the tea.

'I can't make them understand,' Sada said on her way out the door.

Camilla sat there lost in her thoughts for a long time. She didn't doubt that Sada felt trapped in the prejudices about the culture she came from, and somewhere deep down inside she also seemed to feel unsure of what she herself should think about Samra's fate.

As Camilla left the restaurant a little while after that, a crowd of teenagers on the other side of the street caught her eye. They had surrounded Sada and her children, who hadn't made it to the bus stop yet but were trapped in front of the large train station building.

Camilla ran out the door and marched over to the group. Once she had pushed her way through, she positioned herself between the crowd and Sada, and made it loud and clear that if they did not leave this family alone, she would call the police faster than they could repeat the T in towelhead, which was just one of the words she'd overheard them using.

Instead of dissipating as Camilla had hoped, the teenagers started aggressively closing in. They were somewhere between sixteen and eighteen years old, she guessed, and their anger at Samra's mother hung like a thick cloud around them.

'Girl killer!' one of the boys hissed at Sada as she and her kids started backing away from the group. Word of the arrests had spread quickly and, in a small town like Holbæk, the response was quite evident.

Camilla heard Aida crying and, outraged, she stepped up to the group's apparent ringleader.

'What the hell are you doing, you little prick?' she snarled, sensing more than seeing how a couple of the boys jumped. She whipped her press pass out of her purse.

'If one of you has a beef you want to get off your chest, then I would love to hear it. Bring it to me, not to a woman walking down the street with her children. That's just pathetic.'

Camilla heard someone mumbling that she ought to 'shut her ass' and stop butting in where she didn't belong, and she ignored a shove to her left shoulder. She maintained eye contact with the boy she had spoken to.

'Until someone is found guilty of murder, you need to shut up and stop bullying people. But, actually, I'd really like to write about your anger, and maybe I can even get your pictures in the paper,' she said, her sarcasm lurking just below the surface.

Then she turned and followed Sada, who was heading over to the buses. She stayed until Sada and the kids were safely seated. By the time the bus pulled away, the group of boys had gone.

32

The preliminary examination started at three, and it was fair. The whole investigative team attended and listened along as the judge found that there was sufficient reason to hold Ibrahim and Hamid al-Abd, and that they could remain in custody for fourteen days.

'He wasn't sure enough to hold them for four weeks,' Storm said, once they had returned to the command room and were seated around the table drinking colas, which Ruth had retrieved from the fridge. Still, the relief was obvious in his face. 'Well, now we'll have a little space to work.'

Skipper and Dean had finished searching the al-Abd family's home on Dysseparken just before the preliminary examination began, so no one had heard yet if they'd turned up anything new.

'Nothing,' Skipper said, shaking his head. 'No murder weapon, no diary pages; nothing that reveals any new details about Samra's private life. And I think I can safely say that there won't be anything either. There's no place that hasn't been searched, so we need to change tacks.'

'Louise and I are on our way to have a chat with Michael Mogensen,' Mik said, draining his can. 'And early tomorrow we'll bring Ibrahim's brother in. He was with the parents around the time of Samra's death. We need to ascertain where he was when Dicta was killed.'

Louise caught his eye. She left her drink on the table and stood up to signal that she was ready to go. She was having a hard time coming down from the adrenalin rush she'd felt during the preliminary examination, so heading out right away suited her just fine.

Michael Mogensen answered the door quickly when they rang the bell. He lived in a large yellow-brick house, where he rented the first floor from his grandmother and he also had a large room in the basement, which he used for his studio and computer equipment.

'We would really like to speak to you about the two murders that occurred here in town,' Mik began.

A shadow instantly fell over the photographer's eyes and he lowered his head and nodded.

'May we come in?' Louise asked.

He quickly stepped aside to make room. 'Of course. Should we go down to my workspace, or up to where I live?' He sounded uncertain and uneasy with the situation.

'Your call,' Mik said, but when it didn't seem as if anything was happening, Mik suggested that they go down to the basement. 'You knew Dicta as a result of your work, so that seems fitting.' Portraits of babies, couples, brides, grooms and businesspeople from town lined the walls, and there were advertising photos and an enlarged reporting series from the School of Arts and Crafts on the outskirts of Holbæk.

The photographer offered them coffee once they were seated by a small coffee table and rolled his own desk chair over so he was sitting across from them, looking at them expectantly.

'I just can't understand it,' he began. He seemed more exhausted than Louise had first noticed.

'Tell us how you and Dicta became acquainted,' Louise requested, to get him talking.

He seemed to be letting his memory rewind until it found the right instant.

'There'd been a game down at the stadium, and I was on my way home to submit my pictures to my editor. On the way home, I stopped to get a bite to eat, and that's where I saw her. I was standing at the corner by the Kebab House and she came walking towards me.'

'How long ago was that?'

'That was last autumn. She wasn't that old, but we did a few catalogue photos for one of the sporting-supply companies in town and then the rest came later.'

'The rest?'

'The jewellery and clothes.' He pointed over at some pictures showing a hand with various rings and a neck with an elegant gold chain.

'Did you use other models besides Dicta?' Mik wanted to know.

Mogensen nodded and looked over at a filing cabinet. 'But little by little it was actually mostly her that I used. She was good, and my customers were happy with her. But there were some things she was too young for, of course. Women's clothes, for example. I do some work for an optician's, and they really wanted their models to be a little older.'

'How was she as a model?' Louise asked.

'She was great – natural talent and a pleasure to work with,' he said without hesitation.

'Had she ever tried it before you originally stopped her on the street?'

He shook his head. 'No, never. But like I said, I could see that she could become something. Which is why I devoted the time to helping her feel comfortable in front of the camera. Those pictures would just remain in the cabinet. It was an investment for both of us, which ultimately brought in more gigs.'

'What do you know about the photographer she went to see in Copenhagen? Did she tell you about her plans?'

Michael Mogensen shook his head and said a little defensively that she wasn't obligated to stick with him, that they'd never drawn up a contract saying that she would work exclusively for him. There was no way he could have afforded to honour that.

'But if you were volunteering your time and energy to mentoring her, wasn't it a little frustrating that she disappeared just as she was getting so good that maybe there was more money in the gigs you were getting?' Louise asked, eyeing him with curiosity.

He sat for a moment before he shrugged and said, 'That's life, isn't it?'

'Didn't you ever dream about working for some of the big magazines?' Mik asked.

The photographer looked at him and smiled for the first time. 'It's better to be a big fish in a small pond than a small fish in a big pond,' he said, becoming solemn again.

'Were you close, you and Dicta?' Louise wanted to know.

He nodded and said that he thought they had grown close over the time they'd known each other.

'You have to trust each other, otherwise it shows in the pictures.'

Louise smiled to herself. There was something touching about his self-importance, but she had no doubt that he took his work seriously, even if he was unlikely to ever achieve the sort of recognition a photographer like Tue Sunds had.

Mik had got up and was walking around a little. He stopped in front of the filing cabinet and asked if he could look in it.

Michael Mogensen said of course and explained that the pictures were divided into categories, but the top two drawers were portraits.

He and Louise talked a bit more about the friendship that had arisen between him and Dicta over the year they had known each other.

'I got so I could tell if she was in a good mood or a bad mood, if there were problems at school, or if she was tired. It's hard to hide that kind of thing when you're standing in front of a camera lens.'

Louise nodded and listened the same way you skim a book: she picked up on what sounded interesting and let the rest slip right by.

Mik cleared his throat and pulled a picture out of the filing-cabinet drawer.

A dark-haired girl with long, straight hair and large, dark eyes was smiling warmly from the picture. 'You knew her?' he asked, walking over to Michael with the portrait of Samra.

The photographer nodded and reached for the picture. He

sat with it for a bit, as if lost in thought, before he explained that Dicta had sometimes brought her friend along when she came straight from school.

'She was also a pretty girl,' Michael said, setting aside the picture.

'Did she ever pose for you?' Louise asked.

'I asked her to, but she didn't dare because of her parents.'

'But you still photographed her?'

He nodded, but said it was just a personal photo.

Louise smiled and tried to picture Samra. Although she'd never known the young Jordanian girl, Louise knew she would have liked her. She had given herself permission to be photographed and feel the freedom of following the dream, knowing the whole time that the pictures must never be shown. She wanted the full experience. She'd had it, but certainly knew that her parents mustn't find out.

'Did you get the impression that the two girls confided in each other?' Louise asked.

The photographer thought for a moment and then said, 'I'm not sure what you mean by that, but they were best friends.'

'If one of them had a secret, do you think the other would have known about it?'

He mulled that over for another moment and said, 'I'm not sure.'

'When did you last see Dicta?' asked Mik, who had once again taken a seat next to Louise.

'I was actually with her last Saturday, the day before she was found dead. We had an appointment to take a few pictures down behind the Strandparken Hotel that afternoon.'

'Did she seem threatened or scared of anything?'

Michael Mogensen thought about that before he responded. 'I hadn't considered that, but I hadn't really seen much of her lately.'

Once Louise and Mik were back in the car, she said that it seemed Dicta had withdrawn from Michael a little while she tried her luck with Tue Sunds.

'Yeah, you almost wish she hadn't been so ambitious, but had stuck with Michael. She probably would have gained more good experience that way,' Mik said as he pulled up in front of the hotel and gave Louise a quick kiss on the cheek before she got out.

33

Dicta Møller was one of the most talented and promising models I've worked with. She had a natural luminosity that glowed through the camera's lens and stuck. I don't doubt for a second that she had a big international career ahead of her, on a par with other great Danish fashion models like Louise P or Lykke May. It's a great loss for the Danish modelling world that something so dreadful could happen to her.

Oh, just shut up, Louise thought, shaking her head once she had finished reading. She folded up the newspaper and dropped it on Mik's desk. She'd spotted it when she was eating breakfast and had brought the paper back with her. Tue Sunds occupied the whole front page and two pages inside the paper.

'He damn well isn't upset about it,' she said, nodding at the front page.

'No, it looks like he knows how to promote himself,' her partner agreed, pulling the paper over to skim through the article.

'When are we going out to Benløse?' Louise asked and added that they really ought to pick up Ibrahim's brother before he drove in to open his shop at ten o'clock.

'We're leaving as soon as you're ready,' Mik said, tearing himself away from the paper.

There was a relaxed intimacy between them. She had spent a second night out at his farm, and the situation had transformed from being a painful mistake to a controlled attraction, which filled her with warmth. They agreed that what they had together was nice, but that it shouldn't interfere with their work. She watched him as he put on his jacket. He had a calming effect on her, and although his slightly edgy manner and lanky frame weren't things she immediately associated with security, he held her in a way that made her feel like she'd come home.

'I'm eager to hear what he has to say about their being arrested,' Louise said as she led the way to the car.

Camilla was far away, lost in her own thoughts, when the door to her office opened and Terkel Høyer came in.

'What did you want?' he asked, standing in the doorway.

Camilla picked up the clipping and read aloud. '"I'm never going home to my parents again. Their wrath is so great and they're so ashamed of me that it has clouded their minds and warped their hearts. How can people who are tied together by blood be so cold to each other? How can anyone who used to love me suddenly want me dead? I ran into my aunt on the street, and when she saw me she crossed to walk on the other side. I don't know how much longer I can take this."'

'Will it never end?' he said with a sigh. Then he brightened. 'That was good spotting. We'll bring it up again to show that strict rulings and long sentences aren't enough to stop this kind of thing. Find the girl and write her story. If she doesn't want her picture in the paper, she can be anonymous, but get hold of her.'

Since the arrests of Samra's father and older brother, letters to the editor had been pouring in. People were sick to death of hearing about cultural differences and 'honour', and anger was building such that the vast majority felt the sentencing guidelines ought to be made even stricter, a policy the minister of justice had just come out in favour of. A large percentage of the letters basically said that in cases involving crimes based on religious beliefs, cultural traditions or issues involving honour, the judge should order deportation once the sentence was completed.

In Holbæk, anger and frustration at the two killings was so palpable that one night the living-room window and a large, frosted pane in the front door were smashed at Dysseparken 16B, where Sada al-Abd was now living alone with her two youngest children.

'Find her,' the editor repeated. 'Or find someone else with the same story. There are enough of them out there that it shouldn't be that hard.'

'Nah, I guess it won't be that hard,' Camilla agreed, her eyes trained on him. She sensed the rage starting to build within her, but wisely held it in check and instead continued calmly: 'The girl who wrote it is ethnically Danish. Her name is Pernille and she's from Præstø.' Camilla took a deep breath.

'But I won't be talking to her, because she took her own life ten days ago. She was born into a family of Jehovah's Witnesses and had just turned sixteen when she broke with the church.'

Terkel Høyer was on his way out the door but stopped and took a step closer to her.

'And now you just listen here,' Camilla continued, and before he had a chance to say anything, she started reading another account from fifty years ago: '"If I have to bear this child, I would rather end it all."

'That was written by a young woman who came from a fishing family in Western Jutland, where she grew up in an evangelical family. She got pregnant at a very young age by one of the local farmers and turned to Mødrehjælpen, the National Council for Unmarried Mothers, in the hope of getting permission for an abortion. She was denied. That same day, she took her own life by walking out into the waves to avoid having to go home to her family, who wanted her dead anyway.'

'What are you getting at?' Terkel asked, walking all the way over to her desk.

Camilla was geared up for yet another confrontation and was prepared for Terkel to reject the angle she'd found for the current case.

'As a small parenthetical comment on the debate,' Camilla said, 'I want to draw people's attention to the fact that Danish families also expel relatives if they cast shame over the family. Of course, we don't kill them. They handle that on their own. But we shouldn't go around pretending that this could never happen in a Danish family,' she said, noticing her voice getting a little louder.

Terkel sat down on the edge of her desk.

'Those aren't ordinary Danish families,' he objected.

'I definitely think you could meet Jehovah's Witnesses who would be downright insulted to hear you say that,' Camilla said. 'Sure, they're part of a religious community, but otherwise they're completely ordinary, even if the rest of us might think they have bats in their belfries.'

He smiled at her.

'They don't kill their daughters!' Terkel exclaimed.

'No, but that's the only difference. If Samra's family members were expelled by the rest of their Jordanian relatives, they would be treated the same way as Jehovah's Witnesses who were expelled by their community. The difference is that Samra's father had the option of restoring his honour by taking his daughter's life.'

'We can't make that comparison. You're talking about just a tiny group of religious fanatics.'

'Well, it's not that small,' Camilla retorted. 'The current population of Denmark is 5.4 million. That's about the same as the number of Jehovah's Witnesses in the world, so they're not exactly an insignificant group.'

Her boss seemed to consider this.

'Motorcycle gangs,' she said. 'That's not news. If you get on bad terms with them, they'll fucking kill you. Their concept of honour is perhaps more developed than everyone else's, and that has certainly happened in Denmark. During the years when the Great Nordic Biker War was going on, we hardly read about anything else.'

Høyer gave up on saying anything and just looked at her. 'This is about the fact that there are also Danes who feel that their honour has been violated and would expel someone as a result. I think that would be extremely interesting right now, with the debate at its peak, and everyone being so busy distancing themselves from what's going on with Samra's family,' Camilla blurted out. It was very irritating that they even had to discuss this, even though it didn't surprise her.

'A very small percentage,' he repeated.

Camilla tucked her hair behind her ears, looked at him seriously, and said, 'It is also a very small percentage of Muslims who would commit an honour killing. Stop making it sound like you believe it's the whole lot of them who would do that kind of thing. The families who react that way usually come from rural areas and they act the way we did fifty to a hundred years ago, and I can damn well remember hearing my grandmother, who came from tiny Hvide Sande, telling some terrible stories about the girls – and boys, for that matter – who had sex out of wedlock. It annoys me that now we've totally forgotten how it actually used to be here too.'

Terkel was about to say something, but Camilla cut him off. 'I'm still not saying that we accept it. Not that we accept what happened fifty years ago in that West Jutland fishing family either. It's just good common sense to look at the similarities.'

She was totally winded, but could tell by looking at him that he had heard her. It would be complete lunacy not to slap this in as an aside before Holbæk descended into a character assassination of all Muslims.

'Did you also know that the Jehovah's Witnesses' Danish headquarters are in Holbæk?' she asked. 'The *Watchtower*'s office is out by Stenhus, the old boarding school. Not that they have any connection with this case, but since the folks who live out there now are all working themselves into a frenzy about Samra's family and the other immigrants in town, it's a great local hook for this story.'

'I wasn't aware that you had suddenly become so engaged in this specific topic,' her boss said.

'I don't even know if I have,' Camilla replied after a moment's thought. 'But I'm curious to find out what's going on since it occurred to someone to kill a person they love to maintain the family's honour outwardly.'

'Well, get to it,' Terkel said. 'When can I expect your article?'

'You can have it this afternoon. There's just one part I need to read up on,' she said, thinking she wanted to contact the National Council for Unmarried Mothers to see what they had to say about these types of stories.

Camilla had her hand on the phone, about to dial. She was lost in her thoughts about girls who had either knowingly or inadvertently offended their families and what had happened to them as a result. She and Louise had gone to school with a girl who came from a well-respected Roskilde family. She was seventeen when she got pregnant. The family had refused to have anything to do with her. The baby was given up for adoption and the girl sent to France to be an au pair for one of her father's business associates. At the time, Camilla had found the whole thing exotic and exciting, but she was sure the girl probably hadn't seen it that way. Rumour had it that she had married a rich car dealer in Provence, and that she had shocked people by not attending her own mother's funeral a couple of years ago.

Camilla was torn from her recollections when the phone rang.

'He's dead.'

At first she didn't recognise the voice, but then she felt her stomach tense up and her heart begin to pound faster.

'What happened?' she whispered, clenching the phone.

'He managed to hang himself in his cell,' her ex-boyfriend Henning said, obviously referring to his brother.

It felt like a tower of blocks had collapsed in her chest. A loud, piercing voice inside her said she ought to hang up, that this didn't concern her. She had struggled very hard to deal with the break up and had only now finally started to accept that Henning no longer wanted to be with her. So he couldn't just simply call her up with a quick comment and drag her back into his life again.

'I'd really like you to come to the funeral,' Henning said.

'Why?' she blurted out, even though her piercing internal voice was screaming for her to say no.

'He left a farewell note. He asks that you participate in his final journey.'

How pathetic, Camilla managed to think before the voice on the other end of the phone line continued: 'And I think you owe it to him to come.'

Camilla felt the tears and then her throat tightening. 'Do you want me there too?' she asked quietly.

'It's not about me, and it doesn't have anything to do with us,' Henning responded tersely. 'He's going to be buried in Sorø on Saturday at two o'clock.'

Then he hung up.

34

Ahmad al-Abd was thin and immaculately groomed, with his dark hair combed neatly back. He was sitting in the living room with his wife and their three young children when Louise and Mik arrived at the apartment in Benløse, and he agreed right away to accompany them back to Holbæk. Apparently he didn't have anything against talking to the police, nor did he seem to be upset about the arrests any more. Although once they were seated in the cruiser, he did say, 'It's a great tragedy for us all that they're in jail.'

Louise didn't ask him what he meant by that, preferring to wait until they were sitting across from each other and could see each other properly, so she just nodded and looked out of the windscreen as they drove through the countryside back to Holbæk.

'How well did you know your brother's daughter?' Mik asked once they were seated in the office with black coffee in the station's standard-issue white plastic cups.

Louise had asked Mik to take charge of the questioning while she wrote up the witness statement on the computer. There had been something in Ahmad's manner, even when they were standing in his doorway in Benløse, that told her he respected Mik more than he did her, and they couldn't afford not to use that to their advantage.

'I knew her very well,' he replied. 'Our family is quite close.'

'Tell me about Samra as you knew her,' Mik said.

In the car, Mik had made it clear to Ibrahim's brother that the police expected him to cooperate even though arrests had already been made in the case.

'Of course,' the man had said and added that it was his duty to help the police and that he was very sad about what had happened.

'Samra was a delightful child, a happy, easy little girl,' he began now.

'How did things go as she got older, entered puberty, and became a teenager?' Mik wanted to know.

Ahmad drew out his response a little, looking down at his hands, as if he were considering how to weight his words.

'That, of course, is a difficult age,' he finally said. He rubbed his hands together.

Ahmad was thirty-six, seven years younger than Ibrahim, Louise worked out, doing the calculation as she sat watching him.

'In what way was it difficult?' Mik asked, to get Ahmad to continue.

'Yes, well, she did as she pleased. There were friends and boys, who suddenly became more important than her family.'

Louise glanced over at Mik and their eyes met. The uncle

should not be interrupted now. This was an account of Samra's life they hadn't heard before.

It was as though Ahmad had picked up on their sudden interest. He paused for a moment and then started to explain that of course it was fine for young women to live their own lives, but his niece was only fifteen, so it was expected that she would respect the rules her father set for her.

'Could you expand on that?' Mik asked.

Ahmad hesitated a little before he continued. 'There are some guidelines for how young girls should behave,' he began. 'They mustn't run around with boys and they must obey their fathers.'

Mik interrupted, even though it would have been best to let the uncle go on. 'What do you mean when you say that she ran around with boys?'

'Just that young girls should behave in such a way that the family can continue to be familiar with them,' Ahmad explained.

'And Samra didn't do that?' Louise asked.

Samra's uncle looked irritated that Louise was getting involved in the conversation, then he shrugged and fell silent.

Mik took over again.

'It sounds to me like you're saying that Samra was a little more interested in boys than was acceptable. Who did she see?'

Ahmad al-Abd didn't even look up when Mik asked the question, so Louise didn't expect him to answer.

But Mik kept staring at him expectantly, so a long, awkward silence filled the office.

'Did she have a boyfriend?' Mik finally asked directly.

Ahmad raised his shoulders a bit and kept his eyes focused on the desk. After another pause, he nodded a couple of times. 'Was this a relationship other people knew about?'

Again it took a while before Ahmad answered, and it was an answer that was hard to interpret, because he shrugged his shoulders while at the same time shaking his head and mumbling a weak, 'Perhaps.'

'Did her parents know about it?' Mik asked, also wanting to know if it was something that had been discussed in the rest of the family.

Louise was on the edge of her seat. 'Someone did,' Ahmad finally responded.

It was obvious that he was not inclined to provide any more details.

'What boyfriend are we talking about?' Mik asked. 'Was he Danish?'

Louise had leaned back and watched Ahmad. Why he was telling them this, something that frankly would not help Ibrahim or Hamid's case? she wondered. And why was Ahmad the one to provide them with this information, considering how many people they'd talked to who had all denied that Samra had a boyfriend? Maybe the girl had confided in her uncle. Even though he was obviously male and a chauvinist to boot, he was younger than her parents and she had spent a fair amount of time at his house.

Samra's uncle nodded.

'Can you tell us who he is?'

Now Ahmad shook his head and apologised.

Louise caught Mik's eye and held it a second before standing up and excusing herself from the room.

*

Out in the hallway, she headed for Skipper and Dean's office and found them each sitting with a big piece of chocolate cake in front of them. She stopped abruptly in the door, pissed off for a second that they were just sitting there chilling out and having fun while she and Mik were slaving away on the investigation.

'It's Else's,' Skipper said, pointing at the cake, as if that explained how it had ended up on his plate.

'There's more,' Dean said, smiling at her, although he seemed to sober up when he saw the serious expression on her face.

She quickly filled them in, telling them she and Mik had brought Samra's uncle in and that he had just told them his niece had had a Danish boyfriend.

'Or, at any rate, a friend,' she corrected herself, looking at Dean. 'Why do you think he's telling us that? He could just as easily have left that out. All he's accomplishing is he's reinforcing our suspicions of Ibrahim and Hamid, because now we suddenly have a concrete reason for them to have killed her.

'Why is he telling us this?' she repeated when Dean took another bite of his cake as he apparently considered the question.

'So there will be no doubt that the act occurred to restore the family's honour,' he finally responded. 'He's not saying it to help us. It's a signal to the rest of the family and their social circle that the matter has been dealt with.'

Louise pulled a heavy sweater over her head and strolled down towards Nygade to eat lunch at the small local pub, where the beer was every bit as good as the Czech draft beer at Svejk back home in Frederiksberg. Mik was driving Ahmad back to Benløse, and after lunch she would pay the Møller family a visit.

She ordered a large beer and the herring plate, on which the head brewer had left his mark by including a beer-marinated pickled herring. Perhaps it wasn't the best idea to have a meal like this in the middle of the day, but honestly she didn't care. She needed it.

It irked her that Samra's uncle was only now starting to share what he knew. He hadn't said a word that would point in this direction the first time Mik had talked to him. Although, true, she didn't know if he'd been asked, but it certainly would have been nice if they'd known this before they started questioning people, because now they had to ascertain whether Samra's friends hadn't known about any relationship or were holding back and didn't want to get mixed up in anything.

She drank half of her large beer in one go. Then glanced quickly around the restaurant to see if anyone had noticed, but no one seemed interested in the beer-guzzling woman sitting by herself in the corner. Her herring had just arrived when her mobile phone started ringing.

'Hello,' she said when she saw it was Camilla. It took a little while before she could understand what her friend was saying. The sobbing made her voice unclear, and her words came out in hiccups.

'He killed himself?' Louise asked once she'd finally pieced together a bit of sense from the stream of words in her ear. 'Of course I'd go with you, but are you sure it's a good idea?'

She sat there holding her phone to her ear with one hand and drinking her beer with the other while the weeping Camilla explained that she couldn't decide what to do. Finally Louise repeated that she would go if Camilla decided to attend the funeral. That calmed her friend down and then, to distract her, Louise said they'd just brought Samra's uncle in and that he'd told them his niece had had a Danish boyfriend before she died.

'I think you're wasting your time by focusing so much on the family,' Camilla said. 'We're so full of prejudices about the way they behave and in reality we Danes aren't a damn bit better ourselves.'

It surprised Louise that she hadn't piqued Camilla's curiosity more. It just wasn't like her not to ask for more information about a detail like the one Louise had just given her.

'What do you mean?' Louise asked, signalling to the waiter that she'd like a small draft beer.

'You can read all about it in *Morgenavisen*,' Camilla continued.

The beer arrived on her table and Louise asked for the bill. 'Maybe you're the one who should hold back a little until you find out what our investigation turns up, so you don't waste your time on some dead end,' Louise retorted, smiling at her phone. They had eventually found balance in their relationship, the police detective and the journalist, but that didn't stop them from giving each other a hard time when it was justified.

'Yes, well, let's just see which of us is on the right track,' Camilla said, finally sounding a little less overwhelmed. 'Are you going out to sit on that farmer's beer bench tonight?' she asked before they wrapped up the conversation.

Louise felt a little flutter in her stomach at the thought. 'It's not out of the question,' she said, happy that her friend couldn't see the red glow her cheeks had suddenly taken on.

35

Only after Louise had rung the doorbell for the second time did she notice the silence. There was no barking from the garden or from inside the house, but the big four-wheel-drive was parked in the driveway, which confused her.

She rang again, then walked over and peered in through the kitchen window. The house seemed empty. She walked around it once. The curtains were drawn in several of the windows. She stopped for a moment, leaning against the wall, to think. She could call them when she got back to the station. It wasn't because this couldn't wait. She wanted to see how they were doing, given the two arrests, and talk to them about the funeral, which was scheduled for Monday.

An unpleasant mood had taken hold of the town as the rumours had spread that Samra's father and brother had been taken into custody in the case, and in particular, the news that they were also being charged for Dicta's murder had ratcheted things up to a fever pitch. The police were prepared for a big turnout at Dicta's funeral and, along with the local detective inspector, Storm had agreed to send a handful of officers to keep the peace among the many teenagers who needed an outlet for their sorrow and anger. Anne and Henrik had been informed of the situation, but had announced that everyone was welcome and said that afterwards, there would be beer and soft drinks down at the youth hostel for anyone who wished to come.

Louise rang them one last time. When they still didn't pick up, she climbed back into her car and drove back into town; but instead of heading for the police station, she turned down Ahlgade and parked outside Henrik's chiropractic clinic.

She trotted quickly up the stairs and after she introduced herself, asked the receptionist if she knew where Henrik Møller was.

'Yeah, of course. He's here,' she said with a smile.

Louise looked at her in confusion. 'I had understood that he wasn't coming in until after the funeral,' she said, speaking quietly because of the patients in the waiting room.

'That was the plan, but he came in this morning and has been taking patients all day. I didn't really have the heart to talk him out of it.'

The receptionist's hair hung around her head in loose curls. She had warm, cheerful eyes, and when she spoke about her boss her voice contained equal parts concern and care.

'There is actually a break in his schedule when he's finished with this current patient. Because I'm assuming you would like to speak to him,' she said, eyeing Louise inquisitively.

'Yes, please. I'll make it quick.'

Louise sat down and grabbed a magazine, but had only just flipped to the first page when the receptionist called her name.

'I'm sorry to bother you. I hadn't realised you were back at work,' Louise began once she was in Møller's office. She explained that she had actually just come to ask if his receptionist had any idea where he was.

'I hadn't planned on coming back so soon,' he said, tipping his desk chair back. He rubbed his eyes and stretched his arms up in the air and folded them behind his head.

He looked tired.

'I just dropped by at your place, but there wasn't anyone home,' Louise continued.

He looked at her in surprise. 'Anne wasn't there?'

Louise shook her head. 'She didn't answer the door, anyway.' Louise felt bad for a second. Maybe she shouldn't have got involved.

Henrik closed his eyes.

'I didn't go home last night,' he admitted. He brought his arms down from behind his head and leaned forward, supporting himself on his elbows on his desk. 'I actually haven't been home since we found out you arrested the father and brother. She talks and talks and talks and blames me. I didn't tell her I suspected that Dicta might have been up to something she hadn't told us about.'

He rubbed his temples and let his eyes rest on the top of his desk.

'I can't stand talking about it all the time. It's not going to hurt any less just because you keep putting words to it. At least not for me, anyway,' he said.

Louise watched him in silence and when he looked up at her, their eyes met.

'Suddenly I can't stand her,' he said, still looking Louise in the eye. 'She closes her eyes to the fact that our daughter had a life that she wasn't involved in. Which is ridiculous and naïve. The girl was fifteen.'

Louise didn't know what to say, so she didn't say anything. 'Since that morning you came and told us what had happened, she's been walking around pretending this doesn't concern her. Sure, of course the pain and grief affect her. But she won't hear a word about *Ekstra Bladet*, Samra's diary, or the trips to Copenhagen. She doesn't think that has anything to do with our daughter, and I just want to shake her.'

Louise was stunned, not so much because he was so incredibly irritated at his wife. She'd seen that before. It also wasn't new to her that two parents could respond so differently to grief and that the response one of them had could really set the other one on edge. She just hadn't thought it would be a problem for Anne and Henrik.

'The day after you came to our place, we had a visit from a journalist from *Morgenavisen*, who wanted to write an article about Dicta. We spent several hours talking to her, and that triggered something. Suddenly it became very apparent how differently we had perceived our family life and especially our daughter.'

Louise listened to these private reflections a bit uneasily. The man really should have been telling all this to a psychologist if he wanted to get anything out of it.

'Nor do I personally view it as the end of the world to see my daughter appear in *Ekstra Bladet*. She was a pretty girl, and we have no reason to be embarrassed. But Anne thinks she must have been forced into that, drugged or something,' he said with an awkward chuckle, and Louise smiled politely at his attempt to be funny.

'What about the funeral?' she asked.

He took a deep breath and said that he'd brought his dark suit with him when he left the house and wasn't planning to go home before the funeral. He explained that he had a small room and a kitchenette here at the clinic and that that was where he was living for the time being.

Louise gave up on talking to him about the police turnout at the funeral and instead asked if his wife might have been out walking her dogs since she probably hadn't gone anywhere without her car.

He looked at her with his zoned-out but friendly gaze and then shook his head.

'She put all the dogs into a kennel run by someone from the dog club. Even Charlie,' he added. 'That's how it is. She's putting life on hold while I'm trying to get it to keep moving. That's why we can't be together right now.'

There still wasn't any answer when Louise went back to the Møllers' large home, but the bathroom window had been opened. Louise walked around the house, then returned to the front door and left her finger on the bell for a while as she waited.

After ten minutes, something finally happened.

Louise instinctively took a step back when Anne opened the door. Dicta's mother was in a thick red bathrobe and her pageboy hairdo hung wetly down over her ears; her eyes looked small without make-up and bore obvious signs of having cried themselves out of tears. The change was so pronounced that it was hard to believe that it had happened in such a short period of time. Louise wasn't sure she would have recognised her on the street.

'Hi, Anne,' she said. Dicta's mother looked at her but didn't respond.

'Could I come in?' Louise asked, stepping forward, gripping Anne gently around the shoulders, and leading her back into the house. The flowers were still in their cellophane wrappers, the cards still unopened. There were cups, plates and several empty wine bottles in the kitchen.

'I just went over to see Henrik. He thought you were probably still at home even if you didn't answer the door when I was here earlier.'

Louise was talking in an effort to bring some life to the room. She made herself at home and started a pot of coffee and followed Anne into the living room, where she sat down next to her on the sofa.

'How are you doing?' Louise asked. She tried to establish eye contact, but didn't succeed.

Anne made a face. 'What do you think?'

'Yes, well, good point,' Louise consented.

'My husband obviously thinks life goes on,' Anne said tersely, and Louise realised she shouldn't have mentioned that she'd spoken to Henrik first.

'I don't think it does,' Anne said.

'He's not doing that well himself, either,' Louise said.

Finally something that got a response out of Anne. 'Well, then, he's doing a fucking crappy job at showing it. It's like he has no reaction at all,' she said in a more neutral tone.

Louise decided not to explain that that was also a type of reaction, and in the subsequent silence it seemed as if Anne Møller had slipped back into her own world. Her voice sounded frail when she spoke again.

'I only had one child, and she only had one life. I can't accept that it has all ended this way. And I don't want to hear any talk about moving on. I have no desire to move on. Not ever. It isn't fair. She's not even buried yet. No one can tell me to pull myself together. Why should I?'

'I noticed that your dogs aren't here,' Louise said, to get the woman thinking about something else.

Anne nodded. 'I'm boarding them. They don't understand that I feel violated every time they wag their tails or jump up happily to get me to play. They don't understand that we don't do those things any more, so it was better to send them away.'

'Maybe it would've been good for you to have some kind of distraction,' Louise suggested.

'I don't want to be distracted. I'm doing everything I can to hold my thoughts together.'

Her voice was starting to sound shrill.

Louise stood up. 'Isn't there anyone you'd like to have here with you?' she asked as she went to get the coffee. She poured a cup for Anne and placed it in front of her in the living room.

Anne Møller absent-mindedly shook her head.

'Or someone you could stay with for a few days?' Louise tried again, but Anne just shook her head.

After Louise said goodbye, she stood out on the street for a second looking around at all the fashionable homes. It made her sad that Anne was so alone with her grief.

When she got back to the police station, Storm came rushing in and pulled her out into the hall.

'You have to hear this,' he said and led her into the room where the National Police interpreter was listening to the wiretap recording from the al-Abd family's landline.

'Let's go back. Rick needs to hear this sequence from the beginning.'

The interpreter nodded briefly at Louise and was about to start reading from a piece of paper when Storm interrupted him to explain that this was a conversation that had just taken place over dinner.

'Ahmad called Sada,' the interpreter explained. He adjusted his glasses and started translating the conversation.

'I've told the police now.' The interpreter looked up at her and made it clear that Ahmad had said that to Samra's mother.

'Then she asks, "What did you tell them?"'

'"How it's connected."'

'Here, there's a long pause on the tape,' the interpreter noted before he read more.

'Sada says that he's a sick man, and that he shouldn't ruin her whole family with his wickedness.'

Louise had taken a seat on a chair, and she jumped forward a little involuntarily when the interpreter described Ahmad's reaction.

'He says: "You already ruined the girl with all that freedom and you're ruining the rest of our family. Samra's was only one life. We have a whole family to think about. I will not walk around feeling ashamed for the rest of my life because you couldn't control your daughter." Sada sobs intensely and says that he has every possible reason to be ashamed, and that she's going to talk to the police too,' the interpreter continued, addressing Louise, before he read yet another of Ahmad's outbursts and explained that the voices were very heated here.

The interpreter lowered the piece of paper and said, 'At this point, Sada hangs up, and there hasn't been any activity at the number since then.'

Louise let the words sink in for a moment.

'We need to bring the mother in now and get her to tell us what she knows,' Storm said.

36

The front door was open when Louise and Mik arrived at Dysseparken 16B. Mik went in first and waved for Louise to join him. They stood in the doorway to the kitchen, looking at the three people.

Sada was sitting there, ready, her coat on. She was still crying, and her face was swollen and wet. The two little ones were sitting on the floor with a roll of crackers, which they'd spread out, so they were surrounded by crumbs and bits of cracker.

'Hi,' Mik said, walking over to the table where Sada was sitting. 'We would really like to talk to you. Is there someone who could look after the kids while you come down to the police station with us?'

Sada nodded and said that she had already called her sister. Samra's mother had her handbag in her lap and was holding it with both hands.

'Were you on your way out?' Louise asked, stepping into the kitchen as well, so Sada could see her.

The slender woman glanced up at her and nodded. She opened her bag and pulled out a few pieces of white paper. Louise saw with surprise that they must be the pages that had been ripped out of Samra's diary.

Just then, there was a soft knock on the front door and a woman walked in. Aida leapt up from the floor and flung herself at her aunt with a squeal. The woman held the child pressed up against her, but nothing was said. The two women just exchanged a glance.

'Will you stay with them? Or could they go with you?' Mik asked the sister.

'I'll take them home with me,' the woman said briefly.

Sada stood up and closed her bag. Then she stepped over and picked Jamal up off the floor and kissed him affectionately before she placed him in her sister's arms. After that, she stroked Aida's hair, kissed her forehead, and said something Louise couldn't understand. On the way out, the girl blew her mother a quick kiss and blinked her long, dark eyelashes vigorously so the tears stopped before they could truly be seen.

At the police station, several minutes passed before Sada al-Abd got her crying under control enough that she could start talking. As she set down her coat, Louise took a seat across from her to read the pages that had been missing from Samra's diary, and Mik stepped out to inform Storm. Louise had been prepared for the pages she was holding to hurt deep down in her soul, but when she started reading them aloud, she felt a sense of powerlessness so great that something inside her broke.

'My life isn't worth anything any more. I'm dirty and

contaminated and can never be washed clean. He says that if I tell Mother and Father, he will tell what I've done and the family won't be able to live with that. I don't dare sleep. I can hear him coming and feel his arms. If I scream, he'll tell Father.'

Louise could picture the young woman. She almost felt like she could hear the words on the page coming out of her mouth, but the only sound in the small, dark office was Sada's quiet sobs.

'He says that he just happened to see us, but I know that's not true. He must have been following me. I hate him and wish I'd never been born. If I ever have to go to Benløse again, I'll drown myself in the sound.

'I can't take any more. He should kill me rather than letting this continue. I miss Grandma and home. Dear God, I pray that Mother and Father understand.'

Louise glanced over at Sada to see if she was following along with Louise as she read, but the woman was sitting frozen in place with her head bowed, staring at her clasped hands. Only an occasional twitch of her shoulders and the faint sound of deep despair revealed what was going on in her body. Louise had a hard time understanding how Samra's mother could have contained her knowledge of the enormous pain that had filled her daughter at the end of her life.

'I found the pages in her jewellery box after she died,' Sada said quietly, without raising her eyes. 'Where she kept her jewellery and private things.'

Mik Rasmussen walked through the door and stood there for a second, obviously struck by the mood in the small room. Without a sound, he walked over and sat down.

Louise continued to watch Sada.

'Tell me what happened,' Louise pleaded. 'What was your daughter subjected to and why did you cover up something that hurt her so much?'

She spoke calmly. It was as if all the tension had left the room, leaving a heavy calm. In a way, something had been put behind them, even though they hadn't really started yet, Louise thought, looking expectantly at Samra's mother.

'Who is your daughter writing about?'

The woman was silent. Louise thought about Storm and Ruth, who were sitting in the command room, knowing that she was working on something that could resolve the case. She was afraid of being too aggressive with her questioning, or pushing too hard. Piecing together the rest of what happened could very easily depend on how Louise handled the mother, and what she said would have to be able to stand up in court later. In other words, right now it was not so much about getting Sada to confess and sign a statement, because she could recant that once she was facing a jury. That kind of thing happened. Louise knew she had to get Sada to take responsibility for the pain she was feeling right now, to make her feel that, instead of protecting the men in her family, she needed to stick up for her daughter, who had had a right to live.

Louise looked over at Mik quickly, but ignored the feeling that ran through her when he returned her glance. Then once again she turned her full attention back to the woman.

'Something had happened around the beginning of the summer holiday that had turned Samra's life upside down. Something that caused her to be quiet and withdrawn,' Sada said. 'When Samra was home, she mostly stayed in her room with the door closed. She went to school, did her homework, and did her chores at home.

'But she avoided her father and wouldn't join us when the family was together,' Sada continued, her breathing ragged.

The weekend before Samra died, Sada had found her lying on the bathroom floor. She was half unconscious; the paracetamol tablets hadn't totally knocked her out yet.

'I knew what she'd tried to do and got her to throw up all the pills,' Sada said, trying to dry her eyes. 'I gave her tea and a blanket and had my sister come take the kids.'

Sada took a deep breath and Louise fidgeted a little in her chair, aware of how difficult it must be for Sada to tell this story. Mik sat completely motionless, listening along.

'Since spring, Samra had had a Danish friend, whom she saw in secret,' Sada began, taking a deep breath before she could continue. 'She didn't tell anyone about it, not even her girlfriends. But Ahmad found out, and he did something to her that she didn't dare tell us about.'

Finally Sada looked up at Louise and there was something in the darkness of the glance that pleaded for understanding and patience.

Louise nodded weakly in return.

'He raped her,' Sada finally said. 'Several times.' Sada struggled to keep her voice under control.

'She couldn't tell anyone, because then he would reveal her secret, that she'd been seeing someone.'

Louise closed her eyes for a second. 'But seeing a Danish boy could never be as bad as being raped by her uncle and having him threaten her,' Louise said quietly.

Sada nodded.

'Samra knew that he would spread the rumour about what

she was doing, and how bad we were at keeping her in line. So it was better to say nothing.'

There was total silence in the office. Sada's words still lingered in the air, but Louise and Mik tried to understand what had held Samra back.

'It is a much more serious crime for an adult man to rape a girl than for her to be seeing a boy her own age,' Louise tried again.

Sada made a strange motion with her head, which could have been interpreted as both a yes and a no.

'That's not the case where we come from,' she said finally. 'It's worse for a girl to be disobedient, because then she herself is to blame for what happens to her.'

Louise was going to object, but held back.

'When a woman is raped, it's her own fault. She brings it on herself,' Sada attempted to explain. 'Ahmad says that if she can have sex with a Danish boy, then she can have sex with him too.'

Here was a cultural difference that was so impossible to understand that Louise decided not even to try. They had to just let the mother tell her story, and they could go back in later and respond to what she'd said. The autopsy report had not said anything about whether Samra's hymen had been intact, because that wasn't part of the routine exam, unless there was a suspicion of rape. Louise hadn't requested that they do that examination since there hadn't been anything to suggest a sex crime.

'What did you do when your daughter told you what had happened?' Louise asked to bring them back on topic.

'At first she refused to let me tell her father. But I explained to her that my husband would understand. I would no longer consider my husband's brother as family, and if Ibrahim didn't understand, I would leave him and take the children with me.'

She paused for a moment.

'We told him on Monday afternoon when he came home from the boat early. At first he wouldn't believe it and got very angry. He hit Samra and said she was trying to break up his family and ruin things for him. He's a very proud man, and he wouldn't have anyone believing that he couldn't look after his family. She showed him the big marks that she still had on her body, and he blamed her for them, said her Danish boyfriend had made them. But she told him exactly what had happened in her uncle's bathroom in Benløse, and in the end he had to believe her. Several times, my husband's brother had taken our daughter in there and raped her on the changing table by their bathtub, and each time she took it without screaming, even though her aunt and small cousins were just outside the door in the living room.'

Louise understood from Sada's explanation that what had convinced Ibrahim his daughter was telling the truth was her description of a scar his brother had in his groin area. It was from an accident that had taken place when the two brothers were little and had been playing in the river. Ibrahim had accidentally stabbed Ahmad with a sharp knife that their father used to clean fish. The blood had been gushing and Ahmad was practically unconscious before they managed to stop the bleeding. The scar was in a place that could pretty much only be seen when his penis was exposed.

Louise could picture the scene in the bathroom. Samra had been a slight, delicate girl. It would have been almost effortless for him to have his way with her. She hadn't stood a chance of resisting, although she hadn't tried either.

'Then my husband got angry,' Sada continued. 'He hugged our daughter and held her tight and promised that it would never happen again. He also promised that she would be at peace.'

'What did he have to say about her seeing a Danish boy?' Louise asked when Sada once again fell silent, with her head bent and her hands folded.

'He said that she was free to live her life and that she was more important to him than his extended family or anyone else.'

A tremble of discomfort suddenly made the room feel cold and full of sorrow. Louise crossed her legs tightly and folded her arms, huddling up a little.

'Then what happened?'

'He asked Ahmad to come over on Tuesday evening, the night she disappeared,' Sada began and then looked up with an expression so distant, it was as if no one was there. 'They argued. My husband said we refused to be threatened. He had made plans to send our daughter home to Jordan for Christmas. No one in Rabba would turn their back on him. And if she were ever touched again, he would report it to the police.'

Louise looked at her in surprise.

'Ahmad got angry too and said that my husband wouldn't dare because he wouldn't be able to show his face in Jordan once the rumours got there about how his daughter had behaved here in Denmark. My husband didn't care, he was going to protect Samra, and finally he kicked his brother out.'

'The next day, you went to Benløse. What did you talk about on that visit?' Louise wanted to know.

'Samra was missing. We wanted to ask if he'd taken her or seen her,' came the response.

'Had he?' Louise asked.

Sada shook her head and started crying again.

'But you think he was the one who killed your daughter?'

It took a moment before Samra's mother gathered her wits and raised her head. 'I don't know what to think now, but I didn't think she was dead then. I thought maybe she'd run away to get away from him, or so she wouldn't have to be home when her father talked to him.'

Louise had a hard time understanding how the mother could have been walking around with suspicions like this about her brother-in-law – and it was almost worse if Ibrahim had the same suspicions – without anyone saying anything.

She could tell that Mik was already preparing to go and bring Ibrahim's brother in for another round of questioning, but she remained seated when he stood up and let him leave on his own. Samra's story had been more gruesome than she'd imagined, and both she and Sada needed a moment to sit and let everything settle.

37

The scent of flowers was pungent. Camilla chose a discreet bouquet of bright yellow blossoms and contemplated whether or not to include a little card. Maybe she should just leave it anonymous, because she didn't know what to write. Should she apologise because maybe she bore some of the blame for his arrest, and because his life was over now? She didn't hear it when the saleslady repeated her question about a card. Just held out her debit card and finally shook her head. The arrest wasn't her fault, she decided, and she wasn't going to carry that as a burden.

'Just send it,' she said, handing the woman the address of the church in Sorø.

She walked out of the shop and stood on the pavement for a moment, thinking about the funeral. She didn't feel like she could share in grief that didn't concern her, and suddenly it was like something inside her gave in and relaxed. As if the love she'd felt for her ex-boyfriend had finally seeped out of her, allowing her to see clearly again. She didn't have room for him any more and didn't want anything else to do with him. That chapter was over now.

Camilla strolled down the main street. She'd spoken with Louise and knew that Ahmad had been brought in for another round of questioning, and that he had opted not to have a lawyer present because he stubbornly insisted that he hadn't done anything he could be charged for. That was all she'd found out, but that was enough to make her think she might have misjudged the situation and jumped the gun a little with her defence of the family. On the other hand, she was pretty much the only one who hadn't railed against the family and hung them out to dry long before they were ever convicted of anything. If that turned out to have been the wrong call, she was going to have to eat crow.

If it really was someone in the al-Abd family who had killed those two girls, of course the act was completely indefensible, she thought, crossing the wide thoroughfare, whose pavements were lined with planters full of flowers. She had never intended her articles to imply that it was acceptable for recent immigrants to kill their daughters just because ethnic Danes had done the same thing at some point in the past. Of course it had ticked her off that people were so quick to judge the immigrants even though the same phenomenon could be found in other subsets of Danish society, but really she mostly just felt that she owed it to Sada for people to hear her side of the story.

Camilla had visited Sada after she'd been questioned at the police station. Sada had called and invited her over. Still deeply shaken by the experience, Sada had obviously felt that Camilla was the only person she could talk to if she were to have any chance of making someone understand what it was like to be trapped between two cultures. Sada had served her sweet tea, and Camilla had quietly listened with Aida on her lap. While the little girl twisted Camilla's long blonde hair into loose ringlet curls, it slowly dawned on Camilla that the familial schism Sada was talking about was so deep that it wasn't just about being good or evil. This woman's life had been ripped apart, both when Samra died and when her conduct had been called into question, without her having any chance to set the record straight.

Sada might actually have suffered more than Samra had, Camilla thought sadly as she strolled down the narrow walkway that led to the harbour to get a little fresh air.

'Ahmad still denies that he killed Samra, and so do both Ibrahim and Hamid,' Storm said once the team had gathered in the command room, having spent the whole day questioning the three family members. 'But we have to stick with it until one of them loosens up a little.'

'That's going to take a while with this family. They're not going to say shit,' Skipper said, adding that he had the impression Ahmad didn't believe he had anything to hide. 'He actually acknowledged that he'd had sex with his niece, but he doesn't think it was rape because girls who go out with Danish boys are sex-crazed hussies.' He stopped and glanced around at the others as he pulled his hand though his wavy grey hair. 'I was really working on him, but he didn't give up a thing. Suddenly he can't even remember what the boyfriend looks like. Nothing besides the fact that he's blond and way too old for her. Ahmad insists that he didn't see his niece after he left his brother's house on Tuesday night. His wife confirmed that he came right home after the visit and that he didn't leave the house again until the next morning when he went to open his shop.'

'She's not a credible alibi,' Velin interjected critically.

'Of course not,' Skipper said. 'And at this point he doesn't really have anything else to say, although it doesn't seem like he understands how serious his crime is. He's said several times that Samra represents only one life.'

Dean had pulled his chair back a little and was stretching out his legs. 'This all suggests your basic honour/shame scenario,' he said and looked at Skipper. 'One life doesn't matter that much when you look at their entire extended family – the ones living here in Denmark and the ones back home in Jordan – in which this kind of thing generally has ripple effects that people would prefer not to deal with.'

Louise could tell that Mik was going to contradict him, but he stopped himself.

'What about Hamid?' she asked.

Louise hadn't talked to Hamid herself. She had concentrated on Ibrahim and felt that eventually the two of them had built up a decent rapport. Mik had continued with Hamid, even though they still hadn't clicked.

'He's sick of it,' Mik said. 'And I also get the sense that he's afraid of what's going to happen. Whether they end up in jail or get kicked out of the country. He talks a lot about school and his friends, but he says he didn't know anything about his sister having a boyfriend. I had hoped, and still hope, that he could tell us who the boyfriend is. But apparently there isn't anyone who can.'

'What did the techs find? There must be something that can tie them to the two killings,' Louise said, and was immediately followed by Dean, who asked, 'What about the wiretap?'

'Nothing noteworthy,' Storm admitted, 'which is to say, no increased activity; but all three family members consented to let Bengtsen and Velin do a cheek swab on them, so we can check their DNA profiles. No DNA material was found on Samra and we have to assume that any that might have been there was washed away in the water, but we did secure several samples from Dicta. We just haven't heard back yet from the Forensic Genetics Lab if there was enough to construct a profile.'

Storm moved on to the witness statements. 'Several people saw Dicta down on the big lawn behind Hotel Strandparken on Saturday afternoon when she was doing the photo shoot Michael Mogensen told us about. She went home to eat just after six and left her house again at seven thirty to cycle over to Liv's place, where she was going to spend the night. She arrived there fifteen minutes later and stayed with Liv until a bit after eleven, when she left. Dicta said she was going to meet the photographer and promised to come back before the next morning, so Liv wouldn't have to explain to her parents where Dicta had gone.'

'And she was exchanging text messages with Tue Sunds all evening,' Louise interjected.

Storm nodded and continued. 'After that, the father of one of her classmates saw her on Ahlgade entering a shop, and a couple of witnesses also saw her in the town centre at that late hour, but no one can tell us with a hundred per cent certainty exactly where they saw her. But the route fits nicely if she went from Liv's place towards Nygade and then on up to the train station. After that, there's no trace of her. Where was she going?'

'To Copenhagen,' the detectives said, all speaking at once, and Storm nodded again.

'Yes, we're assuming that she went to the station to take the last train into the city at eleven forty-five.'

'But she never boarded,' Bengtsen concluded, lost in contemplation for a moment. 'Should we try to recreate the route she took from Liv's house to the scene of the crime?' he asked, looking slowly around the table.

'We have a good working relationship with *Venstrebladet*,' Dean added, and said the paper had been known to include photos before if the police requested it to jog people's memories.

'That's not a bad idea,' Bengtsen agreed, looking at his younger colleague. 'Let's get one of their photographers to walk the route with us and take pictures of the locations where we know Dicta was seen and of the actual crime scene.'

Storm nodded and thought for a moment. 'Let's do it. But we can't do the same thing for Samra, because she wasn't killed out at Hønsehalsen. She was taken out there after she was killed.'

'The duty officer just received a call from the harbour master that someone vandalised Ibrahim's boat yesterday or last night,' Ruth interrupted, having just walked in through the door. She said that someone had painted extremely crass messages all over it.

'Maybe that means we should start paying attention to the threats against the family. At least as long as the mother is still living in the apartment with those two little ones,' Ruth said, taking a seat.

The group went silent. The newspapers had already described the mood in town as a lynch mob out to get the al-Abd family and other Muslim families as well. People were lumping all the Muslims together in terms of assigning blame for the two girls' deaths. But until now the anger that had arisen had not been manifested in any kind of physical assault.

They discussed assigning officers to protect Sada and her children or maybe moving them out of town.

'Let's contact *Venstrebladet*,' Storm said, concluding the meeting. 'We need to get those photos taken tomorrow.'

They all stood up and trickled out into the hall, heading off to shut their office doors before going to eat, when the mobile phone in Louise's pocket started vibrating. She could see that it was Camilla and answered it with a perky 'What's up?'

Mik stepped on the back of her heel, when she abruptly stopped, listening to her friend's torrent of words. When she hung up, she called her colleagues together before they had a chance to disappear into their offices.

'Aida is missing,' she said, loud enough for everyone to hear her.

'What do you mean, "missing"?' Skipper asked, stopping in the doorway to his and Dean's office.

Camilla had just received a call from Sada, Louise said, and Sada had explained, with some confusion, that the two children had had permission to go down and play in the sandpit before dinner. Dysseparken's minimal playground facility was at the end of the car park in front of the al-Abds' building.

Storm called them back into the command room and asked Louise to finish explaining.

'When Sada went down to get them, Jamal was sitting there alone, playing, and when she asked him where his sister was, he just said she'd left. Sada spent the last hour running around looking for her daughter until she called Camilla a second ago and asked her what she should do.'

'The little girl could have gone to visit someone,' Velin suggested. 'But we have to react, given the threats people have been making against them the last few days. We have to find that girl.'

Louise agreed. They needed to act immediately. It really didn't matter what kind of mischief Aida might have got into. It was embarrassing that the police hadn't responded to the threats. They had talked about providing some kind of protection for Sada and the little ones so many times, but it just hadn't been done.

'Why the hell didn't she call us?' the MTF captain asked, irritated.

'Because—' Louise began, and Storm finished her sentence: 'So far, we haven't done anything besides split up her family. So we're not her first choice to turn to when she needs help. We're going out there.'

38

A small group of people 'of ethnic background' – as Skipper put it – were gathered in the car park. Storm pulled Louise aside with a tug on her arm.

'Find out what the mother says,' he told her and then returned to the others to start a search.

Louise spotted Sada right away. She was sitting on a bench with Jamal on her lap surrounded by a crowd of people. Louise made it to the middle of the crowd and was standing right in front of Sada before the woman noticed her and pointed over to the sandpit through her sobs. Just then Camilla came running up to them and Sada made room for her on the bench.

Everyone standing around moved back a little, uneasy about the level of intimacy they perceived between the blonde journalist and the Jordanian woman. Louise understood their reaction. This was an unfamiliar situation: an outsider was unreservedly offering the same degree of concern and caring they had been providing.

'Maybe she went to someone's house?' Camilla suggested when Sada looked up at her. And at that second, Louise had no doubt that Camilla was there as a friend and not as a journalist.

Aida's mother shook her head. In the background, Louise noticed that Mik and Skipper had started organising the people who had turned out to help into a search party.

'Maybe somebody was bothering her, so she hid?' Camilla suggested, stroking Sada's arm as she spoke.

Louise looked at her. That wasn't unlikely, based on what Camilla had described the crowd of teenagers doing to Sada and the kids outside the train station.

Sada shook her head again. 'Then Jamal would have been scared too,' she said, 'but he was sitting here quite calmly, playing, when I came to get them.'

'When did you last see her?' Louise asked, leaning over to hear Sada's quiet voice.

'Four o'clock. They came down to play when I started making dinner.'

That was over two hours ago. That was a long time for a four-year-old girl to be away, but it wasn't normally long enough to report a person missing. But this wasn't a normal situation.

Louise walked over to inform the rest of the police officers what had happened, and over the next half-hour the local police got a search going that would focus on the area around Dysseparken to begin with. There was still a small hope that she had got wrapped up playing with a friend and lost track of the time or wandered off. It was well past dinnertime, and if she'd forgotten the hour, her hunger would soon remind her that it was time to go home.

Louise was picturing worst-case scenarios. How had the little girl been lured away from her younger brother? Did she struggle, or did she go along trustingly? The thoughts piled into her head, and Louise wished again that they'd managed to do something to provide more protection for Sada and the two children.

Word of the girl's disappearance had started to draw a crowd. Some people were standing off to the side in small groups; others came over to ask if they could help with the search. People were ranting or chatting. Among all those who expressed fear for what might have happened to the little girl, there was also the odd remark that the family had brought the child's disappearance on themselves, that they deserved it after what they'd done.

Storm had handed over command of the search to Bengt-sen, who knew the town and all the local officers who'd been brought in to help. Two canine units were also on their way. His voice was stern and his words succinct and precise. There wasn't any room for mistakes. At the same time, there was a push to appeal to the public so any potential witnesses would step up sooner rather than later. The faster they closed this case, the faster they could calm the anti-immigrant mood smouldering in the town, which had already had too much of an impact.

'Dean will stay with Sada in case the girl turns up on her own. The rest of us will join the search. We'll split the town into zones and each take charge of one area,' Storm commanded.

'Should Ibrahim be informed?' Mik asked, but then shook his head.

Louise agreed. There wasn't anything he could do to help.

Camilla came over to them. The autumn twilight was upon them, and that would only make the search more difficult.

'I'm going to help search,' Camilla said once she reached Bengtsen, ignoring the protests of the local officers. She mentioned the unpleasant episode in front of the train station again. 'Maybe I could recognise those guys if I saw them again. We have to find her tonight, otherwise it means something's happened to her.'

39

They called off the search for the night at 2 a.m., but Louise had trouble falling asleep once she was finally lying in her bed. At eight the next morning, there were once again search teams throughout the entire town, and canine patrols fanning out so they were searching the area from all sides. About twenty to thirty volunteers had shown up to help, and Bengtsen had broken them up into groups and was in firm control of who was in charge of each individual team and where they would be searching.

'All basements and attic spaces, stairwells and bike sheds must be investigated,' he instructed his people.

The missing-persons report ran every hour on the radio news update, but by midday there still wasn't any sign of the girl.

Louise was sitting in her office with a cola and a piece of pizza before the meeting she and Mik had scheduled with a photographer from *Venstrebladet* to retrace the route Dicta had followed late Saturday night after she left Liv's house. Louise pushed the pizza container to the side a little and pulled a padded envelope from the Pathology Lab closer to her. Flemming had sent her the photos from Samra's autopsy, and she flipped slowly through them. When she came to the page with the pictures of the back of Samra's head, she was puzzled by the vellum-coloured yellowish marks on the back of the girl's neck. Suddenly she thought they bore a certain similarity to the rounded marks they had found on Dicta.

Flemming hadn't measured the distance between the marks on Samra's head, because he hadn't considered them relevant. They were so obviously incurred after the girl's death. Now Louise borrowed the ruler from Mik's soccer mug and determined that the distance here was also three centimetres. In other words, both girls had been in contact with the same object. Not that that brought them any closer to what might have made the distinctive rounded marks. Skipper and Dean hadn't found anything in the family's home during their search, nor anything in Ahmad's apartment or his shop. But for the first time they had something concrete that linked the two killings. Louise got up and went to the command room where Ruth was working on her own. The rest of the group was still out with the search teams.

Louise set down the stack of photos and pointed out the marks.

'The spacing is the same as the ones Flemming found on Dicta,' Louise pointed out; and right then she was interrupted by Mik, who had just walked in through the door.

'Are you ready to go?' he asked. 'The photographer's just arrived.'

Louise left the stack of photos on the administrative assistant's desk and they hurried down the hall to meet Michael Mogensen, who was on his way to their office.

'I'm a little late,' he apologised and said that he'd just returned from an assignment with one of the search teams – they were doing a story on the girl's disappearance for the paper.

They took the stairs down to the cars, discussing the missing girl as they walked.

The suburban street where Liv and her parents lived was quiet. Only one lone car drove by while Michael Mogensen set up his tripod and got his large digital Canon camera ready.

'How wide should the shot be?' Louise heard him ask. 'Is it going to be the whole road, or just the driveway?'

'The driveway and a bit of the street so people can recognise the location,' Mik responded, stepping over to hold some of the photographer's equipment as he unpacked things.

Louise followed them at a distance. Mik was the one who'd put together the list of locations they wanted to show in the paper: Liv's house; the kiosk up on the main road, which Dicta had been seen entering; then Nygade; and finally the car park behind that, where she'd been found.

The photographer got ready and did a layout. He suggested that they put a small photo of Dicta in every single picture so readers associated her face with the four locations.

When they'd finished on the street in front of Liv's house, he led the way in his car down to the kiosk on the main street, and they parked right behind him. He jumped quickly from the car, fishing his equipment out of the trunk. He set the camera up on the tripod and adjusted the height so he could get the kiosk and a little of the main street with it.

'I'll take a couple of shots,' he said, moving the tripod a little further out into the street. 'Then we can look at them and decide if we're done.'

Mik had gone into the kiosk to buy something to drink and a couple of bags of sweets, so Louise nodded to the photographer that that was okay. She smiled at his thoroughness. To her it was just a couple of pictures of a kiosk on a main road, but he made it seem like a bigger assignment in which the angle, lighting and width of the shot were crucial to the success of the project.

He changed lenses and said that he just wanted to take a couple more shots with a wide-angle lens, and he asked her to hold the tripod while he squatted down to organise all his various lenses. Every time a car drove by, Louise followed it with her eyes to see if there was a little dark-haired girl in the back seat. The whole time, her eyes were checking front steps, gates and stairs leading down to basement doors. She watched the pedestrians walking towards her and thought: Could they have done it?

'It may make the most sense to leave the cars here,' Michael said when he'd finished. 'Once we've got it all, I think you should come back to the studio and select the specific photos you want to run with. Then I can submit them to the editor right away.'

He swung his heavy camera bag up onto his shoulder, and Louise quickly reached out and grabbed the tripod so he wouldn't have to carry everything. It was pretty heavy.

As they headed towards Nygade, a young couple emerged from the brewery, and she heard them talking about the dead girl's little sister, who had disappeared. Louise turned around to get a closer look at them and tripped over the edge of a pavement slab that was slightly uneven. She was losing her balance and the tripod toppled from under her arm, but her reflexes were faster than her brain, and she stretched her right leg out in an attempt to prevent the plate at the top that the camera screwed onto from smacking against the ground at full force. It hammered into her shin instead.

'Fuck!' she muttered, struggling to rescue the tripod.

'Let me take that,' Michael said, quickly coming over to help her out.

Louise moaned and shot an angry look at Mik when he briskly asked if she had everything under control.

As they proceeded, her leg throbbed, and she felt a drop of blood trickling down towards her sock. Up by the alley, she found a place to sit down and watch the photographer work. Just as conscientiously as before, he got his camera ready, set up the tripod, and took pictures of Nygade and the alley leading into the car park. Once those were done, they gathered up all the stuff and continued down the alley towards the car park to wrap things up at the location where the body had been found.

Mik gave Michael his instructions. There were still flowers there, both recent additions and the bouquets that had been left there since Dicta's savaged body had been found. The photographer was clearly moved to find himself at the scene of the crime and pointed out a large bouquet of white roses that he himself had brought. Still, he remained meticulous and focused as he got started photographing the site, so the readers could see that Dicta had been lying in the rear corner of the car park, down by Lindevej.

Louise reached out to take the tripod when Michael started packing up, but gladly left it to Mik when he offered to carry it back to the cars.

40

They both said yes to Michael Mogensen's offer of coffee, and he hooked his digital camera up to his computer to download the photos before disappearing up into his apartment to put the coffee on. Louise noticed that the gash on her shin was still bleeding and walked over to pull a paper towel off the roll that stood on a small table under the window.

She sat down on the sofa and rolled up her trouser leg. The blood had spread into a smudged stain. She carefully dabbed it clean and held a fresh paper towel up against her leg to stop the trickle of blood. Michael came back down with the coffee, mugs and a carton of milk under his arm.

'Well, are you ready to look at them?' he asked as he sat down in front of his monitor.

Louise walked over to the bin with the paper towel. As she was about to toss it in, she was struck by the familiar and distinctive rounded marks the blood from her wound had made.

This time she didn't need a ruler to know there were exactly three centimetres between them.

For a moment she forgot to breathe. Then she turned around slowly and studied Michael Mogensen, as every piece of the puzzle fell into place.

Mik had not noticed Louise's silence as he poured their coffee. Louise stood and gathered her thoughts for a moment, then calmly walked over and sat down next to the photographer. For a few minutes she watched as he brought photos up on the screen.

Then she asked her question.

Her partner only reacted the second time she asked. Michael Mogensen had his eyes firmly on the screen, but his fingers had stopped moving on the keyboard. He looked at her for a moment, and the look in his eyes convinced her that she was right in her suspicion.

'Why did you kill them?' she repeated, waiting for his response.

Mik came over and stood next to her, but Louise didn't take her eyes off Michael Mogensen, leaving her partner to follow along as best he could. She could see him putting the pieces together as she passed him the paper towel with the two red marks that the screws on the plate the camera housing attached to had left on her leg. His face was serious and his voice calm as he closed in on the photographer.

'Did you take Aida as well?' he asked.

Finally Michael Mogensen turned his body towards them, allowing his eyes to remain locked on the screen and the picture of the suburban street where Liv's home was.

He hesitantly shook his head, speaking in such a low voice that they had to lean close to hear him.

'That wasn't me,' he said.

Louise reached out and grabbed him. She forced him to look at her.

'I don't know where she is,' he continued in the same quiet tone. 'I could never do anything to her.'

He looked down, avoiding her angry face.

'Why should I believe that when you've been so hypocritical – leaving flowers for both Samra and Dicta even though you were the one who killed them?'

He mumbled something she didn't understand, and she glanced up at Mik, who shrugged.

'I'm going to ask you again. Were you behind Aida's disappearance?' Mik said in a voice that Louise had trouble recognising.

'I haven't touched her,' the photographer repeated, this time with more strength in his voice.

The answer came so quickly and clearly that they were forced to believe him. Louise got up and went out into the hallway to call Storm and tell him they'd found their murderer but that he denied having anything to do with Aida's disappearance. She told him that they needed no assistance. They would handle the arrest themselves and he would hear from her again soon.

When she returned to the studio, she felt rage throbbing within her, but she was determined to keep it under wraps and exerted a great deal of effort to make her voice sound relaxed. There was no reason to fight him now when gaining his trust was key so they could get him to talk.

'Tell us what happened between you and the two girls,' she encouraged.

The photographer sat, his back hunched, nearly collapsed

in on himself; but before he had a chance to consider whether or not he was going to say anything, she continued.

'When it comes to Dicta, I'm guessing it was anger that made you kill her – anger that she'd turned her back on you in favour of a Copenhagen fashion photographer. She hurt your feelings.'

Louise omitted to say how small-minded this reaction was, because it wasn't her place to define these things. A forensic psychologist would have the opportunity to do that later.

'She humiliated me,' Mogensen corrected her immediately.

Louise could tell that it wouldn't be hard to get him to talk, so it didn't surprise her when the words suddenly started flooding out of his mouth like loose gravel being tipped out of a truck bed.

'She mocked me and became cruel. She said that I was a second-class, provincial photographer who would never make a name for myself any further away than the village of Vipperød.' Louise nodded. That was what she'd figured. She would get the details later during the official interrogation at the police station. But the answer to the next question wasn't so obvious.

'Why Samra? You hardly knew her, right?' She tried to establish eye contact with him.

Finally something changed in his face. He turned to look her in the eye and what Louise saw in front of her was a big boy who was slowly falling apart.

'I loved her,' he said, his eyes becoming moist.

There was no trace of guilt in his eyes. Just a deep despair that confused Louise.

'You were her Danish boyfriend?' Mik asked. Now Louise was the one left out in the cold.

'If that was the case,' she said hesitantly, 'then why did you kill her?'

Again there was a long pause during which Louise tried to put the last pieces of the puzzle together herself.

'She didn't want me,' he finally whispered. 'She said she wanted to go home to Jordan and marry someone from there. Someone Muslim like herself.'

He spoke softly, but there was nothing tentative about his words. He really wanted to make them understand.

'Why did she want that?' Louise asked, bewildered.

His response took her completely by surprise and didn't fit with the image she had formed of Samra.

'Because she wanted someone who was like her and fit in with everything she knew,' he said, as if he didn't quite understand it himself. 'And then she said that Danish families didn't have the same kind of solidarity that families had where she came from. She didn't want to be part of a family where people never really spent any time together even though they lived in the same house. She thought it seemed empty and wrong that I didn't have more to do with my grandmother, since we lived so close together, and that I'm not really in touch with my other family members. In Jordan the whole family sticks together, they all take care of each other there. If one person is sick, the others bring food. It's never lonely, and she missed and longed for the kind of togetherness she was familiar with. That's why she wanted to go home to Jordan and marry a man from there.'

'But she was happy enough to risk a lot to see you in secret, even though she didn't want people to know about your relationship,' Mik prompted.

'Was it because she knew that her parents would object to her picking you instead of a man from her own background?'

Louise asked and noticed the adrenalin rushing through her body again.

Michael started crying and hid his face in his hands as his shoulders shook.

They let him be until he dabbed at his face and looked up.

'It wasn't like that. She knew that they wouldn't object. She was the one who didn't want it, even though she was free to follow her heart. That's what I couldn't understand. I've never loved another person the way I loved her. She claimed she loved me. But she still didn't want to be a couple.'

'She was much younger than you. Far too young to know who she wanted to share her life with,' Louise interjected.

Michael shook his head.

'Her father had given her permission to go home and visit her grandparents for Christmas. She said maybe she could find someone to marry.'

When he saw Louise's dumbfounded face, he continued: 'She said that on Tuesday night when she came over after her parents were asleep and I gave her a necklace and asked her if she would marry me.'

'You killed her because she said no?' Mik asked.

'Samra tried to convince me that I would always be in her heart even though we weren't together. I couldn't understand that, and for me it wasn't enough either. She was the one I wanted,' he said.

The photographer let his chin fall down against his chest and closed his eyes.

'And when she went home, she said she wasn't following her heart but that it would be easier for her. But it was all just lies. Because if she really wanted to, she could have just moved in here with me.'

Louise cleared her throat. 'Unfortunately, I don't think it was that easy for her,' she began, picturing the pages from Samra's diary.

The room was silent. Only the sounds of their breathing made the air vibrate.

Louise thought of Ibrahim and Hamid. It surprised her that neither one of them had distanced himself more vociferously from the crime. That alone had cast suspicion over them. They had denied it and hadn't wavered on their statements, but they hadn't seriously defended their innocence. Now that it was clear they weren't behind the killings, she realised that each of them must have suspected the other after the crime Ahmad had subjected his niece to.

Ibrahim had suspected his brother of the killing, but didn't want to turn him in until he was sure of what had happened. That was what he'd been trying to work out when he went to see Ahmad the day after Samra disappeared. Maybe he was also afraid that Hamid had acted on his own initiative to make his father and uncle happy, if he knew about his sister's secret.

Ahmad probably suspected Ibrahim of killing his own daughter so she wouldn't cast shame over the family once the relationship with the Danish man was revealed. That would make sense to Ahmad. Louise also knew from Camilla that for a while, Sada had suspected her husband was behind the murder, although later her suspicion had passed to Ahmad. No one in the al-Abd family had ever really suspected anyone from outside the family of doing it.

'I must now officially inform you that the time is six twenty-one p.m. and you are under arrest, charged with the murders of Samra al-Abd and Dicta Møller,' Mik said to Michael Mogensen.

Then he asked the photographer to stand up and he started frisking him, before putting a hand on his elbow and leading him out to the patrol car.

41

'Let's issue a press release right away,' Storm said when Louise and Mik returned to the police station with Michael Mogensen. The photographer was received by two officers who were ready to process him so Louise and Mik could join the others in the command room.

'It's important that we let the media know that this case did not involve an honour killing. Maybe that will make whoever's behind Aida's disappearance come to their senses,' Dean said.

'We'll release Ibrahim and his son immediately and tell them what's happened,' Storm said, looking over at Ruth. 'I wonder if we'll be fined for their arrests. We're sure to receive a claim for compensation for wrongful imprisonment that's going to fucking hurt more than just our public image.'

The administrative assistant raised an eyebrow and nodded thoughtfully before agreeing that he was right.

'But there was no other choice, what with the situation the way it was,' Skipper interrupted.

'All the family members seemed to suspect each other and no one was telling us what they knew, so it's really not that surprising that we suspected them as well,' Louise said, reaching for a can of cola before she started telling everyone about Michael's arrest.

'Late on Tuesday evening, after Ahmad had gone home and her parents were asleep, Samra sneaked out to see her boyfriend. Out of fear that her parents and brother would discover their relationship, Samra hadn't allowed any phone calls between them. Instead they arranged their future meetings in person when they were together. Michael Mogensen thinks it was about eleven when she came over. He had lit candles and bought her flowers, because he had been planning to ask her to marry him that night, so it took him completely by surprise when she said she had come to tell him that she had arranged with her parents to send her back home to Jordan.'

'Ouch,' mumbled Bengtsen, passing the cookies around again as Louise continued.

'He gave her the thin gold chain she was wearing around her neck when she was found. But he didn't understand why she didn't want him, or why she would rather find a husband in Jordan when the time came.'

'Who says that's what she wanted?' Skipper asked.

'That's what Michael Mogensen said,' Mik responded and then let Louise continue.

'Michael thinks it's because Samra wanted the kind of close extended family life she would have had with someone from her own traditional background. After having read her diary, I don't think the family relationship was the main reason. I mean, just think about what her uncle did to her. It might have been part of the reason, but I think mostly she was looking for an excuse to call it off.'

'To escape from the double life she'd been leading, which was making it hard for her to be a "normal" Danish teenager,' Dean added, and Louise nodded.

'I know that a lot of Muslim girls who suddenly choose to go back to their family's traditional values do it to achieve some peace of mind,' Louise continued. 'The struggle is twice as hard, the struggle that the young immigrant girls have to fight, because by becoming "normal Danes" they know they can expect to end up lonely and isolated, cut off from their families and their closest friends. And that network doesn't just get replaced by a new one. In that sense, it's a totally different kind of women's liberation than what Danish women have been through,' Louise concluded, letting her elbows sit on top of the table as she rested her chin in her hands.

'Poor girl,' Ruth said, staring straight ahead.

Mik cleared his throat. 'Michael Mogensen has a boat that he keeps out in Hørby Marina by Cape Tuse,' he said. 'Michael says he suffocated Samra with a sofa cushion, then carried her out and put her in the boot of his car and drove out to his boat.'

'His tripod was in the boot too, and that's where the marks on the back of her head came from,' Louise added. She was annoyed that she hadn't realised the photographer had access to a boat back when she'd seen the pictures of Dicta that had been taken on the deck. She honestly hadn't given it a thought, because their suspicions had been focused elsewhere.

'We'll get it checked out,' Storm said. 'And obviously the same goes for his car and his studio. And you'd better remove the wiretap in Dysseparken now that they're being released,' he added with a look at Velin.

'That also means that those tyre impressions we found out at Hønsehalsen are completely irrelevant, right?' Skipper asked, and Dean nodded.

'But how does Dicta's murder fit into this story?' Ruth asked, looking over at Louise.

'It really doesn't. It doesn't sound like Dicta knew anything about the relationship between her best friend and the photographer. Apparently Samra hadn't told anyone. Dicta was presumably not in the best mood when she left Liv's place after her humiliating rejection by Tue Sunds, and was pretty much primed to take it out on someone. Michael Mogensen thinks it was a little past midnight when he happened to see her crossing the street in front of the train station. He pulled up alongside her and she said that she had missed her train and he offered to drive her home. After she got in, she started mocking him, and he pulled into the car park to let her out. But after she got out, she kept belittling him, and eventually he lost it.'

'You can pin down all the details when you talk to him,' Storm interrupted, then he asked Louise and Mik to start preparing to question the photographer, so they would be ready for the preliminary examination.

An hour later, news of his confession was everywhere. The local TV news team was getting ready to do a live interview with Storm when they went on the air around nine o'clock, and the *Dagbladet* journalists had already started gathering in the lobby of the police station, waiting for the press conference Storm had called for immediately after his television appearance. Louise was trying to block out all the commotion so she could concentrate on Michael Mogensen's questioning, which she and Mik were going to begin as soon as the uniforms had processed the arrest.

The crime-scene specialists had just arrived in town and had started turning the photographer's apartment upside down. The car and the sailing boat at Cape Tuse would be brought in for thorough examinations, but even after just a cursory look at the tripod they had agreed that that was what had been used to crush Dicta's skull. Both the weight and the size and location of the rounded screw heads fitted the lesions with the three-centimetre spacing.

Louise was sitting in her office behind her closed door, reviewing the notes from the first questioning session they'd had when they visited the photographer. So she didn't answer the phone until the fourth ring, and she was dismissive and snappish with her greeting.

'I just heard,' Henrik Møller said, without paying any attention to her stand-offish tone. 'I'm at home and just told my wife. I wasn't sure if she'd heard the news. I need you to come over right away.' He didn't give her any time to object before he hung up.

Louise felt like she'd been stuffed into a deep, black hole. The last thing she wanted to spend her remaining energy on now was Dicta's unhappy, unbalanced mother.

She stood and Mik looked up. 'What was that?'

'Henrik Møller. He just told his wife that Samra's parents are innocent and that the actual murderer has been caught. He wants me to go over there right away.'

'Do you want me to come too?'

She shook her head. 'You don't need to do that. I think he

just wants me there to confirm that the case is really closed. It won't take long.'

Both of the family's cars were in the driveway when Louise arrived, but there still weren't any dogs barking as she walked up to the front door. The dogs' absence left her body with an empty feeling. The doorbell echoed through the house, and a second later the door opened.

Henrik Møller was pale and nodded briefly when she said hello. She reluctantly followed him into the house, and he continued down the hallway towards Dicta's room. There was an open mover's box in front of the door, and a few toys were spread out on the carpet.

Henrik stood there in the hallway and pushed open the door to the room. Piles of little girls' toys filled the floor. The bed was unmade, but at the head end Louise spotted the dark hair.

42

Anne Møller didn't even look up when Louise walked into the room. She was sitting like a statue, watching the little girl who was sleeping in her daughter's bed. Dicta's mother was holding a greyish-white teddy bear in her hands, one that looked like it had seen many years of affection and play.

Louise took a deep breath of relief and watched as Dicta's father nodded at his wife, turned on his heel, and returned to the kitchen without saying anything. Anne appeared to be unresponsive. She hadn't noticed that anyone had entered the room.

Louise walked back out to the hall and found Mik's mobile phone number.

'I need two ambulances,' she said. 'I think Aida is alive, but Anne Møller is in shock or some sort of trance, or whatever the hell you'd call it. I suggest that we call Jakobsen, the crisis psychologist at National Hospital who Unit A uses. I don't know of anyone else out here who can handle this kind of thing. If he can't come here, we'll have to bring her in to him, because she needs help asap, and her family's GP doesn't seem to have seen fit to follow up on her condition.'

Louise went back into the bedroom and said Anne's name. Silently and without startling Anne, she walked over and sat down next to her on the edge of the bed and tugged slightly on the comforter that was covering Aida's little body. The girl was breathing peacefully, and, as far as Louise could tell, there were no signs of violence or assault. She was sleeping with her hair spread out over the pillow.

Louise briefly considered whether she ought to pick up the girl and take her somewhere safe. But there was nothing in the room that gave her a reason to feel any danger.

On the other hand, she had no doubt that Anne Møller was beyond reach. Her grief had taken root in her and was firmly in control of her actions. But there was no sign of evil intent in her face. Anne had taken the child because she'd thought they'd taken hers.

The sirens sliced through the peaceful, upscale neighbourhood. The two ambulances arrived at the same time, immediately followed by police cars. Henrik came in without saying anything, and Louise took Anne's hand and said that it was time for Aida to go home to her mother.

'My little girl came back,' Anne said, looking at Louise through unfocused eyes.

They heard footsteps in the hallway and a paramedic stepped into the room, followed by a colleague. Suddenly the room seemed very small. Anne stood up and bent down over Aida, who had started to stir. The little girl sleepily rubbed her eyes and stretched her small body.

The next movement came as Louise was still sitting on the bed looking at the girl, relieved that she seemed to be unharmed. Anne's hands locked around the girl's throat in a chokehold that squeezed a deep gurgle out of her mouth and made her eyes shoot open in fear.

The two men were on Dicta's mother in a heartbeat, but she had a firm grip and put all her weight into her efforts. The girl twitched a couple of times, and a moment later she stopped moving.

At that instant, Louise swung Dicta's heavy photo album against Anne's head with all her might. The blow flung the mother off the bed, and Louise scooped up the unconscious girl and was quickly out of the room with her in her arms. She laid Aida on the kitchen floor and stayed by her side while the paramedics started CPR. She kept calling the little girl's name until Aida finally opened her eyes in confusion and looked around. Her eyes were bloodshot and radiated terror, but her cries were soundless. The pain in her throat held them back.

Louise heard Camilla at the door and made room as Henrik led her in. Louise knew Camilla had been at the police station along with the rest of the journalists, waiting for Storm's press conference. Maybe Storm had thought she could help, because, with Camilla, the girl felt safe and protected through the shock of waking without her family.

Anne Møller was carried out. Henrik turned away when they walked by with his wife, but the pain in his eyes was so visible that it sliced through Louise.

'Don't you want to ride with her?' Louise asked, stepping over to him.

He shook his head imperceptibly, but walked slowly out to

the ambulance anyway. Louise stood there in the doorway, watching as he climbed in to sit down next to the gurney.

Camilla was sitting with Aida in her lap. She was stroking the little girl's hair and kept saying that there was nothing else to be afraid of.

Louise walked over and tapped her shoulder.

'Let's go,' she said, holding the front door open for them.

There were seven or eight cars outside. Several of them contained members of the press, but Louise ignored them and left it to Camilla to decide how she wanted to tackle the intrusive photographers, one of them from her own paper. They'd worked out that there'd been a massive police response in town and had followed the sirens to the Møller family's house.

Louise held open the door to the back seat of the police cruiser for Camilla, who was holding Aida in her arms. Once the door was slammed shut, Louise got behind the wheel and headed towards Dysseparken 16B.

The couple had seen them from the window, and Ibrahim and Sada were standing in the doorway when they came up the stairs. With tears in their eyes, they reached for their youngest daughter. In the living room, Hamid sat glued to the large TV screen, as if he still weren't ready to accept input from the world around him.

Aida clung to Camilla's neck before she let herself flop down into her mother's arms.

'We need to take her to the hospital,' Louise said from where she was standing in the background.

'But we think she should have a few minutes with you

before she undergoes the medical tests,' Camilla added, smiling at Sada. Then she gave Aida a kiss on the forehead and started back down the stairs.

Louise followed her, but promised before she left that the family would receive a detailed description of what had happened. One of the ambulances had followed them back to Dysseparken and was now standing by to transport the family to Holbæk Hospital.

When Louise got back to the police station, she went straight into her office and shut the door firmly behind her. She needed to gather her thoughts and pack away all her personal and private feelings before questioning Michael Mogensen. It wouldn't do her any good to sit there face to face with the indicted man and his appointed solicitor with all her raw emotions tumbling around in her head.

In annoyance she removed the envelope that had been placed on top of the case file that had been sitting on her desk when she had hurried out the door following Henrik's call. Then she got curious, because it was anonymous, with no police logo on it, nor did it have any name on it. Mik was absorbed in something on his computer, taking notes from whatever he was reading.

Louise tore open the envelope and pulled out a photocopy of a map. Confused, she tried to find Cape Tuse or Hønse-halsen on it. She was assuming it was a map of the crime scenes that she was supposed to use during the questioning, but she couldn't make any sense of it.

'It's Växjö, in Sweden,' Mik told her from the other side of the desk, tossing her another anonymous envelope. 'Here's a little about the route we'll paddle.'

She stared at him, unable to get her brain working and not wanting to be surprised with anything whatsoever.

'I'm not paddling any route,' she finally said.

'Yes, you are. In eight days, you and I are going to Sweden to do a little paddling on a lovely system of lakes. It's right in the middle of mushroom-picking season, and we'll camp and cook our food over a campfire.'

She stared at him with her mouth open and was about to protest vehemently, but he beat her to it.

'That's the kind of stuff people do with their good friends,' he explained. 'If you and I were dating, I'd have invited you to Paris, but we're not, are we?'

Her eyes fell and she closed her mouth as she considered this. She shook her head. No, they weren't. Then she pulled out the contents of the second envelope and started studying them.

'Well, then. I can't wait,' she finally said with a smile, as she stood up with the case folder under her arm, ready to accompany him down to the interrogation room.

ACKNOWLEDGEMENTS

Only One Life is fiction. All of it could have happened, some of it did, but most of it came from my imagination, and the characters in the novel bear no similarity to real people.

I chose to set the story in Holbæk, Denmark, because I've known the town since I was a kid and love it and the area around it. But I used authorial freedom to change some of the locations a bit, as with the police station – I moved the Criminal Investigation Division over into the large, red building even though they're actually on the other side of the street. The micro brew pub at the end of Ahlgade, Dysseparken, Højmark School, Mik Rasmussen's farm and Morgenavisen are not real. The Station Hotel, on the other hand, is, although I've also taken the liberty to permit myself a few changes.

In this book as in my previous books, it was crucial for me to do thorough research so I could create a realistic and credible picture. For this reason I would like to dedicate a heartfelt thank-you to all of you who met with me, spent your time answering all my questions, and offered me insight into your experiences, some of them painful.

Many thanks to Naser Khader, who patiently spent time explaining cultural concepts and differences and helped to flesh out some of my characters, both in terms of their lives and their behaviour. A special thanks to the man on the National Police's Mobile Task Force who was more help to me than I really had a right to ask for. And a big thanks to my friend in the Pathology Lab, who's always game right from the beginning. Without him, there would never have been a book. And to my friends in the Murder Division at the Copenhagen Police Department, without whose help I couldn't have built a world around Louise Rick.

Also a big thanks to my capable editor, Lisbeth Møller-Madsen, who is an immeasurable help. Without her it wouldn't have been fun. And to Lotte Thorsen and Jeppe Markers, who read for me; and to my husband, Lars; his two beautiful daughters, Emma and Caroline; and my wonderful son, Adam, because you put up with me withdrawing to do my work.

Sara Blædel